DANGEROUS DREAMS

GK JURRENS

UpLife
Press

This book is dedicated to "Admiral K"... Designator: *Angel One*

ACKNOWLEDGMENTS

First, I wish to acknowledge the long-suffering patience of my soul-mate, *Kay*. This project required thousands of hours not being her husband, partner and lover. Thanks for allowing me to pursue this dream, my first novel. I love you.

I also honor a fallen comrade and friend for his inspiration, his service to our nation's intelligence services, and his distinguished military career, ***Doctor N. Joseph Thompson*** (Colonel, U.S. Army, Retired). Joe sold us the good ship *Sojourn*, the vessel that helped define two decades of our marriage. *Sojourn* evolved into a key character in this story, and helped me survive the storm-tossed voyage of a challenging and rewarding career. The hours Joe and I spent, sharing wonderful stories shaped him into *the* hero of this story. Sir, I salute you as even in death your legacy lives on within these pages.

And what can I say about *KS?* Dude, you inspired such a rich texture for my air pirate characters. Your consultation, outrageous as it seemed at the time, lent plausibility to these colorful characters' stories. Here's to real heroes everywhere willing to share the lives that may sound like fiction to most, but maybe aren't. At least not entirely.

Judy Howard of Judy Howard Publishing truly inspires me. Judy, I cannot find the words to thank you for your inspiration and guidance as I continue this insane and exhilarating journey with your gentle guiding hand. Thanks for the kick in the old cerebral cortex whenever it's needed, wherever we both wander.

Elizabeth Mackey delivered a gorgeous cover design you will see reflects the story so very well. Thank you, Elizabeth.

Nick Russell, since you're a New York Times best-selling author, I was smart enough to listen to your advice—on occasion, but not always. Thank you, sir.

A special thanks to all my dedicated beta readers: *Sid Treber, GE Thompson, Keith and LaVonne O'Brien, Carol Bailey, Darrell Berg, Tom List* and *Ken Malatesta*. I'm hoping you feel the dozens (?) of hours you dedicated to screwing my head on straight was worth it. If I missed your name, I beg your forgiveness. This was an amazing project because of you all.

I would also like thank *countless others* who contributed to this project, adding their own delicious stories, ripe with personal depth of experience and emotion, not to mention your storytelling expertise and critiques.

Thank you!

Yours,
GK

PART I

THE DOCTOR IS IN

M ay 2001
WINCHESTER, MINNESOTA

Clenched butt cheeks testified to his angst.

Isn't it funny what a self-diagnosed obsessive-compulsive control freak imagines when he's nervous and naked?

Now, with his back exposed to a strange and exotic woman, he was not sure what she would do next. But as a senior technology manager on the darker side of fifty, George Janis was used to uncertainty. Or did he only think so?

George considered himself a sophisticated member of twenty first-century society. Yet his thoughts drifted toward the provincial as he lay on his right side with his pride laid bare, more than a hint of perspiration—everywhere. The rough paper between him and the table stuck to his hip and he wondered if his hair was a mess.

He aimed a noncommittal stare at the sink six feet away on the far wall of the tiny but pleasant room. George hated surprises. And how he loathed that germaphobic smell, although he understood its necessity, perhaps better than most.

Carol Roenssler was a slender and petite Chinese woman with high cheekbones and a pair of all-consuming chocolate eyes. She presented herself as a consummate professional. Her pager beeped, but she ignored it after a surreptitious glance.

George wondered, *Why is it the digital probing of a proctology exam* concludes *the physical? So patient and doctor can both make a quick escape after such intimate and awkward contact? Or so the physician can spare the patient the indignity of watching him wipe the lube from south of the border on the backside of reality? And before the goodbye handshake, sans gloves?*

It was usually that way, but not today. Maybe she didn't know how it worked yet.

Earlier, after causing George to gag with that woody tongue dispenser shoved in too deep, she had asked, "Mr. Janis, I can still ask a male colleague to perform the proctology part of this exam."

He could see her youthful face over his left shoulder in her crisp white lab coat.

"Carol, either you will be my GP from now on, or you're won't. Be gentle, okay? I'm feeling vulnerable."

Had those amazing eyes glistened before she chuckled?

"Thank you. Now please try to…" She half-whispered, her voice breaking as she plunged in with her gloved finger. Or was it more than one? "… relax."

He had researched Carol. She was a good physician. It gave George the tiniest thrill to help this young woman make her bones.

George always made himself available for a comprehensive exam each May in Minnesota. Family history mandated he remain as healthy as possible. A lifetime of gym memberships helped. His long-deceased father suffered the first of his five cardiac events when he was more than a decade younger than George was now. Not superstitious, really, he nevertheless thought, *Knock wood.* There was none to be found anywhere in this antiseptic cell. Certainly none within reach.

Opulent medical centers with marble floors and rich raised

paneling reminded him of casinos. The odds still favored the house, but the stakes were often much higher. George hated gambling. In casinos, anyway. He didn't mind visiting Carol once a year in nearby Winchester. He needed to improve his odds.

This visit began a lifelong professional and amicable relationship.

The odor of hand sanitizer, or perhaps something else, permeated the examination room. A good thing, right? Except it was so strong, it clung to the roof of his dry mouth.

Carol said, "I empathize with you on your high-stress lifestyle. But you must know your job is taking it's physical and emotional toll on you. The latter is not my area of expertise. I can refer you to someone, Mr. Janis."

"George, please."

"All right, George. You've been straight with me. I owe you the same."

Now without contaminated gloves, she referenced the PC's screen to her right where her notes from their earlier conversation glared at her. Traces of talc remained near her wrist visible below the cuff of her powder blue silk blouse where her quick scrub over the sink had missed. She reviewed her crisp summary points, starting with her left index finger bending back its partner before moving to the next.

"So you travel half a million air miles a year, including countless international trips, and you're having trouble sleeping. Your acid reflux has been symptomatic for several years. You admit that your consumption of alcohol is an abrasive topic between you and your wife."

She ran out of fingers, so she punished her right thumb to attack the last point. "You haven't developed an ulcer yet, but it's only a matter of time. Then, it gets more complex."

George's noncommittal gaze drifted downward toward his uncaring feet.

"I can prescribe everything you need to continue managing your symptoms. But here's the punch line, George. You may force yourself to make serious lifestyle decisions. Sooner versus later. That's how I see it."

"Thanks, Carol. No breaking news. Well, please write me a few scripts, and I'll get out of here. I owe myself a few more years in Hell. It's complicated. Then I can go sailing in the tropics with my wife."

Every time things got rough at work, he and Kate would resort to that life-saving dream.

"Okay, George, but I can't count how many times I've heard, 'Mañana.'"

"I'm sure. Say, when I do retire, we're planning on spending time away from first-world medicine. Might be for months at a time. When the time comes, I could use your help to assemble a medical kit for the boat."

"That depends. What did you have in mind?"

Sensing she feared a sticky situation, he explained.

"Nothing fancy. We've had friends stranded in the Caribbean without access to things like antibiotics and regular prescriptions. We want to ensure that doesn't happen to us."

"Sure, George. Let's talk as that gets closer. Soon, I hope. Don't wait too long."

❲❳

MAY 2005
WINCHESTER, MINNESOTA

FOUR YEARS AND FOUR EXAMS FLEW BY.

Time was not standing still for George or Carol. They both grew older and it was obvious that Carol had grown wiser. They entertained variations of the same discussion each May. The conclusion of this latest exam took a different direction.

"George, I'm always delighted to see you. May I make a personal observation?"

"Of course. What's up?"

"Well, I may be stepping over an invisible line, but we share a relationship of mutual respect. I owe you an honest appraisal. As a friend more than a physician."

"Am I going to hate this?"

"George, you're in denial. You're stressed and using your sailing fantasy to cope. You talk about it every time you come to see me. It's not enough to sustain you. Not physically, not emotionally. Make some changes. Soon. That's all."

Carol redirected those huge dark eyes to her new computer screen. She appeared a bit embarrassed as if she had indeed stepped over that invisible line intentionally and had done so at some professional cost.

"Carol, you're a good friend and I very much appreciate your concern. It is not unfounded. Soon… mañana."

George smiled his best conciliatory smile of denial as he fell silent. The awkward thirty second hiatus that followed ended with him rising from the exam room chair. Instead of a cool handshake, he offered her an abrupt but warm hug. She was a good friend, and she was worried.

So was he.

PARADISE LOST

SEPTEMBER 2007
PUNTA GORDA, FLORIDA

It was Autumn in Paradise.

Two years earlier, George and Kate had moved from a conservative cul-de-sac in Minnesota to a marina condo in Florida. They had hoped a change of winter venue would help. It didn't.

George pondered the course he'd navigated through life as he gazed at the tranquil scene just outside his home office window. As he observed the idyllic scene of boats bobbing, tugging at their moorings, the chop driven by a brisk onshore breeze in the marina below gave their movement a comforting randomness. Like him.

He walked the docks to settle that familiar creeping anxiety, grateful nobody could see the tremor in his hands from a distance.

He felt his life had been stolen from him. Snatched by an inexorable series of preordained events as if by a mugger with a knife in the night. Each time he went to bed, his personal nightmare consumed him. Again.

Days were okay. Starting at Happy Hour, though, which began earlier each day as time unraveled, it seemed Kate didn't have anything better to do than to criticize him.

He knew he deserved her discontent, but seemed helpless to change. They experienced fewer surprises after four decades of marriage and his three decades at Greater Global Solutions, Inc. Life simply became more of the same.

George came to realize that the American dream could be every bit as addictive as heroin or cocaine—at least for him. He steered clear of drugs, of course, but not his nightly flight of extra-dry gin martinis. Alcohol wasn't really a drug, was it?

A gin buzz hit the fastest and the hardest. And there was nothing like Bombay Sapphire. Smooth as mint silk that never failed to take his breath away. That thought transported him clear of the ever-imminent blazing heat of battle. At home and abroad.

He wanted to be a good guy, but the decisions required of every hostile takeover delivered a guilty thrill. And that cast him into another depressive state which he knew he must purge. Those decisions usually meant firing people—sometimes good people. He'd tell himself that was the job, and as he was fond of saying, "I *am* the job." Then he'd go home to another world where he'd be embarrassed to even think like that.

What in this Hell have I become?

As George stood at the bar in the condo's spacious living room, he contemplated the necessary but reviled transition from martinis to wine. No, not yet. One more bird bath.

Much to his chagrin, he acknowledged he was the old man in the regular crowd. Billy Joel's song *Piano Man* played in a continuous loop —his personal ear worm with which he'd developed a long-term relationship:

. . .

"IT'S NINE O'CLOCK ON A SATURDAY,
 The regular crowd shuffles in,
 There's an old man sitting next to me,
 Makin' love to his tonic and gin."

BUT HE'D OUTGROWN TONIC, OF COURSE.

Too much sugar, and the diet stuff was intolerable.

Gotta stay trim after all. Doctor Carol says so.

Through this symphony of orchestrated self-medication, he told himself—and believed—the grand lie.

I don't have a drinking problem. After all, I'm successful, affluent, and in command. Aren't I?

He promised soon all would change, when and if necessary. Carol's solitary word drifted back to him—*"mañana."* Another foolish mantra.

A mug of his favorite French Roast coffee occupied the coaster in easy reach of George's left hand on his desk. He managed his GGS business unit from here at least twelve hours each day. These days, as he drained that mug, his thoughts turned more toward replacing that mug, empty more than not, with caffeine in a tumbler on ice, maybe a rum and diet. No, too early. Lunch first.

George considered himself a family man, yet his two grown children seldom spoke to him. Why should they? He was never there for them. He was busy capturing the dream. Though once firmly in his grasp, it mutated into something reprehensible and dangerous. While the kids grew, he flew.

He and Kate met in high school. Theirs began as a love affair for the ages. Then it devolved into a marathon of concessions and compromises. Their arguments had never gotten physical—that never occurred to George. It constantly worried Kate, however. She needn't have worried. Unlike Kate, that's not how George was raised. No violence, no divorce, simple. Having said that, the heart of their abusive affair revolved around corrosive verbal sword play.

Kate remained with him, ever loyal, but now, he wasn't sure how much longer she would carry all the excess baggage he'd piled on over the years.

"George, what happened to you? To us? It's obvious you love the job and the bottle more than me."

While he heard the words, his blue-green Sapphire bottle lied to him with his own voice. Her words were meaningless. So he'd chase the sauce with a powerful sleeping pill or two each night before blacking out. After all, he needed sleep, didn't he?

HOLLOW DISAPPOINTED EYES STARED AT HIM.

Above the foot of his bed floated pools of deepest sorrow.

His employees loved him, except for the few hundred whose livelihoods he ravaged in recent years.

They all visited him every night around midnight—the bewitching hour. He forgot most of their names. He would never forgive himself for that.

So he fantasized about standing at the wheel of his beloved *Sojourn*, navigating clear of the wrecks he had caused, leaving them in his wake, trying to dream of… *mañana*.

A WARM SEA BREEZE TICKLED THE DRAPES.

Most mornings outside the floor-to-ceiling glass sliders of their condo's lanai shone brilliant. He overlooked the marina where *Sojourn* would float someday soon, no doubt unused. But close by.

Salt air here smelled dank compared to the freshwater lakes they were used to in Minnesota, but carried with it a different sort of dream.

George dreamed of sailing to far-flung tropical islands with Kate in their little ship, of leaving the mainland fights behind. Some day. *Mañana.*

Swaying palms and bobbing sailboats just outside belied the tempest that raged within. Theirs was a storm with the sustained energy of a destructive gale. He remained in its vortex each day as the brilliant Florida sunshine faded into dreaded afternoon and evening doldrums.

They'd start near the well-stocked bar, then wandered into the kitchen together to grab a snack or to cook dinner, the conversation always started convivial. Soon their course invariably took a turn toward dangerous waters. And eventually…

"Kate, why must we argue all the time? I know I can be self-centered. That's often what the job demands, what keeps me going. It's hard to leave all that crap at the office."

"G, I can read you like a cheap novella."

He knew she wasn't as mad as she pretended, but the dance wasn't finished, even though the music had stopped.

"You still haven't realized I am not an employee you visit once in a while. You're smart, G, but insensitive as a pail of nails."

He saw her in that short skirt, and the precise shape of those long muscular legs. That was forty years ago.

"But…"

"Look, let's be honest. You've been blessed with lousy long term memory. Not me. I see, and hear, and smell every time you made me feel crappy over the last forty years. They're full-color HD videos, with sound and everything. My eidetic memory is a curse.

"And you've been home, what, fifteen days in the last four months? This is another great example. Both your kids grew up without you. That meant I had to handle all their bad behavior and scrapes with the law. I'm the one who apologized to all the school principles. *I* dealt with all the expulsions, with boyfriend and girlfriend heartaches. I did. Alone. You know why? Because I still love you so damn much."

She picked up speed rolling down a steep grade.

"I see you bought a book called, '*A Thousand Ways to Be Romantic*' a couple of months ago. But the fact that you even *need* such a book is not very comforting. Have you even cracked its cover?"

George rounded the bar and grabbed one of its eight bar stools. He couldn't help thinking, *How much did we pay for* **these** *damn things?* He wasn't winning this round.

So he said, "Remember when you told me I was a worthless Liberal Arts hippy? Not long after I got out of the Coast Guard? That I needed to take classes that would make us a decent living? You were killing yourself working two waitress jobs so we could feed the kids. So I did what I had to do. Got the job, got the degrees, made the money. Then other stuff happened."

Now George's voice pled for even a hint of empathy. He wasn't getting any. It was still all about him.

She responded in a softer voice that was not unkind. "You know, G, those days of waitressing, of squeezing the budget, those were some of the happiest days of our lives. We never had enough money, but you were *home*. You'd splash around in that little ten dollar kiddie pool in the backyard with the kids. You'd play with squirt guns and spray each other with the hose. The kids told me that was pure magic. It was."

As her narrative brought her back to the present, the simmering anger resurfaced.

"Now we have money, but you're always *gone*. Your mouth, still disconnected from your brain, continues to shout that you left all common sense and emotional sensitivity behind. Even when you're here, you aren't. And now people threaten our lives. Is this better?"

THIS ALMOST CAPTAIN OF INDUSTRY SHRANK.

George walked away hanging his head, a lost boy once again chastised by a wiser adult. Every night, after every fight, her visceral response was always the same. She'd compose a list of how to divide their property—their net worth.

Most often, those lists were little more than veiled threats. She left them lying around the house or the condo for him to see. A small retaliation, at least that's what he chose to believe. He had given his heart to this woman, but his life to his career, and that career ripped out that same heart and kicked him in the ass. It was his *career's* fault. He believed that lie too.

Then tallying another point to be made, still keeping score, he wheeled around to face her once again. She had followed him around the bar, but remained standing. Behind him. Forced him to swivel his stool.

"It wasn't as if I set out to design this future for us, Kate. You know? I *always* believed I was doing the next right thing, providing for my family. You expected that. *We* expected that. Especially remembering the dung holes you and I both crawled out of as kids. Remember our promises to each other?

"The next thing I know, you see me as this ambitious ass," He pointed at his chest with all the spread out fingers of both open hands. He made sure he didn't tip his drink at his right elbow. "… someone who will do anything to score the next raise, the next promotion. And for what? So we can buy more stuff? Another new car? You like the Lexus, right? You loved that big house in Stillwater before we cashed out. I ask you, what is the point? I've lost track."

George tried to end many a fight by going to bed alone, mid-discussion, pretending to sleep, pretending he'd had the last word. But that didn't stop Kate if she were in her cups and on her soap box. Worse, her prescription for anti-anxiety meds never lasted as long as intended. Yes, there was a pattern here… a pattern from Hell.

She knew when he wasn't really sleeping. "And now, there's some psycho you fired out there somewhere *trying to kill us both*. Anything for the old career, right George? How's that working out, do you think? I must tell you, I'm always impressed by what you're capable of accomplishing, but I am not impressed with how it's turning out."

He often conducted one-sided conversations in his head. Not that he understood himself any better than he understood Kate. *How did I come to this? Am I a moral pauper? Or just spiritually unfit? God, I need to hit a gym for the soul.*

Although this was little more than a vague concept that often slipped away in the dark regrets of each night's stupor, he wondered if he were just another agnostic flinging a desperate prayer at his affliction?

After thirty years at Greater Global Solutions, George was only fifty-six. He came to realize the job was killing him *and* his marriage. At least that's what he told himself. He could not envision a life without Kate, but didn't know how to live *with* her either. The only way he could sleep at night was to drink and chase the booze with an Ambien or two.

Boy, those sleeping pills were magic. He could sleep through anything. Hotel hallway parties, third world traffic noise, twenty-six-hour international flights... He could even sleep through Kate's yelling... and the nightmares. Even that recurring nightmare—his own personal coffin of despair.

Clutched again in its grip, that dream embraced George, naked and trembling...

My ears jangle in the profound silence.

It smells musty... wherever I am. How did I get here? The clinging blackness is the most terrifying of all. It feels like I'm buried alive, smothering in an all-consuming claustrophobia. How can this be?

Am I finally insane? Is there at least a shred remaining of who I once was? Or is God finally pushing me over the edge to the Hell I know I deserve?

Blinking my eyes, again and again, I try to chase away the ocean of guilt within which I'm drifting. It isn't working. Worse, much worse, I'm unable to move my arms or legs.

I remember often waking up in places with no memory of how I got there. Have I relapsed? No, this is no drunken blackout. Am I drugged? Possibly. Or am I now a permanent prisoner of my worst nightmare? Have I gone utterly and completely mad?

Why can I smell almost nothing? And the waves of pain! There is both old and new pain. Something jars my entire body with violent resolve. Over and over again. I know I'm being lacerated with deep sweeping strokes.

"Remember me, George?"

A cold and bitter voice laced with slivers of ice.

"Remember how you ripped out my heart, and shit on my soul, claiming you were just doing your job, you asshole? Remember what that cost me? You never knew or cared. It matters not. Tonight I return the favor."

That voice...

His box cutter—a rusty and scarred blade, envisioned from his grim narrative—protrudes from a scratched gray metallic handle. It glints with a dull gleam in the ethereal glow of my imagination as it drips with... what?

"I need you to know what's happening here, George. First, let's be clear. You are about to die. Before you do, though, we're going to have some fun. There... feel that? Ouch, that's gotta hurt. Well, I suspect it's too soon for you to feel much, but we're getting you very wet, aren't we? Feel that, George? That's your filthy life dripping onto this dirty concrete floor."

This madman continues to describe what is happening in a professorial tone. As he does so, his chipped blade plunges into the delicate skin and the rough two-day stubble on my neck. As my nerve endings come alive, they give voice to my terror, as does the embarrassing stench of my bowels involuntarily surrendering.

Oh God, I'm conscious and aware. And so very helpless. I'm drowning in waves of nausea and disgust. My head is lower than my body. Why? I can't comprehend. Hearing only pieces of a grisly monologue, I am suddenly aware of a taut blindfold that covers my eyes and nose with coarse heavy cloth... is that the stink of vomit? Mine? My nostrils sting.

I feel a hot puddle spreading near my genitals—urine, or perhaps blood. I hear whatever it is dripping, then splashing, onto the floor beneath the table.

"George, are you still with me? Let's find out how much of a manipulator you are with no fingers. Feel that? Oops, sorry my trusty blade isn't sharper."

A guttural snicker overlays the insistent crunching of bones and cartilage.

"One down, nine to go, asshole. Eight... seven..."

I can neither speak nor scream because something large and round and fuzzy is crammed in my mouth. Is this an old half-bald tennis ball? It is so very tight it's hyper-extending my jaw. It presses so hard against the back of my front teeth that I'm sure they're about to snap. With the coppery taste bleeding gums, my tongue is bunched up behind that awful ball. Some sort of tape is wrapped recklessly around my head and through my beard and hair...

"Are you ready now, George? Say hello to the devil for me, you sod."

I feel what is sure to be the killing stroke of that blade drawing hard across my throat. I can feel it severing what must be my windpipe and jugular as my breath gurgles and whistles through the cuts. The shock of that moment dances through my mind with lightning clarity.

It is still too soon to feel much pain, but I know the blade has achieved its highest purpose. It jerks my head and neck sideways, more than once. I think, Why is he still tearing into me? Lord, are you still there, after all these years?

George jolted himself awake as if tased.

Of all his dreams, he only ever remembered this one vividly. Covered in sweat and soaked in fear, he forced himself out of bed and showered to wash off the memory of all that blood and viscera.

He so wished to not feel dirty... and to forget.

JUNE 2005
PUNTA GORDA, FLORIDA

· · ·

THE MORNING BROKE BRILLIANT.

Almost two and a half years earlier, George needed his game face to prepare for… well, he wasn't sure for what. The mere notion of the next day's meeting in New York churned his ailing stomach. His boss, the Chief Operations Officer of Greater Global Solutions, had summoned him. So he was off to Midtown Manhattan. Again.

After a quick trip to the vomitorium, he brushed off the stench and taste, snagged the garment and computer bags packed the night before, leaving his uneaten breakfast and dear Kate sitting at the breakfast table after a lingering kiss and embrace. They always said, "Just in case, let's make it a good one."

Once more, all was forgotten and forgiven… well, at least suppressed.

The drive to the Regional Southwest Florida Airport would take almost an hour, including the steamy hike to the terminal from long-term parking.

The shoulder strap of his computer bag dug into his right shoulder. The garment bag hooked under his left thumb and slung over the other shoulder grew awkward. Both shoulders sweat like they didn't want to be there.

His flight from RSW in Fort Myers to LaGuardia would take less than two hours. Another night at the Marriott Grand Marquis in Midtown, and then…?

YOUNG TURKS

N EW YORK, NY

"Kɪʟʟ 'ᴇᴍ ᴀʟʟ,"

The first one hissed the bon mot in a somber tone.

With a cruel voice spewing ill-conceived off-the-shelf humor he added in the same breath, "let God sort 'em out."

The second one intoned as if uttering a ritual, "And may the strongest carnivore get the prime cuts."

They never tired of old clichés, nor of butchering metaphors. These two formidable young warriors took pleasure in raping other peoples' ideas. They delighted in exploiting the weaknesses of lesser mortals.

Taking huge risks, they hoped to feel something, anything. Eager for action, they perused Manhattan's East Side skyline. Their perch on the forty-first floor of 555 Madison afforded them a spectacular view.

This morning, they peered into a grim future and contemplated what glared back at them. With relish.

They were newly anointed titans of technology. Both in their early forties, they considered themselves the brutal young Turks of their generation. Behind their backs, people called them the Brooklyn Cowboys.

Not that either would claim that borough as their home. Nor would they admit to coming from such a coarse part of the world. Both were Ivy Leaguers, but they knew how to fight hard and dirty. Their playground was Midtown, with their watchful eyes aimed downtown at *The Street*.

They needed an aggressive growth strategy and required a massive new source of fuel for the ponderous engine that powered Greater Global Solutions. Convinced they knew what to prescribe, they celebrated their predecessors' demise.

These thundering barbarians pounding on the palace gates grew eager to retire outdated traditions.

"The carcass of this bloated old pile is rotten, Mike. We're going to need major surgery, and fast."

The industry was shifting as they spoke. Their newly acquired multinational was in no shape to keep up.

Palmer Xavier, the new Chief Operations Officer for GGS, knew his strength came from his willingness to take huge risks. The ruthless courage with which he planned to attack this job of protecting margins and their sacred triple-A bond rating trumped any fear of failure. He knew his real boss was the almighty *Street*.

Palmer had become particularly enamored of his new acquaintances. *Friends* was too strong a word. Ultra-elite hedge fund managers controlled hundreds of billions within their domains. Some claimed most were little more than upscale mobsters, but they could be useful.

Knowing his boss's desires, Palmer continued. "This family-run-business crap ends now. It's time to retire Uncle Tom's legacy along with the steam engine and other antiquated notions. How long did they think *that* would last?"

Xavier spoke of Michael Martino's predecessor as CEO with disdain. Tom Goodchild often said, "People are our most important asset." Palmer couldn't wait to ditch other implicit traditions too, such as womb-to-tomb employment.

"Okay Palmer, but let's be clear,"

Mike always said that.

"If we're not *way* ahead of the curve, we'll be caught with our pants down. Make no mistake—I will not permit my legacy to look like anything but double-digit growth. At this point, I don't care if it's organic or engineered. Can we make that happen?"

Palmer smiled, for a different reason than Mike assumed. He loved Mike, but his repertoire of clunky axioms? The press, though, loved the dark and serious Michael Martino and his notable quotables.

Time to schmooze.

"Of course. So Mike, how does it feel to be GGS's youngest CEO? And with the board's blessing to exercise a little breakout leadership?"

Palmer knew Mike desperately needed to earn the Board's confidence early in his regime.

"Well, they told me I have carte blanche, and between you and me, we own a CFO who will do as she's told. But the clock is ticking."

Mike never hesitated to make a questionable call. He thrived maneuvering between dark gray and full black—his primary operational zone.

Mike's resonant voice slung shards of glass as he spoke. That voice was a powerful tool.

"We need to outrun our shadows—bold moves. Also, we must pulverize the inevitable pushback from the division GMs *before* it happens. I need insurance. I want serious dirt on every one of those stodgy old relics by month's end. Use Slattery again. And bring me the good numbers, Palmer."

They both knew that most General Managers slowed things down to the pace of a ponderous pachyderm. Mike would tolerate none of that from his GMs like his predecessor. Besides, a little insurance never hurt.

"On it, Mike. I have your back. Like Raleigh."

~

BEAT AT HIS OWN GAME? CLOSE, BUT...

When Mike was GM of the midrange business in Research Triangle Park, the incident concerned a handful of photos. Mike had indulged in one of his junior executive's affections. Non-sophisticates would find his actions objectionable. He would not be someone else's insurance.

On his own initiative, Palmer had dealt with the issue in no uncertain terms. He and Mike harbored no secrets from one another. Since then, Palmer Xavier was Michael Martino's right hand, his clenched fist. No question. He bullied their subordinates into submission. He also sensed he needed to remind his boss now and then.

They earned their stripes leading that troubled division in North Carolina. That had required some serious budget bashing. Product issues remained but they produced stellar financials which kicked them both upstairs—way upstairs—all the way to CHQ. They made a ruthless and effective team, but nobody needed to tell *them*. Martino turned to his keyboard and screen, signaling the meeting's end.

Palmer departed. He knew this would be a business transformation the likes of which this old blue chip turd farm could *never* see coming. Shock and awe.

Yes, this would be a grand game on a grand scale.

~

WASHINGTON, DC

PALMER XAVIER FELT AROUSED AND CHARGED.

As a newly-minted COO, he relaxed in an elite club with a power broker in the midst of western civilization's seat of power. The elder behind-the-scenes statesman sitting to his left commanded influence of untold proportions.

Okay, so I need to up the ante if I want a chip in the grand game. And the only practical way to ensure short-term double-digit growth is to think and act outside the box. In fact, it's time to retire the box.

His down-payment—his ante—was five hundred million, and he needed to deliver it within the next twenty-four hours.

Palmer often conversed with himself. *So what's it worth to own a piece of a U.S. President? After all, we're buying a share of a pro-business platform on the national stage. More than that, Jefferson Davis Redding is a shark, like us. Even better, he's as greedy and has much to gain from helping his new friends help him.* While he didn't say any of this out loud, he felt he could with his elderly friend and mentor.

Palmer was convinced he'd gone straight to that big bank in the sky. The election would most definitely not be a fait accompli, but he tasted the strategy and knew it increased the odds of a win.

He loved the sound of his own pontificating mind. *Besides, the sheep always clamored for change, didn't they? Why not give it to them? There's a simple reason why the rich get richer in this country—we stay focused on one thing: growth.*

He knew business was clean, but politics? Not so much. When he made a business decision, it stuck. Period. *If we ran the damn country like a business, so many problems went away.*

He clung to his favorite quote: "It is not the truth that matters, but victory." This was how the world worked. Not how the unwashed masses *wished* it worked. Poor ignorant livestock. They would never understand visionaries like Adolf.

His friend assured him that the Patriot Brotherhood's money guys would make the necessary transactions disappear into the ether. *Risky, but no choice. Either you are a player, or you aren't.*

The timing for coughing up his ante was awkward. It would take a while to translate R&D budget cuts into cash he could redirect. Until then, he knew he could count on a couple of his favorite fund managers on the street who had made overtures.

They were willing to float the required loans. In return, they expected an inside track. He'd share with them his global product and service strategy for the next five years.

Quid pro quo.

The Brotherhood knew politics. He knew business. Working together, the nation would expose its tender underbelly.

"Sir, I'll communicate the appropriate account information to your representative within twenty-four hours. I know I can count on your utmost discretion."

"Of course. Nice doing business with you, my young friend."

Palmer's *friend* watched the patterns of his cigar smoke snake upward and hang in the stale air. The hand that held that expensive cigar stirred the financial pot called the Fortune 50.

Palmer Xavier observed the old gentleman sitting in his club chair. Both smiled and said nothing more.

What a lovely fire.

THE BIG BITE

GEORGE JANIS GREW UP DIRT-POOR.

In that small midwestern town he was okay with that. But not now.

Sometimes, that history even came in handy. His humble background illustrated how far he'd come despite adversity.

He grew up on the wrong side of the tracks but became adept at crossing those tracks—often against bitter winds.

Today was one of those days.

Ten minutes before nine a.m. he made a quick stop at the cafeteria on the main floor to acquire the best and the strongest coffee anywhere. A stout twenty-ounce French Roast, in a recycled paper cup, black, of course, propped up his courage. He reflected how he had awakened at his customary four-thirty in his sterile suite at the Grand Marquis. The brisk walk to his nine a.m. helped.

Even as the smoky brew slid across his tongue, his stomach groaned in protest. The private elevator in the lobby of 555 Madison smelled of oiled teak. It carried him to the opulent fortieth floor executive suite.

George anticipated an ugly encounter. At the same time, he felt the tingling thrill of being so close to the top. That proximity always bore a price. Always.

He was seldom summoned to Palmer Xavier's office. It was usually a phone call from one of his minions, like the irascible Vinnie Lassaro.

The eldest twenty-something of the COO's three willowy executive assistants, Patchouli, greeted George. They were quick to remind anyone who cared they were *not* secretaries.

Did Palmer's people interview only stunning runway models for his EAs? They had to be more than eye candy, didn't they? After a luminous smile of blinding white and blood red, he took a seat as requested.

The voluminous space appeared Spartan. George knew this was part of Palmer's facade of austerity that always seemed so contrived.

Paradoxically, millions in abstract art stared back at him from the walls in front of him and to his right. George suspected the original oils and vibrant watercolors were nothing more than decor art to Palmer. And these high-end furnishings reeked of trying too hard to look like he wasn't trying too hard.

The fifteen-minute wait beyond the appointed time? Blatant power posturing. He listened to the thin tinkle of contemporary jazz from invisible speakers.

Palmer needed some new material.

As he was being ushered to the inner sanctum at 9:15, before he could even sit down, Palmer impatiently blurted, "George, I need twenty percent." Brutal budget challenges had become an annual Fall Plan event, but *this*…

George blurted, "What? Palmer, you *do* realize that my budget ends with an M and enables revenue that ends with a B, right?" He instantly bit into the side of his tongue so hard he tasted his own blood—an omen.

The COO of the GGS Corporation was *not* going to be swayed with sophomoric excuses.

With faux sincerity, Palmer purred, "Look, George, I understand this is tough. You know what I'm going to say next, right? If you can't do it…"

George gaped slack-jawed for a moment as Palmer straightened his already perfectly aligned yellow power tie with its tiny navy-blue dots. Tiny blue eyes of lost souls. He wasn't even looking George in the eye. Yeah, right. Power.

"Yes, okay Palmer, I've got this." George interrupted, attempting a somewhat anemic recovery.

He was already mentally planning how to cut twenty million dollars from his already ravaged budget. Worst case, that meant two hundred jobs, without impacting business results.

Somehow.

George continued to tell himself yet another lie—that he could wield the sword of doom with more compassion than the next ambitious prick. That he was doing this more for his people than for his own blind ambition.

At the end of the day, peoples' lives got screwed up. And he did the screwing. He took no pleasure in it.

Did he?

Palmer's heavy-lidded eyes, cold and dead, reflecting nothing but black ice, finally met his. George wondered how many other foot soldiers would run this gauntlet.

"You see, George, I have a hundred direct reports, as you know. This provides useful distance, a practical perspective."

The asshole was enjoying this. He needed to peer into the anguish reflected in eyes like George's. He needed to drink in the bubbling bile in George's gut.

"How many senior managers report to you? Twenty? Twenty-five? As you drill down, your lower level guys each have, what, twenty employees? Thirty? Down there, it needs to be five times that or more. This is what I'm talking about. There's always fat, George. Always."

Now a twenty percent precedent was a reality. From now on, this would be a recurring catastrophe. At least under this new regime.

He reached for better times. He envisioned Kate stretched out on

Sojourn's foredeck as he chose to ignore the running knife fight with his high school sweetheart who was also from the wrong side of the tracks.

He was out of his freakin' league here.

Palmer continued the ambush. "Another thing. How many of your employees are in high-cost geographies? The U.S.? Western Europe? Scandinavia? Japan? Singapore? Eighty percent? In two years, you're going to flip that number to twenty percent. The future is in low-cost countries like China, Eastern Europe, Malaysia..."

George didn't mention that India used to be the prime example of a low-cost *geography*. That was thirty-six short months ago. Once those kids in Bangalore and Delhi got a taste of the good life, courtesy of GGS and others, they'd jump ship. They'd head for the next high-tech firm across the street with their updated resumé.

"So I want you to shed your expensive talent. Hire cheaper talent. Increase your span-of-management ten-fold. And convince those who are leaving to stay long enough to train their successors. Or they don't get their severance package. Focus on cutting the troops who are closest to collecting a pension. No need to pay them forever. Can do?"

Palmer possessed a rarified character attribute. It allowed him to go for the jugular in the afternoon and sleep like a baby at night. High functioning sociopathic behavior. George knew he did not possess that attribute.

Or maybe he did but to a lesser degree.

And definitely less with every turn of the soul-crunching crank. Which is why he'd never be a senior VP. Besides, no Ivy League pedigree.

Wrong side of the tracks.

Before George could offer his unconditional surrender, Palmer's desk phone chirped. As a reflex, he punched the speaker button. Patchouli said, "Mr. Xavier, Mr. Enoch Slattery needs to speak with you. Line three."

As he picked up the phone for privacy, Palmer said, "George, I look forward to your plan by next week. Remember, *you're that guy.*"

Dismissed.

What an exquisite micro-sphincter-manager. He is good, but good at what?

～

PALMER XAVIER KNEW DIRTY TRICKS.

His knowledge paled compared to Enoch Slattery's stock-in-trade.

He needed to learn all he could about Slattery and his organization. Rubes from the Bible Belt would be shocked to learn the degree to which Slattery's services were in demand, both domestically and abroad.

Slattery wasn't cheap, but his stink always stuck. Always. For at least the next news cycle, and that's all that usually mattered.

As Slattery would say, "Drive a sharp point, then jump back before getting splattered. Sad commentary, really. Making me rich." Slattery was indeed a colorful character. And useful.

Palmer answered the incoming call from Slattery who said, "Sir, got your message. How may I serve?"

Palmer couldn't help but love this guy. He was professional as hell. Slattery's highly specialized and discreet services produced useful results. Palmer appreciated the irony. For someone whose business was cheating, lying, spying and stealing, he fostered almost unquestionable trust where the stakes were so very high. Palmer still kept a little insurance of his own on Mr. Slattery—a backup bullet.

"Mr. S, you have work. Urgent. Pays well. Can do?"

"Name it, Sir."

"I need some dirt mined. I'll email you the particulars, usual channels. Mr. S, since we're on an encrypted line, may I ask you a few questions? I'd like to understand your range of services a bit better."

"How about I come to your office, Sir?"

"You're in town? Wonderful. Let's say... ten p.m.?"

～

The lights smoldered in Palmer's office.

Enoch Slattery explained his operation.

"Sir, politics is one of my mainstays. Every political campaign uses back-room operators. We do the nasty stuff the big boys can't dirty their dicks on. Same with big business. And Sir, I can't remember a dirtier political campaign—ever—or one that got this intense, this early."

While politics interested Palmer, it puzzled him why Slattery focused so much of his energy in that direction. Although anything that explored the depths of human depravity fascinated him.

Slattery continued. "When I think I've seen every sort of twisted thinking, the crap gets even slimier and more profitable. The work is tricky, but the pay is obscene. And there's nothing wrong with watching—with a recording device in hand. Sometimes, more is required."

That last phrase sounded ominous, but he didn't probe. Not yet.

"And I'll tell you something else, Mr. Xavier. To the job at hand, one of my secondary services involves information leverage. You only need to guess what *that* involves."

He'd been instructed to give this guy a full briefing.

"Well, you've enlightened me with more dimensions to your work than I had imagined, Enoch. Scope?"

"Sir, I use more than a hundred operatives worldwide. Most are ex-military, ex-intelligence, or most often both. They contract with my firm. They've checked their ethics at the door, along with what remains of their purposeless lives, which is often why they work for me. And I only hire by word-of-mouth.

"We've no fancy name, or motto, or company song. These ghosts just get things done, I pay them well, and they never go home. No point. For most of them, my shop is their last stop. And one lap with one of my guys or gals is usually all it takes."

Xavier found it hard believe Slattery was serious, but as he listened he was growing more enamored.

"It all sounds so melodramatic. How do you find these people, Enoch?"

"Sir, you cannot understand how many of these somewhat rusty swords are lying around out there on overgrown battlefields that nobody will ever hear about. I'm the guy who picks up and collects those swords.

"We're a retirement home for active adult spooks. Here, retirement age isn't guys in their sixties or seventies. Most of my operatives are in their forties and fifties. They're at the top of their game and looking to double-dip their pension with side jobs. Or they have no pension and no other options.

"They're hardscrabble as Hell, Sir, with tradecraft oozing from their anal-retentive sphincters.

"Some became disillusioned after losing their sanctions. Because they got their rocks off twisting protected titties, or using the wrong third-world asshole's cat or dog or wife for target practice. Or they screwed the wrong guy's goat.

"Besides my overlooking all that, I pay way better than government service, and I offer a great benefits package. Sometimes they get to burn the stuffed shirts that flamed *them*, and they get to watch it on the six o'clock news. Satisfying work.

"Ever hear of Air America, Sir? They transported everything from personnel to *farm equipment* for the CIA. At one time, AA was the largest airline in the world. Talk about surplus potential.

"It's contemporary counterpart, Global International Airlines, superseded AA. Stupid name, I know. Just doesn't matter. Most of the time, you could not find anybody who could even tell you how many planes were in their fleet! Who do you think flew or crewed all those aircraft, or supported them from the ground? A lot of 'em now work for or contract with me. I get a few hard-core foot soldiers too, but not as many."

Xavier sat and listened without interruption. So far, this guy had always been a straight shooter with him.

Enoch continued. "Okay, so I'm showing off a bit but I don't get a lot of chances to do that. You get the idea, Sir."

Fascinated, Xavier asked, "How discreet are your people, Enoch?"

"Let me put it this way. I'm as discreet as they come, outside of you keeping your own dirty little secrets to yourself. No offense. Everybody has 'em. Everybody. And nobody's secrets are safe forever. Between any dork and his prayers to the Almighty, though, is me with my recorder.

"Until I was referred to you, I'd bet you never heard of me, right? Now we know each other, and are guaranteed mutually assured destruction if either violates our code of silence. That's how it works."

That sounded like a veiled threat, but Palmer supposed that was indeed how it worked.

"You never heard of me until you were referred by another of my trusted clients, Mr. Z, right? And I vetted Hell outta *you* before you received my first call.

"So to anyone but my clients, I am a ghost. My discretion is my trade, but that ain't worth jack unless I deliver results. I'm one of the better-trained spooks you'll ever meet outside government—*any* government—and I get results. Always.

"By the way, Sir, very few of my team know each other. Sometimes a job calls for more than one soldier. That's what I call 'em. They like it. Next job, they either fly solo or work with the same operators, if possible. Outside several of these small on-demand units, nobody really knows anybody else. They prefer it that way, too.

"Spookville is an exclusive community. They might guess others they know are around, but we have no central office, no headquarters, no company Christmas parties. These tight-asses prefer privacy and solitude, so all they can do is guess. Most don't even care to try.

"Operationally, there's nothing. Nothing at all. Deep, dark, empty space. Tight compartmentalization makes for very tight security. The same model used by terrorist cells. In fact, we've taken gigs where clients want it to look like terrorists did the deed.

"Look, Sir, this is more than I've talked in years. Are there any other questions you might have for me?"

"Not right now, Enoch. Thank you. Now here's what I'd like you to do for me next."

JULY 2005

WASHINGTON, DC

THE OLD MAN STARED AT THE FIRE.

He'd heard it said the future belonged to those who lived with intensity in the present moment. Yesterday was a canceled check, tomorrow a promissory note.

He was also perceptive enough to know that canceled checks left footprints in the mud. Promissory notes could be useful leverage, as long as *he* held them.

The 2008 elections approached. His favored party anticipated another humiliating defeat. The opposition offered even less. This would bring his beloved adopted nation to the brink of disaster. A negro in the Oval Office?

Not even a Cuban…

His club was one of the oldest and most exclusive in the District, catering to some of Washington's most influential and anonymous movers and shakers. *And* this was also one of the few remaining bastions of its kind for true cigar aficionados. He preened and fired up a box-pressed *Seleccion Oscuro Piramides Royal.*

While not currently rated the best cigar in the world, it commanded respect as one of the top four or five. He always relished patronizing one of the premier old-world boutique cigar makers from Old Havana, even though Ernesto now wrapped his cigars in the DR. Who knows? It could be that the damn things were still rolled on the thighs of virgins in the Dominican Republic, like the old school Cubano catadors.

Like me, the eclectic blend of tobaccos in this black oscuro is aggressive but nuanced.

Over a not-so-wee dram of smoky Lagavulin single malt—neat, of course—his *Royal* weaved its enchanting spell. A colleague and confidante lounging languorously to his immediate right had whispered a most outrageous bon mot. "If we can't convince our own nation to grow a pair, why don't we import them?" He chuckled.

The club library's ambiance seldom failed to lift his spirits as he conjured visions of greatness. Today was an exception. Surrounded by opulent hand-rubbed cherry paneling and countless leather-bound first editions on shelves with intricate trim, he felt at home.

The old power broker cherished subtle complexity.

He gazed upward at the ornate nineteenth century hammered copper ceiling, embedded within a checkerboard of heavily-sculpted cherry beams. The heady aroma of polished brass and oiled leather gone a bit musty made this room one of his favorite places on Earth.

He nestled a bit deeper into his sumptuous green vegetable-tanned Tuscan leather chair that faced a roaring fire under a small but ornate off-white marble mantel.

He welcomed the punch to his chest as he inhaled the *Royal's* throaty bouquet melded with the complex peaty finish of the Scotch drifting across his appreciative palate. Yet, his dark mood refused to shake loose.

His colleague's suggestion bordered on a less tractable form of treason to which he was accustomed, but...

Desperate times.

Yes, he liked the idea. Greater reward mandated greater risk—for the failing Republic. He hoisted his sculpted Baccarat crystal glass to his colleague. "Za zdorovje!" The old boy next to him smiled in benign ignorance.

Americans!

The raging fire crackled, as did his sulfurous ambition which knew no bounds. After all, he *was* a true patriot uprooting the withering tree.

He defined patriotism different than most.

TEAM WORKS

STILLWATER, MINNESOTA

She was the only female, but...

As their team leader, Nora Mathers could not have been more proud of her guys. Especially her husband Frank Lassiter. He was a brilliant programmer, tester, and outstanding leader in his own right. But he had taken a step back when the team leader job opened up two years ago.

Most everyone knew Frank and Nora were an item, even though company policy prohibited fraternization. Nobody objected. They were that good. Few knew they were married. Nobody on the team, anyway. She was quite sure. They were careful.

One of the guys turned toward the front door of the cozy tavern and shouted, "Hey! Look who's finally here!"

Dent Canfield responded with all smiles. He twisted his considerable frame through the forest of tables in the dim but warm overhead glow of Bertha's Pub. A welcome relief indeed from the ocean of gray-green fluorescents of the lab.

"Well, somebody had to represent *The Unholy Seven* and get some real work done before coming out to play!"

The rest of the test team only recently arrived, smiled, and hoisted mugs of beer in salute. Their favorite prankster spun a heavy hardwood chair with one hand and plopped down.

He crossed his muscular arms on the top of its spindled back, scooted in as far as his ample gut allowed, and nuzzled the chair's back up to the table's chipped edge.

"A Leinie's draft, Dent? Yeah, of course. Barkeep! A mugga Leinie's for what's-his-name here!"

"So Dent, did you burn the lab to the ground before making your futile escape, Big Guy?"

Dent said, "Naw. I figured the mess would be a pain in the ass tomorrow. Might even slow down finishing this frickin' release."

This close-knit team of software testers took their jobs seriously. They were the best and knew it. Like clockwork, the team rendezvoused for beers at Bertha's every Friday afternoon, four p.m. on the dot.

Bertha's was a somewhat obscure after-work oasis. They'd all be back in the lab Saturday before nine a.m. for another ten- to twelve-hour shift. But this tight group of professionals treasured their Friday respite. Tomorrow, Nora had requested they start even earlier.

Dent said, "Oh-nine-hundred tee time tomorrow at Northern Hills, anyone?"

The response was boisterous and immediate. Punctuated with Bronx cheers, mild profanity and good-natured jokes, the team mocked Dent's dubious ancestry.

Dent dead-panned as if he was about to complain. "Hey guys, what do you say to a team leader who tells us we gotta be in the lab at oh-seven-hundred hours on a Saturday morning? You say 'Yes, ma'am! And do you need us Sunday morning before or after church?'"

The group clustered around the cheap circular wood-grain table roared with good-natured belly-laughs and back-slapping. Nora rewarded Dent with a grateful grin.

She hated the name with which he'd dubbed the team—The Unholy Seven. *He brings it up almost ritualistically at every one of these weekly gatherings.*

They always had fun with it, though. Another one of Dent's many quirks. *Oh well.*

Even after all these years, Dent still operated on military time. She could tell the Army and gauzy third-world combat memories still tainted his DNA. *What did this guy go through so the rest of us could be here, laughing?*

Perhaps more than her other guys, he *earned* his seat at this table. And when he was having a good day…

Bertha's Pub sported its own funky sway that appealed to a small but devoted clientele. Mostly to the fun-loving geeks from GGS and a few local wannabes. She viewed Bertha's as the tech version of a cop bar and its flock of groupies.

The warm flicker of votive candles swimming in cheesy brown glass jars on each table appealed to this group. That dim light became more appealing as long Minnesota winters wore on.

The team looked forward to Freaks' Fridays at Bertha's, even though weekend work had become the new normal. This was no different than most every other large high-technology multinational in America, maybe in the world. These were sought-after jobs, especially in a small town like Stillwater. But when you were a professional, it meant you were paid a flat salary, not an hourly wage.

The pay was lucrative, especially the bonuses and stock options, if and when they happened. Not as many these days. In return, employees did whatever was necessary to get the job done. Or that job just might get shipped to a different continent. Most of the team were salaried and proud of their professional status. Few complained about the long hours, but…

Nora worried how long she could press her team this hard. Generous vacation plans collected dust in desk drawers. There seemed no end in sight. She said as much on several occasions to her boss Donny Segwell.

"Donny, the team is running strong, but more and more ragged around the edges."

"Nora, you're a good team leader. Your strength is leading by example. Complain to me behind closed doors all you want. I'll always listen."

Behind closed doors meant within Donny's stifling eight-by-twelve-foot windowless office with lights too bright and outlooks too dim. He stuffed his desk, chair, and two guest chairs into those austere confines. A few family pictures and a computer terminal perched on his otherwise bare metal desk. Jeez. At least managers had private offices. Might she be management material herself?

She said, "Of course, but what's going to happen over time?"

"We continue to do our jobs."

She had stopped going to Donny. He was a good guy, but what was he going to do? She knew every year meant more cuts *and* more work.

She spoke up over the buzzing and clinking at Bertha's, "Guys, next round is on me!"

Her dear hubby Frank broadcast a smile in her general direction.

~

SEPTEMBER 2005
STILLWATER, MINNESOTA

AUTUMN ANNOUNCED ITSELF IN MINNESOTA.

Crispy and crunchy as usual, drifts of desiccated leaves disintegrated underfoot.

George Janis and Maxine Sun sat facing each other, investing a sideways gaze at the maple trees through the window-wall of George's office. This time of year brought spectacular color to the massive Greater Global Solutions Stillwater campus. Their casual demeanor spoke volumes of their relationship.

George needed to seek Maxine's advice and counsel on a matter that was keeping him awake at night. More than usual.

"Thanks again for introducing me to our new team in Singapore, Maxine. While they all spoke English, that Mandarin-speaking cab driver could have really taken me for a ride!"

He chuckled, rather embarrassed by his too-obvious metaphor.

"And I get the feeling that your flawless dialogue with our Chinese and Malaysian senior managers expedited our difficult organizational meetings."

Maxine stuttered a bit in English, but not in any other language she spoke fluently. Curious.

"You always try to speak a few local w-words, butchering them badly, George. Intentionally, I would guess. Never fails to amuse." Maxine spoke with the barest hint of a smile.

"Guilty, as charged."

Low-cost skills were king, requiring sustained focus. The Far East region was ground zero, at least for the next few years. No country remained low cost forever, and that was where Maxine's language skills remained critical as they periodically trudged through that revolving door. Costs always escalated over time in any country, often *because* of their presence. Then they'd move on.

George jumped into the issue he wished to discuss.

"They need another twenty percent, Maxine. Last year we achieved close to that with sleight of hand. But now mere financial re-engineering won't achieve that. I've whacked all the redundant infrastructure across my divisions. And the deadwood's already gone.

"This is going to affect two hundred real jobs held by good performers. I've been working with my peers, some of whom still have budget dollars. I was hoping they could use some of our skills, but…"

He furrowed his brow with worry as he anticipated new nightmares.

"Prospects are grim for placing our folks elsewhere within the company. You know this means another big surplus program."

Surplus—the GGS euphemism for permanent layoffs. Good people would essentially be fired, but given good references and the possibility of a severance package.

"Okay, you n-need to address the team immediately. Share with them the challenge. They'll worry, as they should, but they will also appreciate your honesty. Advise everyone to update their CVs."

George wasn't so sure. He worried about impacting productivity, but agreed. Yes, Maxine was right. As usual. "God, this sucks. We're in for a tough series of ranking sessions with the managers. Sooner is better."

Ranking set the stage, the painful process of prioritizing employees by their performance. Lower performers got the ax. Better performers got to stick around and pick up the slack.

George said, "Please make sure the local managers know that describing someone's performance with statements like, 'he's a good guy' isn't going to cut it anymore. I do *not* want to hear that ever again. Especially from Donny. Let's be blunt. We're going to be firing good people this time around."

Donny Segwell excelled as a people manager, but he often got too close to his employees to remain objective. George understood all too well.

Maxine said. "It would help if the m-managers realized this is no longer about good or bad performers. Now it's about good, better, or best. Let's set that expectation clearly with them. They need to hear that from you, George. And that you're not singling out your Stillwater team."

"Agree. Good. Set it up. I'll be traveling to all my other sites for the same task."

"We'll get through this, George. We always d-do." Maxine's eyes would roll up and to the right as she struggled to speak in her non-native English.

"I'll make sure our teams here understand."

Though she tried to avoid problematic words, she trudged through what had to be said. She gave no consideration to embarrassment over her speech impediment. And even though she was barely five feet tall, she exuded a strong presence.

She fell silent.

"Thanks. As always, I value your insights that, by the way, are always a bit different from everyone else's."

George adopted a deliberate and more formal manner of speech when communicating with anyone for whom English was not their primary language. This was true with Maxine too.

As an afterthought, she said, "It's our little d-differences that can make a world of difference, and if you need *my* job, George, I'd understand. Middle managers are your next logical opportunity."

They knew what had to be done next and parted with a warm handshake. God, he hated this part of the job.

A notion occurred to George. *Maxine is where Confucius meets Mr. Spock, and the two are as one.*

A GRUESOME ITEM DEMANDED ATTENTION.

The group met next door to George's office.

He sat at the table's head in his sunny conference room near the periphery of the sprawling low-rise GGS facility in Stillwater.

George spent summers at his office here when he wasn't traveling. He worked from his condo in Southwest Florida from late September to early May. He would only be in town for a few more weeks between trips to his other locations. Freezing temps threatened to escalate Kate's arthritis to a debilitating degree.

Teams at GGS locations across the U.S. and in eighteen other countries worked for George, although the Stillwater team was his largest. He had begun his career here. Above all, he was one of them and had developed close relationships with this team. So they were very comfortable inviting *the big boss* to discuss what appeared to be a minor problem with the potential for escalation.

George enjoyed the cordial interaction and liked getting out in front of issues with this team. Besides, this was a good precursor to the more difficult ranking discussions to come.

"So what's going on, guys?" The room remained quiet.

With no answer forthcoming, George continued. "I know that picture board was meant to be a team-building exercise. So two-hundred folks could put names to faces as they passed each other in the hallway.

"And now somebody steals a single picture of the best-looking female on the entire team? Not once, but twice? This was a good idea, but now I'm not so sure. We have to hope that someone didn't just jerk the pin from a grenade."

Donny Segwell was not the best technical manager, but brilliant with people. If he envisioned a personnel problem, it needed attention. George turned to him and asked, "What do you think, Donny?"

"No idea, George, but we still think the picture board is good for the team. Since Nora's picture was the only one taken, folks had mentioned it to her. She came to see me and I could tell this creeped her out. Especially after the second photo disappeared this week."

Nora Mathers was jaw-dropping gorgeous. And the technical team loved and respected her. George knew that Donny and the team needed her head in the game.

Donny said, "I'd hate to lose the positive effects of that board. But we need to show Nora and others that we're serious about their concerns. How about we lock it up? Put the whole damn board inside a lockable clear plastic display case?"

George was a courtesy guest, and the hall talk had him curious. He liked Nora too. This was Maxine Sun's meeting. Maxine was Donny's boss who said, "Good i-idea, Don. Let's do that. But let's not post another picture of Nora until that's done, okay guys?"

Other worries plagued George. He needed to hammer out next year's budget proposal with all his sites within the next three weeks.

He knew Donny and the rest of his team were committed to their mission. They developed and maintained a significant piece of the complex software-driven GGS-wide ordering process. Customers could not order most GGS products without their stuff. Even *it* was useless unless updated and tested for six hundred complex new products each week.

Now another complication within an important team.

A CHANGE OF MADNESS

THEY DESCENDED OVER HIM.

Ever since he was a kid, once in a while, often at the worst times, Dent Canfield's vision darkened under an ominous cloud. It seemed to descend over him unbidden—his resident bogeyman.

Sometimes, that murky cloud would take form. Sometimes it drifted nearby. Close enough that he could smell it and hear it snap and pop.

When that happened, it impeded his vision. It reminded him of the pungent smoke from burning flux that sizzles when touched by a red-hot soldering iron. It was like that sometimes. At others, that cloud billowed farther away, less threatening. More like a towering thunderhead off in the distance that never got anybody wet nearby. But it still produced dread and despair.

Once in awhile, Dent felt privileged when a disembodied voice sounded off in his head, almost as if by magic. If he were a religious drone, he might believe this was the voice of God speaking to him, but that would be nonsense. He trusted that small but insistent voice, although he wasn't quite sure why.

Turning to work, he was beginning to think that this team of management stooges had it out for him. He was thinking of that big-cheese ass-hat, George Janis. He damn well dangled his local puppets on a stout string. None of these civilian assholes had a clue what real life was like. Too soft for too long, for sure.

The voice asked him, *"So why do you think his name is Janis, Denton?"*

"Well, I remember something from one of my Humanities cruise courses at SCSU. In Roman mythology, Janus was the god of beginnings and transitions. Like the dark territory between peace and war. No doubt this guy thinks of himself as a god, too. He is a two-faced son-of-a-bitch!"

"You have your answer, Denton. Well done, my son."

"Pisses me off when I think about that stupid promotion party last April. So ten dick-lickers get promoted from associate to senior associate stooge. And everybody's pacified by a hundred bucks worth of cheap beer on GGS at Bertha's Pub. Typical."

"Denton, why is that particular party so memorable for you?"

Sometimes, that voice sounded like the impotent therapist he never saw anymore.

"That's easy. That ass-wipe George Janis has the balls to walk up to me and ask, 'It's Dent, right? So Dent, how come your name wasn't on the list of promos this time?'

"I'll never forget that arrogant smirk on his smug face. He knows damn well I didn't get promoted because of that queen bitch Nora. She burned up her promotion quota on one of her golfing buddies instead of the top performer on her team. I didn't even want a promotion, but the idea..."

An urgent warning issued from his inner voice. *"Keep smiling, Denton. They don't need to know everything, do they?"*

Dent finally responded, "Well, George, I'm keeping my head down, trying to make the whole team look good. My name will pop soon enough. It's nice to have a party for all the folks who're getting recognized tonight. They deserve it. And by the way, thanks for coming."

"'Atta boy! Good for you,' the condescending jerk said. Boy? I've got your boy right here, you empty suit."

Dent steamed in the sounds of silence as he mentally grabbed his crotch in contempt.

"And what about that wife of his, Kate? Jee-ZEUS! Seems smart, but she's not even that hot. She could stand to lose a few pounds. Some trophy wife! And the guys weren't even talking to her.

"Sandy said, 'Man, there's another round of layoffs coming. You *know* there is.'

"And Sherm said, 'Yeah, these managers will do anything to snag their sacred budget numbers.'

"Doesn't matter to them they're screwing up people's lives. Pisses me off.'"

The voice said, *"There's a great deal of anger in your voice, Denton."*

"No kidding! I really got steamed when Mrs. Puppet-Master tried to give us the benefit of her Country Club wisdom. She was trying to make like one of the team. Playing pool with some of the boys upstairs, like she belonged there.

"As if she had a right to say anything to real people, she said, 'No offense, guys, but you have no idea what you're talking about. I've seen George come home with tears in his eyes because he changed a bunch of people's lives, and not for the better.'

'No offense, Mrs. Janis…'

'Kate, please…'

'Well, no offense, Kate, but why is George even in that job if it's so painful?'

'I'll share a little secret with you guys. Because as things get tougher, and they will, George is convinced that he will be able to influence events just a little more compassionately than the next guy who'd move in behind him.'"

Dent continued to confide to his inner friend, *"The suckers actually bought that line. She must have practiced that little speech for awhile. It was like shouting into a five-gallon bucket and hearing only the hollow reverb of your own voice. And… wasn't it a hoot watching the managers scramble today? They finally realized her pic was missing from the board!"*

Dent retreated further into his own silent reverie. *Jeez, that picture board! The best part? Her Polaroid was up there too. What a picture. A fingernail under the head of one thumb tack and she was his. Happy day. And, oh man, what a weekend.*

The voice eased into therapist mode again. *"It is obvious that picture is important to you."*

Dent said, *"Yeah, especially what it represents. These managers are all about teamwork. They want to encourage social interaction among the team. Kum-Ba-Yah!*

"Remember that first picture?" He smiled as he addressed his therapist, his confidante. *"It was so flimsy that it only lasted a few days. But then I discovered a wonderful new use for Ziploc bags. Remember?"*

"Yes, I remember, Denton."

He needed another snap of her. Then he got the second one.

"That one-quart bag protected her and gave me edges to grab. Handles. Perfect during the heat of passion, huh?" He didn't want to obscure a single square millimeter of her gorgeous head shot. *"Besides, it made cleanup easier."*

The voice whispered to him, *"She does want you, Denton, but that hasn't yet occurred to her. Until then, why not enjoy her every night at home? How about at work? You deserve it. You deserve her."*

What a delicious secret between two conspirators.

"It makes me happy to see you're amused by the uproar over that missing picture, Denton. Imagine the conversations!"

Dent's imagination ran riot.

"Yeah. That delicate thing drives me insane. Every guy on the team tries hard not to gape at her whenever she's around."

THE DAYS AT THE LAB WORE ON.

Dent could not get Nora Mathers to leave his mind alone. Even her own attempts to downplay her natural allure proved futile. She wore little or no makeup, baggy blouses, blue jeans—not baggy—and no jewelry. She wasn't fooling Dent.

"She can't hide all that, especially when the camera adores her. I can't believe any work gets done at all when she's around."

He noted she was, in fact, the only really attractive woman in a sea of female nerds as he scanned the test floor. He visualized her a super nova amidst a sea of dark matter, bright lab lights notwithstanding.

"Do you think you indulge in fantasies about her too much, Denton?"

"Hell, no! She's even soft-spoken with a smile so hot it melts chocolate from across the room. And the best part of all? She doesn't even seem to care much for her own beauty, even though she takes really good care of herself. How is that even possible? She always smiles at me. That's good, right?"

Then she was right there in front of him. Right in front of *his* workstation.

"Good morning, Dent." And he *did* have a bar of chocolate in his front pocket.

The voice said, *"Say something, Denton!"*

"Hey, Nora. You look great today." She stood *right in front of him.* From his seated position, the best of her taunted him. He told himself, *Don't stare at her, you idiot!*

He loved her long blonde and slightly frizzy hair that draped in loose curls around her shoulders and down the middle of her back. And those brilliant pale blue eyes? They threatened to hypnotize him into speechlessness every time he dared gaze at them. Or worse, inspire him to say something stupid. Her perfectly sculpted nose and long creamy white neck—

"Uh, thanks, Dent. Have you seen Frank around?"

He could see she was trying to move on. His awkwardness around her seemed to creep her out a little. He never failed to say exactly the wrong thing. But she seemed to accept him for who he was.

Frank Lassiter was Nora's perfect safety net. He was never far away, but far enough. Since management discouraged team members dating, Frank tried to make himself scarce once in awhile. But everyone knew he and Nora were not only an item outside work, some of the team suspected they might even be married. Nobody pressed the matter. Not even management.

They're way too perfect together, aren't they? Doesn't matter. Frank is too slick, in a down home country boy sort of way. Of course, everybody likes him. He's quiet, lanky and far too witty. Yeah, that's it. Too damn self-assured. I can do something about that one day. I have important plans. On so many levels.

His inner voice shouted, *"Denton, you must say something out loud. Now!"*

Dent finally responded. "Um, yeah. I think Frank's in the lab supervising the team testing the latest compile."

Frank doubled as Nora's second and was responsible for preparing each weekly release. This was a massive body of intricate software called the configurator. Everyone, including Dent, knew this work was critical to generating billions in corporate revenue.

"Thanks, Dent. Well, I gotta run. I have a ten o'clock."

She hurried off, as Dent looked on.

After ensuring nobody was watching *him*, over his shoulder he whispered to the voice as if it were standing close behind, *"Can you believe how she swings those little hips that look like they belong on a teenage nymph? Of course, it's all to tempt me. Bitch."*

DESCENT INTO MADNESS

D**ENT FINGERED THE SMALL SILVER AMULET.**

It featured a delicate turquoise inset and hung from a fine silver chain.

That amulet remained a treasured reminder of an erotic dream in which he indulged now and then.

H**E SHIVERED IN THE DARKNESS.**

Late one mild September evening in Southeast Minnesota, a gentle breeze swept across the cracked asphalt. He wasn't thinking about the weather. Or the asphalt.

The immense GGS parking lot was well-lit. Dent parked his aging white Cadillac next to an immaculate red three-year-old two-door Malibu. Her car. Theirs comprised a two-car island in a desolate dead sea of black tarmac and white lines.

Nora Mathers and Frank Lassiter often drove to work in separate vehicles. He parked his expensive blacked-out Harley Road King

Custom close to the buildings in a small lot designated for motorcycles only. They called that 'rock star parking.' *Seriously?*

As Nora approached, his heart skipped a few beats, not just because she was his team leader, but for far more intimate reasons. He could not get her out of his mind.

The fantasies always started well, but never ended that way. There was almost always copious blood splatter involved. This confused and excited him.

"Hey, Nora. Another late night, huh?" He sauntered around the hood of his car to hers and leaned on the top edge of her driver's door with his left hand, his fingertips resting on the roof.

"Hey Dent, can't get your car started? Need a ride?" she chirped.

Dent thought she sounded like a clueless parakeet about to be snared by a ravenous hawk. "Naw, just want to catch you for a sec."

"You gonna be at Bertha's tomorrow with the rest of the team?"

"Sure, but maybe the two of us might wanna hook up before then. Heard ole Frank's burning the midnight oil tonight."

"Um, Dent, you know Frank and I are together, right? Not a good idea here. At all."

Now, he towered over her. It was obvious she felt he was way too close. He knew she could smell his provocative musk. She was obviously trying not to overreact.

Then he shocked her by gliding the fingers of his right hand around the edge of her delicate left ear. He swept her hair back suggestively. He lingered, taking his time to slide the backs of his hairy fingers down the left side of her fragile neck. He contemplated slipping his palm behind her neck with a small turn of his wrist to draw her in…

She froze in fear.

Reminded him of Liz's neck.

The purr he intended came out more of a croak. "No harm, no foul, right?"

Her fear aroused him.

Finally, she recoiled, trying to force his considerable bulk away from her, using her hip against the car as leverage. Not much moved.

"Dent, *I gotta go.* See you tomorrow." He made no attempt to remove his left hand resting on her driver's door, which she tried and failed to open. Might as well have been welded shut.

"Dent! Move! Now!"

Her harsh words startled him. It was his turn to recoil.

"Oh, right. Sorry. No offense. See you tomorrow."

He watched her fumble with her keys in amusement. He could see her shaking in shock—enough to scratch the edge of her door with her fist full of keys as she violently swung it open. She looked either pissed or scared, or both. Good.

He sauntered back to his car thinking, *Man, she can get ugly in a hurry.* He did not like that. At all. *Pretty queen bitch.* Her sudden shift in attitude, for no good reason, reminded him of his ex-wife, Liz. That was, what, eighteen, nineteen years ago?

Yeah, it was almost twenty years ago already, wasn't it?

APRIL 1988

HARTFORD, CONNECTICUT

It had been magic... at first.

He remembered how they met.

"How do you *do* it, Dent?"

Liz Warden stared at him with admiration. "You must absolutely *think* in numbers. This is so elegant!"

He knew his military experience turned her on. She had asked if she could see him in his Army uniform and his sexy brown beret sometime. And she couldn't stop asking him if he'd *been through a lot.*

Liz said her father had always taught her the importance of honor and service. She said she knew service could extract a horrendous price.

A soldier groupie. He could use that.

"Hartford is a small town, and Southern Connecticut State isn't that big. Why is it we've never crossed paths before grad school?"

Dent more or less mumbled, "Well, truth is I tested out of most courses without attending many classes. I'm not much of a people person."

That night, their five-person study group was analyzing an HBR accounting case study. Dent always said most Harvard Business Review articles covered ludicrous real-world business scenarios. This one described two companies that used different inventory accounting practices. The question on the table: which company performed better and why?

After the entire group sat dumbfounded for several minutes. Dent lectured the confused little group with a few quick pronouncements as if anyone not getting this was an idiot.

"Look, it's the first company. No question. A far more interesting question? How could that company avoid paying their more costly tax bill? *And* without anyone noticing."

"Um, as long as it's legal, right?"

Elizabeth Warden was adorable. As long as it's legal. He knew the place for legalities in accounting was when you were taking a CPA cert exam. Not in the real world.

Dent's mind worked like that of a criminal. He wasn't one, of course. But he figured the way he was wired, he could catch bad guys fudging numbers. This explained his attraction to Fraud and Forensic Accounting. The ultimate opportunity to show he was the smartest guy in the room over and over again?

He even amazed himself how he could see things in numbers nobody else did. Lesser mortals. Dent knew he could leverage his unique perspective to make a great deal of money. He just knew he had to do this. Besides, he loved exploiting other peoples' weaknesses.

Yes, this would be his life's calling.

The fact that petite Lizzy Double-U found him brilliant? Well, that was just too much. That little turned-up nose and her twenty-something-going-on-seventeen body of hers? That pushed his V8 revving into the danger zone.

Six weeks later, a JP married them in Hartford. They parroted standard vows printed on a laminated three-by-five card—his on one side, hers on the other.

Their demanding class schedules preempted the newly minted couple's honeymoon. Dent's accounting internship further complicated things. They did manage to squeeze in a romantic weekend at a B&B in Mystic Seaport.

"Oh, Dent, this is so beautiful! I wish we could stay here forever."

"C'mon, kiddo, you know how loaded up I am with the ole internship at Vernon-Westphal. And you carrying over twenty grad credits? Kudos, but... Hey, let's enjoy this while we're here. We'll take a real honeymoon once things settle down, okay Sweetness?"

A 360-degree curtain crowned the ancient cast-iron clawfoot tub in a corner their room near a rear window. It hung with fatigue from a tarnished oval brass rail by dozens of clear plastic S-hooks so they could either bathe or shower.

"C'mon, Mrs. C, let's grab a shower together. Save water."

"Okay, Mr. C, but no funny stuff! We have reservations."

He took his time soaping her porcelain doll's back, marveling that he stood over a foot taller. Like bathing an innocent child. Ever since the study group, she frequented his erotic dreams, asleep or awake.

"Don't you ever take that thing off?"

The small silver amulet with a delicate turquoise inset hung from a thread of a silver necklace. It suited her tiny neck, obscured here and there by his energetic sudsing.

"It belonged to my mother and her mother before her, Dent. My mom gave it to me when I told her we'd married. It's a family tradition. And no, I'll never take it off, not until *our* daughter gets married to the love of *her* life. It's a whole sacred thing with the women in our family."

"That's sweet, Liz. Everything about you is adorable. You know that?"

They missed their dinner reservation.

~

MARCH 1989

ARLINGTON, VIRGINIA

LESS THAN A YEAR LATER...

Events conspired against Dent with frightening rapidity. Deep concern consumed Liz.

Though small, someone had tastefully decorated their rented apartment within the last decade or two. But visitors, which they never had, might have noticed peculiarities.

Fist-sized impressions marked at least one wall of each of their three rooms. Something had pressed the heavy velvet Victorian wallpaper into the sheetrock underneath.

An otherwise spotless white area rug in the living room exhibited several large overlapping stains. Deep four-foot jagged gouges scarred the varnished maple floor planking around the edges of the rug as if made by giant claws. Scratches in the off-white six-panel door to the bathroom would have begged questions too.

And a subtle but curious odor permeated the air. Not quite pungent, but sour, like curdled milk and vinegar.

"Honey, you need more help than I can offer."

"That's a load 'a crap. I'm not the one that..."

"Listen to yourself! It's never your fault. Never! How is that even possible within a relationship between two reasonable people?"

"Look, don't even try to understand me, okay? You have no idea what I'm dealing with."

"Dent, there's something wrong. You can't see it. I can. We should see someone..."

"For crying out loud, Liz. We don't need to see someone!"

"Well, what about…?"

He closed his eyes, a feral growl came from deep within his constricting throat through gritting teeth. He tasted bile. The annoying drone of her voice once sounded so lyrical. Now the very notion of it, when he listened, caused his head to vibrate in sync with the slow motion of the planet's rotation. Somebody told him that's, like, seven cycles per second.

He seemed guided by that old familiar voice beyond himself. Or that reverberated from somewhere within his lizard brain. He wasn't sure. Now it annoyed him that he was forced to listen to her *and* it. They seldom agreed. On anything.

"You refuse to take your meds, which you do need so very much, and I don't know what to do about that anymore! I used to love you so much, Dent, but I can't handle your crazy mood swings! I… just… can't…"

She was sobbing a soft apology, her shoulders convulsing up and down in rhythm to the abyssal depth of her pain. Tears tumbled onto the front of her stained silk blouse.

He could smell the disgust she felt for him at that moment.

"*Used* to love me? And did you actually just use the c-word? Those damn pills make my goddamn dick limp, and then you bitch about no goddamn sex! Which way do we twist this thing, *Elizabeth?* You're trying to launch my balls into space while they're still clamped in the jaws of a vice in Virginia! Will you… GIVE… ME… A… BREAK!"

As if by magic, her shoulders and head pressed so hard into the wall repeatedly to the rhythm of his rant, they ripped the wallpaper. The sheetrock underneath tried to crumble.

Dent's huge hands encompassed her throat, his fingers connecting at the back of Liz's little neck. Her tear-stained cheeks now inches from his mostly white eyes widened in terror.

Not able to meet his maniacal glare, she looked down. She saw the chords and bright blue veins on his muscular forearms distended. Somehow, there was blood flowing from her left nostril and from the back of her head. Her blood now dripped onto the hands still clutching her tiny neck.

"I'm sorry, baby," he said, but it came out much louder than he intended—a pleading screech.

He relaxed his grip as he allowed his arms to fall. Like they were tree trunks felled and rough-stripped of their bark. How could she do this to him, getting him so cranked up? All he wanted was some quiet.

He knew it was over. It was in her eyes. Nothing remained to be said. That was clear. The blessed silence thundered through his temples, like an earthquake in deep space.

And then she was gone.

THAT WAS 1989.

Now Dent saw Liz in Nora's eyes as he fingered the small silver amulet with a delicate turquoise inset hung from a silver thread.

MANAGING CONSEQUENCES

S EPTEMBER 2005
STILLWATER, MINNESOTA

Nora knew she had no choice.

Frank needed to know what happened in the parking lot with Dent an hour earlier now that they were home safe together.

"He did *what?* I'll castrate that slimy bastard!" Frank was as lathered up as she'd ever seen him.

"Frank, I think there's something wrong. He was like in a dream or something. Let Donny handle it. You steer clear. You hear me? He was a *Ranger* for God's sake."

This wasn't soaking in. Frank exuded swirling clouds of malevolent fumes as he paced… stomped.

Nora knew Frank had a temper, but she'd never seen… He wasn't listening to anything she was saying.

"Damn it, Frank? I'm thinking serious medical or mental issue."

She was petrified at who might do what to whom.

Frank settled down. Or so it seemed. But his voice—low and even, nostrils flaring—alarmed her like never before.

"What exactly did he say to you?"

"Oh, Frank..."

"Damn it, Nora. Tell me."

"Well..."

She proceeded to tell him, word for word, everything that transpired in the parking lot with Dent.

"Did... he... touch you?"

"Frank,"

"Nora, exactly *how* did he touch you? Please."

"He touched my cheek, my ear, brushed my hair. That's all."

"And what were you doing during this time, Nor?"

"I was backed up against my car. He sort of hovered over me. I could smell him. I tried to open my door. He wouldn't let me. I shouted at him and he seemed to break out of a dream or something. That's all, Frank."

Now his lack of visible emotion scared her even more than his earlier bluster.

Her gentle husband looked dangerous.

At the risk of making matters worse, she told him one more thing that she found most frightening of all.

"Frank, you need to know. After I yelled at him so he'd wake up or whatever, there was something very spooky in his eyes. I was looking at a different person. I saw something sinister, something savage. Dent directed that look *into* me."

That got Frank's attention. He turned introspective.

"Okay, yeah. Sick. We may be out of our depth here. Babe, I won't do anything stupid, but if he makes another move..."

Nora took a deep breath and exhaled slowly with relief.

❧

NORA MATHERS CONFRONTED HER MANAGER.

The next morning, she started to describe what they now called the parking lot incident. Donny Segwell stopped her mid-sentence and phoned his boss. He wanted more horsepower involved.

A few moments later, Maxine Sun glided into Donny's office, greeted Nora with a subtle nod. She took a chair beside Nora.

Without preamble, Maxine spoke. "Please s-start from the beginning."

As Nora relived the bizarre event by speaking of it, her fear and shock approached a consuming paralysis. She repeated what happened in a quivering voice they listened hard to hear. Her eyes cast toward her feet.

Donny gently half-whispered, "Nora, are you alright?" This was not the Nora they knew. If she had been watching her bosses' eyes, she would have seen Donny and Maxine connecting dots. The missing photo now made complete sense.

Nora gathered her fortitude as she spoke and became assertive once more. "I'm fine, you guys. I've never had anything like this happen before. There's something very wrong with Dent. His eyes..."

Later, Nora retold her story yet again to George and his entire staff, now with her old confidence. They were drawing on the entire management team's experience now. Any reticence due to Nora's concern for Dent had evaporated. Ms. Team Leader was back.

A half-hour later, one of Nora's testers called her from the lab. Jay's voice cracked as he spoke. She met him in the hallway with offices on one side and the test lab on the other. The lab's lights illuminated the hallway through the frosted glass wall.

She agreed to meet him near the test lab's door guarded by a security badge reader. Jay had found a defiled photo. Unknown to him, however, she now assumed with certainty that Dent did this.

When she first saw the condition of her own picture, she surprised herself with a sense of shame. The shame of what? Of her own attractiveness? Shame that she might be the cause of Dent's perverted behavior in some small way?

But that was silly. No, he's ill, or something. Those glazed eyes haunted her. Then that undeserved sense of shame morphed into raw rage, still tempered by pity, but not much. Not anymore.

Nora looked deep into her tester's confused eyes. Jay's own confusion and disgust were evident. She could see it had been difficult for him to bring this object of revulsion to her. He didn't even want to touch it and presented it to her sandwiched in a flimsy tissue.

Without offering to take it, Nora said, "Jay, you take that to Donny right now. Tell him exactly where you found it and when, okay? And please don't talk about this with anybody. At least for now. Thanks. I know this was hard for you."

Within the hour, with a recommendation from Maxine, Donny invited Nora, Claire, their organization's HR manager, and Claire's upline manager to an emergency staff meeting. They discussed a decision of consequence.

Today would be ugly.

After Nora brought everyone up to speed, they agreed that Donny would interview Dent, to hear his side of the story. Donny would then expect him to submit to a medical exam and a psychological evaluation. Donny made no secret that he was apprehensive about this interview.

Maxine made it clear this must all happen as soon as possible while the incident was fresh. But she also solicited any other guidance George might feel warranted.

George's alarm was visible. He'd seen variations of this theme before, but not to this degree.

"I want a security team involved. Ask them to equip Donny with a wireless panic button."

Donny became more anxious the more he listened. Most of this was new to him. "Is all this necessary? I mean, I'm just going to talk to the guy."

George explained, "It's only prudent that we plan for the worst. Okay, Donny?"

"Uh, sure Boss, I guess. Jeez." He felt way out of his depth, but this was the job.

"Not to worry. Donny, you're a good manager. And remember, you have an entire team behind you here. Do the best you know how, and you'll be fine."

George then directed his attention to the HR manager. "Claire, I need your team to perform the deepest background check possible on this guy. Fast. We need to learn as much as we can about his emotional state upon his discharge from the military and his time since. Can do?"

"Yes, of course. We need to manage the risk here."

She left without saying another word. But her tone revealed a sense of culpability. HR's initial background check of Denton Canfield surfaced no mental health issues. And if he turned out to be dangerous…

The wheels turned faster now.

George counseled Donny and Maxine to ensure they were up to this unpleasant but necessary task. Donny was too sensitive about this stuff, but it was clear he was glad to have Maxine backing him up.

This team had executed surplus programs that affected dozens of employees. George's experience in such matters went much further. He had implemented a wide range of programs that affected hundreds of employees.

Nobody with a strong sense of humanity ever got used to this.

DIVORCING ENMITY

THE WEAPONRY SEEMED OUT OF PLACE.

Maxine Sun and a three-person armed team from Security stood at the ready in the hallway around the corner from Donny's office.

Donny launched right into the core of the matter.

"Dent, you frightened Nora last night in the parking lot. She didn't want to say anything, but she was so shaken, she had no choice. Whatever happened is unacceptable. What can you tell me about that?"

Dent said, "Yes, I talked with Nora last night, but I did not do or say anything inappropriate. She must have misconstrued my concern for her safety."

Donny could see Dent was either distorting the facts or lying outright. This was now Nora's word against his. But the charge of harassment came from a credible source and had to be investigated. It could not end here.

"Well, um, whatever happened got her pretty upset, so I need you to avoid any isolated one on one contact with her going forward, just to be considerate of her feelings, okay Dent?"

He simmered in anger but agreed. "Hey, I just want what's best for the team."

"One more thing. I'm sure you understand this, Dent. GGS takes these sorts of situations very seriously. What's best for the team right now is for us to explore why Nora felt as uncomfortable as she did. I know you like Nora. I need you to do something for her and for the team."

Donny watched Dent squirm in his chair. Then he squared off. The body language shouted this was not going well. Dent clenched his fingers into fists before relaxing them again, clenched and unclenched, his grinding jaw bone visible at his cheeks.

And Dent's eyes, those eyes, turned cold, hard, flinty.

Donny was mad at himself for the beads of sweat popping out all over his own forehead and flowing down the middle of his back, and at his own feeling of personal dread. Dent's amiable facade had faded, like the colors of an old ragged flag.

Donny braced himself. The words refused to come. For thirty seconds, the two men stared at each other.

Dent now wore a translucent mask of practiced neutrality, but it cracked at its edges.

Donny's mask was no mask at all. He oozed empathy, or was it sympathy? No, it was fear.

He finally forced the nervous words from his throat in an unsteady voice. "Dent, protocol in situations like this mandates you meet with the team from Medical. That would include an interview with a psychologist. I'll set that up for later today."

Through gritted teeth and a shallow smile that barely creased his lips grown thin, Dent said, "Donny, I'm sorry. I can't do that. I've done nothing wrong. To me, that would be an admission of guilt for something I didn't do."

Donny was at a loss for words as Dent rose, turned, and left. They both knew the team's dynamics would now mutate toward a very dark direction indeed.

Donny now worried about Frank confronting Dent. He worried

about Dent confronting Nora again. And he worried about Nora's effectiveness to lead her team with this disturbing distraction.

He just worried.

At the same time, Dent had just refused to comply with a clear mandate, a direct order. What he'd ask Dent to do was not optional. He knew he needed help. Everyone liked Dent, but they protected Nora. This was going to disrupt everyone. But protocol must be followed.

Donny asked himself for the hundredth time today, *Remind me again why I got into management?* This was volatile. Now he worried about the roiling magma chamber about to erupt into a deadly pyroclastic flow. He had a bad feeling about what was likely to happen next.

Damn!

~

WHEN HE THOUGHT THE WORST WAS OVER...

The next morning, no fancy words could describe the worst day ever, and it was only ten a.m. Donny Segwell knew it would be a long one.

First, one of the testers spotted the tattered remains of a photo in a dark corner of the test lab behind a waste basket yesterday, and had just brought that... artifact to him. Although almost unrecognizable, there was no doubt it was the first missing Polaroid of Nora Mathers.

Someone vitiated that photo in a most disgusting manner. Medical guessed the layers of desiccated material on its surface were dried semen.

Then Nora caught Dent glaring from across the lab. She told Donny she was petrified that Frank would notice and lose it.

Much worse, HR's thorough background check on Dent discovered a disturbing surprise. They had dug much deeper than mandated by standard employment procedures. Dent's claims of military service were a complete fabrication.

At GGS, lying on an employment application was considered an inviolate COE, or Condition of Employment. This was acronym-speak meaning incontrovertible grounds for immediate dismissal.

GEORGE WAS STILL IN TOWN.

For a few more weeks, anyway. Donny asked to meet with him, Maxine, the rest of their local management team, and Human Resources—Personnel—once more.

Later that afternoon, they met to discuss this new development, the discovery of this desiccated photo. Maxine led the discussion, having already made up her own mind with input from Donny and the rest of his staff.

"George, w-we must dismiss Dent immediately. Even if we believed him with respect to his altercation with Nora, which we do not, he has violated a COE."

George said, "I agree, Maxine. Exit interview this afternoon? Okay. I suggest you guys be prepared to walk him out. I'll hang nearby too if you'd like. Let's also get the security team teed up: panic button, armed team standing by, the works.

"HR, any further input? No? Okay, folks, we're doing the job for which we were trained. This cannot be personal. I know, easy to say. Let's stay strong for our team. They depend on us for this."

George wished his feelings were as cut and dried as his peppered commands. He pulled Maxine aside and apologized. "Sorry, your meeting. I got carried away." Maxine said nothing, but it was obvious from her silent smile and subtle nod she appreciated George stepping in.

Three hours into Dent's exit interview, the sun had long since set in a cloudy sky. Donny came out of his office, unkempt, tears streaming down his burnished cheeks.

"He's curled up *in a fetal position on the floor in the corner,* for God's sake. Says this was his last chance, whatever the Hell that means. I don't… know… if I… can… see this through, guys."

Donny's voice shook with emotion, and so did his hands, unable to look neither Maxine nor George in the eye. He didn't even try to hide his shaken demeanor from the three grim Security guys who just couldn't understand.

"You're almost there, Donny. The hard part's done." George exuded confidence. He anticipated this would be hard on Donny. But that was the job. He'd been there himself many times, and it never got easier. The manager's mantra—*empathize, never sympathize.*

In a smooth tone Maxine said, "Donny, r-remember, Dent made choices. Remember Nora and the rest of the team. When you're done here, I'll help you walk him to his office and then to the door. You're doing fine."

"He keeps repeating, *'You have no idea what you've done!'* You'd think we delivered a death sentence or something."

"Get it done, Donny." George patted his shoulder with firm empathy, sending the guy back into his own personal Hell. The good news? It would not last for an eternity.

Upon exiting Donny's office, the gelatinous Dent had solidified. He now exuded a rancorous resolve of a condemned man now resigned to his fate. He looked surprised to see them all waiting, but only for a moment before his dead-eye mask re-surfaced.

Donny and Maxine walked Dent to his shared office while George stood by. The security team hovered out of sight but moments away. It was almost eight p.m.—the timing was not coincidental. Dent's officemate left hours earlier.

The painful process of giving the condemned man time to make his peace became more and more awkward. As he emptied his desk drawers with ponderous deliberation, Dent dwelled on every artifact of his eight years at GGS. Every object received minutes of his attention before placing it in his box of shame. Dent seemed determined to make this process as difficult as possible. Was he actually relishing their collective discomfort?

Finally, after sixty minutes of this torture, George's abrupt voice was a gun shot in the silent room, his patience gone.

"That's it. Time to go." George felt a dreary blend of pity and disgust but retained his disguise of neutrality.

Donny and Maxine both appeared grateful for his demonstrative intervention. Finally, the maudlin pity party within which Dent seemed immersed came to a merciful end.

The small group approached an exterior security door that opened onto the sidewalk. The security team followed. As they walked out into the crisp Minnesota evening, they trudged through connected pools of garish mercury-vapor light.

Dent clung to his meager box of memorabilia. He was performing his best don't-give-a-crap act, not quite pulling it off. George placed a paternal hand on the side of Dent's upper arm. He leaned in close and in a not unkind voice whispered, "Dent, please seek professional help. Good luck to you," hoping to spare him any more embarrassment in front of the others.

Equally discreet, mouth to ear, he responded, "Oh, I'll get help alright, Janis. I'll get professional help. Say goodbye to Kate for me."

George shuddered as Dent pulled away and levied his glassy dead-eye glare before turning and strolling toward his car. What was left unspoken behind that malevolent jagged-edged glare? He flashed on that movie, *The Green Mile* and recalled the iconic phrase, *'dead man walking.'*

But Dent's thinly veiled threat left George wondering who that might be. *Was **he** looking at **me** thinking, 'dead man walking?'*

Dried red maple leaves crunched underfoot on the sidewalk. Were they trampling dead leaves, or crushing the remains of those whose lives they'd ruined?

Virulent malignancy radiated off Dent in white-hot waves, like buckling pavement shimmering from the merciless blast of a desert sun in late summer. Revulsed, George thought, *So many levels to that sick and suffering soul.*

Dent isn't the first, won't be the last, George lamented. *God in Heaven, forgive me for having become so callous.* George's hands trembled as they cowered within the shameful privacy of his pockets.

Nine-thirty. They were all anxious for a succinct end to this prolonged drama du jour. After a wrinkled moment with knitted brow, George turned to Maxine and Donny. He whispered, "Please see Mr. Canfield to his car. Take security."

Then to the security team leader in a quiet voice, "Take no chances." The security chief rewarded him with a purposeful nod, the heel of his right hand resting on the holster of his compact sidearm.

Thirty minutes later, the management and HR teams met for a debriefing in George's conference room. They often used this room even in George's absence during the winter months. Even then, George was often piped in via video from his condo in Florida. Or from wherever his travels found him. It was a pleasant room from which they couldn't escape soon enough.

"This poor head case is sick, alright. He might even be dangerous. Why are we just letting him go?" A noticeable quake in Donny's hands betrayed the bluster in his voice. When he saw others looking, he tucked them under the table. His ragged voice and tear-stained grimace broadcast a vein of emotional turmoil. It ran far deeper than his histrionic tirade.

They trusted Donny's humanistic sensitivity but also sensed his profound relief now that Dent was gone. This series of events affected him to unexpected depths. As it had all of them. George intuited it was far from over.

Claire Peterson, the HR manager, responded to Donny's question.

"Look, folks, I've seen thousands of troubled souls in my thirty-six years wading through the underbelly of this business. Especially in the last few years. But what has the guy really done?"

Donny did not like where this seemed to be going.

Claire now sounded more like an attorney than an HR manager. The disgust in her voice was clear, however.

"He lied on his application. That's no criminal offense. We fired him for that. Next, he jacked off to a picture of a beautiful girl."

She swung a knowing maternal glance around the room. Claire was on a roll.

"We tossed the guy a lifeline for evaluation and potential treatment. He threw it back in our faces. He's an adult. He's entitled. One thing we should discuss is a restraining order. An RO might give Ms. Mathers at least a veneer of legal protection if we believe we have enough to get one. Might she want help with that, Donny?"

"She was clear. She wants this all to be over and doesn't want to pile on. Thinks it was puppy love, innocent or not. Sounds like she still feels a little sorry for the guy. He was a good team member until…

"Look, I don't feel very good about what I think right now. I actually liked the guy myself."

"That's it then. We're done. Good job, guys. These are never easy."

Claire snapped her folder shut which visibly startled Donny. She placed it on her lap as she deftly spun her wheelchair around. The practiced maneuver was impressive—a swift one-eighty arc. Claire sped from the room. George knew she needed to feed her cats.

At ten p.m. everybody decided to end this long and hard day, everyone except George, that is. He was the only one who heard Dent's ominous threat: *I'll get professional help, alright. Say goodbye to Kate for me.'* He sat alone in the darkness of his office for a long time. Kate would already be asleep. She wouldn't ask him about his day until the following morning. He needed that time to think.

This guy Canfield was different from the others. It was times like these when George wondered whether his natural style of getting close to his teams was tactically naïve.

Dent knows Kate.

Dear God, George implored, *am I losing perspective? Is that all I'm losing?*

～

A LOADED SHOTGUN WAS JUST A TOOL.

George never imagined needing such a tool within Corporate America. He hated guns.

Shoulder-to-shoulder across the fence, George didn't exactly whisper. "Jerry, can I borrow one of your guns and a few rounds to go with it for a couple of weeks? Until we head south anyway? How about a shotgun?"

Living next door to Jerry in Stillwater was always exciting and interesting. A bit of the Wild West. The lovable lone-wolf Harley dude never failed to intrigue George. And now he was grateful for their friendship.

"Sure, man. What's going on?"

"Aw, just some BS at work that could follow me home."

"I hear that. Dangerous times. I'll bring it over later. Under the table?" Jerry owned an explosives company and, on occasion, traveled in rough circles. No stranger to danger.

"Yes, please. What Kate doesn't know…"

"Copy that, brother."

George reported a white Cadillac parked down the street across from a construction lot after seeing it there three nights in a row. A cruiser showed up—no Caddy. Jerry offered to tail him next time, but George didn't think any good could come of that.

George analyzed their situation. The time had come to sell this house in any event. The damn thing sat empty all Winter anyway.

Jerry would be disappointed.

After work, usually around nine p.m. or later, George often enjoyed hanging out for a while with Jerry in his garage next door. The ultimate Minnesota man cave, that garage. A full bar, heat, ribald conversation and provocative posters of motorcycle babes—little more than soft porn posed on high-octane hardware. A relaxed respite from the GGS pressure cooker. If the door was up, the party was on.

And for Jerry, hanging out with a white collar stiff was an amusing diversion. Hell, Jerry would move to Florida too if he could afford it. If *he* wanted to relax, he'd just blow up an old refrigerator in an open field on his company's dime. Even around explosives, Jerry's omnipresent beer and cigarette signaled job satisfaction. The simple life.

Time to turn the page, to start the next chapter.

They'd be heading South in another week for the winter. That would provide some distance between them and this sick madman. George had to wonder, though, how sick and how mad was this Canfield?

George thought, *Just in case...*

COVERED OR BURIED

P OTOMAC, MARYLAND

A BRUTAL THUG HE MIGHT BE.

But he was a well-educated thug. Enoch Slattery's parents may have been narrow-minded, but their focus had always been a better life for their son.

Their world view to make that happen? Higher education, of course, which was not optional. Threatened with disinheritance, he decided to check out the campus parties at NYU.

Turns out he actually enjoyed learning… anything, and everything.

With no clue for his future, as a teenager on the verge of adult-hood, he gravitated toward the Liberal Arts. The best courses? Those that explored the vagaries of the human condition.

Enoch enjoyed philosophy and abnormal psychology. That's where the needy chicks hung out.

He came to understand that the human animal, in general, was always hungry. He knew his fate—he would feed the animals and get rich.

~

ENOCH SPENT QUALITY TIME WITH MALC.

Malcolm Frieberg, his second-in-command, was an experienced level-headed operative. An aggressive young man, Malcolm Frieburg shared his own ruthless leadership style. Malc also shared his rather unique political proclivities.

Enoch said, "Do you know what people in this country lust for most, aside from pleasure? They need to be led, so they can be self-indulgent lazy citizens."

He amassed considerable wealth over the last thirty years harvesting the fruits of this cynical epiphany.

"As a great man once said, 'How fortunate for governments that the people they administer don't think.'"

Enoch believed America's political system had grown antiquated.

"We are a nation ungoverned. The animals are now starving. Malc, democracy has become little more than a fickle illusion, a meaningless mirage.

"Now, this is where it gets interesting, my friend."

He grinned at how much he'd intuited the state of humanity in the country today. It was so obvious if you cared to observe. If he weren't such a hard-nosed opportunist, he might even be saddened.

"Every thinking man knows beliefs are far more compelling than facts. In any event, facts these days are nothing more than lies told with conviction, over and over again. What's most interesting is the erosion of critical thinking.

"Look around, Malc. That's assuming you're not one of the tens of millions whose heads are voluntarily buried in the green, green grass of home."

Malc jumped in. "As the rich get richer, the sheep making up the other ninety-nine percent of the population help them do it."

The upward-then-downward inflection in his voice exhibited a mocking tone.

He continued. "Tough jerky—chew harder, peasant! Right? It means the less educated gulp from the old propaganda pump of their own free will."

Enoch liked discussing this stuff with Malc.

"Yeah, and that pump is called social media and online news sources. Our life's work gets easier *and* more profitable."

Enoch was on a roll now.

Playing a respectful devil's advocate, Malc said, "Agree, but doesn't all this technology everywhere also make our job harder?"

"Not if we're careful, Malc. While there's a lot more watching going on, there's lots more to watch too. Look around. The constant introduction of seductive technology is out-running society's ability to absorb it. At least, in a way that makes sense to the average gadget geek. That's our edge. The demand for gadgets is high.

"The sheep are so addicted to it, they've no choice but to use it and believe whatever we feed 'em through their high-tech toys. Feed 'em 'til they choke, baby!"

He clarified that *we* meant the two of them. In conjunction with the monumental resources of the Brotherhood, of course.

Now lecturing, Enoch continued. "It's simple. Kids who are growing up with a more absorbing persona online than in the real world? They spend the majority of their excessive free time gaming or texting instead of talking. To actual people, face-to-face, that is. They get neurotic about having fewer Facebook friends and Twitter followers than their peers, or fewer views of their videos or likes or shares. And that's the very small tip of a very large cyberspace iceberg."

Malc picked up on the rhetoric. "And most folks now depend on Twitter and YouTube as their trusted sources of advice, news and *wisdom*, right? Two-thirds of Americans don't even vote anymore! Is that so surprising when their attention span is shorter than a single news cycle, or a hundred-forty-word Tweet? Could the citizens of this great country make our job any easier? Baaah…"

Enoch said, "Right on, Brother Malc. And Mr. Z's playbook is inspired genius. I've taken enough political science and history courses to realize he is orchestrating his own revolution. Like the Bolsheviks.

"He might even be related to one of those old Commy bastards. The man knows history, and how to swing it like a sword!"

Malc said, "So why do you think so many Americans don't seem to care, Enoch? Come to depend on some crazy rich bastards to tell 'em exactly what's good for them. That's why. And like Mr. Z says, *'The solution? Create fear. Then replace it with order, even at the cost of lost freedom, for the sake of personal and public safety.'* Right?" Even though Malc quoted Mr. Z, word-for-word, he still seemed to need someone to affirm that he got it right.

Enoch said, "Yup. Take a few small skirmishes on the other side of the planet or near one of our own borders. Escalate them to full-on conflicts to boost a failing economy at home. Then tell the sheep what they need to hear. Appeal to fever-pitch patriotism and fear that keeps 'em dizzy and busy."

"Yeah. Then give them only what they need before they realize they've been had. Again. And redirect the inevitable blame."

"Easy. Fund the revolution. Doomed to repeat history? Damned skippy!"

The kid was definitely coming along. His plans for a successor…

They looked at each other, and simultaneously chanted, "Baaaah!" like a couple of bleating sheep before breaking out laughing at their own elitist genius.

~

JANUARY 2006
MINNEAPOLIS, MINNESOTA

. . .

The weather wasn't all that chilled him.

Outside the apartment Dent rented by the week, a dirty accumulation of snow couldn't decide whether to melt or re-freeze into a treacherous crust. A warm spell hovered just above freezing.

Dent's cell rang. He heard, "No job again? So what the Hell happened, dick-wad? Couldn't keep it in your pants? This gonna happen every few years?"

Dent only knew him as Dawg, short for watchdog or some such nonsense. He did not like that this guy knew him, but not vice versa.

"Look, Dawg, I know the Brotherhood values cover and concealment. But now I can dedicate myself completely to the cause. What's wrong with that?"

"Will you please just shut *up?* You just used two names on a cell, you idiot, even if it *is* encrypted. Don't talk. Listen. Now you have no cover. That's what's wrong. We have rules for a reason. Where you gonna live? How you gonna pay? You, of all people, grasp the concept of a plausible money trail. What are we gonna do with you now?"

"Okay, sorry. Look Daw-, man, I'll find another job, even without a reference. You know I have skills. You need what I can do for you, right? I'm a patriot too. Give me a chance to score another gig, and nothing else has to change. Meanwhile, I keep working. I'm begging you, man."

"Fine, but we warned you when you got booted from E&Y back in 'ninety-eight. We covered for you so you could get references. We buried that thing with your wife. I'm starting to think you're more trouble than you're worth, dick-wad.

"What about this guy you worked for at GGS? He keeps digging. There may be hairline cracks in your cover if he looks hard enough. Anything happens to him, gotta be accidental. Follow?"

"Okay, sure. No problem. Renew my contract and we're cool, okay? Please?"

"This is it, man. Don't waste it. We like your work, but priority one? We do *not* risk exposure. We've been around a long time. You,

you're just today's news, brother. Don't forget it. Watch your damn back, because we are."

A mind full of tornado twisted him into a knot. So, was that it? Would he still be alive tomorrow? And Janis's name was flagged all over the deep check that got him fired, almost whacked. Might still.

Dude's definitely gotta go, but how? I need to think. I almost blew it for real this time. Janis, you did this to me!

PITCHING OR FLOATING

M AY 2006
WHITE PLAINS, NEW YORK

Riding an elevator at corporate HQ?

Such a ride with a senior executive could be a boon or a bane.

Depending.

"Yes, George, I'm all too aware that division is in the red for over a hundred a quarter. Product issues, right? By the way, I hear congrats are in order. You made your budget numbers. I knew you could."

George flew from Minneapolis the previous afternoon. Corporate Headquarters existed in a different world. It was one into which he inserted himself so often these days it seemed second nature.

Was being a chameleon honest work?

He was still astounded by how casually a guy like Palmer Xavier—GGS's Chief Operations Officer—could mention a one hundred ten million dollar loss per quarter, for *years*, as if it were a mere inconvenience.

And, in the same sentence, he abdicated personal responsibility for the mess *he* left behind as Operations VP of that division until recently.

Palmer's customary modus operandi mandated a spasmodic knee-jerk. Get the quick returns—on paper at least—by firing a pant-load of good people to reduce costs. Then post stellar earnings and move on. With full deniability, the backfilling swamp will be some other schmuck's problem later.

If George were less concerned about his job and possessed a little more intestinal fortitude…

Okay, so Palmer the slasher had descended from his tower at 555 Madison in Manhattan to mix it up with mere mortals at CHQ in White Plains. The two of them happened to be in the same elevator at the same time on very different missions.

George felt good that he had dangled the bait of his pitch to Palmer on his way to a status meeting. All execs worth their salt carried a thirty-to-ninety-second pitch in their hip pocket. Ready to quick-draw at a moment's notice, *the pitch* lent visibility to one's cause célèbre. An elevator's confines created the perfect short-term captive audience, sans interruptions.

Having said that, every exec knows that when flying close to a flame, there exists the very real danger of scorching one's wings. The trick was to shove fear to the back burner and forge ahead. At least that was the conventional Exec 101 wisdom.

"May I assume you have a recommendation, George?" Palmer kept his eyes locked on the lighted floor indicators above the door.

He knew Palmer had no idea how to fix the product problems. He also knew that Palmer continued to receive disappointing and conflicting recommendations from within his old division.

George flashed to a bleached old bone on which a hungry coyote couldn't quit gnawing. Palmer knew how to emaciate a technical team to the point of ineffectiveness. *But* he'd get his precious financials. He was also smart enough to know he was clueless on the technical product stuff, and he had George here who wasn't. So he was listening with greedy intent despite the lack of eye contact and an air of aloofness.

Time to butter the muffin.

"Palmer, you had great success re-engineering that division from a financial perspective. Unfortunately, as you know, product issues remain. That division's middle managers always present a good story about how great it's going to be in the future. But the future never arrives. They spin ever deeper into the ditch, stuck in the mud of the past."

George was now a locomotive picking up steam on an incline. "The flawed nucleus? Their product line is so different than the rest of GGS that their infrastructure has to be unique. At the same time, they must accommodate a forest of ill-behaved third party software providers. That stuff is always plagued with error-prone application programming interfaces and flawed function.

"In contrast, all other GGS products are manufactured on mass production lines and run on their own proprietary APIs. Think Apple. This model allows more intuitive and cost-effective integration with the hardware in-house. And that's all enabled with a single cross-platform business process infrastructure. Investing in unique production lines and using third party stuff is expensive on so many fronts.

"That division's PC heritage has always been innovative. It satisfied a market niche but created an outlaw garage band culture. Think one-off where the rest of the company is streamlining mass production. That made sense for the first quarter century of its life. No longer. We need different thinking now as times get tougher.

"GGS is now in an artillery battle down on Wall Street, and these guys are bringing Saturday night specials to a party up in Washington Heights."

George thought, *In for a penny...* He now must carry the ball across the goal line, as he mentally smiled. He knew Palmer loved sports similes, distant recollections from his glory days.

"Only two choices as I see it, Palmer," as he looked up at this tall arrogant jerk standing to his left. Palmer's eyes were still locked on the floor numbers above the door. All in the span of a fraction of a second, he observed Palmer's perfectly trimmed hair and face of granite. His upturned nose was bursting with a gin bloom or chronic use of something else.

"Plan B: Corral the product design to be more in line with the rest of the company's offerings. This will be expensive and span years of effort. That's why this is Plan B."

"So what's your recommended Plan A then, George?"

*He **is** listening.*

"Divest. Sell it off. At least the client side. Desktop computers are messy and no longer have a legitimate slot in our big-iron portfolio. Decide on its merits whether to keep the server side. They're more in line with our distinctive competence and mainstream infrastructure.

"Palmer, our payday is high-end servers and enterprise systems, along with the stuff that goes with 'em. Ditch the scrap metal, Boss. With less than 5% margins on the desktops, we could make more profit selling lettuce, *if* that were our business.

"We brought the personal computer to major markets in 1977. Got the footprints. The time for kudos is long past. It's likely time to lose that costly tradition before it drags us down any further. We need a touchdown, Palmer. I recommend an in-depth analysis of a divestment strategy for all or a part of that division. If that becomes the right play, we grab the cash and run. That's the pitch."

George's last words gushed out faster than he would have liked, but they were approaching Palmer's floor.

After the doors opened three seconds later, Palmer thanked him for an interesting ride with a disinterested nod.

I can't believe I just did that.

Immediately, he wished Palmer would just forget that ever happened.

~

STILLWATER, MINNESOTA

. . .

WHAT HAD HE DONE?

The next day, back in his Stillwater office, George spent some time thinking. He wondered about the pitch to Palmer, and where that might lead, if anywhere. He'd proposed a bold plan. But had he gored Palmer's ox?

Screw it.

Now he had moved on to considering the delicious logistics of moving aboard the boat for the summer. He and Kate had sold their large four bedroom, three bath house near the river in rural Stillwater. It seemed superfluous.

The plan was to spend summers on the boat berthed at the Lake City Marina, less than an hour's drive from his office. And he'd work from his home office in their Florida condo from October to April until he hung up his spurs.

He eagerly anticipated spending the summer on the good ship *Sojourn* with Kate. He felt good about getting outta Dodge. Especially with Dent Canfield potentially still skulking around somewhere.

He'd never forget that day almost eleven years ago when he had bought *Sojourn*. He'd also made an influential new friend who would one day save his life...

~

OCTOBER 1995
BALTIMORE, MARYLAND

THE EAST COAST SWELTERED THAT AUTUMN.

Kate made the money work. The boat was theirs. It was time to transport her twenty-ton splendor by truck to Lake City, Minnesota —a twenty-mile-long wide spot on the Mississippi River.

George took some rare vacation days. He flew alone from MSP to

BWI armed with enough socks and underwear for a week's stay aboard *Sojourn* in the dubious Inner Harbor waterfront district. He'd contracted for the use of Tidewater Yacht Service's lift and crane to haul the boat from the water to the bed of a truck's trailer.

They'd remove the boat's substantial sailing rig for shipping. Her fifty-four-foot mast, boom, tackle and nine sets of heavy stainless cables that held it all in place needed to lay down and get wrapped. All would be truck-ready before he preceded her back to Minnesota to await her arrival.

Annie, from Annapolis Yacht Brokers, had connected George and Kate with Dale from Tidewater Yacht Services. That's where they had initially discovered the boat. George procured the services of a truck broker who would arrange transportation and permits.

While preparing her for shipment, George intended to learn as much as possible about this magnificent vessel and her many systems. Dale stopped by with an offer George couldn't refuse.

That's when everything became a great deal more interesting.

"Mr. Janis, congratulations again on your amazing acquisition. I can't believe Dr. Braxton accepted your offer. He seemed pleased by your respectful promise to give his vessel a loving new home, despite your somewhat low-ball offer."

"Thanks, Dale. I'm feeling blessed. What's up?"

George refused to engage in that low-ball discussion again. It seemed Dale would not let it go. He obviously felt cheated out of a few commission bucks.

"Well, I dropped by to see if you need anything. I also came to ask if you'd like to meet Dr. Braxton. He's offered to spend the afternoon with you on the boat tomorrow if you're so inclined."

"Are you kidding? Yes! I have so many questions!"

Late the next morning, as George stowed the canvas bimini that protected the cockpit from sun and weather, he spotted a nondescript rail-thin gentleman sauntering down the long concrete pier. This stranger stopped at *Sojourn's* transom. The old man appeared so ordinary, he was almost invisible. George met his analytical gaze for a couple of beats.

"Howdy!" came the mellifluous drawl of a southern gentleman. His eyes were cast in deep shadow by a frumpy beige sailor's hat. It was bleached almost white by the sun and featured a ragged fringe around the brim. His eyes twinkled behind a pair of old-fashioned round spectacles with tinted lenses.

The crow's feet outboard of those eyes either came from age or from smiling or both.

"I'm Sam, and you are George. Mighty fine to meet you, Sir. I'm pleased to see you're getting to know my best girl. Permission to come aboard?"

"Hello, Sam. A real pleasure. Yes, please. I can't tell you how much..."

"Of course, of course. Would you object to my smuggling a few handcrafted micro-brews aboard? To lubricate the launch of our relationship, Captain?"

It was at that precise moment that a twelve pack of local Union Crafts appeared in his left hand, as if by magic. George couldn't tell whether this genteel patrician's demeanor was sincere or contrived. No matter. He pulled it off with aplomb.

"Say no more. Please join me in the shade and comfort of *our* pilothouse."

"You're too kind; however, she's all yours now, Sir." It came out all Texas, as in "how-evah," and "Suh." Or was it Georgia?

After twisting the caps off two bottles and handing one to George, they now sat in the warm glow of the pilothouse, the boat's living room.

THE OLD GENTLEMAN SWELLED WITH PRIDE.

Sam immediately asked George his impressions of the little ship.

He wanted to know of her new home port, and of any long range cruising plans.

He watched George's eyes rove over the Rubenesque features of *their* best girl.

George responded with unbridled enthusiasm. The ease with which they conversed seemed preternatural.

THE BRILLIANT AFTERNOON EVAPORATED.

The two *boys* puttered around engine and generator spaces, bilges, and cockpit lockers on into a cool crimson evening. They spent some time in the hold. They sat cross-legged, knee-to-knee on the wood floor, engaged in congenial conversation. Later they lit the lamps.

Reconvening in the pilothouse, George smiled at the sight of all the empties accumulated down in the galley's waste bin. George cracked open the third of three massive four-inch binders. These books contained the ship's detailed documentation. He was eager to ask more questions.

"So, Sam, you were with the NSA?"

Time stopped dead.

Steely blue eyes bored deep into George's. Leaning forward, palms face-down on his knees, elbows braced outward, now way too close to George's face, Sam's voice transformed to echo his aggressive posture. The convivial country gentleman disappeared in a Dallas nanosecond. His next words became coarse gravel grating into a bloody wound that had just begun to heal.

"And how is it… you… are aware of that… George?"

Those eyes!

George's mind stumbled in shock. He trembled.

"Ah, um, your name was, ah, on a sheet of NSA letterhead with, um, this, ah, sketch of an electrical diagram for the lower helm."

He blurted this out louder than he intended, waving a crude hand-drawn diagram on a five-by-eight-inch sheet of notepad paper he'd extracted from the binder in its plastic sheet saver. He fluttered his arms as if he could soar above the dense cloud of visceral fear that threatened to smother him.

Silence.

And then…

The switch flipped back to genteel as if the previous twenty seconds were nothing more than a distant anecdote. The smile returned, a little apologetically.

"Sorry. Rough business at times. Before I retired, I was Director of Medical Services for the Agency. Job damned near killed me. Now that I'm retired, I'm privileged to serve as Chief of Surgery at Walter Reed in Bethesda. Still keeping busy. Mostly an honorary position."

While reticent to discuss specifics, George did unearth a few more nuggets about Sam and his wife, Mary.

Their budding friendship began to blossom, and the beers continued to disappear.

"Sam, I only know one other guy affiliated with the intelligence community at one time, an old friend named Calvin Pierce. The two of you couldn't be more different though. But you'd like him. He was in air transport."

"Yes, I've worked with a few of those boys over the years. Maybe we'll get a chance to chat some day."

And that was that. A rather abrupt end to a fascinating day.

George later learned the rank of Full-Bird Colonel was one level below Brigadier General. If Sam's rank wasn't impressive enough, his job was. He couldn't remember how he'd discovered Medical Services Director was NSA-speak for Chief Worldwide Interrogator.

Too many beers.

~

MAY 1997

LAKE CITY, MINNESOTA

. . .

T̲HEN TWO YEARS LATER...

Their beloved ship *Sojourn* took a palpable hit.

She suffered significant damage while tied to her dock with nobody aboard. And through no fault of her own.

Lawrence, the Lake City Marina harbor master called George at his office in Stillwater. "George, are you sitting down? Good. Hey, the great news is that *Sojourn* is still floating."

"What! Lawrence, what are you talking about, and this had better not be a joke."

"No joke, George. A drunken pilot at the helm of an Army Corps of Engineers tug lashed to a work barge lost control in last night's storm. He took shelter in the sailboat harbor. Came in hot due to strong cross-winds and lost his steering. Dumped over a hundred gallons of hydraulic fluid into my harbor.

"This, ah, incident, ah, destroyed the ends of a couple of my floating docks out there, and chewed pretty hard on your port quarter. It appears to be no more than cosmetic damage, but she took several pretty hard hits. That's one stout vessel, George."

"Son of a bitch! Okay, I'll be down. I'll spend the night on her... sleep in the frickin' engine room watching for leaks, I guess. Thanks, Lawrence."

"You have my home number, George. If she starts taking on water, we'll line up the lift. Call anytime, Skipper. Not a happy day."

George learned later the tug's crew took a full twenty minutes to secure the barge. It had run aground on the rocks ahead of it.

During that time, the rusty steel tug bounced around in the choppy water while she laid right up against *Sojourn's* port side. After chewing on her for almost a half-hour, the crew finally pried that rust bucket off George's beloved little ship.

Sojourn did indeed suffer cosmetic damage only. Unfortunately, the repairs would cost twenty-two thousand dollars. George assumed a simple arrangement between perpetrator and victim could be arranged, but he was wrong. The Corps would not take responsibility for the incident. George assumed they were trying to prevent yet another citizen from fleecing the government.

Uncle Sam self-insures. After months of runarounds and double talk, George's insurance company also grew frustrated. So he appealed to the good Doctor Sam for help.

"Sons-a-bitches won't stand up, Sam."

In his patient drawl, Sam said, "George, we need to yank a few tactical levers. I'll email you the draft of a letter this afternoon. It'll contain the names to whom y'all will send it, along with a list of copy and blind copy names. I want you to leave the blind copied recipients visible on all copies you send. These mid-level weasels can't stand the kind of Hell we're gonna rain down on 'em. No worries, Old Son. You'll have a check within two weeks. Guaranteed.

"But now, you say our girl took the hit and just snickered at the raunchy old rust bucket that tried to defile her? Yessir. *Yessir!*"

Two weeks later to the day George held in his hand a check for twenty-two thousand dollars signed by a contrite Uncle Sam. He endorsed it and sent it to the repair facility. Paid in full.

Who are you, Sam?

~

Pleasant memories.

Enough nautical day-dreaming of the past for one day.

Back to business.

WAR ROOM

M AY 2006
STILLWATER, MINNESOTA

Life aboard the boat? Yes!

He knew it would be therapeutic to return to Minnesota and live aboard *Sojourn* each summer. He could visit family and work out of GGS Stillwater. And he relished going home to Kate and to the boat every night after work.

All Summer.

Then, when the temps descended toward atrocious next Fall, they'd pull and winterize the boat, load up the SUV and aim it South. Snowbirds... just like the older folks. Recently, Kate had developed rather severe osteoarthritis. The unrelenting Minnesota winters made it painful for her to get around. Prescription? Other than pills? Tropical warmth. She still had the mind of an eighteen-year-old gymnast, but the body? Not so much.

He remembered those bittersweet days of passion and battle as he reminisced. *Ah, the memories.* But her almost-sixty-year-old body reminded both her and George of their mortality.

Sometimes pain trumped fanciful visions.

George's desk phone shrilled, not caring that it startled him out of his reverie's warm embrace. A delicious afterglow lingered.

"What on Earth did you say to Palmer in White Plains the other day, George?"

The caller didn't need to announce himself. That irascible voice was unmistakable. George shared a "dotted line" relationship on the org chart with Vinnie Lassaro, who was on Palmer Xavier's staff. In essence, Vinnie was George's direct boss with whom he almost never had contact.

"Hey, Vinnie, nice to hear from you. I'm fine. Kate's fine. Man, we gotta work on your people skills."

"Kiss my ass, George. He's all revved up about something you said to him yesterday. In an elevator? That old gag? That's rich. Nobody still does that, man."

Vinnie was venting a full head of steam, "He's establishing a *war room* in RTP starting *tomorrow*, for God's sake! He wants you and your top fifty or so best and brightest on a plane. *Tonight.*

"Folks from a dozen other teams are also now converging on RTP. Son, you got his motor revving in the red on whatever the Raleigh guys have been force-feeding him.

"Seems to trust you more than his old team. Unbelievable. What the Hell did you say? All joking aside, you got to the guy, and now it's time to follow through. Can do?"

All joking aside? That was Vinnie's idea of a joke? Neither humor nor people skills were his strong suits.

"Uh, wow, yeah Vinnie. I'm on it. Might not all be there at 8 a.m. tomorrow, but we'll start mobilizing the teams. Great, I guess. I've been bitching about that division for quite a while. Not to the right people, until now, obviously. Wait and then hurry, right?"

"Yeah, quit screwin' around, kid. This is serious stuff. Piss off the wrong people, and...

"Look, I'll assume this train has left the station, and you're already on it. Jee-ZEUS, George! And 8 a.m.? Think more like 5 a.m., okay? You're in for a wild ride, m'boy, knowing the Cowboy. Not sure who his on-scene guy will be, but it won't be a vacation."

He ended the call like he started it, but George could hear the smile, or smirk, in Vinnie's voice before the click. Vinnie liked people who got things done. *Why do these younger Turks insist on calling me kid, son or boy?* He smiled. He liked it. A lot.

"Hi, Kate? Guess what, Babe?"

"Aaaah… G, how long this time?"

So much for romantic summer sunsets on dusky Lake Pepin, listening to the loons at twilight. He knew she liked the money George was making, but she also wanted him to live long enough to enjoy it with her.

George knew this was not doing his marriage any good, but what was he going to say? No? And being out of town for awhile might actually help. The tempestuous ebb and flow in his relationship with Kate never seemed to be what either of them wanted.

~

RESEARCH TRIANGLE PARK,
NORTH CAROLINA

WAR ROOM MODE WOULD BE UGLY.

This meant taking extraordinary measures to make emergency business changes using the best resources available. ASAP, of course. In this case, ground zero was the once-bustling GGS facility within the park.

RTP encompassed hundreds of high-tech firms sprawled through seven thousand acres of aromatic pine woods. The cities of Raleigh, Durham and Chapel Hill comprised the Triangle's points.

Not that the lovely rural setting mattered. At all. The entire team worked seven days a week, fifteen hours a day. From before sunrise until several hours after sunset.

George gave each of his newly arrived team members a personal orientation to their home away from home within one of the sprawling GGS lab complexes.

Invariably they asked, "What *is* this place? Jeez, the only thing missing is the tumbleweed. It's kind of creepy, isn't it George?"

"Yeah, but it has all the comforts of home. Except for our families and our actual homes."

They called this particular office complex the *Ghost Town*. Comprising hundreds of empty offices, conference rooms, and quarter-mile hallways, broken and stained acoustic tiles in the ceilings hung askew everywhere. Phones sat neglected in corners on the floor at the end of long tangled cords amidst dust bunnies the size of softballs.

The entire area appeared long-abandoned as if the apocalypse had occurred in the not-so-recent past. No doubt these were artifacts of Palmer Xavier's handiwork when he and Michael Martino still ran GGS RTP.

Cowboys...

George advised, "Eat if you can."

He told each new arrival, "Food is catered in, morning, mid-day, and evening every day. Pretty good stuff, too. Strong coffee, fresh fruit and pastries are available twenty-four/seven."

He knew from personal experience—the fare was sumptuous, over the top. Most would either be too busy skidding off the rails, or too nauseated from stress to care. Or even to partake at all.

He'd already lost twenty pounds. All the nearby restrooms alternated between the odors of vomit and industrial disinfectant.

One of George's team members from Poughkeepsie asked the same question that every new arrival asked. "So why all those cots and blankets in empty offices off *Broadway?*" That was what they called the widest hallway a hundred yards from *Times Square*. And *that* was where *The Gauntlet* was set up.

Those offices with cots featured clear glass windows, waist-to-ceiling, on the wall that faced *Broadway*.

"They're available for anyone to use. They're not assigned. Fair warning, though. It's not cool to be caught napping except between the hours of midnight and four a.m."

"George, is it me, or is this whole scenario surreal... like an existential Hell in the woods?"

"Yeah, a lot of pressure, for sure. The message is clear with those cots, though. Sleep here if you want to save commute time, but only when the senior execs are off-site. Otherwise, somebody will blow you smoke.

"I know, I know..."

~

SEPTEMBER 2006
RESEARCH TRIANGLE PARK,
NORTH CAROLINA

IT HAD ALREADY BEEN A LONG SUMMER.

George and his best people from various locations had literally not seen daylight in months, except for brief interludes in an interior courtyard to sneak a smoke or a quick cell call to a loved one. No signal at all inside. George didn't smoke.

The entire affair wreaked of a bad joke: *"What happens when you lock a hundred geeks up in a dungeon in the dark and scary woods with a pack of ravenous corporate wolves?"*

GGS experts from several other areas of the business shared the same fate. George did his best to stay in touch with the rest of his organization not sequestered in RTP. The Cowboys could not have cared less.

The team managed six daily senior executive updates on a standing schedule every day of the week. They started at six a.m. and took place every two hours through noon. Each lasted fifteen minutes. Precisely. The last two took place at four and eight p.m.

If an issue caused any schedule delay, the guilty party brought a status report with recommendations.

For these meetings, every project manager dropped everything and headed to the *Gauntlet*. This was the not-so-affectionate term given to the conference room at the heart of *Times Square*.

The *Gauntlet* was a cobbled-together impromptu video conferencing center. This was where all teams updated a half-dozen execs in person, as well as at least that many piped in.

Regular bludgeoning was the norm—a full-on blame game whenever the team failed to fulfill unrealistic expectations.

Between updates, the senior execs yelled into phones in offices surrounding the *Gauntlet*. This area within *Times Square* always hopped with activity.

Usual corporate war room stuff.

THE RTP MARRIOTT IN DURHAM...

Those were George's digs.

He snuck down the road for at least a few hours most non-cot nights over the last four months. He tried to sneak back to Lake City for a conjugal visit to Kate on the boat every month or so. But he'd get jerked back to RTP after fifteen or twenty hours. Every time.

Without exception.

On principle.

Kate didn't try to conceal her loneliness and disappointment. But she tried to make the best of it. Whenever George did manage a quick flight to Minneapolis, she'd pick him up. The forty-five-minute drive to the boat in Lake City comprised the bulk of their quality time together.

"George, I see this project taking more of a toll on you than any of your projects over the last thirty years at GGS. I am very worried about you. I'm also worried about us."

"Look, Babe, it's a tough gig. I've missed being with you more than anything. The only thing worse than bickering when we're together is missing you when we're apart."

To him, it seemed like some sort of a test.

"Dunno, G, every time you come home for a visit, you're immediately called away again."

And every time he left, with his overstuffed garment bag over his shoulder, he felt her watching him walk the dock toward shore. He'd catch an airport express back to MSP. He wondered, *How long can this go on?*

They'd been fighting less lately. No doubt because they'd been spending so little time together.

Absence makes... what?

～

LAST NIGHT WAS NO DIFFERENT.

A little after ten p.m., George drove back to the hotel in Durham. He'd made his customary quick stop in his leased Taurus at Taco Bell for a Crispy Crunchwrap Supreme.

As always, he brought it back to the room. Once stripped down to his PJs, he'd wash his Crunchwrap down with a plastic tumbler of decent gin—no rocks or olives or any other useless accoutrement.

Sleep remained elusive. He'd have to be back to the *Ghost Town* in a few hours, so no Ambien. Then up in the dark, a quick shower and shave before the ten-minute descent back into Purgatory. After all, he had asked for this with that elevator pitch. He could feel his wings diminishing to ash.

George spoke at a six a.m. vid-con. He orchestrated an update in the *Gauntlet,* a performance for Palmer Xavier and a few other CHQ celebs. Palmer was the focus. Three of George's project managers reported success in overcoming some key product issues. Then George picked up from there to summarize.

"Palmer, as you likely already know, we've reached consensus with your business ops team. We are indeed recommending divestment of the client business.

"Our teams have completed the technical homework. As you know, *Renoun,* the Chinese remarketing firm, is demonstrating interest. Now your financial guys need to hammer out the deal. Ah, what? One moment, Palmer. Sorry."

Marty, his senior project manager, was waving for him to disconnect. He looked frantic.

"Palmer, we'll talk again. The team is pretty ragged, but making good progress tying up the stragglers. Thanks."

He punched END on the vid-con link. That rude departure would cost him. Palmer remained a first-class hard-ass.

"Marty, what's going on?"

"George, it's Kate. She's talking crazy! It's only five-fifteen there." Marty knew Kate from social gatherings at their Stillwater home before they sold it. He liked Kate.

Marty's expression went far beyond frantic. He looked scared. For him to interrupt a senior exec call...? A mortal sin.

An instant headache bombarded George.

He could feel his face flush. This job was killing him, and he missed Kate. He even missed their bickering. He roughly snatched his cell from Marty to whom he always surrendered it before entering the *Guantlet.*

George bolted for the outdoor courtyard for a solid signal.

"Honey, why are you up so early? What's going on?" He didn't intend to near-shout into the phone. "Are you *okay?*"

"G, Caitlyn is dead!"

She was their dearest boat neighbor, across the dock. She looked a lot like Kate. Everyone on the dock called her *Cate with a C* to distinguish her from *Kate with a K*. George called her Catie. They had had fun with their names.

"She drowned, George. Makes no sense whatsoever. She and Fred have been live-aboards for twenty years! No way she just falls over the side, bumps her head and drowns, right?"

Immediately George feared the worst. His gut was aflame with doubt and raw fear, and fourteen hundred miles prevented them from a badly needed embrace. His own frazzled state of mind started to shred like a soggy beer napkin.

"What, Babe? Catie is… what? I don't understand." He heard what she said as his mind raced through a convoluted maze, trying to catch up. "Oh, my God! Aw, man."

Denial evaporated before it could take root. He knew.

"And George, the police suspect foul play."

He knew. His anxiety level bumped up another order of magnitude. Those words confirmed his suspicion. Yet…

No, I refuse to go there.

His hand twitched with a visible shiver all the way to his shoulder. "What happened? Why do they…?"

She gushed as she interrupted, unable to hold it back.

"Something about… far too much force behind the… the blow… that caused her to go into the water unconscious?"

The words, once hesitant and interrupted by intermittent sniffling and sobbing, now tumbled out of their own free will.

"George, her neck was *shattered!* They could tell by looking at her after they retrieved… And George, she was found under *Sojourn,* not under *Wind Walker!* Oh God, this is… too…"

Sobbing and trembling consumed her. She obviously struggled to hang onto her phone.

George was shaken to his core but with a low tone kept repeating, "Oh, Baby… Oh… Baby…".

He strangled his Blackberry while he listened to Kate's tortured sobbing. In a low-level voice, he said, "Okay, Hon. You're gonna come down here and stay in my room for a while. I won't be there except to sleep, but it's nice, spacious, has a terrific mini-bar, and I should finish up here in a few more weeks. Then we go from there. We'll take a trip or something."

He was a fighter preparing to pounce… on, what? He cared little the concerned looks he was getting from the few others in the court-yard, including a frightened Marty. They had disappeared into a cloud of irrelevant mist.

"No, G, I'll be okay. It just happened sometime late last night or earlier this morning. Fred's a mess. I just need a little time… to… to process… And, G?

"Yeah, Baby?"

"I just remembered… it might not be related, but it's strange. The Police asked me. Do you know someone around here whose name starts with a D?"

The trap door to the bottomless pit under his feet dropped open with a loud *bang*. George fell in a full-tumble, a dizzying free-fall. He dropped backward onto a bench fearing he'd collapse and continue falling.

This is not happening!

"Why, Kate?" He tried to mask the choking panic from his quivering question.

It wasn't uncommon for boat neighbors to use a thumb tack to attach a note to the post on the left side of the dock steps that George had lovingly built and painted. Those four steps up onto *Sojourn's* starboard side deck…

"Because there was a printed note nailed, George, *nailed* to our step post. It read, '*G, Sorry I missed you. Best regards, D.*' And then there's a little smiley-face scrawled at the bottom. *George?*"

Her voice was now the pitiful plea of a scared little girl. "What in God's name is going on?" Deep wracking sobs followed. He knew she was soaking her cheap little flip phone as well as the depths of

George's suffering soul with tears of terror.

His blood turned to slivers of ice that would never thaw.

Dent Canfield.

Dead serious, he enunciated in a slow and clear tone that shocked and stabilized her… a little.

"Kate, listen to me.

"First, ask the police officer nearest to you right now to call me *immediately* on my cell.

"Second, I want you at the condo. Fred's no good to anybody right now, I'm sure. So get Lawrence or one of his marina staff to drive you to the airport. I'll have a ticket waiting for you at MSP. Pack your toiletry kit and three days' clothes. Nothing more.

"Third, I want someone with you at all times from now on, and *I need you out of Lake City in the next thirty minutes.* That's it. Get that cop. Now. Can you do that for me, Kate? Do you understand?"

"George, what…?"

He almost shouted. "Just do it! Babe, I'm not kidding. I'll explain later. This is deadly serious. Right now, *move!*" He waited for her taciturn reply.

He punched the red button and waited.

REVELATIONS

P UNTA GORDA, FLORIDA

Kate preceded George to Florida.

She retrieved him from the Fort Myers airport a few days after Caitlyn's death. They drove for over an hour through heavy traffic via Veteran's Parkway and Burnt Store Road back to their condo at Burnt Store Marina.

She could see her appearance shocked him. She was so very tired, smaller somehow, diminished. Once they arrived at home, he demanded she take a nap. She did not argue and fell into a restless sleep within minutes. She knew he laid by her until she nodded off.

Her heart weeped.

She must be dreaming. She was looking into those unseeing eyes.

"Oh God, Catie, I loved you so much, but you shouldn't have been my friend. You'd still be... alive."

Catie responded in a shimmering voice free of any malice.

"Kate, don't you dare blame yourself over this. That ugly man is to blame. Not you. And you tell George for me it's not his fault either. Don't worry about dear Fred. He can't stand to be alone. He'll grieve his loss, and then he'll move on. That's Freddy. Protect George from himself, though. He's a good man who's lost his way a little. Can you do that, *Kate, with a K?*"

The ghost of *Cate with a C* smiled and dissipated in an ethereal vapor.

~

KATE AWOKE FROM HER TROUBLED NAP.

She and George decided to spend an early happy hour together. Portobello's overlooked the south basin of Burnt Store Marina.

They enjoyed their little piece of Florida's gulf coast. And Portobello's waited for them a short one minute walk across the parking lot from their condo. They sat in superficial tranquility on the covered deck facing the marina, watching the boats.

They both sipped their fourth cocktail—Kate enjoyed her vodka and tonics as George continued diving into his most recent extra dry gin bird bath martini. No words were necessary or useful for a long time.

Then, "It's good to be back at South Shore, G, and especially away from Lake City. After everything that's happened."

"Enough said. I couldn't agree more, Babe. By the way, *Sojourn* is out of the water, winterized, covered and stored on her cradle in record time."

George had arranged for Kate's flight from Minneapolis to Fort Myers. As she was settling into the condo, he'd flown from Raleigh to Minneapolis to put the boat to bed for the cold Minnesota winter. Kate knew he had concluded his work at RTP. She had been waiting at RSW where theirs was a tearful reunion.

Both were making a mighty effort at small talk. But their words couldn't differ more from their unspoken nightmares. Finally, Kate blurted out, "George, I can't get that horrible vision of Catie's broken body out of my mind. It was all so surreal. I've never seen a dead person before, much less someone I knew. She looked so... *wrong!*"

In a soft and tender tone, he said, "You guys were two peas in a pod, alright. Well, if there's any positive news from the ME's report, it's that Catie didn't suffer. But old Fred is still a ship without a rudder. She was everything to him."

She thought, *Kind of like you are to me.*

"G, WHO IS 'D'?"

You were completely spooked when I told you about your friend's note that day. It's clear you believe it's connected somehow to her death... her murder. Do they think he might be a witness or something?"

"Aw, Honey. I don't know. Dent Canfield was this odd duck we had to fire about a year ago. Haven't seen him since. He worked for Donny Segwell in Stillwater and reported to me through Maxine Sun. It was a rough one. He's sure no friend, more like a disgruntled ex-employee who's also very ill.

"We tried to help him, but I don't know. If Catie was murdered... God, I can't believe I'm using that word about a dear friend of ours."

His voice cracked. He was trying to be strong over an impossible topic. He sniffled and rubbed his left eye with his knuckles like a little boy recovering from a spanking.

"If someone did murder Catie, and the evidence points in that direction, I have no idea if this Canfield guy is capable. But I was not going to take any chances. And I'm not sure who else would... take it out on poor Catie."

Kate said, "I do feel safer down here. I felt, well, kind of exposed on *Sojourn* out there at the end of the dock. At least here, we have some distance and a couple layers of security."

"Let's play it cool for a while here anyway. I'm gonna be pretty busy with work, so..."

They drifted into an uneasy silence, each held captive by their own imagination.

A short while later, they fell under the spell of syrupy sunset reflections on the glassy water. He said, "Let's go home and grill a couple of gigantic, artery-clogging rib-eyes. And we'll switch from the hard stuff to an unhealthy bottle of Bogle Red Zin while we cauterize the steaks. How about we slather on some secret sauce, Babe? You nuke a baker, and we'll be good to go."

"I love you, George. What's going to happen next?"

"Uh, steaks, wine, and I hope some tom-foolery on the lanai. I'll queue up your favorite Andreas Vollenweider CD. Beyond that, I don't give a damn."

He barked over his shoulder, "Check, please!"

THE POLICE INVESTIGATION STALLED.

In light of the skeletal evidence, the local police looking into Caitlyn Potts's murder in Lake City was going nowhere. Dent Canfield was a person of interest but nothing more. He was nowhere to be found in any event.

Besides, it wasn't clear to George how much more that small town cop shop could accomplish. Even when assisted by the ill-funded Minnesota Bureau of Criminal Apprehension.

Calling from the condo, "Sam, I have no right to ask for your help again. I'm asking anyway."

Ever since George purchased *Sojourn* from Sam, they kept in touch now and then, mostly by email.

"A dear friend of ours was murdered. Kate and I are still stunned in disbelief. Caitlyn Potts's shattered body was found wedged between *Sojourn's* starboard side and her dock."

Even after almost two weeks, his voice broke as he spoke of it.

"I'm convinced this sicko's target was actually my Kate, but he missed. I don't think he's done. I must tell you, Sam, I'm scared."

Once Sam had absorbed the details, he drawled, "Of course I'll do what I can, Old Son. First, we need to know who we're dealing with. I maintain a decent network at the Agency."

George then shared with Sam the details of the deep background check acquired by GGS Human Resources manager, Claire Peterson.

"I'll get back with you when I have more info, alright George?"

"Thanks, old friend."

~

OCTOBER 2006
PUNTA GORDA, FLORIDA

GEORGE'S CELL JANGLED, STARTLING HIM.

That old-fashioned ring tone is best reserved for folks whose hearing isn't what it once was. Eleven p.m. He was still finishing his work day in his Florida home office.

Office was too grandiose a term. Little more than a large window-less walk-in closet off the rear bedroom of the condo, it was a pleasant space where he could concentrate.

These late-evening office hours had become more frequent. He often needed to get a jump on the following day. They'd only come south for the winter three weeks earlier, and he was catching up from his war room summer in North Carolina.

"George, it's Sam. I have some disturbing news for you, Old Son. About your friend Mr. Canfield."

"Hi, Sam. Well, it's good to hear from you again, despite the topic. Must be urgent as well as disturbing at this hour. What did you discover?" George couldn't help thinking that Sam sounded like Clark Gable playing Rhett Butler in "Gone with the Wind," but less reso-nant. Thinner and shorter.

"Well, it's mighty curious, the hornet's nest I stirred up at the agency. This Canfield character has some very dark connections, it seems. Not to mention some serious help fixing at least one altercation in his past."

"What? Sam, exactly what language are you speaking? Can you give me an example I will comprehend?"

"His wife, George. She disappeared in the late eighties. My contacts drilled hard and deep enough to discover the artifact of a marriage record that someone with juice expunged. That was accomplished in a way not too many folks are capable.

"He went to school with a young lady named Elizabeth Warden. They had a romance. Shared an address. Some evidence of a marriage license, but only an impression. Then after a year or so, she disappeared. Completely. So did the paper trail. Very curious.

"For all intents and purposes, this asshole was never married, but in fact, he was. My guys cross-correlated tampered data with local law enforcement interviews and civil records. They scoured the two venues this couple haunted—Hartford, Connecticut and Arlington, Virginia.

"George, so many irregularities seem likely the result of some high-level tampering. My colleagues validated this assertion by scanning transcripts of interviews with family members and friends circa December of 1989. This guy's wife just disappeared almost two decades ago. Appears professional cleaners got called in.

"Net? This guy is a career psychopath with very powerful friends who are short on ethics.

"Even though we've been treading slowly, I'm afraid this drill-down was not as subtle as I had hoped. More like a digital machete. Unlikely, but could be an issue if someone's watching.

"Now, this is where the old weird-o-meter jiggles on up into the red. My guys say there's something strange about how this particular incident was erased. It feels more like outsiders with serious help from *within* the intelligence community. Could be with a law enforcement nod and some politicos too. Guy's mom was a Connecticut state senator. May not all be relevant, but it's all mighty strange."

George said nothing.

"I don't know, George. This raises some sophisticated questions. This creep has hooked his wagon to some smooth operators. If it's not the Bureau or any of the major agencies, it could be rogue elements which seems more likely, but orchestrated from outside.

"Either way, it's of concern to me. This will require some additional resources. If my suspicions are correct, we must be very careful about who we trust from here on out. I'll work on that."

George listened in dumbfounded silence.

The guy he fired was a murderous spy? How...? Then he remembered Dent's prophetic parting words, *"You have no idea what you've just done."* And, *"Oh, I'll get help alright, Janis. I'll get professional help. Say goodbye to Kate for me."*

"So why in Hell was this guy working for me at GGS as a lowly tester?"

"Not sure, but I'd guess it was a benign cover mandated by his handlers for whatever else he was doing on their behalf while he was working for you. Clever—hiding in plain sight."

Handlers? Oh my Lord, please rescue me, along with my sanity!

"George, you must remain vigilant. We're not sure how mobile this guy is yet, but please assume you're in danger. Meanwhile, I'll keep digging, see if we can't get a bead on this clunker."

Click.

~

DECEMBER 2006
FORT MEADE, MARYLAND

Sam Braxton remained apprehensive.

He'd been working a few contacts on behalf of his friend George. The wheels finally started turning more rapidly. Patience might be a virtue, but only to a point. Now was the time to turn up the volume, to recruit more help.

Sam smiled. He decided to take his research to the next level by reaching out to his most trusted agency analyst and friend, Andy Nantzfield. He took Andy into his complete confidence.

THE RUNNING GAG NEVER ENDED.

Back in the day some of the older guys cajoled Andy about his last name. Comparing it to a fifties movie star and sex goddess of her day, Andy usually played along.

"No, we're not related, so I can't introduce you to Jane. Besides, idiot, her last name was *Mansfield*!"

His teammates would tease, "Oh yeah, that makes sense now. She's a luscious blonde bombshell, and you're a balding brunette bomb!" They'd often turn to that schtick to dampen the obscene stress.

Sam smiled again, picturing old Andy with an hourglass shape and a rack of ribs.

Before Sam retired, Andy worked for him, back when they were both wild men. They were invincible back then. They both split their time between the field and the fort. Andy was still in the mix back at Meade and was glad to hear from his old friend and mentor.

"HEY, YOU OLD FART, DIDN'T YOU RETIRE?"

"I may be retired, ole buddy, but I still have some juice. And I have a problem."

"Sam, you know anything I can…"

"Yes, Andy, I know, which is why I'm talking with you, one-on-one."

While Sam missed la vita—the life—he knew his health was starting to fail at age seventy-nine. Mary had made him promise not to go back, and he hadn't. But this increasingly nasty den of snakes in which brave George and sweet Kate were entangled could not be ignored.

Mary would have to understand, recent cardiac event notwithstanding. She always did, bless her heart. Even when they'd gone in-country together so many years ago. Sometimes as partners, even though she was a civilian.

Ah, those were the days, eh old girl?

Besides, he was feeling better again.

He met Andy for a beer that night at Buck Murphy's Place on Telegraph Road in Odenton. What they had to discuss had to be quiet and private. Off book. The dim and smoky ambience of Buck's place fit Sam's mood.

"Andy, I'm involved in something that looks to be ugly, and not sure who I can trust. I do know that you and I trust each other. Neither of us would be alive today if we hadn't. I've been dancing around the edge of a mine field that's bigger 'n potentially more explosive than I anticipated, but now I gotta cut 'n run through the darn thing."

"Spit it out, Doc. You and I are as one. You need a deep inside man. I'm deep inside. Whatever you need, Boss."

AND SO IT BEGAN IN EARNEST.

After sharing with Andy the story of escalating intrigue, Sam implored his old friend to exercise extreme caution. He warned him only to deal with those in the community whose motives they could both be one-hundred-percent confident.

So Andy and his team of select confidantes within the agency and across the intelligence community quietly went to work. Out of network.

On behalf of their legendary colleague, Doctor Sam, a short but intense fishing expedition revealed a few more surprises. They confirmed that someone had pulled Dent Canfield's sanctions.

Further, someone posted a generous non-exclusive contract. Somebody was shotgunning and wanted Canfield dead.

THE NEXT DAY, ANDY CALLED HIS OLD BOSS.

On as secure an outside connection as was available, he said, "Sam, it would appear you're tangling with a nasty bit of barbed wire. Not sure who this character is, but he's not shy about who he hurts, *and* he's pissed off the wrong people."

"Well now, this smells like a possible break!"

The most surprising factoid uncovered? Canfield really *had* served —three years in the *Marines*. He had *not* been in the Army as he'd claimed, *but he had served.* The motivation behind that deception still escaped them.

There was little doubt now that some well-camouflaged agency or organization had funded his education. His parents had disinherited him. The trail evaporated with the last remnants of his honorable discharge. The rest? Mere speculation. This affirmed in Sam's mind that this guy had some juice of his own, and was definitely an operator. But for whom?

Andy continued briefing Sam on the team's findings.

"Our analysis of this character, so far, uncovered at least three interesting factors.

"First, chatter confirms the subject is still alive and has more than one agenda. Second, he is now a wounded animal, naked of his sanctions, on his own, prowling to survive. This makes him even more dangerous, but less of a ghost. And third, the falling out with his benefactors either resulted from his personal bloodlust, or because he developed a shred of conscience."

"That's great progress, Andy. Many thanks to you and the team."

"Okay, Doc. Please let us know if we can help further. Be careful colliding with this cat. You aren't so young and invincible these days, you old fart, and he looks to be unpredictable. That could well mean… messy."

Sam knew lots of jarheads.

Marines tended toward patriotic fervor flowing through their olive drab veins. If this guy felt betrayed, that could be the nucleus of an opportunity to figure out what was going on.

Now convinced they needed to confront this guy, they'd offer him salvation, even turn him if possible. His blend of motives, though, was like a stomped-in mud puddle.

He needed to somehow get Canfield face-to-face with another operator, not another victim. He feared for his friend George and his bride.

But how do you set up a meeting with a ghost?

I gotta hang out in the house he's haunting.

TOOLS OF THE TRADE

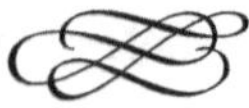

F EBRUARY 2007
MINNEAPOLIS, MINNESOTA

IN THE BEGINNING, THE WORK EXCITED HIM.

Jobs for the Brotherhood once exhilarated his sense of forensic adventure. But now... He still liked being part of something greater than himself. He *was* a patriot, and he buried residual doubts under a mountain of invisible money he could not spend.

Dent found an apartment in an anonymous rundown neighborhood near downtown. It was ideal—low profile, rented by the week. He moved here from his almost new town home in Stillwater, which he could no longer afford. Too much and too visible.

This dump needed paint, stunk of boiled cabbage, old ash trays and featured ancient wallpaper peeling at all the seams. Velvet wallpaper, no less. Reminded him of... what? It had been elegant a century ago.

He found the building's shabby federal row house architecture appealing. Rare in the midwest, it reminded him of more expensive squat brownstones in some of the older neighborhoods in Hartford. It just felt... familiar.

He paid top dollar for the fastest residential cable-based Internet connection available in this part of the city. It could be better. But it would suffice as a small but adequate doorway to cyberspace. He just needed acceptable service since most of the compute-intensive operations he'd perform in-house. Beyond that, he'd adjust to time-consuming uploads and downloads.

Dent made contact.

He received his next mission via the week's black-web ListServ Internet site used by his technical contact within the Patriot Brotherhood. The nature of this complex digital search-and-destroy job reminded him of the old adrenaline rushes this work used to provide.

He'd employ a few invasive software patches injected into a network of secure servers. He'd spice up the job with several subtle and dubious tricks from his *gig bag*—his repertoire of forensically stealthy accounting hacks—many of his own invention.

It was never much of a challenge for Dent to hack secure networked servers given his remarkable aptitude and level of experience. Especially given the ineptitude of public sector IT dorks who pretended to manage "sophisticated" government information technology.

The artistry? He ensured nobody ever knew he was there at all. The same was true for online accounting systems on which a mediocre analyst could cover or uncover money trails. Unless Dent performed his counter-magic, of course.

Dent took his genius to the next level by finding ways to perform the same magic on offline accounting systems. The only accounts immune to Dent's finesse were those systems that remained quarantined forever. These were the few machines with no Internet connection whatsoever. Nor were they attached to other machines that maintained a connection.

Even then, most machines backed up their books to online storage servers occasionally. If he could access some of *those*, he could create doubt. Doubt in accounting was the kiss of death. At least this could buy valuable time for a client to take other action. In short, this stuff was the pinnacle of elegant and devious forensic countermeasures within the accounting milieu.

His skills were rare and in demand. They needed him... as long as he didn't lose his mask of obscurity, that is.

~

DENT ADMIRED THE RUSSIANS.

They subverted their enemies in Ukraine by shutting down power grids with remote triggers at will. This was hackware called *Dark Energy* or *Crash Override*. Very cool stuff, but they hogged their way across a network—like tanks and missiles. *His* stuff remained invisible before, during, and after—dark energy in deep space with no trace.

The current mission took Dent the better part of a week working around the clock to finish—slow and meticulous and methodical. Creeping under the cloak of invisibility took longer than running and stomping around.

When he finished, no paper trail or digital footprint existed between dozens of offshore business accounts and hundreds of elections supervisors' personal accounts. Officials within select counties in Michigan, Wisconsin, and Pennsylvania grew suddenly a lot richer.

His earlier missions were similar involving various code-named government officials and contacts in several foreign countries. Dent hid the money, those who paid, and those who got paid.

The numbers astounded even his considerable imagination. If he harbored any doubt about the magnitude and reach of the organization to which he had hitched his wagon, that doubt was now extinguished.

He knew the Brotherhood employed dozens, hundreds, maybe thousands of contractors like himself. He could only speculate how big this whole thing was, and his curiosity threatened to get the best of him.

But that curiosity may have saved his life. He was picking up chatter that made him nervous.

Someone was hunting.

Him.

***

Undetected and at will, Dent skulked.

He crept into and out of cyberspace. He slid under a cloak of black technology contained within three trunk-size AmeriPack hard cases that went everywhere with him.

These cases appeared benign but road-worthy, lined up against the front wall of his shabby-chic apartment. A cheap white plastic folding table he bought at Walmart sat in front of them. It supported his monitors, twin keyboards, and trusty paper tape calculator.

That antiquated mechanical desk calculator was his sentimental touchstone with the past, and with better times, although he seldom used it. Come to think of it, he wasn't even sure if it still worked. But this clunky device afforded an ever-present reminder of his personal white whale—a paper trail-maker.

The three bulletproof cases comprised lightweight electronic equipment enclosures. Available to any high-end civilian buyer, the military also employed them in various field applications. Ubiquitous. Untraceable. Quick egress if necessary. Unplug, lug, and run. Or burn and forget. You never knew...

There were potent electromagnetic and incendiary devices in each case. He could trigger them from his cell, independent of external power via powerful short-duration batteries. This last resort option would only be used should their contents need instant neutralization.

Employing devices of his own design and implementation, there would be no military or agency hardware to be traced.

He couldn't afford all this.

So he was glad he didn't pay for this high-tech luggage, much less the gear stuffed inside. All shock-, vibration-, altitude- and EMI/RFI-resistant, per Mil-Specs, or military design specifications, made them costly tools of the trade.

Dozens of purpose-specific state-of-the-art blade servers on ultra-fast PCIe backplanes provided the brains in the first case. A battery-powered UPS—an uninterruptible power supply—with integrated batteries would supply instant juice in the event of a power failure, at least long enough for an orderly shutdown.

Twenty years ago, the second case, full of a dozen high-density huge-capacity hot-swap mass storage devices configured in redundant arrays for data integrity would have filled a dozen floors of a skyscraper.

And the third case contained equipment that communicated to and from cyberspace via redundant high-speed routers with IP-address-masking and encrypted redirection capabilities. In case someone started sniffing around the net, even if they saw him, they wouldn't locate him. Time enough for effective egress, anyway. Nobody stayed hidden forever. But he would buy a few precious minutes... *and* he'd see them coming.

Ultra-quiet high-CFM fans delivered efficient cooling to each case. Quick-disconnect umbilicals tied together the three broad coffin-like enclosures—kid-sized coffins, that is—to external power for normal operations.

The raw high-horsepower hardware delivered bleeding edge computing speed, protected mass storage, and stealthy connectivity. The spooky-smart stuff, though, came from millions of lines of specialized code. There was also some exotic hard-wired magic, much of which even Dent didn't understand. Didn't want to. Dark, dark stuff. You could lose your head.

Literally.

The apartment, the equipment, and his own virtuosity? The stuff of survival and victory. And he *was* a patriot, despite his foibles. He would *never* stop trying to prove it.

Now he needed a precise plan for concluding his unfinished personal business. Might as well have a little fun too. But he had all the time in the world.

Or so he thought.

He was invisible and he had a hit list to address.

SUBURBAN CLEANSING

N OVEMBER 2007
OAK PARK, MINNESOTA

Bedtime and warmth approached.

Sandra Segwell suffered from a perpetual chill. Donny complained that she was too skinny, and that was why. She looked forward to slipping into a warm bed with him, especially near his toasty feet to warm hers.

She let their miniature Schnauzer out the back door of their suburban home. He barked three times in rapid succession from the recesses of their fenced yard, and then he fell silent. Sandra called, "Oscar! Oscar?"

She went down. No preamble, no warning, a single extraordinary blow to the back of her neck.

She folded like wet origami.

~

"No hard feelings, Sweetie."

Dent Canfield's bloodshot eyes, filled with a total absence of malice, peered over her lifeless body toward the interior of the spotless home.

As he stepped around the dog's food and water dishes on the tiled kitchen floor, he smiled at how obsolete they now were. He hated little dogs. They splatter when the thumper strikes. Now he was tracking its blood across the kitchen floor.

Frickin' pocket dogs.

Donny Segwell wasn't OCD.

Having said that, meticulous personal hygiene was a source of great pride for him.

Of course, his last wishbone flosser snapped before he could get to that troublesome spot behind his upper right-rear molar. Then it occurred to him the house was seldom as quiet as it was right at that moment.

"Oscar? Sandy? Everything okay?" An unusual rhythmic thumping noise on the stairs further alarmed him when an apparition glided around the large bathroom door's jamb.

"Omigod. Dent? Is that you?"

In a reflective moment, Dent considered how far he'd tumbled down the rabbit hole. He whispered, though he wasn't sure why.

"I'm truly sorry, Donny. In all fairness, I did try to warn you when you fired my ass, but you wouldn't listen. You couldn't hear. You couldn't see. You were always a pretty good guy, Donny."

A dark cloud descended, obscuring all rational thought. Like the rest, but especially for good ole Donny, he'd be merciful and make it quick. He tightened his grasp on his beloved thumper. He was hoping for another thrill before another kill, but…

"Dent, you left us no choice! Please…"

Then, as if he had keyed the microphone to report the first score of the last game of the season over the stadium-wide PA, "*And* his last words are a lie. Typical."

Erotic rage fulfilled him, a violent abandon now his very breath of life. He breathed deeply that night, cleansed once more.

Donny would never know that his wife and pocket dog preceded him to Heaven, or wherever. Or that Dent had been merciful with them too. If only Donny and the rest of those on his shopping list hadn't destroyed his life.

COLD CASE

M AY 2008
LAKE CITY, MINNESOTA

TIME TO MOVE ON.

The job no longer fulfilled George nor was it tolerable. Worse, it was killing him, and now his friends. His life had become downright frightening in light of what Doctor Sam shared with him a few months ago.

He had become a lightning rod for a crazed killer, as well as those around him, it seemed. He might even be at the top of Dent's list. Both he and Kate would duck and cover at every unexpected noise. He could not focus. Poor Kate seemed in a perpetual state of apoplexy.

They found this galloping paranoia excruciating and exhausting. It also exacerbated tensions already running high between Kate and him. Again. They were drinking more, much more, every day, each of which they felt could be their last.

George remembered the feelings of his childhood. He'd lay in his bed, awaiting Armageddon, orchestrated by a vengeful god of toxic religiosity. Donny and Sandra, for God's sake? As well as poor Catie?

Even though he was only fifty-eight, George earned his full pension after almost thirty-two years of service. They needed space and time. Hell, he no longer had any idea what they needed. Other than change.

~

A TRADITIONAL RETIREMENT PARTY?

That did not seem appropriate. So a few of his managers, key team leaders, a few employees, and friends assembled in a private party room permanently festooned with nautical wall hangings and aquariums at Waterman's Restaurant in Lake City.

George was as close to this small group of favorite employees as anyone anywhere. Kate returned with him from Florida a few days earlier to provision and fetch their boat. Then they would be leaving again, this time aboard *Sojourn*.

Six months had passed since Donny and Sandra… those memories were still too painful. And fear still scratched at the growing collection of wounds that refused to heal.

None of Donny's team even tried to pretend there was any hope for emotional closure—even six months downrange. Police protection for select Stillwater employees dragged on for two uneventful months. Then that was gone. A grief counseling practice in town thrived.

Donny and Sandra's story had been big news. The lurid local headlines, including the Twin Cities' rags, compounded the team's pain at the time. The news outlets hinted at sensationalistic and presumptive conclusions with no basis in fact. That pissed off the team.

The small group did agree to celebrate George and Kate's escape from GGS. The endearing couple would be missed. Still hungering for a modicum of personal closure, they assembled to celebrate the life of manager Donny and his innocent wife.

At the same time, George sensed they also wished to reaffirm their own lives and purpose. Nonetheless, the affair felt contrived. Quiet polite laughter at one-dimensional humor failed to reach their darting eyes or uneasy posture. The funerals and wake last November had not been enough, yet had been too much too soon.

NO DOUBT REMAINED.

Law enforcement confirmed it. Their disgruntled ex-coworker was an icy psychopathic serial killer. The very idea overwhelmed all who had known and worked with this erstwhile likable teammate, the card-carrying prankster of *The Unholy Seven*. They made every attempt not to speak of that. Instead, they focused on memorializing his victims, their friends.

The Minnesota Bureau of Criminal Apprehension had interviewed everyone and kept George and Kate in the loop on their investigation.

THEIR DRINKS REMAINED UNTOUCHED.

Sitting on the foredeck of *Sojourn* before the party, Kate and George watched with suspicion as a man approached.

Upon arriving at the end of the long narrow dock, he looked up at them through the boat's starboard lifelines. George was grateful that he hurried to identify himself when he observed their anxiety.

Looking every bit the epitome of an overworked state employee, the short firebrand named Agent Seamus O'Brien announced himself and his purpose. Yet another BCA agent. The Irish name seemed consistent with his messy mane of flaming red hair worn too long and curling back on itself atop his hatless head.

George granted him permission to come aboard. At least the man possessed the decorum to ask, as dictated by nautical tradition.

As the supervising agent on the case, his update on the investigation sounded like an apology. He twisted the ends of a ridiculous handlebar mustache, waxed beyond all reason. A nervous habit.

They had made precious little progress.

Agent O'Brien reminded George of a rodeo bronc buster who stayed on the circuit a few too many seasons. Complete with cowboy boots showing under the cuffs of his jeans as he boarded.

He seemed professional and considerate even to the extent of removing his boots so he wouldn't scuff the gleaming deck paint. George respected him for that small courtesy. He must be a boater too.

An overworked but courteous Irish cowboy cop boater?

Agent O'Brien spoke after taking the proffered empty deck chair.

"Folks, I figured I owed you the courtesy of filling you in, face-to-face. The MO of the Segwell deaths appear identical to the murder of your boat neighbor, Mrs. Caitlyn Potts.

"We found no trace evidence, which is curious, as there's always trace. The Segwells' necks were shattered from overwhelming blows by a tapered cylindrical object. These caused their instant deaths. The only variation was a defensive wound discovered on Mr. Segwell. His left forearm was also shattered, and the killer's final blow impacted the left side of his neck, not the back. Mr. Segwell saw his attacker approach."

George shuddered.

Donny had looked into Dent's eyes before the final blow. Did they speak? Dear sweet God...

O'Brien continued. "The note printed on computer paper found at the Segwell scene matched the one found at Mrs. Potts's scene."

That scene wasn't more than ten feet from where they currently sat, since that was one of the few berths long and deep enough accommodate both *Wind Walker's* and *Sojourn's* depth and length requirements. They'd be moving the boat out of the state within the next few days anyway.

Agent O'Brien continued, "Same common paper, same font,

similar words. This one read, 'Sorry. Best Regards.' That was it. Mr. Canfield might as well have autographed it."

George wondered… *'Sorry?' Regret, maybe? A growing powerlessness over his own actions? Their inevitability? Seeking absolution?*

That poor sick lethal son-of-a-bitch.

DOCTOR SAM HAD RECOMMENDED SECRECY.

He was adamant that George keep their NSA probe to himself for the time being. No telling where that would lead, or who they could trust. George trusted Sam. O'Brien seemed like a good guy, but then, so did Dent. Before…

Agent O'Brien further muttered in a low monotone, almost as if he were talking to himself instead of to them.

"This guy has to be busted broke. Yet he hasn't used a single credit card, and he's attempted no contact with his parents in Hartford, not that they would help him in any event. He burned that bridge, we're told. He does have a meager savings account and a pathetic 401K. All are frozen. Nobody seems to care. Plain and simple, we are at a total loss."

George continued the diminutive agent's line of reasoning.

"And nobody hires a skilled programmer without a Social Security number or references these days, do they? What is this guy doing for money?"

"Must have some other source or a stash. If he does, we can't see it, and the BCA is pretty good at that stuff."

George could tell by his next words what Agent O'Brien felt in his gut.

"Something else is going on here. Very polished executions. He has skills, but the note 'n all? That's some up close and personal business. Amateur hour. Now six months, and nothing?"

O'Brien shared a few hypotheses, which was about all he had to offer. It was obvious he wanted to toss these folks a bone.

First, he said, "One possibility might be he offed himself. But no body? Possible, but unlikely. More likely, somebody offed him. But why? And who?"

He was asking himself these questions more than of Kate or George. His frustration was hard to miss, in his expression and his voice now raised almost an octave and those squinted eyes underneath his prominent and bushy red eyebrows.

O'Brien then dropped his bomb. He admitted he'd had no choice but to back burner the entire investigation. No leads for so long meant no funding.

Then, offering a sliver of consolation, "Dead end, hopefully, with emphasis on the word, *Dead*, guys. But… if he's not dead, he's not done. His type never is. So leaving town is a good idea. Wish I had more to offer.

"Say, does the water around here always smell like rotten fish floating in egg salad gone bad?" He smiled a little, at his feeble attempt to lighten the mood.

George responded, thinking about sinister scenarios.

"Algae bloom. Stinks sometimes. Not dangerous."

He and Kate watched that diminutive overworked but courteous Irish cowboy cop boater grow smaller with distance as he shuffled down that long dock.

With the sound of his hard boot heels echoing on the dock and growing softer by the second, they knew they were witnessing the death throes of an official investigation.

Rest in peace.

They hoped.

A RETIRING PARTY

A wake for a murdered *couple?*

Most normal people have never attended the wake of a murder victim, much less for a couple whom they knew and loved. There was so much left unsaid.

The prevailing mood? Awkward, emotionally lethal, a desolate landscape scarred by too many battles. This was a breeding ground for sustained and profound post-traumatic stress. The Segwell wake preceded their burial six months ago. Seemed like yesterday.

No, this gathering today was more about renewing hope. Nobody wished for this more than Nora Mathers, Donny's attractive team leader. Her charge of sexual harassment started this entire horrific chain of events.

Her husband Frank applied for and received a concealed carry permit for his new KelTech .22 handgun with a thirty round clip. Frank was fond of saying, "Small caliber, but with thirty rounds? It's called learning through reinforcement."

Nora took self-defense classes and achieved her yellow belt in Taekwondo. She was well on the way to her green. These days the two of them never parted. Life changes once threatened. They felt good about doing something, and that helped a little.

It was definitely time for all of them to move on, if they were able. George's retirement event was subdued but cathartic, at least for some. Maybe now, Donny's team could take at least one more step forward. Maybe George and Kate could breathe a little easier and a little deeper. They all needed to be less afraid, to refresh their spirits.

Still, was Dent dead? If not, had he given up? Would not knowing nibble at the edge of their sanity for the rest of their lives?

GEORGE INVITED DENT'S SURVIVORS ABOARD.

He whispered they required absolute privacy. He told them he wished to share new information they needed to hear—as a matter of survival. That grabbed everyone's full attention.

After the party faded into a reluctant funk, five of them huddled together inside *Sojourn's* pilothouse at the end of the long floating neighborhood known as the 800 dock.

Nora and her husband, Frank, along with Maxine Sun, whose husband stayed in the car, awaited their boss's next words as if their lives depended on them. Soon they would learn they did. Kate sat beside George.

Before saying a word, George reached over to insert a Steely Dan CD into the stereo which lit up the pilothouse with sound. It seemed appropriate they were listening to the song, *"I Guess I Just Got the Goodbye Look."*

George turned it up past a volume that almost eclipsed his conversational tone. The small group exchanged perplexed looks, except for Kate.

"Guys, it's time we share with you some rather scary stuff. You deserve to know, but I must ask you to keep what you're about to hear to yourselves. I am deadly serious about this. If what I tell you now is picked up by anyone outside this trusted group, we could very well be gambling with each others' lives."

"George, it's been a wild six months, but aren't you being kinda dramatic? Isn't the craziness behind us?" Frank obviously felt George was scaring Nora and Maxine more than necessary. But his voice broadcast that he would listen with an open mind, and would do anything to get their lives back to normal. George was taking them in the opposite direction.

"You'll understand in a few minutes. Please let me get through this. Gonna sound crazy, but we're all playing with the highest personal stakes possible - our very survival."

George charged forward without keeping this loyal little group in suspense a moment longer than necessary.

"First, we need some operational assumptions. We must assume that Dent is still alive and is not done, merely inactive. Foolhardy to assume otherwise. There's much more to what's going on than you know."

Donald Fagen's distinctive and pensive lyrics seemed a fitting backdrop to their somber conference.

"I have a friend who is well-placed in the US intelligence community."

Everyone in the room now escalated their emotional state from a known fear they assumed was now history to wild-eyed anticipation of what surreal revelation George would deliver next.

He needed to settle them down before they could start asking questions, while they were still just looking around the room.

"I'll remind you again before I go further. Nobody must hear of this outside this group. I assure you this is not needless melodrama. Maxine, if you wish you may share this with Shen Ma with the same caveats should you feel the need, but that's it, guys. Before you ask, we currently don't know any more than what I'm about to say."

Maxine's husband had chosen to wait in their car. Since Shen Ma was very shy and struggled with all social interaction, not to mention with the English language, he and Maxine agreed to his absence from this meeting.

"This is key—my friend and I don't know who can be trusted, but I trust him with all our lives. Some details I'm sharing with you came from the Minnesota Bureau of Criminal Apprehension. Even they are not aware of Dent's activities outside the… homicides, and have suspended their investigation. So here's the net.

"Dent works—or worked—for an organization that's likely a non-government organization. This NGO commands a broad and deep reach, including intelligence, possibly even law enforcement. Dent is a spy. His job at GGS was a cover—a disguise.

"Dent does not appear to be an assassin; rather, he's a remorseless serial murderer who is unhinged by any normal standard. We believe he is ill and needs treatment that he's not getting."

Nora and Frank exchanged knowing looks.

"We don't know what his real job was or is. He does not think like us, guys, and is on a path of irrational vengeance. His killings are a personal matter. We don't think they have anything to do with his… work as a spy or whatever he's up to.

"Further, while we can't know for sure, we must assume all of us *and* our loved ones are on his, ah, hit list.

"Now, you might think it crazy, but my friend has warned me we could be under surveillance, either by Dent or by someone else. That's why we're enjoying some soft rock right now. I know it all sounds like this could only happen in some cheap movie, but remember Donny and Sandra, gang."

If it weren't for that music pulsing over the top of George's words, the silence in *Sojourn's* pilothouse at that moment would have been deafening. The group was in shock. George knew he needed to draw them back into the present moment.

"Guys, I know this is a lot. We are all way out of our depth here, but we're smart, and now we're informed. Can't call the police. Since the BCA told me two hours ago they have nothing to go on, there's nothing to be gained by talking to the wrong cops.

"Besides, they think Dent is dead based on his dormancy. *We* cannot afford to assume that. Plus some scary-smart folks at the NSA and elsewhere aren't either. But they *are* humping this thing on the down-low. They're making progress, but it's not fast. It is big. Bigger than us."

Frank said, "The NSA? George, you're dead serious, aren't you? So… what should we do, Boss?"

Even though he was now retired, he was still the boss. And now they knew he was seriously connected.

"Guys, I can share with you what Kate and I plan to do. Dent may or may not be anchored to any specific geographic area; nevertheless, Kate and I are driving our boat down to Florida and will disappear out onto big water for a while. The BCA guy told me that since Dent's first murderous stop was right outside this very boat, relocating seems prudent. His first victim, that we know of, lived right across the dock.

"Here's a scary corroboration for you. She bore a strong resemblance to Kate here, spelled K-A-T-E. The victim, our friend, was Cate, C-A-T-E."

George paused for a long moment, remembering. He shook his head hard from side to side on an impulse as if that might allow him to shed the memory. The others stared at him as if at a man already in Hell.

"Dent addressed his first note to me. He wrote that he was sorry he missed me. Agent O'Brien thinks I'm still Dent's number one priority. I'm taking that to heart. It would be a bonus if we were able to draw him away from you guys.

"You all still have jobs, and can't just leave Stillwater. But I suggest you remain hyper-vigilant. If you hear or see *anything* unusual, call 9-1-1. Don't be afraid to cry wolf. Report a suspected home invasion, someone following you, whatever.

"Tell the police you believe a disgruntled ex-employee suspected of being a serial killer may be stalking you. Refer them to Agent O'Brien at the BCA. That's important, but *tell them nothing more*. Okay?"

"George, how much danger are we in?"

"I wish I knew, Nora. It's less than we fear. Again, local and state law enforcement seem to think this guy is history. You know how laser-focused Dent was at GGS. I can't tell you what to do, but Kate and I are going to still plan for worst case best we can.

"My agency friend says *'when ordinary people are thrust into extraordinary circumstances, it's prudent to exercise extraordinary care surrounding ordinary events.'*

"He also advocates *'situational awareness and response'*, whatever that means. I guess we pay attention and prepare to act. Maybe even practice.

"A few more things for your consideration that I haven't shared with anyone except Kate and the local police. Shortly after we released Dent from GGS, I spotted his white Cadillac parked down the block from our house in Stillwater on three consecutive evenings. We only knew he was pissed at that point, but that still spooked me.

"I called the police, but he disappeared before they showed each time. Even though I'm not what you'd consider a gun aficionado, I borrowed a shotgun from my neighbor for a few weeks. Kept it loaded. In the bedroom by my bed. Just in case.

"I also stopped off at Cleary's Fire and Safety back then. I bought several small canisters of pepper spray. I got one for my keychain, one for the glove box of each car, and one for Kate's purse, along with a few refills. I tried to buy MACE, but that's not available to paranoid civilians.

"I worry a lot about you guys. You might think this is weird, but I stopped at Cleary's again yesterday to pick up a bunch more pepper sprayers."

George unlatched the door to a closed cabinet. He retrieved two small gift-wrapped boxes. Each was the size of a thick paperback book. He handed one to Frank and the other to Maxine, accompanying each action with a deliberate look that transmitted the message, *This is serious.*

"You'll find four pocket-sized spray canisters in each box. The split ring on top of the little black leather holster for each allows you to hang it or secure it to a key ring. Do me a favor. Learn to use them. Sprinkle them around your house and cars. Carry one on your key chain. For the Hell of it, for me, okay guys? Consider it a personal favor.

"I guess my net message to you is to be very careful *all the time*, at least for the foreseeable future. It is warranted. And when I receive more info, you'll have it too.

"Any other questions I won't be able to answer right now? Then God bless and protect us all from this crazy son-of-a-bitch, if he's still around."

VEILED AND UNVEILED

W ASHINGTON, DC

"One hundred, seventy-two days.

"That's how long to election day. We are not on schedule."

The venerable voice transmitted an air of supreme confidence and utter disdain.

"We will recover."

Unmitigated fear in the other's voice did not match his words of unqualified braggadocio.

In sotto voce, as one might use when ordering a bottle of fine wine in an exclusive restaurant, "Please ensure you do. Much is at stake."

The veiled threat was not lost on the senior minion who responded into his phone, "Of course, Sir."

While flattered to be placed in a position of such awe-inspiring influence, he knew he now flew too close to the flame. His wings were already singed, although he did not yet plummet to earth.

Lost credibility was a death sentence at this level. He would leverage the reprieve he'd been granted with all the gusto at his command.

THE OLD MAN ENDED THE CALL.

The younger man sitting to his right simply smiled. How he loved the scent of fear. These two had sequestered themselves in a small but impressive library in an exclusive DC men's club.

The tectonic plates shifted beneath a subterranean dimension of global politics. Those plates kept grinding without remorse. The group to which these two elitists belonged had gone undetected for a half-dozen decades.

The liberal application of financial lubricant placed in the required hands enabled such unprecedented secrecy on such a scale. Into little hands, lots of them. And then there was the death oath of silence and invisibility.

This organization's policies often ran counter to Politica Publica. Ironically, that was the very source from which this dark Doppelgänger drew its strength.

The older gentleman answered his phone again, accepting another report from yet another minion. Before he ended the call, he said, "Yes, Comrade. We both win. I congratulate you on your daring and vision. Do svidaniya." He disconnected to a concerto of chirps and beeps—laid his encrypted cell face-down on the glassy surface of the Victorian table to his immediate right between him and the younger man.

The ancient patriarch reflected on the encouraging words he'd heard. The graveled voice on the phone belonged to a comrade from the highest levels within the Kremlin.

"As always, absolute discretion is critical. Now if our friend is competent and sincere, we're almost back on schedule."

"Of course, Sir." The young man looked up to this senior statesman with eyes of ardor.

"We must keep reminding ourselves. Nobody outside our circle must ever guess they're unwitting subjects of our grand social re-engineering project."

The upward inflection of his voice on the word *project* hinted a subtle betrayal of his calm countenance.

"And all without the need to pull a single trigger, or the loss of a single life."

The student addressed his master. He knew which words must come next.

"Well, in principle, anyway. We must continue to go to any lengths, no matter the collateral cost."

"Right you are, my young friend."

"Will we buy the time we need?"

"When awareness of our current episode surfaces, and it will, a new day will have already dawned. Nothing can stem continued redistribution of wealth and power at that point. A fait accompli."

These were two high priests of power and influence feeding on each other's patriotic fervor. Or was it nothing more than greed? Anyone listening without knowledge of their current episode would likely have labeled them lunatics. But they were deadly serious. These men, unfettered by ethical, legal and constitutional trivialities, accessed vast resources; however, they discovered they needed still more.

Their strategy was simple and ingenious involving a bold and steady cadence on several fronts. All led up to and played out underneath the normal bluster of the public parade toward election day. The risk of exposure was high, but so were the potential rewards. Their entire shadow campaign leveraged the bulk of their extensive network. This network comprised dimensions private and public, domestic and international, physical and psychological.

"So you've put a great deal of thought into this, haven't you, Sir?"

The old man took a moment to draw the smoke of his ever-present cigar deep into his lungs and exhaled. The pungent smoke flowing over his vocal chords thickened his voice.

"First, on the political front, we will ensure fewer nationwide polling places remain open, and only on weekdays. So fewer opportunities for the impoverished masses who will need to drive a greater distance to vote. They tend to vote for mainstream candidates, given the chance, and that usually means the opposition.

"Even if they do show up to vote, they will lose time from work. That is if they're even able to get the time off. We're betting this will likely trump their desire to vote. Besides, if we play them with care, they'll believe their vote is irrelevant.

"Second, orchestrating increased political and racial gerrymandering of several key districts in a half-dozen swing states will add another level of insurance. This will deliver a high level of confidence that our candidate will win in those districts. They are fundamental to capturing important electoral college votes in those states should the general election be close."

"Sir, are we skirting legalities, or can we make these moves without fear of interference?"

"Ours is a broad spectrum strategy. Some transactions need to be masked, others do not. The beauty of this strategy is built on the general public's profound ignorance. They have little or no idea the electoral college is the real linchpin, not the general election, as long as the spread is thin. Knowledge is power."

The patriarch continued.

"Third, and this is critical, we will provide massive intelligence and financial support to a handcrafted populist candidate. He will be unfettered by the constraints of any major political party, or the broader brush stroke of traditional politics. A comprehensive nationwide poll will enable us to sustain our candidate's popularity.

"This involves the critical harvesting of personal information from millions of social media accounts. That data will be important both before and after the election, as long as our man adheres to our script.

Our motivated candidate knows this, and is counting on our support. We will continue to remind him of his role.

"And finally, we will leverage the genius of *importing brass balls,* a pearl of wisdom a colleague suggested to me almost two years ago. This is now the most significant leverage point of our entire strategy.

"We will use every available private and public source of information which a small army of *disinformationists* will manipulate and communicate. They will tailor our mass communication agenda as the foundation for our blanket micro-marketing campaign using our harvested social media data.

"This is already underway and we are making substantive progress as it shapes our candidate's agenda *and* his court of public opinion. He will espouse exactly what people want to hear and how they need to hear it.

"Then, by leveraging every form of media, especially those unconstrained by the traditional vetting of facts, this throng of disinformationists will further shape voters' opinions."

"That seems awfully bold, Sir, even for us."

"If you know your history, we are expanding on a strategy that's been employed for decades by worldwide intelligence services. They've used this strategy to disenfranchise individuals and organizations, even to destabilize governments. What's good for the goose…

"Now, however, we're privatizing and weaponizing those strategies, aiming them toward our own agenda. The proliferation of ubiquitous communication technology now affords us an unprecedented opportunity.

"So more than ever, we shape our vision of a profitable future in the minds of voters. You will tell your grandchildren that you were a part of re-engineering American democracy, my young friend."

The younger man responded with enthusiasm, "Change people can believe in? Indeed, whether they already know what they need to believe or not." He bowed his head deferentially to his legendary mentor, Mr. Z.

ABRAHAM ZELOKOV PULLED LEVERS.

Proud of his heritage, Mr. Z was not above using it as a lever in negotiations. Quick to change the subject, once he got his way, he'd then build bridges necessary to initiate or shape world events. His stock-in-trade—his genius—extended back to his years as a homeless teenage prodigy in Leningrad.

Surviving in the streets of Mother Russia was easy for him during a difficult time in her history; however, his family was persecuted to the point of extinction. *He* would not go so gently...

Appearance was important. He stole what he needed. Food and clothing were easy. So were influential friends, equally important sustenance. Such was the nature of his demeanor.

When he was a devastatingly handsome lad, he learned the power of simply telling people what they wanted to hear and then finding a way to give them at least a taste of what they desired before either befriending them further if they were useful, or eliminating them if they were not. In short, that described the history of Mr. Z's life.

It was so simple, yet so few understood.

Ensuring he always positioned himself near seats of power was his gift—a preternatural anticipation of world events.

Abraham had been in Moscow, by way of Leningrad, when Perestroika and Glasnost finally metastasized, ending the Great Experiment, at least for a while. He befriended disenfranchised intelligence operatives of the FSB and KGB who became the new generals of the Russian Mafia. He'd delivered to them an exclusive network of street-smart operators from across their land.

Later, he happened to be in Berlin when that wall came down, and borders were opportunistically redrawn. He endeared himself to Eastern European leaders, hungry to embrace Capitalism, providing them, and himself, opportunities to join the ranks of the nouveau riche through the brutal exploitation of information and application of force. They lusted for a free market, but only free to their own ranks.

Now, a surprisingly vital centenarian, possessed of obscene wealth and influence, Mr. Z had not only witnessed great historical changes in his lifetime, his hand was instrumental behind the scenes that made many of them happen. America was now where the action could be found, at least for the next few decades.

~

Mr. Z loved his cigars... and power.

One of the few vices he could still relish with relative impunity was a lit cigar, whenever he was awake.

Next, he adored his beloved club, where he also owned and occupied a private wing. None of the members knew. With limited mobility, but prepossessed of a reputation drawn in broad strokes of near-mythical proportions, the few elite power players who knew Mr. Z, including kings, despots, presidents and prime ministers, regularly sought his advice and counsel.

A few of these world leaders would even view him as a threat, except for his advanced age. Some, however, still sought his leadership, including his network, as an agent of change.

Some revered him as the ultimate bellwether, although nobody still alive knew precisely why, other than his formidable aura. The few who knew him considered him a puppet master, and could tell you precisely why; his network of inference and influence remained unrivaled among his contemporaries.

"Look, my young friend, I am all too aware that my days are numbered. I wish to leave a final legacy as a strong platform for my successor, yet another bold move that will never find its way into the history books, at least not with my name on it."

~

His mortality crept up on him.

Mr. Z reflected on the long and distinguished history of his Patriot Brotherhood, a centrally-led consortium of like-minded businessmen, law enforcement officials, key bureaucrats, and politicians. Many were motivated by either large-scale profits, their version of political power, or visionaries who were convinced the laudable experiment of American democracy had run its course.

"I'm sure you'd agree that America now seems little more than an ugly hybrid of quasi-socialism and emerging anarchy. The result? An idiocracy… apathetic idiots governed by self-serving idiots with illusions of grandeur.

"With so many already intellectually numb leading the myopic masses, the Brotherhood is an essential stabilizing magnum opus. I'm sure you'd agree."

He continued, his voice filled with patriotic fervor.

"We are the purveyors of a new patriotism, bred to assist the now-ugly worm known as America emerge from her cocoon as a fresh and vital butterfly. The Brotherhood has long existed in the dark corners of human frailty. We've wrought desperately needed change when and where it was required through time. Always through time."

Yet again, Mr. Z chanted his most sacred mantra. *"Recognition grows restraints; invisibility breeds power,"* for the benefit of his young mentee, Palmer.

~

JULY 2008
WASHINGTON, DC

Palmer Xavier sat at his master's side.

The young chief operations officer of Greater Global Solutions, Inc., wondered why he was here again today. They lounged comfortably, side by side, facing the fire in the library of Mr. Z's opulent apartment within the embrace of his precious club.

As far as Xavier could tell, it was the *only* apartment, and it featured its own underground exterior entrance.

Curious, and impressive.

He had visited Mr. Z here many times before over the last three years. He was Palmer's most highly valued mentor, bar none.

There was always the fire.

They did not face each other, which Palmer thought strange, but he must have his reasons. *Almost as if he sees the future in that fire, and its relevance to their current discussion.*

He wasn't sure why, but Palmer almost felt like this might be a coming out party.

They had discussed Mr. Z's business with the Brotherhood many times, but always at a relatively abstract level. Palmer respected unbridled power and had made it abundantly clear—he wanted in. Or more precisely, he wanted what the Brotherhood could offer. He could not have anticipated what Mr. Z said next.

"Palmer, you are about to assume the helm of the most formidable source of visceral power and influence on Earth."

Is it possible?

Palmer actually experienced the early stages of an erection.

"You will have the ability to change the course of history, to act with impunity, employing resources so vast even you cannot yet comprehend.

"Today, you are constrained by your board, investors, customers, the court of public opinion, and the law; however, tomorrow, these constraints will simply become your pawns to manipulate as you wish."

Unbelievable!

~

Mr. Z swiveled his squinted gaze.

He peered with intensity toward his mentee as he said, "Be solemnly warned, however, there is one immutable law of this mise-en-scène, as you've often heard me say: *'Loss of concealment will always be our Achilles' Heel.'*

"Can you swear to this blood oath of invisibility should the day arrive when it is your turn to lead the Brotherhood?"

Abraham Zelokov was taking a chance on this young man and his ill-fed ego, but time was running out, and Palmer possessed the raw materials of this mantle. He just needed experience. He was about to get it.

PALMER HID HIS JOLT OF DISAPPOINTMENT.

Mr. Z dangled the carrot just out of reach.

Should *the day arrive? It's a test, cowboy, don't screw it up now!*

"To my dying breath, Sir. Your life's example is my duty. There is much work to do, and I stand ready to serve our Brotherhood."

Palmer realized his position at GGS, while formidable and near the top of that heap of withering carcasses, was still very finite in scope within the grander scheme.

It was always about schemes, wasn't it?

He hungered for more, ever more. His long-standing relationship with this awe-inspiring survivor and leader made him realize he had clearly yet to achieve his own pinnacle. There was still much to learn.

Palmer admitted to himself he *would* miss drinking in the fear pouring from the eyes of those who had no choice but to submit to his will. He'd get over that by replacing it with influence over world events, even though from beneath the cloak of invisibility. *He'd* know.

That should be enough.

Abraham's sponsorship had made Palmer's swift ascension to his current job at GGS possible, but they both subliminally acknowledged that was a mere stepping stone.

That job was also his first big league test, perhaps the first of many, which simply strengthened his resolve. His ante in the game was five hundred million. He'd delivered based on a couple of handshakes. Mr. Z confided that now he was nearly ready. God, how he loved this! Nothing else mattered. If not today, then...

Mr. Z had been observing Palmer's reaction to his words, visibly pleased.

Then, there it was.

"So, my young friend, as of this moment I consider you the provisional leader of the Brotherhood. It is time to officially promote you from Palmer Xavier to Mr. X.

"I will continue to serve as your confidante and adviser. You will always give considerable weight to my guidance, but your decisions will stand, unless I decide to override them, privately, of course, at which point, you will always understand why.

"My remaining time on this earth is now limited, so use this time wisely. This is a pivotal period for us. You must have a hand in it. Are these conditions understood and acceptable to you, Palmer?"

"Yes, Sir. I will not fail."

"Very well, then, Mr. X. Now you must meet your generals. First will be Mr. Slattery."

"Forgive me, Sir, but I already know Mr. Slattery."

"You only think you do. Please set it up. Meanwhile, you'll need to arrange your exit strategy from Greater Global, of course, as well as from any other distracting entanglements."

CAREER CHANGE

NEW YORK, NY

MIKE ANSWERED THE PHONE PERSONALLY.

Hmmm... "Mike, we need to talk. Do you have ten minutes some-time today?"

"Palmer, why don't you swing up to my office now? I have twenty minutes."

The uncustomary instant access surprised Palmer. As he entered the austere office suite of GGS's CEO on the forty-first floor of 555 Madison, the elderly of two EAs ushered him directly into Michael Martino's office. Another precedent.

"Mike, I'm leaving."

"Yes, Palmer. Mr. Z instructed me. Time is short."

"*What?*" Palmer wasn't sure if he should feel astounded, flattered, manipulated or impressed. He instantly regained his composure.

Mike just smiled. "Look, Palmer, you've been chosen to lead the

Brotherhood. It was my job to prepare you. You're moving on because you're needed. I already have my dream job. You're just getting started. I know you want this, and you deserve it. This is top shelf, next level. We won't be strangers. I'll expect your resignation on my desk within the hour. Give me two weeks. Can do?"

Palmer's foundation trembled, but held. The Brotherhood's reach, and this, yet another taste of their compartmentalization, amazed him. He made every attempt to hide his astonishment, only partially transforming his demeanor to that of gratitude, all in a few milliseconds.

Mike noticed. Palmer said, "Can do, Boss, and…"

"Shut the Hell up, and get out of my office."

They both knew this was perhaps Mike's last opportunity to speak to his mentee in such a manner. He smiled. So did Palmer.

As Palmer strode from that office, perhaps for the last time as *just* a multinational COO, he symbolically entered into yet another sphere of power and influence. Even though he'd be tying up loose ends here for a couple of weeks, he could feel a metamorphosis taking place as he floated toward that elevator door, his portal to a parallel universe. *Shock and awe,* as he knew his friend and mentor Mike Martino might mutter, given the chance.

Shock and awe.

IN THE DOLDRUMS

D EMOPOLIS, ALABAMA

SOJOURN PERFORMED FLAWLESSLY SO FAR.

George expected it. That was saying a great deal.

They had traversed the Upper Mississippi, Ohio and Cumberland Rivers. Now en route to the gulf via the Tennessee-Tombigbee Waterway and the Black Warrior River, a flooded watershed had them holed up at a tug re-fueling station.

The cold weather forced them to hunker down inside the pilothouse. And until the Coast Guard officially opened the river again, they weren't moving.

George used the time to reflect.

Just as he'd flown frivolous flights of fancy over the swamps of his childhood religion, so he similarly approached the quagmire of American politics. Simply not relevant.

He knew he was over-educated, but never well enough informed to sustain an intelligent debate concerning all things political. So he abstained from expending what he viewed as wasted energy.

Admitting that he was a political agnostic usually evoked one of two reactions. First, "What's an agnostic?" Fair enough. Or second, "That's downright un-American!" to which George would think, *Screw you, and mind your own business, thank you very much.*

After all, George believed, like most Americans, the fervor exercised over one's right to vote, was an exercise in utter futility. Wasn't it?

To truly believe that a single citizen had any impact on the overall political landscape, was that not little more than obtuse optimism?

George believed politics entailed little more than a frail and endless thread of rancorous compromises, further diluted as self-serving agendas proliferated in perpetuity.

Shortly before he retired, a squeaky clean junior employee had dared to approach him to ask what he felt was a very personal question, "Mr. Janis, how do you feel about the prospect of a black President?"

"Really? You feel we need to weigh in on the color of a candidate's skin? I have two words of wisdom for you, my friend, 'Who cares?' Get a life, man."

George may have been a political agnostic. He was not a racial agnostic and had little patience for anyone who appeared to be.

His favorite bumper sticker said it all, *"Don't Vote, It Just Encourages Them!"* Of course, he voted, because it was his right as a citizen. He was all about exercising his rights.

An obligation, though? He resisted that notion because it inferred that someone *expected* him to vote, and that's not how his mind worked.

Acting on someone else's expectation was the antithesis of personal control; worse, it exemplified a lack of control. There was enough of that in his life already.

When he voted, however, he did so as much to get the little sticker that proudly proclaimed, "I Voted Today," so people wouldn't blow him smoke for not voting or suck him into yet another meaningless discourse.

Most importantly, they could see that he had indeed voted and would leave him alone. A merit badge that professed at least cursory patriotism. He served his country, now wasn't it somebody else's turn? An apathetic prickly pear's defense mechanisms that perhaps he doth protest too much?

Besides, a black President would be a piece of history, of which he'd be a part. A story to tell to his grandchildren. Yeah, that would be a good story.

At one point, George was more involved, but after really looking at the political process, he knew you could spin any issue in any direction. Consequently, facts were as clear as homemade dandelion wine in a dirty glass. Facts were the last true bastion of fiction. Weren't they?

EVERYBODY'S GOT ONE

C LEVELAND, OHIO

Roxy's stank of bad beer and stale smoke.

Nestled in a dilapidated waterfront building on the shores of the Cuyahoga River, Roxy's was one of the few remaining tenants in the heart of the town's heaviest industrial district.

Dim incandescent lights shone from plastic faux-stained-glass Tiffany-style lamps hung low over the shiny but heavily scarred bar. They were the major feature of the decor.

Roxy's Tavern catered to a handful of regulars who frequented this neglected neighborhood watering hole.

Zeke Wilson peered at his yellowed finger tips from smoking too many butts so short his callouses were spotted with burn marks. It was as if this afternoon was the first time he'd noticed them.

His clothes stunk of stale smoke, his shirt reeked of old beer stains, and it seemed something black or brown clogged every pore on his face. But he didn't seem to notice any of that. He viewed himself just another hard-working well-informed citizen.

"Hey, Miles! How about another round over here?"

Zeke straightened his slump over the bar slightly from the exertion of ordering. He leaned on his elbows, a half empty mug of Schlitz draft between his cupped hands, chilling those mill-calloused fingers and cracked palms.

These frickin' cracks finally stopped bleeding. A small smile crept onto his creased face to acknowledge that small victory.

Zeke felt it was important for the next round to arrive *before* he ran out, but not so soon that the new mug got warm. It was all about timing, which could be tricky for the less practiced. He sprinkled a bit more salt on his napkin.

If the front windows of Roxy's hadn't been blacked out, he and his post-shift drinkin' buddy, Pete Moorhead, might have enjoyed the late afternoon sun sinking into a bend of the Cuyahoga. Several decades ago that river got so polluted it ignited, and a legend was born—the river of fire. Now, after pulling a double shift at American Steel, all they wanted was a cold beer and a heated discussion.

Pete said, "Thanks for the beer, Zeke. I don't care what the boys at the mill say about ya. You're almost as generous as your mama, but better looking!"

"You're welcome, and kiss my handsome butt." The blast of the furnace, but none of the heat. "You takin' any more shifts this week, Pete?"

"Yeah, whatever I can get. It's gettin' harder every year just to feed the crew."

Zeke knew this to be true. He could almost see it happen as he watched the news each night before dozing off in his crusty old brown-plaid La-Z-boy recliner in front of his new Samsung Smart TV.

That chair had belonged to his dad. Lifetime warranty on the mechanism, been re-covered twice. He was proud of that.

He'd grouse out loud, whether there was anybody in the room

listening or not, "The rich get richer, the poor get hungrier, and them's in the middle get poorer too. And forget health or dental insurance anymore. Now, Union's no good for nuthin' except BS."

Pete said about the only thing they *could* do was bitch to each other. Then he added, "Can't afford not to, ya know? Go crazy."

Zeke prided himself on being one of the more intellectual guys at the foundry. He even read some books and stuff. Mostly, he monitored a lot of YouTube channels. His Smart TV was connected, HD and everything.

Figuring himself well-informed, he said, "Yeah, there's somethin' really wrong when the top one-tenth of one percent in America owns more'n the bottom ninety percent combined, ya know? That's us, brother. If you ain't John D. Rockefeller, or one of his snotty kids or the like, you're the bottom. *We're* the bottom."

"You tryin' to depress me, man? But you got a point."

Zeke knew how to impress, quoting numbers 'n all. Got Pete every time.

"Yes, I am, Brother Pete! Tryin' to get you off your lazy ass to vote. Comin' up!"

"Aw, who in *the* Hell has time for *that*? Besides, ain't gonna make no difference anyhow."

"See, that's the sort of lazy attitude what got us here in the first place. It's Washington DC and New-Freakin'-York against the rest of us, man.

"And I don't give a hang which party we're talkin' here, either. They're makin' laws out there that's stackin' the deck against us. Like they forgot about us, or never cared to begin with."

Zeke knew he amazed Pete. He considered himself the exception to the old mill worker's saying, *Strong back, weak mind.*

I even have a two-year college degree! Almost.

Pete said, "So what do we do about it, smart-ass?"

Zeke was ready. He did not hesitate, ticking off his points by extending one finger at a time, now whispering conspiratorially, which only compelled Pete to listen more intently.

"First, we make sure we get out and vote next election. This is important, Pete. We get all our brothers and their families to do the same.

"Second, we vote for an independent, somebody in the middle, like us, who ain't gonna suck up to Wall Street on the left, or them rotten corporate lobbyists on the right."

Zeke was on a roll with pearls of profound YouTube-inspired wisdom. Pete smiled, just a little.

"Well, I sure don't know what right and left means. But I understand middle like us, as in caught in the middle - nowhere land, right?"

"Exactly. And we vote for a candidate who will use American steel 'n piss on the boots of them Chinese bastards. That's what we do, Pete."

Zeke could see Pete was now overwhelmed.

"Hey, man, my head's starting to throb. Been fun, but I gotta go grab some zees before next shift. Thanks for the brewski."

"See ya, *brothah!*"

Zeke spoke exaggeratedly to Pete's back as his friend trudged heavy-footed outta the dim Roxy into the hazy late afternoon light without another word.

Pete just waved once over his slouched shoulder as he walked out, head hung low. Zeke sang out, "Don't forget, pass the word!"

He planned to sit and think some more. Political activists like him always had a lot more to do. He'd go home and monitor a few of his favorite videos from his La-Z-Boy command center before hitting the sack. Knowing exactly what needed to be done ignited the fire of righteous indignation in his belly.

Zeke considered his responsibilities.

After all, knowledge is power.

GRAND DESIGN

UGUST 2008
WASHINGTON, DC

Palmer Xavier sat in his sweat.

He lounged comfortably in front of Mr. Z's ever-present fire in his apartment's library at his club, even though a steamy Washington summer had already long-since taken the starch out of his once-crisp Egyptian cotton shirt. Even his button-down collar sagged, his French cuffs hung limp. But there was the omnipresent fire six feet away.

Palmer had been invited here for the third time within the last week, each time with no clue he'd be back so soon. Commuting between LaGuardia and Reagan National now felt like little more than a limo ride through the Midtown Tunnel.

"Mr. X, it is critical you absorb some historical touch-points of the Brotherhood and its many forms, along with where this will take us and this country. You need this specific context as you assume the mantle of leadership.

"We are implementing a long term phased strategy comprising four stages. We are currently in the throes of phase two.

"The foundation of the first phase employed a spectrum of physically aggressive actions in order to establish selective footholds in business and government. You should retain some degree of plausible deniability here for now. Just be aware that at one time, it was necessary. Think *grassy knoll.*"

A meaningful wink and a nod in return closed out the discussion of Phase One.

"The second phase, that of political influence and ultimately, restructuring the American political system, requires far more time and resources than phase one.

"The third phase will see us assuming the reins of American government. Plans are in place. We are posturing for the installation of our own unconventional presidential candidate, as you know, in addition to numerous other key elected officials, both on the national stage as well as at the state level. Most of the latter have been in place for many years, some for decades.

"The fourth phase, international expansion, will be highly dependent on our success in this country. We look to America as our guinea pig, our seventy-year test program."

Palmer—Mr. X—really didn't know how to take all this in. So he just said, "Examples, please. I need a plausible context."

"Of course. First, a history lesson that you probably assumed to this point was just American democracy running its natural course. Nothing could be further from the truth, at least for the last sixty-five years or so.

Mr. Z launched into a long-winded lecture outlining how the Brotherhood led the way for sixty years redistributing the wealth of America to the top one-tenth of one-percent of wage earners, but more interesting was how this wealth was but a cog in their machine to control American politics and the US Government. The international stage would follow.

Unbelievable!

~

Mr. Z squinted. Looked Mr. X in the eye.

"Now this is of immediate relevance. The US citizenry is already disillusioned with both major political parties. They believe the parties and their candidates are to blame for their pitiable plight. How delightful they're not even aware they participated in their own financial ruination. So we are now positioned to advocate our own presidential candidate—*this year*.

"He will run independent of the shackles inherent in the barely still-extant two party system. We only harbor about a thirty percent chance of victory, but our best odds will be achieved by aggressively running the dirtiest campaign imaginable.

"Shaking confidence in politics as usual will play to our advantage. We are running countless operations to reinforce our reality. Then, our plans for attacking annoying checks and balances that still remain will start to coagulate.

"Whether we win or lose this election, those of our operatives already on board who euphemistically think of themselves as Senators, Congressmen, and lobbyists, will craft additional legislation over the next few years that will essentially remove the few remaining obstacles for unrestricted corporate spending on future elections, and for preventing, or at least diluting efforts to restrict financial markets.

"I'll reserve the topic concerning our international partnerships for a future briefing."

Mr. Z was done speaking.

~

Palmer's mind swirled.

While he appeared to calmly contemplate the astounding history lesson of political debauchery he'd just heard, his mind struggled to absorb too much, too quickly, even for an intellectual sophisticate. *My*

God, this all sounds like plausible fiction, dripping with national and international intrigue!

He couldn't help that his business mind was already evaluating huge risks offset by unbelievable rewards.

Mr. Z patiently observed Mr. X processing this mass of data. Finally, he said, "Questions?"

After a full minute of silence, Palmer said in a low and steady tone, "Obviously, this is a lot to take in. I'm not sure I'm able to pose too many intelligent questions at this moment. Perhaps if I try to summarize all that you've shared with me in a simple statement, which you could then either affirm or correct. Is that reasonable for now, Sir?"

"Imminently!" He sounded pleased.

So far, so good.

PALMER—MR. X—LAUNCHED HIS SUMMARY.

"Beginning in the middle of the last century, a loose coalition of like-minded business leaders came together in a covert cabal. They began implementing a staged multi-generational strategy to subvert the American political process in order to take over the United States government. And they're robbing the wealth of America to fund that coup, as well as to enrich their own estates. If I understand correctly, it probably would follow that we'd eventually want to move the Capital from DC to lower Manhattan. Mostly correct, Sir?"

Mr. Z grinned, a mad clown. From his throat emanated a macabre high-pitched warbling squeak that reminded Palmer of a rusty hinge on a dungeon door that protested movement.

Finally, after a slow and ill-disguised gasp to feed wrinkled lungs that had laughed more than they deserved, but less than almost anyone, he croaked...

"Precisely! I am pleased that you made no feeble attempt to camouflage the true nature of our naked avarice. Having said that, I would contend that avarice is the new politic required to rescue this failing republic.

"We are ambitious men, Palmer, willing to stand on the shoulders of lesser men to elevate not only our personal status but more importantly, our collective strength. That does not mean we are not patriots. We simply believe that American democracy has run its course.

"Now is the time for strong men to create a stronger nation. Move the capital to the new seat of power? Fascinating idea—for the future. Shortens the financial supply lines. Plus, it creates a clear line of demarcation between the old symbolic regime and the new practical one. You're thinking like a general, my young friend. Well done."

"Thank you, Sir."

For the first time in his life, Palmer hoped he wasn't getting in over his head. His antennae wiggled. He wished Mr. Z would stop referring to him as his young friend.

MR. Z PASSED THE RING OF KEYS TO PALMER.

"What are these?"

After such a grand and glorious dissertation on money, politics, and power, this seemed a trivial and mundane act to Mr. X.

"The keys to your new home and office on Chain Bridge Road—here in Washington. Your Camelot. You will find the mansion comfortable and commodious. There are several nice automobiles in the garage. The grounds are lovely; although, I think eight bedrooms and nearly a dozen bathrooms wasteful, especially when appearances are useless to an invisible man. It was available. Complete."

Mr. Z was enjoying himself, particularly with this symbolic passing of the baton.

"Please use our discreet moving company to relocate whatever is necessary from your Manhattan apartment. The estate is nestled in a very private area just northwest of the downtown area, should you need to conduct a physical meeting; although, most of the Brotherhood's business is conducted either by phone or computer, all anonymously and heavily encrypted, obviously."

"I am moving to Washington." Not a question, a statement, with a hint of eagerness.

"At least until you move the Capital north again!" There was that mad clown screech again, a soprano chatter like the squeaky scraping of a brittle diamond on rebellious glass.

A whistling wheeze ensued.

"I will be at your disposal, Mr. X. Please consult me, day or night, on all significant decisions, at least for the next few months. I will spend as much time answering or asking questions as might be required.

"God bless us all."

Palmer thought, *Who?*

TAILORED AGENDA

N EW YORK, NY

Jeff Redding wanted more.

The sixty-two-year-old agriculture mogul from Nebraska had never held an elected office. Yet. How hard could it be? He was independently wealthy, already possessed the ego required for public office, so why the Hell not?

If politicians only ran the country the way I run my businesses, America would be a lot better for it.

At least, that would be his platform.

"Ladies and gentlemen, here he is...

"Please welcome the next President of the United States, Jefferson Davis Redding!"

As applause from the live New York audience of over five hundred rang through the giant studio in the Ed Sullivan Theater, Redding marched, waved with both arms high above his head and smiled, showing off his unnaturally white teeth and board-straight back. He sat down, shot his cuffs and turned on his thousand-watt grin.

"Thanks for having me, Jesse. It's a pleasure to be here with you all tonight."

"Mr. Redding, let's get right to it. What is it you want the American people to know about you?"

"Well, Jesse, I need everyone to know that I break rules. I'm a political outsider and bad boy. As such, I don't owe anyone any favors. I plan to run this country like a business. There's so much fat in Washington that our political system is dying of morbid obesity. For cryin' out loud, it's already on life support.

"That ends when I become President. We're gonna get lean 'n mean 'n turn a profit again. We'll be the model for the rest of the world to follow."

"That sounds great, Mr. Redding. But an efficient government? Isn't that an impossible ideal?"

She'd been prompted to ask that leading question.

Redding addressed the American people directly; his intense pale blue eyes bored into the very soul of every TV viewer. He knew Jesse's massive network audience was sympathetic to his platform.

"Elect me as your President and I'll show you that it's entirely possible. Not only possible but inevitable. Look, I didn't get to be a successful businessman by not achieving my goals. Like any good American, I know the value of hard work, and hard-working Americans shouldn't have to pay for fat politicians to get fatter by robbing America's piggy banks. I will transform DC into an efficient machine, and put money and power back into the hands of the people."

"Assuming you're right, Mr. Redding, what's your secret?"

"First, I've been blessed with success, but I'm basically a blue collar guy who wants the same thing for America that every American wants for his own family. I started as a farmer and my businesses are now the largest agricultural concern in America.

"I want every single American to have a shot at the dream that I made happen for myself. I also want ironclad law enforcement and stronger security for our borders. Who doesn't want their president to address these basic issues?

He continued to beat the drum.

"So why hasn't any administration, including that of President Stevens, already done that for you?" He switched his gaze, never missing a cue for each of the three cameras focused on him, as if challenging the current president, wherever he was hiding, to answer him on the spot. Of course, he didn't. So Redding continued his shameless monologue unopposed.

"I'll tell you why folks. Because instead, they've all focused more on lining their own pockets and dedicating themselves to getting re-elected.

"Look, I don't need your money. I have all the money I could ever want. You can take that to the bank. Let me make America that successful by using my proven skills. I know how to trim fat. I know how to get to the heart of an issue and resolve it before moving on to the next one.

"Let me ask you. How much confidence do you have in any politician in Washington today to be able to do that for you? You don't. But I will do that for you, and for the future of my own children and grandchildren—and yours—growing up in this great country.

"Yes, I'm a Washington outsider, just like you, and I know exactly what's needed. No waffling, no compromises, just action.

"We need a new and honest agenda. No longer can we afford to be the world's policeman. No longer can we allow terrorists to migrate to our beloved homeland and set up shop in our neighborhoods. And no longer can we afford to pay for a welfare state for those too lazy to work. We're going to trim fat, rebuild our military, *and* cut your taxes.

Applause.

"Look, folks, everybody knows our government's way too big, and it costs us taxpayers way too much. Worse, all this bloat provides too little real benefit to you and me, but nobody seems to know how to fix it. Well, I do. I will return power to the states and to the people.

"Here's another thing. I'm going to pay for my campaign out of my own damn pocket, not yours. Have you ever heard that before from a presidential candidate? So let's roll up our sleeves and get this job done—together. What do you say, America? *What do you say, my dear friends and neighbors? You give me your vote, I give your government back to you!*"

After the applause finally died down again, being careful to let it run its course, Jesse said, "What would you say to your critics who suggest you're perhaps a bit old for such an aggressive political agenda?"

"Jesse! You obviously haven't kept up."

He flashed his disarming grin and held it a second too long.

"You didn't know that seventy is the new forty, did you? Well, now you do. Spread the word. And I'm not anywhere near that old yet!"

He delivered an exaggerated wink. Was it aimed at her, or at the camera, or most likely, at both? Was he flirting with a national TV celebrity on camera?

"Well, you have my vote, Mr. Redding. I'm sure we all agree that sounds pretty darn good!"

"Thanks, Jesse. I'll look for you on my side of the ballot. Thank you all, and God bless *our* America!"

At the end of what had turned into a shameless infomercial, the applause sign lit up, but it would not have been necessary. The applause from the studio audience was thunderous and spontaneous. Jeff Redding had them greedily slurping out of his trough.

Then he rewarded the suddenly wide-eyed anchor, who was known as a tough nut to crack, with a playful hug. His purposeful stride off stage gave viewers the impression that this man of the people was seriously off to the races. It seemed only a trivial detail that he had not yet captured a nomination. Every viewer knew it was only a matter of time.

～

REDDING INTUITED THE BIG GAME.

He didn't envision himself all that different from other political candidates, at least in terms of his Machiavellian mind. He *did* know that he clearly stood out in almost every other way, and guessed that's what most voters would be looking for in the upcoming election. Different, even if they didn't precisely know in what way.

He'd leverage that doubt in his campaign. He knew most people were simply fed up, continually disappointed by politics as usual. Actually, by politics—period. This would be his most lethal weapon—at least as far as his opponents were concerned.

But that wasn't enough. A presidential campaign required an obscene deluge of cash. He needed to outspend everyone by at least an order of magnitude. But they'd orchestrate the optics to appear the exact opposite. The linchpin, of course, was massive but invisible injections, directly into the vein of his campaign. Like an addict who received injections between his toes. He was rich but knew he wasn't so rich he could afford to buy the Presidency alone.

He and the Brotherhood were made for each other. They just needed to know that too. To be honest, which still happened occasionally, he wasn't sure whether he was courting them, or if they were courting him. Didn't matter.

Privately, Redding expected to get elected, no matter what the cost. He needed this next mountain to climb. He was willing and able to jettison his few remaining ethical standards, but not his ego. That was non-negotiable. After all, that was his stock in trade. He fancied being the man most ordinary men wished they were.

Because of his big business roots, billing himself as a self-made man of the people who had successfully captured the American dream, even though that dream was built on a foundation of good old

Dad's third generation cash, his leaned toward the conservative right, but he was not willing to acquiesce to party mandates. That was also non-negotiable.

He decided he'd run on a renegade ticket if necessary. That now seemed likely.

~

POWER BEGETS POWER.

Two hours later, in his midtown Manhattan penthouse on the top floor of one of his own high-rise co-ops, Jeff Redding met with six Fortune 50 CEOs... *his people.* They shared common goals.

"Gang, let's not mince words. Y'all need an ultra-pro-business president. I am that guy. I need a bigger war chest to pull this off. What say you?"

"I like the sound of that. We need a government that thinks in terms of profit and loss, rates of return, prudent investments and aggressive inventory control. But how exactly do you plan to get there by November, Jeff?"

"Simple. Money and mood management. With massive enough funding, we will manage voters' moods. We play to their fears. Get them so scared of a grim future, they won't view going with an outsider like me a gamble. They'll see me as their savior. They'll think they're hedging their bets against the end of the damn world by the time we're done conditioning them before they get to the voting booth.

"We continue to apply maximum leverage via social media where we're free to sow weeds of disinformation and discontent, and we bombard the buffoons with our own platform any way we damn-well please.

"Think *customized micro-marketing.* Everybody's soft spot is exposed, and nobody fact-checks out there.

"Look, most people don't know what they want, but they do know what they have isn't it. We tell 'em what they want to hear, and then we promise to give it to them. What 'it' is, really doesn't matter. Get my drift?"

"That's pretty radical stuff, Jeff. Could easily backfire."

"So what? You all wouldn't have achieved your positions if you weren't world-class risk-takers, right? Roll the dice, kids. We're on this yellow brick road together. If it doesn't work, we still have our day jobs, and our investors all across our great land will have paid for this little adventure.

"Then we bide our time until the next election if need be. Just a matter of time, whether we win now, or if I or someone else is your candidate for the next election. But if it *does* work this Fall, well then, gentlemen and lady, then… it's a payday of planetary proportions— for all of us. This is our time."

Risa D'Antonio, CEO of Flanders Information Systems, Inc. said, "Look, Jeff, you're our guy. A generous war chest won't be an issue, but with what party do you intend to align as the nomination process evolves? Let's be practical here."

"Which party? Our own party, Risa. Look around. Today there is a standing majority of voters who are pissed off at both the majors who have sucked 'em dry for the last thirty or forty years.

"Look at the piss-ant ninety-nine percenters, and the *Occupy Wall Street* flunkies. The so-called *Independents* damn near outnumber both major parties now. There's a reason for that. If we align with either the Dims or the Pubes, we've already lost. We go our own way, and if they line up with *us*, fine.

"If they don't, we run on a *screw big government* ticket. We break all the rules, and we just keep repeating our version of the truth until voters become believers. Then, Risa, we have 'em. Because belief is more powerful than fact any day of the week—not just on Sundays.

"And by the way, the more we sound like anarchists, raging against the corrupt DC machine and the big business assholes on Wall Street —no offense—the more hungrily the neglected majority will slobber it up.

"As for the rest of the voters, I'm assuming the Brotherhood can pull some strings with the Super-PACs, a little gerrymandering, whatever, so we can more easily lean into our own vision for the future of government. I don't understand all of that. I don't need to.

"Once I'm in the West Wing, y'all, woe be unto anyone who pisses us off. Know what I mean? Look, I'm your guy. We gonna do this, or not?"

He already knew they were in—he was just making them feel good after the sale.

Risa seemed to be the de facto spokesperson for this small group of industry titans. She said, "We know what your public platform is, Jeff. Your performance on Jesse's little love fest earlier tonight was impressive. What's your back door plan?"

"Back door plan? Yeah, I'm your back door man. I like that. People want change they can believe in? Well, I say we plant the seeds of doubt about just how little they really *can* believe in, and take 'em to a whole 'nother place by helping those seeds blossom.

"Doesn't really matter what, just as long as we profoundly scare the crap outta every single voter in America. Then we wait for the returns. Not great odds, but better than the house odds.

"During the campaign, we make 'em doubt the vanilla *and* chocolate candidates on the ballot, and get 'em to go for the twist.

After I'm in, we make 'em fear for their safety, for their incomes, for their health care, anything they hold dear. We play to the voters who want a street fighter in the White House, somebody who talks and thinks like them, and we render the rest of them irrelevant or better yet, impotent. I'm convinced that people want a winner in the White House, not another career politician."

"Then it's more of the same. We start rolling back anything that stands in the way of increased margins, for all of us, including my own global holdings, and yours, Risa. And yours, James. And all y'all. We start neutering anything in that town that still stands in our way.

"Meanwhile, I deliver a few campaign promises to keep the loyal herd in a tight bunch at the edge of the cliff. Maybe beef up the military machine and serve 'em up a shooting war here and there, start the process of rolling back the touchy-feely stuff in order to pay for it, and the best of all? Big tax cuts for us'ns 'n ours!"

If sharks could smile, especially after tasting chum in the water, this six-pack of predators would look just like that. Yes, they would indeed shower their candidate with cash.

Well-hidden, of course.

HEAVEN ON EARTH

C LEVELAND, OHIO

ZEKE WILSON ORDERED ANOTHER ROUND.

Pete Moorehead nodded in thanks for the Schlitz draft. Miles had the night off. Just as well. He couldn't tell a raging conservative from a bleeding heart liberal.

In his place behind the bar, their favorite bartender of all time, Lester, never hesitated to enthusiastically insert himself into a lively discussion, *and* he actually knew a few things. He always tickled the discussion in interesting directions. Zeke needed the intellectual stimulation tonight.

After their shift ended thirty minutes earlier, Pete and Zeke had trudged over to Roxy's for their nightly discussion. Zeke was excited by who he called the outlaw presidential candidate who appeared on Jesse Whittaker's show last night. True to form, Pete missed it. Zeke knew it was his moral obligation to bring Pete up to speed.

"You gotta see and hear this guy, Pete. Even though he owns a gaggle of zip codes, he's one of us. He's a frickin' farmer! Lester, you catch Redding on TV last night? I only saw a clip on the eleven o'clock news, but found the whole interview on the *America for Real Americans* YouTube channel."

From behind the bar Lester said, "Here we go again. Seems everybody's talking politics these days, even turkeys who never voted before in their lives. Yeah, I saw it. Impressive. He's no politician, so I guess he doesn't know what can't be done. I'll be interested to see how he's gonna do everything he's proposing, though."

Zeke defended his candidate. "Well, he's gonna cut the fat, and we all know there's a lot of that. Should be plenty to build up the military again while cutting our taxes at the same time. I tell you, he's one of us, even though he's one rich mother."

Time for Pete to weigh in. "Uh, whaddaya mean, Zeke? Can't trust nobody's got that kinda bread."

"No, seriously Pete. It's like this guy knows what I'm thinkin'. He's smart and wants the same things for the country that we want. I'm not kidding, man. We've been waiting for a guy like this with some balls to shape up government—take out the trash—so it can afford the kinda things we *wanna* pay taxes for."

"You mean like a raise and less OT?"

"Well, sorta. He knows how hard it is out here, man! He built a business empire outta nothin' but hard work. Says he's gonna pay for his campaign out of his own pocket. When's the last time you heard *that*? Plus, he wants to run the government like a business. Man, I like the sound 'a that."

Lester chimed in.

"Yeah, me too. Although something ain't quite right. He says he's spending his own money and a lot less than the other candidates, but you see all his ads? Jeez. And not just the cable channels, he's on all the networks too, every day: morning, noon and prime time. He's spending really big bucks. I like what he's pitching, though."

"S'pose you're gonna vote for this guy and expect me to do the same, right?"

Zeke already knew Pete would lean wherever he was leaning.

"C'mon, Pete, quit screwin' around. Think about it. Wouldn't it be great to have a guy who thinks and talks like us in the White House? I'm tellin' you, man, this guy is the one to watch. Specially when you look at the alternatives, if ya know what I mean."

"Great, you say? Okay, Zeke. I could go for a little *great* for a change, specially if it would make our lives easier."

Pete had finally jumped on board. Zeke smiled. Lester wiped out another beer glass, shook his head.

"And a black President? Can you imagine? They say he wasn't even born in this country! Doesn't that make him, like, not a legal candidate? Somebody's cookin' the books!"

Even Lester was coming around. "Well, considering the alternatives, I see your point, Zeke. Let's see if he gets a nomination. That would take a miracle, so all this might not even matter."

But the seeds of greatness had been planted. And it smelled like hope and old cigarette smoke.

All three fell silent, sipping their beers, as they conjured dreams of Heaven on Earth, brought to them by Jefferson Davis Redding.

PARADISE ROAD

SEPTEMBER 2008
LAKE CITY, MINNESOTA TO PUNTA GORDA, FLORIDA

GEORGE DESCENDED INTO REFLECTION.

During their thirteen years in Lake City, a small cadre of gawkers and requests for tours of *Sojourn* never failed to amuse him and their boat neighbors. After casting off one last time, they had entered the Mississippi River in Southeast Minnesota late the previous May...

HE FELT A LITTLE LIKE HUCK FINN.

Their three-month trip down the river system began with sunny skies, a moderate breeze out of the northeast, and a small crowd of well-wishers on the dock.

They passed through several more aboard a few boats out on the lake. All offered a silent salute with a few envious waves at the permanent departure of *Sojourn* from Lake City en route to the tropics.

As the only ocean-going pilothouse motorsailer in the largest marina on the entire length of the Mississippi from St. Paul to the New Orleans delta, *Sojourn* was a fixture of some note, her permanent departure momentous.

Sojourn's traditional design—with a foredeck that swept upward several feet to an elegant bow platform, richly appointed in highly varnished teak all around, and her glossy white painted fiberglass hull that presented the illusion of a finely-crafted planked wooden hull—never failed to turn heads.

Had George and Kate known they would be stalked, they might've chosen a lower profile boat back in 1995.

Relieved finally to be underway, the sailing couple smelled the wind. It carried the scent of hope. They allowed their reddish-brown tanbark main and jib sails to lay open their eager bellies to a gentle close reach.

That first tack was the last time those gorgeous sails would caress the breeze until they entered the Gulf of Mexico at Mobile Bay some fifteen hundred miles south and east. They'd be far too busy dodging river traffic and a hostile shore fifty yards to either side of their little ship.

So they navigated only under power through America's inland rivers, interrupted by flood delays, forty locks, and numerous moments of high anxiety. Once *Sojourn* gained the gulf, she was instantly in her element. Full sail at full speed to the southern end of the Florida peninsula.

They arrived at Sojourn's new home port.

At the entrance of Burnt Store Marina on Charlotte Harbor, several neighbors greeted them warmly by waving from the shore as they entered the marina's south basin.

After a few weeks of provisioning and resetting their emotional clocks to island time, they began the adventure they'd talked about their entire adult lives, ever since George's discharge from the Coast Guard over thirty years earlier. They departed BSM and headed south to the Florida Keys. From there…

In years past, they chartered or leased boats for a few weeks at a time, mostly in the Eastern Caribbean, but also in the Pacific Northwest and in the Mediterranean. Now they cruised tropical waters in *Sojourn*.

Time to live the dream that enabled George to retain his sanity during all those years when stress threatened to crack his brittle soul.

They had made a host of emotional withdrawals. Now came the time to make a few deposits.

~

FLORIDA KEYS

THEY STRETCHED THEIR SEA LEGS.

"I just love hanging on the hook, don't you, G?"

George did not say *his* favorite part of this adventure was their relative safety—far away from that poor deluded lunatic, Dent Canfield, who still prowled out there.

Somewhere.

Anchoring just offshore was free; a slip in a marina almost anywhere in the Keys could cost a fifty to a hundred-fifty a night. More important, privacy was often absolute when hangin', especially when tucked into the secluded cove of an obscure tropical key like the small unpopulated lumps of grassy sand on the gulf side of the Middle Keys.

Seclusion, however, required provisioning in advance because there would be no shopping anywhere close by ashore.

But enjoying quiet hours during the day, sometimes sans clothes or inhibitions, lounging or partying on deck, day or night, playing loud music on a whim with no neighbors to piss off, howling at the moon at will, with a simple offering of too much red wine and not enough brownies? What was not to love? Why had they deferred living until now? What had they been trying so hard to achieve… and why?

How about now?

"Yeah, Babe, livin' the dream. Like being rocked in Mama's arms."

The inflection in his voice, however, was more akin to mild cynicism than enthusiasm.

He continued. "This is *finally* the good stuff, huh? You okay even though there's no Walmart within a hundred miles?"

That was Kate's definition of civilization—reachable proximity to Wally World.

She said, "We're good for another week or so, but I just listened to the latest NOAA forecast. Sounds ominous. They're projecting a low-pressure cell that could turn into a nasty depression. We're *really* exposed if that system moves in from the southwest. Could get ugly fast."

Kate was the weather planner. George mostly handled and maintained the ship.

He agreed. "Too much of a good thing, anyway. We better beat feet to Boot Key Harbor and snag a mooring ball. We can re-provision there whenever. And for God's sake, no more grilled hot dogs for a while!"

I like hot dogs, but seriously…

THE WEATHER POUNDED LIKE ARTILLERY.

A tropical depression rocketed across the straits toward their position shortly after they abandoned their anchorage west of uninhabited Sawyer Key. This dangerous system struck before they could seek shelter. Wind and waves attacked with frightening ferocity.

"Are we alright, G? I've never felt her heel this hard before! George, I'm really scared. Feels like we're gonna capsize!"

She literally had to scream over the screeching wind as it whistled through the rigging.

A wave hammered their port-side Bimini window. Seconds later, that window shattered as a succession of breaking waves weighing hundreds, maybe thousands of pounds, spanked them without mercy.

Kate's paper charts were drenched in salt water, as was her neck-to-ankle rain suit. Rivulets of sea water dripped from her nose and trembling chin. Hundreds of dollars of nautical charts now lay forgotten in the cockpit sole in a foot of water slowly draining out of the scuppers. George could see the terror in Kate's eyes by the dim reflected light of the instruments.

She repeated her screaming plea. "George, are we alright?" He was the boat-handling expert, especially in heavy weather. He had seen it all from his four years in the Coast Guard. She always admired his courage and fearlessness. At the same time, she chastised him for what seemed like foolhardiness at times.

He shouted, "The boat should be fine. Not sure we've got everything secured well enough down below. Too rough to check now. Just hang on!"

Strong integrated harnesses in their life jackets connected to stout tethers of two-inch nylon webbing. These, in turn, attached them to the boat in case waves or gravity washed them overboard.

They had anticipated this storm and deployed only the barest amount of sail for a steady ride, while their motor idled with the transmission in gear so their propeller slowly churned through the water. The combination of power and sail—motor-sailing—allowed for a more direct course to Boot Key, which meant less time exposed to the vicious storm.

They rode on the merits of George's heavy weather checklist completed *before* they weighed anchor back at Sawyer Key. But this system was more aggressive than he anticipated.

"A lot of lightening, G! Oh God, it's all around us, non-stop!"

The air crackled and tingled their skin with omnipresent energy. They knew a major discharge would *not* be a slight 'tic' that zapped them when they touched a metal door knob on a dry winter's day.

They both knew a direct strike to any of the boat's metal fittings could instantly kill anyone standing too close to any metal, or blow holes through the hull, or even start a fire. George's nostrils filled with the metallic-vinegar odor of ozone.

At a minimum, touching any metal aboard during one of these strikes will set us on our asses.

One of his USCG piloting instructors had implanted a vision of a lightning strike in his mind's eye that he never forgot: *eyeballs boiled dry.*

GEORGE CHEWED ON ALL OF THIS.

He perched in his captain's chair less than fourteen feet behind an aluminum lightning rod that towered fifty-four feet directly up into the angry clouds.

"Just keep your distance from the backstays or anything metallic for now, Babe. Should be okay."

But then…

"OH SHIT! You gotta hang on tighter, Babe."

Petrified with fear, Kate said nothing. She couldn't. Her expression was a study in terror as she tried to recover from the tumble forward and to her right out of her navigation chair on *Sojourn's* port side, the high side for the moment.

She fell to the watery deck inside the partially protected ten-by-twelve-foot cockpit. A rogue wave caused the boat to heel far enough to starboard for the spreaders on the mast, twenty-five feet off the water, to kiss the wave crests on George's side of the boat.

That left her dangling like soap on a rope from her high-pedestal chair on its elevated platform with nothing but air beneath her for a few eternal seconds before she touched down onto the waterlogged cockpit sole five feet below as the boat righted itself atop her seven-thousand-pound keel.

Thankfully, Kate's tether had shortened with an unintentional wrap around the left arm of her stout navigator's seat. This turn of events prevented a bone-breaking descent all the way across the cockpit toward George's padded but unforgiving captain's chair.

The next boat will have seat belts and quick-release shoulder harnesses like the Coast Guard Columbia River diesel surf boats.

Several intense hours later, when they finally yawed their way into Moser Channel under the Seven Mile Bridge and plowed into the protected channel toward Vaca Key, barely visible buoys guided them toward the entrance of the protected harbor called Boot Key.

Soaked, exhausted and grateful for the absence of damage that could have impeded limping to the safety of calmer waters, they grabbed a mooring ball in the dark. The twin spreader lights still dripping with salt water brilliantly illuminated their foredeck; however, the ball's mooring pennant remained largely in the shadow of *Sojourn's* upswept bow.

Since their bow sprit towered seven feet off the water, George snagged the pennant's eye using an extendable boat hook with the aid of a handheld floodlight aimed by Kate.

Once they secured their little ship to the floating ball tethered securely to the bottom, Kate said, "Well, *that* was interesting!"

What a gal.

How he loved that magnificent high-spirited woman, even though she could frustrate Hell out of him at times. He was sure *Admiral Kate* felt the same about him. At least he hoped.

PARADISE DISPLACED

BOOT KEY HARBOR, MARATHON, FLORIDA

However, spending time in isolated anchorages meant frequent interim sorties to more populated anchorages or mooring fields that catered to live-aboard boaters. Boot Key Harbor was such a refuge.

Nestled in the heart of a series of small connected islands called keys, the Municipality of Marathon, Florida, BKH was a well-protected and popular enclave of some two hundred mooring balls. Boats could securely moor here, safely away from any dock that could damage a boat during rough conditions. And balls were much cheaper than dockage.

Hanging on a ball presented challenges too. Small tasks became arduous, including transporting garbage, trash, empty water jugs, and dirty laundry to shore; groceries, full water jugs and clean laundry back to the boat.

Moving multitudes of empty wine, gin and vodka bottles to shore and full ones back aboard strained one's back and patience. Full five-gallon water jugs were heavy as Hell and a bitch to lift six feet up onto the deck from the dinghy.

Since the dinghy was more heavily loaded upon their return to the mothership in the inevitable chop, cargo got wet. So protecting their bags of clean laundry and groceries from salt spray took priority. Once sprayed with saltwater, clothes never dried until rinsed out with lots of soap and fresh water which was in short supply aboard.

Once precious provisions were onboard and stowed, Kate and George were refilled with renewed hope knowing they'd once again be self-sufficient and completely off the grid for another week or three, living in selective and safe isolation.

Sanctuary in Paradise. They ventured further down-island to a place with no name on the charts. Didn't matter. Anchor down, they settled in, and time passed.

This seemed all very exciting at first. Later, not as much. Isolated togetherness extracted its price. Their dinghy, a rigid inflatable boat, or a RIB, served as their family car. Lowering the five-hundred-pound RIB from its stern cranes, or davits, where she would hang faithfully until needed, was a non-trivial task. The stuff of sore backs from cranking manual winches.

"Tell me again why we didn't get *motorized* davits, Kate?"

"The minor matter of money... a few extra thousand we didn't have because you retired about seven years too early, remember G?"

"Oh yeah. Well, I could have worked another seven years at a job that was sucking the life out of me, I guess. More moolah for the widow, right? Not to mention there was a madman trying to kill us."

"Would that have been so bad? At least it would bring this endless bickering to an end. George, it's not always all about you. We promised we'd never be poor again, remember? You retiring this early screwed up a lot of our plans. I'm the one who has to figure out how to pay for all your grand dreams, aren't I?"

"Look, we've got serious six figures in our IRA, and we're living mostly off the interest. What's the harm in spending a little more of our own money? The kids told us they don't want our money, so what's the deal?"

"I'll tell you what the *deal* is, George. If I die before you, you get a raise. But if you die before me, *I take a fifty percent cut in total income.* That's why I have a huge insurance policy on you. But not too many years in the future, even that won't be affordable. So you tell me. What happens if you die before me?"

Son-of-a-bitch, she was always thinking ten years ahead of this mere mortal. Here they were, living fat, and he was bitching about not being able to spend more. *What an idiot I am. And I'm not even tanked—yet.*

"Sorry. You're right, I know. I'm gonna shut up now and try to retrieve my size elevens out of the idiotic mouth on this idiot's face, okay, Babe?"

"Aw, G, how can I stay mad at you, ya big buffoon? After all, you are *my* buffoon."

He sheepishly added, "By the way, I started to ask. Did you hear anything of interest on the piracy report this morning?"

"Yeah, they say the Frenchman is out of jail. I've heard stories. Reported operating near here. I think we'd better boogie, weather or not. I like it here, but I don't like that color of trouble. They say that guy's also known to wave a gun around sometimes."

The Frenchman was a regional ruffian known for intentionally crashing his crappy ninety-foot multihull into private yachts, then demanding cash in return for just leaving. George mentally agreed with Kate's assessment. Discretion being the better part of valor, and all that.

Land lubbers might just refer to these nefarious characters as criminals. Sailors, however, never fail to paint their eccentric lifestyle with splashes of primary colors and high drama, particularly in their vocabulary. They called such criminals *pirates.*

Much to the befuddlement of most lubbers, sailors also lean toward emotionally entrenching their psyches in picturesque post cards dripping with nautical history and ribald tradition.

Sailors were dreamers.

~

Island time meant full-slow.

The backyard for Kate and George was the Florida Keys, the Gulf of Mexico and the Eastern Caribbean. The stuff of drunken naps on the beach and lounging nude on deck without a thread of chagrin.

They were the envy of most of their weekend boating friends *up north*. If they only knew the rest of the story.

Kate and George pursued *everything* to excess, sucking the juice out of every day, as if, well, as if every day were their last.

They were still putting distance and water between them and Dent Canfield, so they felt sufficiently insulated out here and justified in blowing off steam. There wasn't a party at which they weren't the central fixtures. Friends and even strangers around them noticed the symptoms of quiet but growing desperation. The two of them could not see that in themselves.

Now that their own kids were grown and gone, and now that George's job no longer kept them caged, they were the ones who ate too much, drank too much, moved around too much. And then, there was that other thing. Always that other thing.

For a short while, this hedonistic regimen was the epitome of romantic novelty and the kernel of George's lifelong dreams. He recalled countless nights of *boat dreaming* after a stressful day at GGS when he couldn't sleep after yet another horrendous day of hiring, firing and Machiavellian maneuvering. Boat dreaming took place *before* he fell asleep. And there was always that other dream too, *after* he fell asleep—his signature nightmare. The dangerous one that kept haunting him.

After traveling and living aboard *Sojourn* for several months, however—he'd lost track of time—with all that peace and tranquility, and then the not-infrequent verbal brawls, their daily lives became not only painfully mundane but physically and emotionally arduous.

They both missed real life and being around other people they'd actually see for more than a few inebriated hours at a time.

Gazing at a non-stop sequence of a couple hundred photogenic sunsets, between river banks and behind tropical islands, and over far too many extra dry martinis and bottles of wine, they finally succumbed to the mendacity of their wet dream: it had become worse than merely routine. It had become tedious.

They grew numb to these sweetest spots of their dream, dreading the task of hoisting the RIB every night so local ruffians couldn't steal it. They dreaded the next salty trip to shore, or whenever they'd need separation from each other to avert suffocation from isolation in such close proximity.

Diving into the bottle replaced diving into the water. Shouting at each other in frustration, sometimes in anger, replaced loving touches whenever they were within arm's reach. They worried constantly—Kate about the weather, George about their safety.

The dream ran its course. For the thousandth time in recent weeks, George quoted the old Peggy Lee lyrics, asking himself, *Is that all there is, my friend? Then, let's keep dancing...*

More and more frequently, they wondered silently, "What in the *Hell* are we doing out here? Are we trying to prove something to ourselves? To somebody else? Do we plan on running away from ourselves and our future, or our past... indefinitely?"

One night, during a quiet and uncontentious moment, they caught each other's eye. Unspoken, they reached a tacit agreement that it was time to turn the page, to write the next chapter. After a spontaneous sideways wiggle of their heads and puckered cheeks, at the same time, and without saying a word, they both nodded their affirmation.

First Kate, and then George, simply arose from their customary low chairs on the foredeck, and started securing gear in preparation for weighing anchor at first light.

They claimed success, despite the steady advance of their twin life-threatening diseases of alcoholism and boredom. They'd achieved a lifetime of incredible memories—both good and not so good, but very real.

Now it was time to generate others with renewed hope elsewhere.

Now it was time to face their fears and decide whether it was important to do something more meaningful.

HOME AT LAST

O CTOBER 2008
PUNTA GORDA, FLORIDA

They were going home.

With renewed anticipation, George and Kate Janis looked to the northeast. Only the upper floors of the few high-rises at Burnt Store Marina reached above the horizon. The Gulf was a mirror, a positive reflection. A beautiful sixty-five-foot dock awaited them and *Sojourn,* not fifty paces behind their luxurious condo.

Don't worry, old gal, you'll get to drink all you want soon enough. Wish I could join you.

He affectionately whispered to his trusty vessel of memories, *I'll personally give you the longest and most luxurious soapy bath you've had in months. Then we'll rest for a while.*

It's amazing what you think of after a period of dramatic change. He located her seven mooring lines buried in a top-loading cockpit locker, hoping they wouldn't be moldy from salt, humidity and lack of attention.

Moored at the end of G dock, he could almost hear *Sojourn* breathe a deep sigh of relief after the engine was secured. She finally looked relaxed and ready for a rest before eagerly venturing out again.

After getting their feet dry, as sailors are fond of referring to a time on shore after a voyage, George and Kate planned to spend long weekends, maybe some short weeks, exploring their home waters of Southwest Florida aboard *Sojourn*. Maybe they'd play some golf between sorties. It was time to check on the condo, anyway. Maybe they'd ready it for sale. It was nice, but so under-utilized.

Those first few days ashore unsettled both Kate and George. A certain unsteadiness accompanied the lack of constant wave motion beneath their feet. Sea legs took time to acquire and time to shed. The two thousand square foot condo seemed an obscene waste to them after living in less than three hundred for months.

So they continued sleeping on the boat each night. Their excuse? After a prolonged absence, they needed to clean the condo before moving back in. The reality? The boat just felt more like home than anywhere ashore.

Besides, what was the rush?

DEFECTOR

O CTOBER 2008
       BALTIMORE, MARYLAND

Time to renew an old acquaintance.

"Hailing motor vessel *American Dreamer, American Dreamer,* channel one-six, copy? Over…"

"Tug *American Dreamer, Sojourn Portable,* do you read? Over…"

Sojourn Portable, American Dreamer, copy… seven-two?"

Sam Braxton smiled, it sounded like *"SO-jorn Por-tah-bull, Ah-MARE ee kahn Dreumer."* He rotated the knob on his handheld VHF transceiver to channel seventy-two.

"American Dreamer, Sojourn Portable on seven-two. I am one hundred yards off your port quarter. Permission to approach, Captain?"

"Sojourn Portable, please to state your business, over…"

He still had trouble with pronouncing some English words… "beez-noos?" Adorable.

"Suggest discussing off the air, over…"

"Roger. Please to be on port side, Sir. Toss a painter. I secure."

Doctor Sam Braxton's joints creaked. *I'm too old for this tomfoolery. No choice.*

As he looked his friend in the eye for the first time in over twenty years, even the dark of night couldn't mask the delight they both felt at the sight of one another.

"Sergei, old friend! It's Sam Braxton! Permission to come aboard?"

"Doktor Sam! My dear old friend! Permission granted, you kid me? I recognize hail by *Sojourn Portable*, but no *Sojourn*. Good move, Doktor Sam."

A bit embarrassed at the difficulty with which he negotiated the relatively low railing atop the tug's gunwale, Sam carefully climbed aboard the '*Dreamer*, greeting his old friend with a warm, prolonged embrace and hearty back-slaps. Was that a tear in Sergei's eye?

"Sorry, Sergei, my frailty is showing. I'm not getting any younger, you know."

"So yes, yes, I am so much happy to see you, Doktor Sam. Come, Come, we drink some wodka together! Anchor secure, pilothouse warm, wodka cold."

As they settled into two comfortable helm seats mounted on stout stainless steel pedestals that were bolted into the steel deck of the bridge at the forward section of the pilothouse, they swiveled inboard to face each other.

The panoramic view of the harbor from fifteen feet above the water struck Sam. They overlooked the stubby but equipment-rich foredeck of the hundred-foot sea-going salvage tug. A dark trawler lamp hung overhead gently sculpting the air, gray-on-dark with its slight swinging arc. Sergei kept the cold deck from penetrating his soles by wearing sheepskin-lined slippers. Another smile.

"I light lamp."

Sergei declared this with his wide-mouth Russian pronunciation. As he did so, the smoke dissipated toward the ceiling, offering a slight lemon scent to the pilothouse. Once he dialed it down to a strong, but controlled flame, the light danced delicately with the movement of the tug on the mild chop of Baltimore's expansive inner harbor.

Sam noticed the circular light glowed evenly thanks to a well-trimmed wick as it sipped clean kerosene-based fuel. The trawler lamp delivered a soft honey glow, casting a set of undulating shadows around the edges of chart tubes, portholes, and hatches. Locking hatch dogs protruded from the slightly rusty bulkheads that surrounded them on three sides.

Sergei ensured that a traditional *bucket* of smooth iced Russian vodka magically appeared at Sam's left elbow on the tug's flat dashboard. A bucket was larger than a tall shot glass but smaller than a highball glass.

Before Sam took an obligatory sip, he raised his glass toward Sergei in toast, "Na Zdorovie," carefully avoiding the American movie pronunciation of "na-STROH-via."

It was obvious that Sergei felt a tinge of disappointment that Doctor Sam only took an American swallow. A bucket traditionally survived just two manly gulps. At least Doctor Sam drank *some*.

Sergei echoed the traditional Russian toast, smiled broadly, as he opened his practiced throat, throwing back his entire bucket with naked Russian pride. He continued smiling.

He said, "To waste good Russian wodka, worse than treason! Say, Doktor, how you find me? Aw, what I'm saying to Super Spy himself! Hey, Doktor, why you carry the daggers in cloaks? So secret?"

Sam spent a moment to parse Sergei's broken mix of English idioms. "Sergei, I love ya with all my heart, Old Son, but y'all need to learn the local language just a bit better."

"Doktor Sam! I take night classes! Doing wary good, too!"

"You're doing fine, my friend. Besides, your English is far better than my Russian. I trust Amelia is well? I'll never forget your wedding on *Sojourn's* foredeck. A grand affair.

"Listen, Sergei, I must cut the chit-chat and get to the reason for my intrusion. I need your help, my friend. Am I still good for a favor from my favorite defector?"

"Doktor Sam, I owe my whole life in America to you, my friend. My citizen, my business here in Bawl-tee-mor, everything. You need, I do. I must! What you need, Doktor Sam?"

"Sergei, I'm involved in an operation, and not sure who I can trust. So I'm here because you I trust. I need someone completely outside the intelligence community, but someone who still possesses some tradecraft. There may be danger involved."

"Danger? Hah! I laugh at this danger. You lead, I follow. Amelia, she understand too. Okay, so let us roll 'n rock, no?"

"Thank you, old friend. Yes, let us roll 'n rock."

Smile.

"We must root out a group of traitors leaking confidential mission information. I need you to carry variations of the same message to twenty-seven different assets who my guys have identified in three different US government agencies. They are all, ah, persons of interest.

"You'll fit the profile of a standard cut-out, a runner. No reason for them not to trust you. They'll eagerly communicate the message you'll deliver. Shouldn't take more than a few days."

Encouraged by Sergei's enthusiastic nodding, Sam continued.

"Then we watch for each variation of the big news to show up where it shouldn't. Based on which versions of the message gets leaked, our broad-spectrum electronic surveillance of the POIs should reveal who can or cannot be trusted."

Sam cringed internally. He was about to spy on American intelligence assets as if they were terrorists, which may very well be true. He chanted a portion of the oath to himself, *Foreign **or** domestic...* Painful, necessary, need to know.

"This will allow us to weed the garden. Can do, Sergei?"

Without hesitation, "Good plan. Roll 'n rock, around the clock, Doc!"

You just *had* to love his enthusiasm, his grit, and his marginal English. No doubt some people unquestioningly accepted what he said just to get him to stop talking.

Good old Sergei. Sam still remembered as if it were a recent memory—Sergei's defection to America over twenty years ago—during the heat of the cold war. What must have it been like for him? Sergei had tried to describe what it was like back then...

~

JUNE 1985
ANACOSTIA RIVER, MARYLAND

COLONEL SERGEI ROSTOV WAS A PATRIOT.

But he was no fool. Trust was a rarity in his country, betrayal was not. He faced false charges of high treason levied by an ambitious rival. The outcome? A fait accompli as the Union of Soviet Socialist Republics splintered.

Rostov felt alone and abandoned, despite his loyal service for almost two decades, the most difficult choice of his life made for him. He always fantasized about living in America. It seemed America wanted him when his own country did not.

Very well.

Sergei closed his eyes. *I like the sound of it, Ah-MARE-ee-kah.* He had heard the stories. Now he'd discover for himself.

A funny little American doctor threw him a lifeline. In exchange for what Sergei considered some relatively unimportant statistical data, Colonel Samuel Braxton brokered a deal for his travel to Washington, an offer of employment, opportunity for advancement, and ultimately, citizenship.

~

FEW WOULD MISS HIM.

That Sergei was single, entertained no current romantic entanglements, with no living family, and he possessed a working knowledge of English made his hard decision easier.

Sam debriefed him aboard his private fifty-one-foot pilothouse motorsailer moored in an isolated semi-commercial marina on the southern shore of the Potomac River, well outside of Washington.

In his genteel drawl, Sam said, "Sergei, you will be comfortable here until we make further arrangements."

Sam sometimes used the boat as a short-term safe house for valued assets. He felt gratified to see *Sojourn* put to some use. He and Mary stayed so busy these days.

Sergei scratched the jet-black hair he started to grow after shaving his head every day for the last twenty years.

"Does everyone own a private vessel in America, Doktor Sam?"

Colonel Braxton came close to a rare smile. "No, Sergei, but you could if you work hard and save."

Now Sergei smiled. He would miss Mother Russia, but he would like America. No relationship lasts forever. Not even between a man and his country. He kept telling himself that.

HE COULD IMAGINE A GREAT DEAL.

But indulging in his wildest dreams Sergei would never have imagined that in less than ten years, he would own a small but profitable marine salvage fleet in Baltimore, with Doctor Sam's sponsorship, that he'd marry a beautiful American girl on this very boat, and that his best man would be the wonderful little man sitting before him once again drinking good Russian wodka.

God bless Ah-MARE-ee-kah!

Since then, Sergei and Sam shared over two decades of camaraderie, despite no direct contact in recent years.

Now Sergei finally had the chance to pay Doktor Sam back in a small way.

LETHAL LINKS

O CTOBER 2008
STILLWATER, MINNESOTA

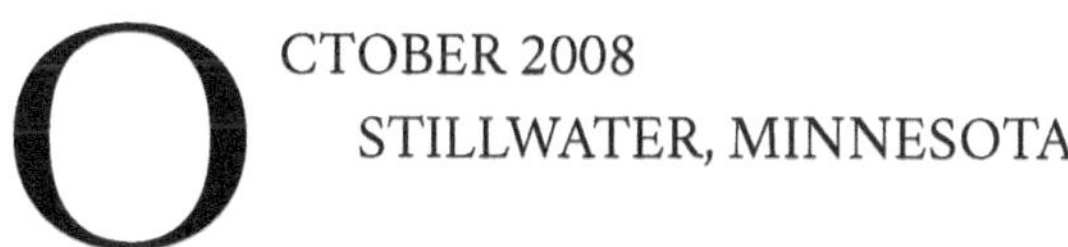

They tried so hard to forget.

Nothing really worked.

Frank Lassiter and his wife Nora Mathers hadn't tramped the links in a very long time. Nora still lamented her decision to accuse her GGS team member—Dent Canfield—of sexual harassment that started a string of brutal murders. Nothing her husband Frank said or did consoled her.

"C'mon, Nor, tee up and let's get this tour underway."

He worried about her. She seemed sullen and worrisome all the time now. Waking up in the middle of the night, he'd find her pacing in front of the living room window, watching the street.

With more enthusiasm in her voice than she felt, she said, "Yeah, let's do this."

She desperately needed a droll distraction. Although neither of them really ever put together a complete round they'd be truly proud of, that now seemed so inconsequential. They used to take the game so seriously.

Hidden Hills remained one of their favorite courses. It featured few water hazards and wide fairways, but lots of trees. Fall colors burst everywhere, although now mostly on the ground. Picturesque. They bundled up against a nip in the air, thankfully not much wind blew. In a few weeks, the course would close for the season.

At the tee box for the first hole, Nora chose her three-wood for a lay-up on a dog leg to the left. Without preamble, she teed up and demonstrated her beautiful swing. Frank felt like he was admiring Annika Sorenstam's swing on the Golf Channel. Her drives always exceeded 150 yards, although these days, seven out of ten enjoyed scads of shade in the deep woods, especially on this old Minnesota course, and it would seem, especially today.

They shared atrocious short games. They didn't care, as long as they were together. And it wasn't raining much at all. A good walk not totally spoiled. Frank appreciated misty days that matched his mood. Everything was an intense gray-green and smelled freshly mowed. Evidence: shredded leaves.

They walked the course to save a cart fee and to produce a few badly-needed endorphins from the exertion. By starting after three p.m. they cut their green fees in half. Not that they were likely to play too many more rounds anytime soon.

By the time they arrived at the seventh tee box, improving weather highlighted their mood. Longer shadows foretold twilight creeping toward them. They'd need to pick up the pace.

Frank nailed his drive, precisely down the center. Nora was less fortunate. While he approached his ball, preparing to address it, she went searching for hers.

A lone golfer aboard a fast-moving cart quickly approached on a vector that appeared to cut between them. Frank signaled him to play through if he wished.

Instead, the lone golfer veered toward the point at which Nora entered the trees, her bag still slung over her shoulder. Alarm bells jangled in Frank's brain. He immediately unzipped a side pocket in his carry bag, extracted something small and heavy, and frantically began running full tilt.

Before abandoning his cart on the fairway's fringe, the stranger pulled a club from his bag. No, wait… Frank shuddered.

Instead of extracting a club, the stranger snatched what appeared to be a short fat baseball bat, expertly twirling it like a practiced baton twirler.

Frank's knees weakened. "Dent? DENT! NO! JESUS GOD NO!" Frank screamed so loud it came out as a hoarse vocal-chord-shredding croak.

Dent heard Frank, still fifty yards away, but paid no attention. Nora remained oblivious to the approaching danger in the whispering wind and the damp rustling leaves. He could just see Nora between a Maple sapling and an aged Oak. She focused on her difficult shot. Frank watched the scene unfold as he sprinted into his nightmare.

Dent closed in seconds, approached her purposefully from behind, and raised his lethal weapon high over his right shoulder. He struck without uttering a word. She collapsed, crumpling straight down.

Hard.

Dent's thumper twanged upon impact.

The short aluminum bat—designed for truck drivers to test tire pressure on their eighteen wheelers by *thumping* them and listening to the echoed sound—was badly scarred, scratched, and stained, but still efficient.

When it hit its mark, that is.

He misjudged the force required to shatter Nora's tiny neck. More notably, his arrogant backhand blow had landed a bit low, shattering her left shoulder instead. Profound pain threw her into immediate shock and unconsciousness. But during a treasured moment of gloating, he saw she still exhibited shallow and rapid breathing.

Realizing his mistake, Dent reared back with his trusty thumper and prepared to finish what he had started.

How appropriate the queen bitch should end her reign in the dark woods of a golf course. Dark woods, dark heart.

After finishing this tasty bit of business, he'd turn and confront that wiry little piss-ant husband of hers. One more well-aimed swing downward and…

CRACK, CRACK, CRACK! A sledge hammer slammed into the backside of Dent's left shoulder.

That little dick shot me? Son-of-a….

Dent fell like a green sapling from a heavy hatchet, more from the shock and surprise than anything, but also to escape further fire. A jarhead's reflex.

He dropped directly on top of his prone team leader who was face down, exactly where she toppled. A horizontal hostage. Only her right cheek and the back of her slender neck were visible.

God, she's even more beautiful up close…

THE SHARP REPORTS STARTLED FRANK.

His little pistol barked louder than he would have imagined. But he recovered quickly as he rushed toward Dent piled on top of Nora's inert form.

He feared the worst.

God, is she still alive? Did I just kill a human being? The intensity of pulling the trigger, not once, but three times? Madness!

He had blown through the small cloud of cordite smoke that hovered around his head where he had abruptly stopped to assume a firing stance. As he was trained.

Frank fired from farther than he'd ever practiced. They taught him to aim for center mass, and only fire with lethal intent in a deadly situation, always for real. His instructors said, "Don't pull a weapon unless you intend to use it. To kill." He had done that. Instant regret, and visceral fear, and bloodlust all threatened his sanity at that moment.

He shook uncontrollably.

Is she dead? Oh God! What do I do?

He approached the heap of bodies, stacked like twisted cordwood, whipped out his phone to call 9-1-1.

That's when it happened.

DENT ROLLED AND SWUNG HIS DEADLY BAT.

As he completed his roll from his prone position, he struck upward with another backhand stroke at Frank's right arm, the one holding that nasty little pistol—he recognized the KelTec. Accompanied by the sound of breaking bones and the sight of that gun spinning off into the deep grass, Dent prepared to hit a home run after he picked himself up.

He saw the wimp was close to fainting, but remained on his feet. Somehow. He was reaching for something in his right front pocket with his left hand. His right arm now useless thanks to his thumper, he struggled to coax out a little black canister. Was that MACE?

Dent snarled. Frank would be too late.

"Hey! Asshole! Back off!"

A foursome astride two carts pulled up from an adjacent fairway after hearing the shots. A big guy hefting a menacing three-iron advanced swiftly with what appeared to be iron resolve. That three-iron was now just a few yards away as Dent stood over the two prone figures. So he bolted. Shoulder bleeding, left arm useless—time for a tactical retreat.

Spewing a string of profanities, he stumbled into the trees, leaving his rented cart behind.

MINNEAPOLIS, MINNESOTA

Sometimes the light bulb shines late.

I'm a patriot, not an ignorant drone, you greedy fascists. I may indulge in justifiable vengeance, but do not think me dishonorable or traitorous!

He muttered to himself, felt charged by articulating his venomous sentiments.

His left shoulder hurt like a bitch. Fortunately, Frank was a lousy shot. A little soap and water, a little triple antibiotic ointment, a gauze pad held in place with sticky white tape, and the deep groove on his bicep would heal in a week or two.

Still hurt like a hot poker.

Next time, ass-wipe.

He felt good about the progress on his shopping list.

With Queen Nora Bitch gone, not many more to go.

When Dawg basically told him that the Patriot Brotherhood no longer needed him to serve, or perhaps even to live, Dent trusted his gut. In fact, he had started years ago acquiring personal insurance. One never knew. His latest snooping revealed his gut's reliability.

Dent affectionately fingered the rough tape's surface on the side of the 4TB memory stick. With his black gel pen, the same white tape on his arm made a handy label.

This little stick contained his ironclad policy. He made no copies. Too hard to control. He smiled at the neatly printed label he'd trimmed to size with a single-edge razor blade: "Feebs, Best Regards, D."

He didn't know yet precisely what he would do next, but a plan began to crystalize.

His understanding had dawned. This wasn't about patriotism at all, nor anything whatsoever to refresh the fundamentals of his beloved Republic. And he discovered a non-exclusive contract on his ass, even as he worked that last job for the Brotherhood.

Dent's rage inspired his plan.

Despite their rhetoric to the contrary, these guys were nothing more than whores in three-piece suits—serious profiteers setting up the entire country for their own big score. Democracy didn't even appear on the dance card. *Sons-a-BITCHES!*

The rich get richer, which is fine. But when the other 99% are placed under the avaricious thumb of greed-mongers with no souls who are mere patriot-posers, fuck 'em.

The lights finally turned on. They were playing the populous for suckers, including *him*. He now knew his insurance policy was essential.

Maybe the piss-ant one-percenters know something after all.

He tingled at the alien feeling of self-righteous indignation.

Is this what it feels like to be a good guy? Well, let's not go crazy.

Over several years, the Brotherhood directed Dent to repeatedly apportion and obfuscate mountain ranges of cash as it flowed into the greedy hands of politicians, election supervisors, social media experts, law enforcement officials, members of the military, intelligence operatives, and foreign constituencies. Further, he sourced cash from dozens of big-league contributors—enough to buy a handful of third-world nations.

Something assaulted his acute sense of smell a while back. Something was so very rotten. So very wrong.

That's when he *knew* having taken out a policy—just in case—would pay off. Over time, he employed software sniffers and concealers of his own invention to not only hide financial transactions for the Brotherhood, but to collect his own brand of intel on them and their benefactors.

Thousands of account numbers, IP addresses, currencies and amounts, from whom, to whom, incriminating emails, transcripts of encrypted phone calls, surveillance briefings, stock manipulations, and a complete outline of the grand strategy, he piece-mealed from hundreds of sources—this was the master high-resolution mosaic of a world-class conspiracy. All compressed on this little memory stick.

*Now **this** is some insurance policy!*

Dent didn't even have immunity in mind. Now, it was simply a matter of reconstituting his innate patriotic spirit. Long overdue, anyway.

He concluded that the Brotherhood, or more likely, whoever was pulling *their* strings, was not simply engaged in a few political dirty tricks to properly inflate their party's candidate. Everyone does that. This was something very different and far more nefarious.

These slugs were laying the foundation for a palace coup by a pack of fascists. For fucking profit!

And the obscene amounts of foreign dollars pouring in from the world's Number One Thugocracy? He drew the last straw, right there. He wasn't so old he didn't remember the Cold War. Dent wasn't sure of all the legalities, except for the one right in front of his nose—sixth-degree black-belt treason.

Dent's brilliant abilities in forensic accounting and technology manipulation aside, he wasn't quite sure what to do with the armed thermonuclear device he held in the palm of his hand.

Perhaps for the first time in his life, he didn't know what to do next. He knew one thing for sure, though. He better acquire one serious back channel if he wished to survive. Now he grinned, He had a higher purpose.

Best regards, D.

~

DENT PUSHED THROUGH THE PAIN.

Despite his injured shoulder bleeding again, he packed and loaded his cases into the back seat of his slightly rusty snow-white Caddy parked on a tree-lined side street off Hennepin Avenue.

Good old American car manufacturers really knew how to build space into these gunboats in the old days. You could keep those crappy little foreign compacts. And while this baby rusts, there's enough heavy steel behind it to last for two more decades.

The ten p.m. call on his encrypted cell grabbed his attention. This was not going to be good. He trotted back into the apartment as he poked the green button.

"Okay, dick-wad, so tell me why flags are shooting up at Fort Meade. Somebody at the N-S-bloody-A is digging way too deep on you. Extremely not okay. And is that trail of bodies in Minnesota your handiwork, you temperamental ass-wipe? We're seeing fireworks with your name on 'em from the fuckin' BCA!"

Oh, how nice. The bloody Brotherhood's blustering again.

"Look, Daw-, the Bureau of Criminal Apprehension here doesn't know jack. I mean, I'm simply tying up some loose…"

Dawg blasted in, "Seriously? Kiss my ass. *You are done.* Have been for a while. You just didn't know you were a dead man walking. Wanted to tell you myself. Have a nice life… what's left of it, dick-wad."

Click.

Dent was running out of time. As he often did these days, he conversed with himself, *I gotta clean things up fast and take off. I'm nearing the end of my runway.*

FIRE'S PASSION

P UNTA GORDA, FLORIDA

Change in the air smelled sweet. Yet...

Summer's heat and humidity surrendered to cool sea breezes typical this time of year.

Late their third evening back at Burnt Store Marina, George reclined in luxury on *Sojourn's* foredeck at the end of G dock in the south basin.

He thought, *G dock—how appropriate.*

He had scooted closer to Kate than was comfortable for either of them. But somehow, it still felt right. They were lounging in legless padded deck chairs called Sport-a-Seats.

Recent days seemed reminiscent of their teenage battleground. He grew reluctant to make small talk for fear it would be redundant with something she'd already said that he'd unintentionally ignored. Or perhaps not so unintentionally.

Now tied to a dock, he wished they were still hangin' on the hook somewhere. Funny how you want whatever you don't have; nevertheless, the martinis tasted particularly rich with innuendo tonight, and George's libido was thankful for the prospect of a worry-free night of relaxation with his best girl. His only girl.

"Didn't you hear me just tell you that? Damn it, G, isn't what I say important to you?"

"I just didn't hear you, okay? Jeez."

"And I suppose you're not wearing your damn hearing aids again, are you?"

At which point, George would have some off-the-shelf excuse that neither of them believed.

"George, I love you, but *you* are losing *my* mind. Something must change."

Resentments once again began to fester, usually after the third martini, and somewhere into the first half of the second bottle of wine. But not tonight, no matter how many martinis and glasses of wine to which they'd willingly subject themselves. Tonight was a night for reparations.

"Baby, we're both under a ton of stress and adjusting. Let me try… At least for tonight. I know I need to try harder."

After thirty seconds of steamy introspective silence, she turned those incredible bedroom eyes to her right and bored directly into his mushy cerebral cortex.

"Aw, G, you make me melt like soft butter in the sun. Let's go below and discuss further how you're going to change to make me a better woman."

Regardless of good days or bad, *Sojourn* was their baby girl, even though she was almost half their age. That was a lot in boat years. They would never give up joint custody, except to rights of survivorship, should one of them pass, as it ominously warned on the ship's mortgage they had yet to pay off and burn, as was the tradition.

She was more than their home, she was a member of their family.

Having said that, Kate purred suggestively, "Wait… I have a better idea. We have an awesome California King Sleep Number in the condo. I like *Sojourn's* Queen too, and sex is always better afloat, but hey! Are ya with me, Skipper?"

Just like that, they were thrust back into the sweet memory of their first time in that crappy green '62 LeSabre, lubricated with Wild Turkey, serenaded by Jimi Hendrix and *Purple Haze*.

No sooner had they stumbled through the condo's front door, which still yawned wide just inside the glass storm door, than they started peeling each other like tender grapes.

She pressed him against the door jamb for support as she pulled his t-shirt over his head. He reciprocated. Somehow, that seemed more erotic—and for them, more spontaneous—than undressing themselves, although not as efficient.

Stripped of everything but his boxers, his butt cheeks pressed against the cool glass of the windowed storm door.

George felt the heat on his bare back and shoulders just before the condo's concrete floor shuddered beneath his feet. Thunder cracked so near that they could feel the sudden blast of air pressure that threatened to shatter the glass. He stared at her in shock as her eyes glowed.

Kate peered back into his suddenly frightened eyes, then over his shoulder as terror resurfaced from somewhere within her battered soul. The sky became molten magma.

No! Please. God!

George pulled up his cargo shorts, t-shirt and boat shoes with abandon. He didn't mean to shout, but did.

"Lock the door behind me with the deadbolt, Kate, and all the windows. Don't assume. Check 'em all. Right now, Babe. I'll be back!"

She stood there, half naked, not comprehending.

As he finished tugging down on his t-shirt, he half-shouted into her face, "RIGHT NOW!"

His sharp words galvanized her into action, even though she wasn't sure what just happened, or for that matter, what he expected might happen next.

Crimson and orange flames tore across the clear black skies still tinged with twilight blue. Background stars and entire galaxies faded to insignificance. Already gathering on the balcony overlooking the marina's south basin, a few neighbors stood and stared in shock.

George sprinted, rage oozing from every pore, as he saw the flotsam of *Sojourn's* fifty-five-foot mast and a tangle of rigging cast down, half across the adjacent dock, the top of which already submerged in the inky waters on the far side. The stench of burning resin assaulted him.

He stabbed 9-1-1 and screamed, "Burnt Store Marina, boat fire, fully engaged, south basin, end of G dock, also in flames. Need the fire boat. NOW!" He didn't bother wasting time offering his name or with disconnecting.

The Cape Coral Fire Department was only minutes away by road. Too late for *her*, he knew. He'd seen entire marinas melt down at light speed from his time in the Coast Guard. Maybe they could still save most of the south basin.

CCFD maintained a purpose-built fire-fighting vessel in the north basin. But it would need to be lowered into the water from her lift, manned by the same crew now en route, launched and navigate the quarter mile canal between the north and south basins before arriving on the scene.

Inaccessible by road.

George remembered. First to burn would be the mooring lines. Then a burning hull would become a migratory funeral pyre, an infernal contagion carried by any whimsical breeze. Fortunately, it was a still Southwest Florida evening.

Sojourn's once curvaceous hull already burned halfway to her waterline casting off waves of unapproachable heat.

George knew that while fiberglass itself doesn't melt quickly under the onslaught of fire, the super-heated resin that holds it together does, and can cause a boat to burn like rice paper.

He and Kate were supposed to spend the night on her.

It dawned on him with a flame of recognition brighter than the burning hull.

Attempted double homicide.

Dent.

Sunrise: ash and the stench of despair...

The birth of the next day broadcast an ugly light on the horrid aftermath. Three badly charred and damaged wooden docks, one of which was no longer a dock at all, just six pilings standing still-proud at futile attention in the water—blackened like giant spent match-sticks. Four yachts worth a few million were badly damaged.

Nowhere to be seen? *Sojourn.* The detritus of her rigging had sunk with her hull. And the last remnants of G dock's incinerated planking and creosote pilings were reduced to floating cinder scum.

George sat slumped on a short retaining wall separating the condo building's grassy slope from the boardwalk at the root of G dock, elbows on knees, chin cradled in his sooty palms.

The CCFD fire boat loitered with its water cannon poised to pound any still-smoldering material with sea water pumped from the basin, guarding against a re-flame.

The rotund Doctor Saul Menendez sedated Kate even though she proclaimed she was fine, but couldn't stop shivering convulsively. Doctor Saul normally didn't make house calls, but he was their long-time Florida GP from Port Charlotte. When George called, he'd driven the twenty miles south to BSM in the middle of the night as a personal favor.

He'd offered George a sedative too, and was visibly frightened by what George said next. "Naw, Doc, I need to stay sharp for what I'm about to do."

She was just gone, after almost fourteen years, just gone. George sat there on the knee wall muttering to himself, numb to the profound pain, but contemplated, "Dent, you asshole, how'd you know?"

So this wasn't over.

It soon would be, George solemnly vowed.

"MAXINE, IT'S GEORGE."

"George! It is so wonderful to hear from you! It has been too long. I'm glad you kept my cell number, even after you escaped GGS. How are you, Boss?"

George could hear her enigmatic little smile. Then he realized that Maxine had spoken several rather complex sentences, articulating them perfectly with impeccable inflection, without a single stutter.

All things change.

"Maxine, you sound wonderful. Forgive me for skipping the pleasantries for now. First, Dent is alive. He's on a rampage, tried to murder Kate and me here in Florida last night."

"What? Are the two of you alright? What happened?"

"We're fine… physically, at least. I'm convinced Dent planted some sort of explosive device near the large propane tank we carry in our boat. Only fate saved us. We had just walked up to the condo minutes before she blew at her dock.

"First, a warning. Be very careful. Inform the team to do the same. Better contact our friend Claire in Human Resources as well. This guy's madness and resolve exceed our worst fears.

"Then, I need you to contact Agent Seamus O'Brien at the BCA. I believe you met him at our retirement party in Lake City. Please ask him to call me on Kate's cell. You already have her number. My phone with his number is at the bottom of the harbor. Clear?"

Instantly all business, Maxine confirmed, "Yes, George. Understood. I'll warn Nora, Frank, Claire, and the rest. I'll ask Agent

O'Brien at the Minnesota BCA to call you on Kate's phone. I assume you'll connect him to your local law enforcement. I'll also inquire after physical protection for the team, including Claire. Anything else?"

"That's it. Thanks, Maxine. And you really do sound wonderful. Everything okay there? How is Shen Ma?"

"Everything is fine here. The team remains devastated over the loss of Donny and Sandra, even after almost a year, and we miss you and Kate terribly, but we must go on."

Maxine continued, not missing a syllable.

"We have some college new-hires. In light of the debacle resulting from hiring Dent, the pro-hire program is suspended until HR analyzes weak spots in their vetting process.

"Oh, by the way, I've been promoted, thanks to you. Please address me as Director Sun now! Thank you again for your sponsorship, George. Shen Ma is... visiting his family near Taipei ... indefinitely. Nothing more to be said about that."

"I understand. Congratulations on your promotion, Maxine. Well deserved. I'd love to talk more, and we will do so very soon, but now we both have urgent work to which we must attend.

"*Xièxiè. Zài jiàn*, old friend," as he thanked Maxine and expressed the wish they'd see each other soon, at least as well as his rudimentary Chinese would allow.

An hour later, Kate's phone rang.

After his call with Maxine, George received a call from Agent Seamus O'Brien from the Minnesota Bureau of Criminal Apprehension.

Once George had updated him on recent events, a dumbfounded Agent O'Brien said, "At least now we know the asshole is still operating and moving around. I gotta ask this, Mr. Janis. Any possibility this could be someone else?"

The implication was clear. O'Brien wanted to know if George had other serial killer enemies.

"What? *What did you just ask me?*"

Now very subdued, and in a soft, almost contrite tone, Agent O'Brien repeated the question.

"What do you think? No… wait. I'm sorry, Agent O'Brien. I know you need to ask. No. I can't imagine… son-of-a-bitch."

Taking no offense, O'Brien continued.

"Okay, you're in Lee County, right? I looked it up. I'm going to connect with their sheriff's office and the Florida State Police. You're gonna be busy with the boat fire stuff, but you'll also receive inquiries on the attempted murder stuff. Lots of folks are gonna be asking a lot of the same questions again. That's how it works. Just be patient. We're all in this together, Mr. Janis.

"This is also solid Fed fodder now, so the Ft. Myers FBI field office needs to be involved too. This is gonna be a three-ring circus. I'll keep you updated, Sir."

And he disconnected.

THE NEXT DAY, "GEORGE, HAVE YOU HEARD?"

Nora Mathers? Oh God. Hadn't talked with her for months… since the Lake City party. His gut lurched so hard, he tasted bile so strong it burned his throat.

He barely understood her, only anguish and a drastic upward inflection in her voice that grated on his already exposed nerves stretched out over sixteen hundred miles of pain. It was damn near a squeaky scream. Oh no, not again…

He feared for Frank.

She was sobbing so hard, she apparently dropped her phone. He heard someone recover it. Off the floor?

Nora's husband Frank said, "George, Dent attacked us yesterday on the golf course, we both suffered some broken bones, but we're okay. I winged the son-of-a-bitch.

"And George, Maxine's body was found at her house this morning."

Frank stopped. Took a few seconds to steady his voice.

"Oh, man, looks just like Donny and Sandra's. George, this was Dent too."

George crushed Kate's pink-shelled iPhone so hard in the fist of his right hand the glass screen spider-cracked. He struggled to listen.

He wasn't sure he'd heard what Frank just said. Dreaming? Can't trust... Full-on nauseous, drifting... then he tumbled into a free-fall, nightmare plots of vengeance terra-forming somewhere deep, dark... Drifted back, again, he heard Frank's voice quavering, words that started to make some absurd sense again.

"... O'Brien just called us. Had a city patrol car right out in front all night. Dent musta come through the back. The cop knocked to escort Maxine to work. After no answer, flags went up. She busted in, found Maxine dressed for work in the kitchen at the rear of the house, and the back door was open."

George continued to half-listen in shocked silence as Frank uttered little more of substance. He now calculating consequences of future desperate actions.

Frank struggled to continue, now almost a pitiful whine, a sound that shouldn't come from a grown man's throat. He was entitled. His friend and leader was gone.

After a while, Frank continued. "Poor Shen Ma. He's gonna disintegrate. They're calling him. We're being placed in hard core protective custody..."

This is where George tuned back in, and he heard, "No idea where... After the agent told us what almost happened to you guys, it's gone to a whole 'nother level, hasn't it? George, who *is* this guy? *What* is he? He must've caught a direct flight to string these attacks so close together!"

Both Frank and George just sat there in stunned silence, staring straight through whatever was in front of them, witnessing the same horror movie in a ghoulish loop. They both needed at least a little time to process.

Nobody asked, "Are you still there?" A full minute later, George croaked, "Um, do whatever they say, Frank. This... monster is... Um, you guys okay?"

After another ten seconds of smoldering silence, "No offense, George, but that's a pretty stupid question, ya know?" He had *never* talked to *The Boss* like that, instantly acknowledging George was in shock, just like him. Regret punched him hard in the gut. "Aw, George..."

"Yes. I'm sorry, Frank. I can't help but feel like this is my fault. Our friend Catie? Donny? Sandra? You guys? This week, here? And now Maxine? It's... just... too... aw, Frank... *Suffering God...*"

Sobbing openly into Kate's damaged phone, unable to speak, even though he tried before giving up completely, alternating between punishing himself with guilt and fantasizing sorrowful nightmares of what he'd do to Dent if he ever got the chance.

Who was he kidding? What would he do to this poor tortured asshole that obviously someone hadn't already done to him? Someone seriously damaged him.

Maybe it was God, put him on this Earth to punish mortal sinners like me.

George truly considered the possibility that this was indeed God punishing him for abandoning Him as a child. It was all that fire and brimstone coming back to pile on the pyre. *They* were right—Karma's a fickle bitch.

Who did he loathe more right now - Dent or God? Civility, legality, morality, all evaporated in a muddy fog of anguish and vengeful despair.

He'd never felt this profoundly sad or angry before. An evil alien invaded all of who he was, or ever would be—the convulsing death throes of a disenfranchised child of God.

Tough guy Frank's heart cracked wide open without warning.

Hearing George sobbing was a first for him. Now *two* grown men bawled like wronged innocents, locked in an emotional long-distance embrace. Such was the depth of their grief and guilt and camaraderie.

"George, the asshole broke Nora's collar bone and there's a lot of damage to her shoulder. He broke my right arm after I shot him—before he ran off like a coward. They just released us after two days of setting casts and observation. Wanted to hold me longer. Told 'em to go screw themselves."

Tough guy was back.

Suddenly, after trying unsuccessfully to process all of this, George just stopped. A high-voltage breaker crackled with a serrated sizzle as it flipped, fried his tears dry, tempered his voice hard and slivery like brittle flint, his eyes grown black-iron dead.

Clearing bitter phlegm, he said in a low and ominous voice, "Frank, you guys get safe and let me deal with this maniac.

"This… will… not… stand."

WHOSE VOICE WAS *THAT?*

Frank, still drying his eyes on his shirt sleeve, stopped in mid-wipe. He deferred blowing his nose because of the surprising bolt of lightning that tingled his every nerve ending. Suddenly he was not at all sure who exactly was on the other end of the line—someone, um, different.

Whatever George had just become, it frightened and encouraged him.

"George, be careful, man. What're you gonna do? George?"

Click.

SHARK BAIT

FORT MYERS, FLORIDA

Sam couldn't reach George for hours.

He'd heard from various sources that another of George's team had been murdered, and of the explosion in their marina.

Surprised when George finally answered Kate's number, "Oh, thank God. George, I'm up to speed. Deepest condolences. Time is critical. You and Kate must seriously run for cover, my friend. No other options. I've arranged it.

"I'm told you're still at your condo. US Marshals are en route to y'all. ETA twenty minutes. Pack for a two-week trip. Nothing else. Be ready."

"Sam, thank you. Kate will be ready. I've made a decision. I need to be part of this. Use me as bait. Nobody on the right side of the fence, who's still alive anyway, knows this madman better than me. Before you say it, my mind's made up. How can we do this?"

"Ah… damn, George,"

Sam had heard that voice many times before. Hard as nails, mind's made up, highly motivated, fearless.

"Fine. I won't insult you with attempts to discourage. First, you and Kate get in the marshal's car when it arrives. This is not up for discussion. You must trust me. I'll meet you at their field office in ninety minutes. You and I will go from there. At least I want Kate safe."

"Wait, what? Where are you, Sam?"

"I caught a non-stop into RSW. Arrived two hours ago. I have additional news which requires a plan. I can tell you're serious about attending the party. So be it. I must say this, George; we can *not* guarantee your safety in the open."

"No shit! … Aw, damn, Sam, I'm sorry. I'm still getting a handle on my grief and anger. You don't deserve attitude. Thank you for your concern."

Eighty-three minutes later, George could not stop embracing Kate in a small and exceptionally drab conference room in the marshals' field office in downtown Fort Myers. She was medicated, as Doc Menendez had prescribed. Mandatory. No discussion. His incredibly strong woman was in such a fragile state, it threatened to emotionally paralyze him as well.

George realized, at that moment, the essential life-giving force Kate exuded. She sustained him. She always had. He flashed forward, maybe not all that far forward, realizing how important it was that he precede her in death.

They said their silent goodbyes as she was whisked off to a safe-house.

Sam convened the briefing.

"GEORGE, I HAVE DISTURBING NEWS.

In light of the difficulty tracking Mr. Canfield, our small cadre of trusted intelligence operatives spanning several agencies—don't ask, need to know—have uncovered some alarming trends."

Sam tried to tread lightly. His first impression of George was shocking. Despite their countless email and phone conversations, they hadn't met face-to-face in almost fourteen years, but the ravages of age weren't what appalled him.

The face of happier times had been subsumed by the visage of an emaciated veteran of countless campaigns behind the lines, scarred by circumstance. His skill as an interrogator enabled him to see inside this semi-battle-hardened soldier of sorrow and pain.

His heart went out.

But on to the business at hand. Time to haunt Dent's house.

George said, "Aw, Sam, just spit it out."

"Okay, let's get to the heart of it. Y'all need to know what our trusted friends in Intelligence now know."

He courteously included the three well-vetted marshals present, all sworn to utmost discretion, all briefed on the trust issues. The fact that Sam possessed the latitude to read in these civilians spoke volumes about his juice.

"First, we've discovered Mr. Canfield has deep ties to a shadow organization, as a low- to mid-level operative of some sort."

George had to say it. Even though it added no tactical value. He quietly injected in a calm but icy voice.

"The sicko's name is Dent, Sam. Please don't afford him a title of respect. He's damaged goods. That name suits him much better. Thank you, Sam. Please continue."

Sam could smell the searing pain fermenting in George's wounds, but surprisingly, he no longer sensed fear. The decisive leader he suspected George had become at Greater Global now resurfaced, but with a core of ravenous brutality awaiting an opportunity to feed.

"Alright, George, in any event, his designation shall be *Bandit One*, but definitely not *Mister* Canfield... as of now.

Sam went on after receiving George's grateful nod.

"Chatter reveals very few and surprisingly obscure references to a group called *the Brotherhood*, mostly from phone and email snippets we've spoofed out of Meade. This group is likely a loose consortium, with lofty leadership, a specific charter, and with deep roots that go back decades.

"That an organization of such scale and longevity has remained so obscure for so long points to powerful cover. Your ex-employee seems to be the minuscule tip of a very large iceberg."

Sam regretted his reference to the murderous Canfield as George's ex-employee the moment he'd uttered the words. A grimace of guilt flashed into George's now nearly wasted eyes, far more deeply set than he remembered from softer times. That expression evaporated as fast as it appeared. Those used to be laughing eyes. No more.

At the corners of George's mouth, Sam observed an erratic flicker of subtle twitches. To Sam, they seemed a billboard of bitter resolve, framing pinched lips stretched hard against countless regrets.

At that moment he felt a deeper kinship with this erstwhile desk jockey than he'd ever felt before. This guy might be a virgin, but he was on the verge of becoming a virgin operator.

Sam continued, "We may surmise, much through innuendo, that this name, the Brotherhood, is an abridgment of some longer name, perhaps possessing a military or paramilitary connotation. As y'all likely know, soldiers affectionately refer to those with whom they've shared the field of battle as *brothers*.

"From this, we've deduced that this may be some sort of ultra-patriotic cabal. That might further suggest either a military and/or political focus. But this organization is no simple group of para-mili tary fanatics marching through the woods with antiquated weapons. They seem to possess that which no lesser group has ever possessed: continuity spanning multiple generations."

"GOT IT, SAM. WHAT'S THE PLAN?"

George was delighted to finally see Sam again after all these years of communicating by phone and by email. He was old when they'd met in Baltimore in 1995.

He hadn't changed all that much since then. Still genteel on the surface, however... with George's new fire-tempered eyes, he now sensed in Sam's eyes jagged obsidian shards that threatened to slice through any falsehood, threat, or evil that might wander too close to his resolve. Few would see that coming.

George would. Now.

He remembered a flash of that dangerous edge when he had asked him in *Sojourn's* pilothouse if he worked for the NSA...

Sojourn! Oh God, she's really gone. Does Sam still feel it too? That sick... stole her, my friends, almost... Kate. Ah... well, back to business.

With zero inflection in a voice void of emotion Sam stated, "We use you as bait, George. This lunatic's hard-on for you is our best play, and that will be his earthly demise."

George had never heard Sam talk like that. He visibly shivered.

Sam continued, "I need to burrow into his twisted psyche to gain more intel. That might become very physical."

A warning to the faint of heart.

"I fear there's a perfect storm brewing on the horizon, and we must know its magnitude, speed, and heading. Of course, we'll also bring him to justice for murder, but that must be secondary."

"Let's do it." No hesitation. Dead eyes, and electricity in George's voice.

"Good, George, you're on board, now a member of the team. Okay, then. Here's what we do. We determine who we can trust. I have an operation running that you need to know about."

PROBE REVEALED

THE DRAB CONFERENCE ROOM CLOSED IN.

Sam lectured, "George, before a sniper aims his scope on full zoom, he needs to know where to start scanning for individual targets, or he aimlessly scans a rapid blur until he goes blind or crazy. That's why he uses a spotter with a lower resolution scope before zeroing in on a target."

Sam then patiently explained the results of his probe using Sergei Rostov as his spotter. George found this interesting and relevant, but his claustrophobia crept up on him. He continued to listen with his scant remaining patience.

The inflections in Sam's voice indicated his escalating excitement.

"As we zoomed in using the results of Sergei's probe, we discovered more than a few anomalies in the actions of several suspects within the intelligence community. I chose this technique to focus our investigation, to narrow our search. It paid off handsomely, George.

"Nineteen of our twenty-seven suspects illegally passed Sergei's hot information. What info doesn't matter. In doing so, my guys discovered several communiqués that smelled rotten.

"An unusual code name for someone—*Rusty Sword*—popped

several times. A focused search revealed this same designator used by a few of our older suspects going back decades.

"Code names never last more than the duration of a single mission, or at most, a tactical group of operations.

"Where we'd designated Mr... ah, Dent as *Bandit One*, we're now designating *Rusty Sword* as *Bandit Two*. This guy, whoever he or she is, made a serious tactical error by retaining such a unique code name for so long. We're going to leverage that, George.

"Our suspicions grew even more acute by what we could *not* see. Turns out that *Rusty Sword* is not an official designator, and appears nowhere in any official mission documents, but does appear repeatedly on several password-protected and heavily encrypted *civilian* dark Internet sites we were able to spoof—superficially, anyway.

"User names themselves, usually fictitious handles like *Rusty Sword,* exist outside the protection of those sites' internal encryption schemes for the most part. That was our knot hole in the fence.

"Beyond spotting the designator, most of these leads were not traceable further and led to dead-ends, but that was enough. Because a very deep probe could not identify additional intel on this designator, its very invisibility and obscurity identify it as an extremely provocative nugget. So *Rusty Sword* is on the board as *Bandit Two*."

George had been patient but finally could remain silent no longer.

"Sam, this is a fascinating primer in PI 101, or Spyware 505, for all I know, but so what? C'mon, cut to the chase will you, already?"

"George, you need to know how we got to where we are. You said it yourself. Nobody knows *Bandit One* better than you. That's the *only* reason you're out here listening to all this, and not in protective custody with Kate. We now have a significant key to the first of many doors. We need to find more keys. We will. That's how this works, my friend. One clue leads to another. Now do you wish to be an operational member of this team, or not?"

Sam wasn't being as harsh with George as his words and tone of voice might reflect. It was an act. He knew his friend simply needed a splash of cold water in the face to retain his focus.

Admonished, George said, "Okay, Sam. I get it. I'll shut up and listen."

Sam rewarded him with the smile of a confidante before continuing.

"Several years ago, one of my guys was suspended after a mission went horribly wrong. An acquaintance of his, no longer with the agency, suggested a profitable career change, that he might want to contact someone using the handle, *Rusty Sword.* He remembers his acquaintance saying, *'Call Enoch. He's a really good guy.'*

"Our analyst was exonerated shortly thereafter, against some pretty steep odds, and never pursued the matter. He also chose not to return to the field. But that handle was so unusual, plus he remembered the word *'profitable.'* Nobody uses that word in conjunction with any sort of *legal* intelligence work for the government, so it had to be a reference to private or off-book contract work. That spells *merc,* George, short for *mercenary.*"

"Enoch? That's an unusual name… Wait, I've heard that name. But where?" George dug deep into his memory, but couldn't retrieve it.

Sam tucked away George's query in his 'interesting, but obscure' file within his highly analytical mind before continuing.

"At any rate, since our investigation was strictly off the books, it took some time to follow the threads of our nineteen questionable agents, now in deep guilty, as far as we are concerned.

"There may be more, but this allowed our sniper scope to zoom in on known bad guys, thanks to our spotter, my old and trusted friend, Sergei."

Sam had told George the story of the likable Russian defector who was stashed on *Sojourn* during the cold war and later married on her foredeck. Better times…

Sam looked George in the eye and said, "One day I'd very much like you to meet Sergei. He's a prince of a gentleman. You and he would be great friends."

George smiled gratefully at the pleasant diversion, however momentary.

The marshals just glazed over at the inside comment between the two spooks, or at least that's what their body language broadcast.

"The really good news is that as we followed the threads of transgression, while some mid-level agency honchos and others appeared to be involved, there was no evidence that implicated any major agency heads that we know of.

"That said, we'll have to decide the timing to involve some or all of them—after further vetting—and as the good guys clean their own houses. We are not there yet.

"Based on the chatter the team's broad-spectrum surveillance is picking up, though, we may not have much time. Something significant is about to take off on a short runway."

Sam could see George's head was spinning. Suddenly he looked like he had been jolted by a bolt of lightning. He violently leaped out of the cheap hard plastic swivel chair. As it up-ended, the chair clattering to the tile floor behind him startled everyone in the room. He shouted, nearly screaming. The marshals reached for their sidearms.

"Holy shit-on-a-shingle, Sam! I just remembered where I heard that name! Not sure whether it's significant or not, or even relevant, but it could be important, right? I heard the name, *Enoch Slattery*, or *Slatterby*, something like that..."

Now intent, Sam looked deep into his eyes.

"George, this is very important, if for no other reason, to eliminate one more possibility. Exactly where and when did you hear that name? Think carefully..."

Without hesitation, now standing over the conference room table leaning into his certainty with his knuckles on its surface, he pictured clearly in his mind a painful memory subliminally buried and now resurrected at some cost. He shouted as the words tumbled out, further startling all three marshals. His voice now a machine gun on full auto.

"555 Madison Avenue, Manhattan. Fortieth floor office suite of Palmer Xavier, Chief Operations Officer of Greater Global Solutions, Inc. Fall of... 2005!"

He stole a quick breath.

"Xavier raped my budget for tens of millions..."

Then, after a badly needed deeper breath, "...That pillager was an artist at jerking cash out of the business. His MO across the board. Always to justify more focus on R&D. Or to contribute more to sales and marketing."

Breathe, George!

"But frankly, I had my doubts. I can't speak to the sales stuff, but I cut my teeth on Research and Development. The blood flowed freely from deep cuts there too, and I mean *everywhere*."

Now George's head pounded from his revelation and he puffed from adrenaline-fueled excitement as possibilities dawned on him.

"The slime-ball forced me to fire good people, Sam!"

He fell silent, but continued to breathe heavily through his mouth from emotional exertion, excited at uncovering a new piece of intel. He realized his legs were shaking, threatening to fail him.

Looking sheepish, he picked up his chair from the corner where it landed. He sat down carefully, unsure of his equilibrium, and waited expectantly.

The grumpy marshals' demeanors relaxed.

George took several deep cleansing breaths as the wheels continued to spin.

Sam sat down too, contemplating George's epiphany. The only sound came from the air conditioning panels flush in the acoustic tile ceiling of the cheaply furnished conference room—a syncopated background rattle from above.

Finally, Sam spoke slowly without much inflection in his voice as if he were one of those computerized text-to-speech voices.

"Interesting. Very interesting indeed. George, you may have just connected a couple of important dots."

Another two full minutes elapsed, during which time the three marshals in the conference room began squirming and looking around, not accustomed to Doctor Sam's trance-like analytical style.

A jittery look from George with a subtle sideways shake of his head settled them down, realizing important progress in the investigation was occurring within this little man's scintillating intellect.

At last, he croaked, "Tell me more about this Mr. Xavier."

So George did.

While he tried to sound objective, the loathing he felt for this character sculpted his face with sneers and squinted eyes of hatred. At one point, he noticed drops of spit flew onto the table in front of him as he spoke. He unapologetically wiped them up with a quick swipe of his left hand's heel while he spoke.

George described this ruthless, avaricious senior executive near the top of a hundred billion dollar multinational corporation. He now appeared to have connections to some dark character whose purpose was, at best, dubious. This painted Xavier the color and texture of another person of particular interest. George speculated, *Bandit Three?*

As he fell silent once again, his new input considered and analyzed, Sam said rather excitedly, "Okay, George, we're jumping the zoom on our scope to near maximum. We're designating Mr. Xavier *Bandit Three.*

"Let's review what we know, or just as importantly, what we suspect, or are able to deduce."

DOCTOR SAM PACED MADLY AS HE SPOKE.

Now a tenured professor, he delivered a well-structured lecture to a small group of eager graduate students.

No, that wasn't right at all... he consulted with his full partner in an intriguing case of potentially monumental proportions. He threw himself into a strategic briefing to his partner and trusted field operatives, the trio of marshals.

If they only knew...

Sam continued to pace back and forth on the other side of the small table in that tiny room as he summarized what they knew. He ticked off his points by extending the arthritic fingers of his right hand, one by one.

A single crooked finger extended.

"First, it may be a remarkable coincidence that your ex-employer's chief operations guy has some sort of relationship with a shadowy operator outside the official intelligence community. We now know this character is connected in some way to rogue elements within the government's intelligence community.

"There also appear to be entanglements with at least some elements of various local or regional law enforcement organizations. This likely also extends to more than a few political operators as well. We'd also be prudent to now place Mr. Xavier and his closest associates at GGS under scrutiny."

Another finger popped out of his liver-spotted fist.

"Second, it may be a coincidence that your psychotic ex-employee worked for the same large company until you fired his twisted ass. Perhaps it is yet another coincidence that he's a serial killer with apparent ties of some sort to a longstanding powerful and very well-funded ghost organization with extensive intelligence access. But I doubt if that too is a coincidence. We only know this group as the Brotherhood.

"Further, this cabal, failing a more appropriate mot juste, is also outside official purview, a veritable cancer that has at least partially metastasized in the lymph nodes of our system of governance and seemingly, at least in some arms of law enforcement. Same group? TBD."

Yet another finger extended to join the first two.

"And third, we may be collecting yet another 'coincidence,' however unlikely, that our new friend, Mr. Xavier, may be skimming tens of millions, even hundreds of millions, out of his business, targeted for some unknown, potentially nefarious purpose. Questions? Comments?"

"That's a whole lot of coincidence, Sam. Full zoom?"

"Full zoom, my friend. Let's go hunting."

FRIGHT NIGHT

OCTOBER 2008
PUNTA GORDA, FLORIDA

Nobody expected an attack.

Nobody except George and Sam and their team, that is.

The South Shore Condominium Association, just referred to as *South Shore* within the boundaries of Burnt Store Marina in Southwest Florida, was George's principal home now.

A housing community surrounding a boating and golfing haven, BSM comprised 2,000 homes ten miles south of the small coastal town of Punta Gorda on the shore of the ten-mile-wide Charlotte Harbor. West of the harbor lay the Gulf of Mexico's southeastern coastline.

South Shore, a sixteen-acre peninsula, was bordered on the north by BSM's southern boat basin where *Sojourn* once moored. The enclave was guarded to the south by an impenetrable tropical jungle of mangroves and Brazilian pepper trees. An automated security gate operated by vehicle bar code controlled access from the east. The west end of the peninsula jutted out into the harbor.

South Shore was more private than secure.

WOULD FRIDAY NIGHT BE A TARGET?

George and Sam both thought so.

The weekly *Drunk and Disorderlies* at South Shore were BYOB parties at the community clubhouse and open to all owners and renters. The name *D&D* had become a geriatric tradition, an attempt to vicariously recapture memories of impetuous youth.

These 'spontaneous' events at the clubhouse each Friday were well advertised on exterior bulletin boards near the elevator of each of the eight three-story concrete buildings in the colorful South Shore compound.

These events were popular, and no more so than at the advent of each snowbird season. A delegate from most of the one hundred-twenty-three units' residents would optionally bring a dish to share. That became a low-key culinary competition of sorts.

Near the center of the large main room of the clubhouse, Sophie Landers glided over. In her obvious New Jersey accent said, "Welcome back, George! Too bad about *Sojourn*. Condolences. Propane can be a dangerous proposition. We are *so* glad you and Kate weren't aboard."

George heard the words, but wasn't really listening.

Too bad about Sojourn? My God, she has no idea, nor does she care in the slightest, how devastated we are over this, or that there's a psychopath bomber in the neighborhood!

"Thanks, Sophie. A pretty frightening affair indeed. I can't believe our little ship is gone, but it is good to be safe, home, and among friends and neighbors again. We've missed South Shore."

She didn't seem to hear a single word he'd said.

"So where's Kate?"

Sophie and Kate were cordial but didn't really get along. George suspected Sophie saw much of herself in Kate, only she perceived that Kate was less educated, and didn't much like what she saw. Two North Poles. He could tell this gazillionaire's wife was about to regale him with some pearl of useless trivia. He pre-empted.

With a drink in his left hand, a club soda on the rocks with a twist of lime, George casually replied, "Oh, she's taking care of some family business."

"You know, Kate's a nice gal. It's just unfortunate that she sometimes sounds like a truck driver's wife. That must be trying, George. You seem so much more articulate."

Remember why you're here, George. Be civil and let this old cotillion queen's bitter tongue wag. She's probably sailing her feeble mind three sheets to the wind.

"You know what I really love about both you and Kate, Sophie? If I want to know what either of you is thinking, all I have to do is *listen*."

"Well, aren't you the sweet one. Oh, hello, dear!"

And Sophie drifted off to the next pair of ears needing to be victimized. She obviously hadn't heard or understood a word. Typical. A different reality.

THE SEASON HAD BEGUN.

Each late Autumn to early winter in Southwest Florida saw snowbirds arriving in droves. Those present were getting reacquainted by slinging ritual conversation starters, such as, "When did you arrive?" or "Did you have a good summer?"

These refrains resounded repetitively all over the clubhouse's large main hall. The chattering of sea gulls reclaiming their social turf in the tropics grew steadily louder as cocktails continued to disappear at an astounding rate.

Whenever George returned to Florida from Minnesota or New

York each Winter, he felt like a movie extra slipping out of a subtle black and white film into one recorded in outrageous full Technicolor. Not in Hollywood, but nearby Miami, maybe.

A blinding array of dazzling hundred-dollar Tommy Bahama silk shirts circled him. In his mind he winced at designer-label yellow and teal Bermuda shorts that tried unsuccessfully to obscure knobby northern knees.

The sight of glittering flip-flops designed to tastefully display expensive pedicures amused him. 'Up North' he never saw such ostentatious miniature art, replete with rhinestones (?), on acrylic toe nails.

One mature but vivacious woman wore what appeared to be a cheap costume necklace with oversized coral-colored beads around her generous layered neck. This necklace offered a remarkable contrast to the lady's rose gold Rolex President on her left wrist, set off by a princess-cut channel-set diamond tennis bracelet on her right. She clearly hadn't played a round of tennis in several decades. He couldn't help but smile.

Even the younger renters who could only afford a month or so in Paradise enthusiastically participated in the fashion parade.

Nowhere in evidence, however, were two of the three grumpy marshals with whom he and Sam had met earlier in the week to plan this operation. They were convinced this soft target-rich environment with George at its nucleus would be too tempting for Dent to pass up.

George learned these marshals were members of an elite felony criminal apprehension team. No wonder they seemed both grumpy and good-natured at the same time.

The local FBI office was briefed, and wanted to attend the party, but agreed their four agents would hold their perimeter position on a side street just outside South Shore's gate to the east, off Matecumbe Key Road. Just sixty seconds out. They insisted on constant radio contact, however. The marshals agreed. They comprised a tightly controlled low-key presence.

Anxious to do something other than wait around to be brutally murdered, George engaged in some meaningless banter to serve as utilitarian camouflage. He approached an old acquaintance with Sam in tow.

"Rand, this is my dear old friend, Doctor Sam Braxton. Sam, Rand Parrish is the president of our home owner's association."

Sam fit right in. Not only because of his tradecraft. He was also, well, age-appropriate.

"Delighted, Sir!"

Sam exuded southern charm, instantly captivating Rand who asked him about his retirement and his medical career. The intense situational awareness in Sam's eyes remained, even though the genteel old spy dispensed charisma intrinsic to the nature of an accomplished social chameleon and quasi-retired spook.

While George knew sixty or seventy of the owners in the large room, as well as a few of the perennial renters, dozens of strangers joined the party, placing their potluck dishes on the open counter between two hotspots inside the clubhouse—the large kitchen and the larger main room.

Less ambitious attendees, usually the first-time monthly renters, brought chips and salsa to share, but *everybody* brought at least one bottle of booze. A few brought beer. Accomplished cooks offered a tray of deviled eggs, or hot dishes known as casseroles outside the Midwest.

Nobody *ever* brought a cake or any elaborate desert, as that would be viewed as over the top. Besides, cake and cocktails? Gauche.

Except for tonight.

A larger older gentleman with an unusual spring in his step entered the clubhouse with an oversized three-tiered cake to share. He placed it gingerly on the counter alongside the other four dozen dishes.

Several residents stared. That cake was *way* over the top. He didn't even bring a knife with which to cut it, which would have been decent etiquette. Nor did he greet anyone. As he drifted back through the front door he just entered, George's motor revved past its redline. Odd…

Oh. My. God!

Externally, he forced a calm facade so as not to start a panic. George sauntered, rather more quickly than he'd intended, toward that cake. Drawing a few stares from those nearby as he brushed through the densely packed room, including past Jersey girl Sophie Landers, George crudely stuck a finger deep down into the middle of the top tier, up to his wrist, and felt something hard. Digging around, he then felt at least one wire.

Has to be a bomb.

Gently picking up the cake with both hands, one now covered with frosting, he walked with deliberate purpose to the rear door of the clubhouse, ignoring jokes and questions.

Balancing the cake on one hand, he used the other to slide open the patio door already partially open, leaving a smear of frosting on its handle. Once out, he *ran* thirty feet toward the edge of the pool, heaving the heavy cake as far to the other side in mid-stride as…

Whump!

The concussion knocked him flat onto his back, blown out of his high-fashion flip-flops with their decent arch support. A poolside deck chair flew overhead crashing into the glass patio door to the clubhouse twenty feet behind him.

Then it rained chlorinated water. George would have been relieved to just lay there and recover, just to let his ears ring for a while, but no time. He sat up, dizzy. Blood dripped onto his Tommy Bahama shirt. Kate would be pissed. Then…

That was Dent!

Their gambit had almost cost a hundred or more lives, but now they had him… didn't they? He must alert the marshals with a description of Dent's disguise.

Still disoriented and bleeding from his ears and nose, hair plastered to his dripping face, he recklessly got to his now bare feet, almost falling over again onto the drenched and now-slippery pool deck. George bolted through the flock of disoriented party goers, some bleeding from flying shards of glass, some knocked over by the concussion, most already on the floor and descending into shock.

He ran straight through the front doors which were still propped open to receive the warm and breezy night. He began shouting in all directions. "It's Dent! He's here! Black shirt, black shorts! Salt and pepper wig, fake mustache! He's here! *HE'S HERE!*"

Apparently, Dent wanted—needed—to observe the object of his desire, not anticipating George's creative and rapid response. Caught hungrily drinking in the chaos from across the small parking lot between the clubhouse and the path to the docks, he suddenly turned and ran full tilt.

Even under the deep shadows of swaying palms, that sudden movement across the well-lit lot caught George's eye and he took off after it toward the docks. George could see that Sam tried to follow, but could not keep up. Before he sprinted off, he could hear Sam barking commands at the marshals and the agents, directing their movement over his secret-service-type radio.

In pursuit of Dent, George approached the seawall and the docks. He watched, horrified. In a single practiced motion, Dent leaped into a nearby center-console runabout whose engines already idled, cast off, and headed toward the marina's exit channel into the harbor at full throttle.

George knew that neighbors Jeff and Cassandra kept their high-speed center-console fishing boat behind their condo adjacent to the seawall and never removed the keys. He'd apologize later.

Hopping aboard, twisting the key resulted in the gratifying grumble from the 250 HP four-stroke Yamaha outboard.

He looked back toward the clubhouse and the path from the parking lot, hoping to see his friend Sam or the marshals. Nobody there.

No time.

Under a dark and threatening sky, George cast off and gave chase to the madman who killed his friends and just attempted to murder his entire neighborhood.

This asshole just graduated from serial killer to terrorist.

PURSUIT AT SEA

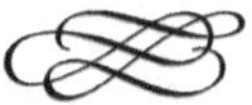

O N CHARLOTTE HARBOR, FLORIDA

I CANNOT LET THIS ASSHOLE ESCAPE!

Heading toward the harbor, George pursued Dent at full throttle. His gigantic wake, like Dent's, wreaked havoc on the boats tied to the docks. The charred remains of G dock, where *Sojourn* once berthed peacefully, passed by in a blur on his port side. A bitter pill.

Once he hit the open water of the harbor less than a minute later, a three-foot chop driven by a rising headwind made for a vicious ride at thirty-five knots in the small but powerful bay boat. A three-quarter moon lit Dent's wake like a long arrow that might just as well have been labeled, *Bad guy, this way.*

George's mind whirred like an empty blender on purée as he interrogated himself: *He can't hide from me now. Would he have a gun? He's already tried to kill me, at least twice. He'll try again, now that I'm out here all by myself. If I come face-to-face with him, what will I do? He's killed friends of mine. He tried to kill Kate. He killed Sojourn, and he's not done.*

Now out loud, also to himself, "He's some sort of traitorous spy. I better decide what I'll do when I catch him. Okay, no question. I put the mad dog down. It's my duty, after all. But can I do it? I better decide now."

He was catching up. The murderous chop coming in off the Gulf and across the harbor was building and made holding a course difficult. He knew he was a more experienced rough-weather boater than Dent. After all, he'd survived as a boat cox'n—skipper—in the USCG for four years. He'd assume that was his advantage. He needed one. Dent was a big boy.

George tracked a course dead-center of Dent's wake where it was smoother, and faster. He also guessed his boat had at least 50HP more than Dent's. The gap closed to less than a hundred yards.

This was it.

Dent *seemed* to be running for his life.

But his real plan was to draw Janis away from his safety net in case he survived his party popper. Did they really think he wouldn't spot the law enforcement types sprinkled in the weeds?

During his recon the previous afternoon, he noticed at least a half-dozen runabouts on the sea wall with keys in their ignitions. He assumed that since this marina was Janis's turf, he'd know he could grab a boat and pursue. How could he not?

Sucker.

Now that he was only a five or six boat lengths back, seven miles offshore, it was time for this chunk of dried street crud on the sole of his shoe to get scraped.

Remember when you fired my ass, I said you had no idea what you had done? Well, you're about to find out, boyo!

With his tactics decided, Dent jerked back on his rental boat's throttle and shifted into neutral, simultaneously spinning the wheel to starboard. Just like that, he presented the length of his boat directly to the path of George's vessel, still screaming directly toward him.

Dent hit the deck, braced himself, and waited. He didn't have to wait for more than a second or two of greedy anticipation as his boat bounced violently on the waves in the interim.

~

"What in Hell?"

George considered jerking back on his throttle as the starboard side of Dent's boat suddenly filled his field of vision, but then thought better of it. He might be able to take him out with momentum. This was going to be nasty.

After George's bow slammed into Dent's boat, it continued to grind viciously up over its right side. He crushed the starboard railing, stopping abruptly as his bow slammed into Dent's stout steering console amidships.

Dent rose as soon as he saw George's hull ceased its forward momentum. He vaulted up and over the bow of George's boat just as it slid off and away from his now-sinking rental from a huge hole at the point of impact. He clutched George's bow rail for stability.

Neither combatant took his eyes off the other to watch Dent's boat drift away and disappear beneath the building waves. George half-crouched at the helm behind his console, clutching the chilly stainless wheel. The seas threatened to whimsically toss them both over the side and into the tempest like the cracking of a giant whip.

The two men stood less than six feet apart in the tiny boat, facing each other with nothing but the console and naked hatred between them.

Precarious seas rose to five feet. Cresting waves in the shallow waters broke with violent resolve through the pass from the Gulf into the expansive harbor. White-caps blew off the waves' peaks in the darkness. That signaled that winds from the northwest exceeded thirty knots and approached gale force.

Dent Canfield, a traitorous serial killer and Geo's ex-employee, held a stubby little bat in his right hand. The considerable paunch he carried around his six-foot-three-inch frame did not diminish his deadly intent nor his cat-like movements.

Geo wondered, *Is that bat the nasty instrument of death that killed four of my employees? My friends?*

DENT'S RAGE WOULD NO LONGER BE CAGED.

His two-year-long erection verged on eruption. There were no adequate words, even if anyone could hear them in the tempest.

His most heinous personal adversary stood right where he needed him—isolated and within swinging distance of his precious thumper. Dent's fulfillment was at hand. It consumed his soul with lust. He took a step closer to his wet dream being fulfilled.

Without warning, lumpy clouds delivered a tropical deluge to punctuate the angry wind. The two men became ghosts, shimmering in the wind-whipped brackish salt water from the harbor that blended with fresh water from the sky. The soggy scene became a stroboscopic nightmare, barely believable.

GEO HAD ALWAYS BEEN A PACIFIST.

He focused on saving or salvaging human life. Or at least dwelling on compassion, not chaos.

Now, though, fury flowed through him like a watery toxin. At first, he felt guilt at this unmitigated wrath soon to be unchecked. Then, he accepted and reveled in its delicious abhorrence. He spoke out loud, although he knew the storm swallowed his words.

"This is a defining moment. I must find the strength to stop the killing."

~

THE MAELSTROM'S FEROCITY ESCALATED.

That did not seem possible.

Now punctuated with thunder and lightning every second all around them, Dent advanced on Geo. He raised his lethal bat above his head and right shoulder in a two-handed death grip.

A cancerous malice sculpted his face with water dripping from his nose and untrimmed eyelashes. He was within reach of Janis, of fulfilling his dream. He swung.

Geo raised the borrowed pistol within that same moment, aimed at center mass, and pulled the trigger before he dropped to the deck. Dent fell too.

There was nothing left.

Nothing at all.

~

SAM FEARED THE WORST.

The marshals, two firemen, and he battled the building wind and waves of a vicious late Autumn cold front sweeping in across the Gulf from the northwest. They searched for George's boat.

The radar-equipped Cape Coral Fire Department's vessel, the same boat too late to save *Sojourn*, honed in on two targets nearly lost in sea clutter on the screen. Then they resolved into just one fuzzy target.

As they approached, Sam recognized the profile of the fishing boat he'd seen speeding out of the marina with George driving. Sam spoke loudly into the ear of the fireman at the helm.

"If you please, bring her alongside, Lieutenant."

Lieutenant McBride of the CCFD was reluctant, knowing there

might be a murderer aboard. Even though the two marshals with Doctor Braxton carried rifles and sidearms. He and his emergency medical technician, Sergeant Sorley, did not.

He cautiously brought the port side of their thirty-seven-foot fire boat alongside the twenty-five-foot fishing boat's starboard side. He kept the boats tight against one another with his wheel to port and slight forward throttle—no lines. Even with McBride's expert helmsmanship, the two boats did their best to chew on each others' gunwales, spurred on by the tempestuous harbor.

From the higher deck of the fire boat, looking down into the smaller boat taking on water forward, they could make out two bodies separated only by the boat's walk-around console.

Sam's heart lurched at the sight of George on the deck aft of the helm, face down. He recognized his colorful shirt.

"Oh, Jesus, please let him be okay!"

He could see the other body just forward of the console on his side, with a dark bloom spreading on his chest. Had to be *Bandit One.*

"Nice shot, Old Son."

Sam and one of the marshals jumped aboard as soon as the seas momentarily aligned the boats' gunwales. Both marshals held their sidearms at the ready as they braced themselves. Too rough to hold a rifle with both hands.

Sam was relieved to discover that George just appeared to be bruised and unconscious. Dent bled from a gunshot to the chest, but had a strong pulse.

Then CCFD Sergeant Sorley—Sarge—swapped places with Sam. Armed with two backboards, Sarge and the marshal strapped a victim to each board for transfer to the fire boat's cabin bunks.

As soon as the two combatants were secure aboard, McBride immediately cast off to prevent further damage to his boat and held his bow stationary, facing into the oncoming wave crests at an angle. Otherwise, he feared a wave could force them to ride on top of the victim's half submerged hull. His boat was stout, but with so much kinetic energy behind these waves, and this many miles offshore, he saw no sense in taking chances.

Sarge secured each victim and his board to a bunk below decks on the fireboat against the violent lurching wave motion. He then focused on stabilizing Dent as best he could in the rough conditions.

The Lieutenant awaited a signal from his EMT before beginning the slow trek back to shore in a waddling sea now coming from behind—on his port quarter.

Once Sarge was confident he'd performed all the triage he was able on the victim the slender doctor identified as Dent, he turned his attention to the other one he called George. Sam assisted best he could, but he wasn't current nor familiar with Sarge's kit.

Ten minutes later, Sam sat next to George who remained prone and strapped in—forehead to feet. He laid an affectionate hand on George's chest just below the neck brace and kept it there. He drew comfort feeling his friend's chest rising and falling.

Half shouting over the din of the storm, he said, "Old Son, I can't tell you how happy I am you're okay."

Sam's voice shook with emotion and effort. Suddenly, he felt his age.

George, still disoriented, nauseous, and in a great deal of pain, croaked a single word, "Dent?"

"Well, Son, he lost quite a lot of blood, but he's alive, likely to survive if we can get him to the hospital in Punta Gorda in time. We're headed directly there now."

Sam could read George's expression without a single spoken word to explain it. He knew without a doubt that George was experiencing a deep-rooted relief, maybe even spiritual comfort that he hadn't taken a human life after all. He'd been given a second chance.

George bawled like a baby, tears pouring down over his temples onto the yellow-fabric cover of his neck brace and the nonporous blue rubber pillow velcroed to the backboard.

"You cry, Son. You cry like that because you *can* cry like I never can again. You go ahead and have a good cry."

Sam was envious. He knew he could not be wet from tears this night, just rain, and spray, and years of sweaty regret. Never having taken a human life was a gift not to be squandered. For him, that ship had sailed.

After a few minutes, George's sobbing dissolved into weak questioning.

"Did you find… anything… on… *Bandit One?*"

Sam looked both pleased and perplexed.

"*Bandit One?* Old Son, you are now officially an operator requesting a post-action brief. Son-of-a-bitch, boy! Makes me proud.

"After we got him strapped to his board, I searched him and found a wallet, rental car keys, a hotel key card and a flash drive on a silver chain around his neck. Your shot just missed that trinket by an inch or two! And if he survives, we'll have *him*. This could be a real break, George."

"I'm just glad we've stopped the killing, Sam. Thanks for finding me. Maybe you'll get your chance to, how did you put it, *burrow into his twisted psyche to gain more intel?*"

"Yes, George, but the first order of business is to get the two of you to secure hospital beds, and then to figure out what's on that flash drive."

They entered the broad mouth of the Peace River. After rounding the fat point of land for which the city of Punta Gorda was named, they fell under the wind shadow of the shore. Smoother water enabled higher speeds.

An ambulance awaited at the small marina tucked under Laishley's Crab House to transport them. They arrived at Bayfront Hospital near the shore a few blocks away minutes later.

GUILT TRIP

P UNTA GORDA, FLORIDA

An opioid caress embraced Dent.
   He resisted consciousness.
   But now...

Where am I?
   Now... the smooth walls of the pit where he lay prone, face down in rotting vegetation, were slick and greasy with countless layers of rancid blood. The stink of it all consumed him as he clawed upward toward a shred of sanity.
   The cloying atmosphere, damp with the musty fumes of innocent death, was so thick he could taste their acrid bitterness in the back of his throat. Blood flowed from his every pore...

The storm outside had subsided—was that just last night? Why, then, did he harbor this feeling of a turbulent atmosphere right here at the bottom of this pit as if waves of desolation were still crashing in, smothering him?

Then it occurred to him a cloud descended, settling in the pit like dense sludge, consuming him. Might this be a strange new emotion, equally clutching and cryptic? Was this guilt? Shame? Could that be it? That, and love were both so foreign.

Now there were *more voices* down here with him. *No! Liz? Oh God. You? I know, you were an innocent. I just lost it. I'm so sorry, Babe. And Ms. Potts? I thought you were Kate Janis that day in Lake City. Honestly!*

Liz's ethereal whisper reached him.

"Dent, I told you ignoring your meds would make you ill. You wouldn't listen to anybody though, would you? I loved you and tried to care for you. For that, you strangled the life out of me."

To her equally deceased counterpart, she turned away from Dent and said, "Hi, I'm Lizzie."

Caitlyn Potts turned her spectral death mask toward the ephemeral shimmer addressing her from the space directly above Dent's head.

"Hi Lizzie, I'm Catie, another innocent. *He* shattered every bone in my neck and threw me in the water. And we're not the only ones. Where's poor Sandra?"

"I'm here too, with Oscar, my little puppy and his squashed head, thanks to *him*," whispered a mere shadow of slender and shivering Sandra Segwell. "I wish I could say it was nice to meet you all, but... what are we to do, girls?"

"Why, we haunt *him* until the end of *his* pitiable days. That's what we are to do. Then, when he joins us, we'll haunt him for all eternity. Dent, you may have felt justified murdering all those other folks, but *innocents*? Seriously, Dent, you desperately need some perspective here."

Dent was sure he'd finally succumbed to total madness. He shouted, then screamed, "I don't understand... go... go *AWAY!*"

"Dent, for once in your life, try to do the right thing. Believe me, you want to at least try to make things right before... you know..."

The ghost of Liz pleaded with him before her voice faded.

Then suddenly and enthusiastically, almost cheerfully, as if she'd just discovered a path to redemption for the man she once loved, she sang out lyrically. "Get back on your meds, so you can think more clearly, *gain some perspective!* Do this for me. I still love you, Dent. Do this for..."

~

DENT STARTLED HIMSELF AWAKE.

He drowned in the throes of a cold sweat that drenched him, his gown, and his bed clothes. Now, even awake, the multitude of some of his victims' voices would not release him from their grasp. The haunting pandemonium overwhelmed him.

Confused and scared, he didn't know what to do. Then he remembered Liz's words, *"Get back on your meds... try to make things right before..."* Yes, that'll be a start. Oh God, all of these *voices!* That horrible place.

Now smothering within a dense fog in his hospital room, wide awake, his head pounded. His ears stung from a cacophony of horror. Make them stop!

"Doctor! Nurse! Anyone!"

~

TWO DAYS LATER HE STILL REELED.

A plenitude of virgin emotions appeared as if by magic. He remained strapped to his hospital bed, but the swollen purple rage, fear, and anxiety steadily subsided, until Dent possessed more clarity than he had experienced in years.

The wound in his chest had been a relatively clean hit from a small caliber pistol, he was told. His chest still burned, but the OxyContin helped.

Dent politely asked to speak with someone in authority. He learned that George Janis survived their violent encounter. He felt some relief at the news, but did not know why.

Then he turned profoundly introspective with respect to the Brotherhood. It occurred to him *they* were the real enemy, not only his own, but his country's. Looking back, he realized they weren't patriots at all. He not only needed to do something about it, he could.

Maybe that would help, just a little.

Once a jarhead...

Four serious men filed into Dent's room, an hour after he invited them. They introduced themselves as an FBI agent-in-charge-of-something, a US Marshal, his attending physician and another man simply introduced as Doctor Braxton, obviously a spook of some sort. He closed the door and spoke first.

"Mr. Canfield, please call me Sam. What would you like to share with us?"

"Well, I'm not sure, Sam. I know I've been bad. No excuses. I'd like to do a little good now if that's okay with you guys. This isn't about confessing, but maybe explaining."

Desperation drizzled from every pore as if he was still in a nightmare from which there was no escape, except maybe for a small measure of potential redemption ahead. For his country more than for himself.

Sam presented his genteel side. "Of course, Mr. Canfield. You're a Marine. Once a jarhead..."

"Yes. It's a lot. I wanted to help my country. That other stuff, I don't know. It got really bad... in here, ya know?" The index fingertip of his left hand viciously pounded his left temple four times so hard it bounced his head to his right. A self-administered pistol-whipping.

"May I call you Dent? Good. We'd like to help. How can we do that?"

"You found my flash drive, right? You will find it illuminating. But you'll need my twenty-six-digit decryption key to gain access. There's this organization called the Patriot Brotherhood.

"It started out as a contract job. I really did think I was performing my patriotic duty. Turns out these slime-balls are fascist power mongers, out to suck our country dry before moving on to the next. You won't be able to stop them, but maybe you can do some damage, slow them down."

"How do we do that, Dent?"

"The data on that drive is a compilation of all the Brotherhood's greatest hits that I could gather over the last two years. You'll find details for thousands of domestic and international financial transactions, code names, account numbers, IP addresses, like that. It includes hundreds of specific acts of treason of the highest order.

"I found a lot of this stuff after I realized they weren't really patriots at all. Not like me.

"I also spoofed encrypted email accounts, names of account holders, dark Internet sites they used, list servers, the whole enchilada. Just in case these guys ever decided to dump me in a landfill, I analyzed the contents of my insurance policy and found what they were really up to… treason.

"It was not just about giving the edge to their purchased political candidates, including their guy for President, which was my original assumption, but their strategy is to subvert our entire American political process for profit.

"They're funding that long term strategy by skimming savings accounts of two hundred million Americans by way of Wall Street. It's a coordinated ruling class subjugating the rest of us poor grunts. No, I cannot just let that happen.

Sam swelled with pride at how much of this they already intuited, but was grateful for confirmation, amplification and hopefully data needed for convictions.

Or for taking more definitive measures.

"Dent, you're going to prison for your crimes, obviously; I can tell you privately right now, however, that you've performed an indispensable act of patriotism right here, right now. Your nation thanks you. Is there anything else you can offer us? Don't answer right now. Just think.

"Deputy Tillotson here is the senior U.S. Marshal tasked to protect you. He can get hold of me twenty-four/seven. I will be your overall intelligence liaison.

"Ultimately, when we have a bit more time, we'd also like to learn about your training, your methods, and anything you might think useful as we combat these traitorous dogs in the field, and online.

"Again, Dent, thank you. Just two more questions: First, does anyone know you've acquired this mass of data? And second, are there any other copies?"

"No, Sir, to both questions. First, my stock-in-trade is invisibility going in and getting out. That's my specialty. I'm very good. Second, I had intended to secure this, the only copy, but never got the chance."

"We are in your debt, Dent. Thank you. Now, if you'll excuse me, it's time I go to work."

Sam couldn't wait to escape that room.

He hastily left that psychopath under heavy guard with the encryption code scrawled on a torn page from Deputy Tillotson's pocket notebook. He now sat beside George's bed just down the hall.

"George, we got the goods, Old Son! *Bandit One* cracked like a rotten melon. Actually seems to feel guilty *and* patriotic, if you can believe it. Must've had a spiritual awakening. And medication the last few days. The staff here has been spoon-feeding him anti-psychotics and he actually sounds quite sane, even remorseful."

George's enthusiasm did not yet show. He still struggled with the idea that he'd fully intended to kill a human being.

"That's great, Sam. Most of that is so far above my pay grade, but I must admit, he's one sick asshole. I think I understand at least some of his pain. I've seen other employees at GGS with this sort of affliction.

It consumes them. He's the most extreme, but I don't quite know how I *feel* about all this yet, about my intent to kill. It's hard. Just so we're clear, I never want to see him again."

George winced from the massive bruise on his neck and the back of his bandaged head. Fortunately, a fortuitous wave threw off the force of Dent's blow just enough. He was told there would be complications.

"Well, I've had some experience in this area," Sam knew this poor soul had no idea how differently he'd feel if he had succeeded in killing another soul, even one as sick as Dent, "and you'll learn to live with what you *intended* to do. You will simply come to grips with that. Be thankful that the poor sick son-of-a-bitch survived your lousy marksmanship. Who knows? Maybe *your* heart guided your bullet *away* from *his*. Take your reprieve and run, Old Son. It is a gift. You're hearing this from someone who knows."

"Thanks, Sam. I'd like to think Dent discovered a new lease on life now that he's getting proper treatment. And if I'm totally honest with myself, I'm grateful that he'll spend the remainder of his days and nights in prison, especially the nights. He'll wrestle with his own demons. Now that he seems to be exhibiting some remorse, I suspect they will visit him regularly."

SAM SENSED IT WAS TIME.

"Okay, to business. The guys at the agency would not have been able to crack Dent's drive anytime soon without his crazy complex decryption key. The wrong key would scramble and delete, as in rewrite and reformat.

"That boy really knew what he was doing. Given the full resources of the intelligence community, it might have eventually been cracked, but we still don't know what kind of timeline these jokers are on.

"Within minutes of opening that drive, George, they found manna from Heaven. Since we're intelligence types and hunger for simplicity, true to form, we've designated Dent's drive and its contents *Shiny Sword*, or just *Sword* for short.

"The first pass analysis lists who is clearly on the payroll. Interesting, to say the least. But who *isn't* on there is most important to us right now—reveals who we can trust. There's still a risk, but now it's smaller. We'll save the rest for later, and determine for whom we should be lining up firing squads.

"Now we can confidently engage the intelligence community, and its resources, above the radar. While the team continues their analysis and surveillance of *Bandits Two* and *Three* via a joint NSA/CIA team known as *The Special Collection Service*, with the FBI's blessing and participation, we need to concurrently start briefing the agency heads and their trusted circles, also vetted by the info from *Sword*.

"George, this is an international intelligence coup of monumental proportions, Old Son."

"Okay... let's see, *Bandit Two* is Slattery, and *Bandit Three* is Xavier, right?"

"Correct. We can't risk either of these characters ghosting on us, so the preliminary info I've personally passed on to my old boss's successor at the NSA gave us carte blanche for full spectrum eyes on the two prizes.

"*Bandit Three* was easy. With *Bandit Two*, however, we required some fancy footwork to initiate and sustain contact without discovery. This guy is really good, but our guys are better.

"Now, George, this is where we need high-level clearances you do not possess, but I'll keep you in the loop informally, fair enough?"

"Understood, old friend. I get the clearance issue. Plus I'm fairly certain you'll likely employ tactics I might find objectionable, but endorse enthusiastically as long as I don't have to see it... God, what does that say about my standards? Besides, I'm not much use to you until I at least partially recover from Dent's love tap, assuming these pain killers don't consume me first."

❧

ANOTHER BRILLIANT SUBTROPICAL MORNING…

But that was not the reason her face was flushed nor the reason warmth radiated throughout her body. Kate was never so happy to see George.

Sam told her of his injury but that he was okay, *and* that they captured that madman.

When she saw him on the sofa, fully reclined and sleeping in front of the TV on the lanai, her heart raced as tears streamed down her cheeks. She quietly sat across from him and just stared for a while.

They sat in shadows. Forty-eight feet of ankle-to-ceiling glass admitted very little light thanks to the drawn blinds and drapes.

She forgot all the fighting and bickering, at least for now. Here was the crazy motorcycle-riding teenager she'd fallen in love with, ego and all. After Sam briefed her personally, she realized how close she came to losing him the previous night.

Her husband, the adventurous spy who saved most of the people in South Shore and shot the bad guy on the open seas, almost losing his own life in the process.

She just stared, her heart shattering in gratitude and love for this geeky pirate who was all hers.

Momentary panic set in. The bandages on the side of his head and the neck brace scared her even though the hospital had only kept him overnight for observation. She bit her lip as her heart began to race. How badly had he really been injured? Or affected?

She checked his chest to make sure he was breathing. Okay, just sleeping. Her pulse began to slow.

George, don't you ever do something so stupid again!

Or so brave.

~

GEORGE SENSED KATE'S PRESENCE.

He slowly awoke with a stiff full-body stretch. God, he hurt all over. In a soft voice, he said, "Babe! C'mon over here!"

Right now, he desperately needed his suddenly-once-again-perfect soulmate... his eighteen-year-old gymnast with those perfect muscular legs and her deep well of courage.

Admiral Kay... designator: *Angel One.*

They embraced with rediscovered warmth. She worried about hurting him. She needn't have. He was already there.

"Hey, my neck stings like it's been stomped on, I'm a little dizzy, and I have some pain in my back, but I'm fine. I love you, Kate. Sit with me awhile, okay?"

The lump the size of Lee County in his throat revealed how badly he'd missed her over the last few weeks. And fearing for both their lives had frazzled him.

"I'm kinda fuzzy from the Oxy but clear-headed enough to know that we're really good together, Babe."

"George, Oxy?"

"Okay, I have more than just some back pain. Doctor Shepherd says I may have some pinched nerves, but we'll deal with that. And I'm watching my use."

She'd learn about the rest soon enough.

"Babe, I've been waiting for Nora & Frank to get home from work in Stillwater. I need to share the good news with them. They don't deserve one more second of worry."

She took the hint. She excused herself, gently kissing the new creases on his forehead, just below the bandage.

The last few days... so much change.

"HI, FRANK? GEORGE HERE, OLD FRIEND."

"George! Um, it's really great to hear from you, but the last few calls we've exchanged have all been bad news. What's up, Boss?"

"Frank, only good news today. We got him. He's in custody, and he's cooperating, even exhibiting remorse, if you can believe it."

"Ah Jesus, George. That's really great. Who got him?"

"Well, uh, I actually shot him at the end of a high-speed boat chase in a storm after he tried to blow me up along with about a hundred of my neighbors."

As soon as he said it, he regretted what sounded like bragging.

Maybe it was, just a little.

"George, you old sea dog! You shot him too? So it's over?"

"Frank, none of us will view the world quite the same ever again. That's unfortunate, but we can choose how we will react to it. For me or Kate, it'll never be, ah, over, and we'll likely be more vigilant about our personal safety from now on. But I am hopeful. With this guy locked up, we're all a lot safer. So, yeah, it's kind of over."

"Boss, thanks for the call. I can't wait to tell Nora. Thank you for giving our lives back to us… Sir."

Did Frank just salute me over the phone? Aw Jeez. Why did he have to…?

"Ah, you're welcome?"

Lumps all around.

Click.

PART II

GRAND COUP

O CTOBER 2008
FORT MEADE, MARYLAND

"OH, MY GOD, SIR!

"This Brotherhood reaches *way* beyond anything we could have imagined."

Chance Brewster gaped at his monitor—at the intelligence contained on the high-density flash drive they just received from the field. He was the lead analyst on the project code-named *Shiny Sword*.

His boss, Brigadier General Anthony Flannery would kick this upstairs, like yesterday.

"General, this is a frickin' shadow *government!*"

Leaning in over Brewster's shoulder for a quick scan of what was displayed on the screen, General Flannery stalled his next breath. He hadn't seen anything like this in his twenty-five years as a Marine and seven years at the agency.

"Settle down, Mr. Brewster. Let's follow protocol. Continue your analysis. Eyes only."

With a slow, disbelieving shake of his head, the General returned to his office and opened a secure internal line to NSA Director, Admiral Gregory Mannheim. "Sir, we have a big problem. We need to talk *right now*."

General Flannery took pride in his stalwart demeanor under extreme pressure. He was troubled that his voice contained a not-so-subtle element of barely-controlled panic. His boss, Director Mannheim said, "Tony, my office, ten minutes."

❧

Shiny Sword was more a shiny bomb.

Now ensconced in Director Mannheim's glossy walnut raised-panel office, still out of breath from hoofing up three flights of stairs, General Flannery said, "Sir, the preliminary analysis of *Shiny Sword* needs to be escalated as soon as possible.

"This Patriot Brotherhood has penetrated everything from Wall Street to the Fortune 50 to the White House. Upon cursory examination, We see confirmed evidence of foreign involvement as well. We're seeing evidence of *billions* in funding.

"Sir, we are under attack."

The Director's face paled as the General spoke. He muttered, more to himself as he gazed at nothing but incalculable implications in mid-air, *Oh, Sweet Jesus.*

Upon regaining his command voice he barked, "Okay, General, we need to know how far this thing goes, and what is left to play out. Continue your analysis. Nobody sees this material except you and your lead. Any additional eyes will be cleared by me. Personally.

"Meanwhile, my office will coordinate an NSC briefing for the President. Prepare a running brief for me with key talking points."

"Yes, Sir!"

Even though both officers were now civilians, he snap-saluted, spun and marched out.

The General's hands shook every so slightly before he plunged them into his trouser pockets to steady himself. *This is huge. None more so.*

GREG MANNHEIM WANTED HANDS ON.

Since Doctor Sam Braxton had cracked this egg wide open, and since his clearances were already of the highest level, he decided to pick his brain for exogenous insights. Personally.

The doctor's former position of senior leadership on his predecessor's team and his role in bringing *Sword* to the agency also factored into Mannheim's decision to include him.

This was more than just a courtesy. Sam Braxton had interrogated *Bandit One*, eye to eye.

"Doctor Braxton, can you get here within the hour?"

Sam anticipated this, already booked for an extended stay at the Quality Inn, outside of Jessup, Maryland, just a few miles from NSA HQ. Of course, the Director already knew this.

Sam was retired military, which is why he verbally saluted.

"Yes, Sir. On my way."

THE DIRECTOR MADE A DOZEN MORE CALLS.

None lasted more than thirty seconds, and none to any names on this bombshell list of now-known traitors. Invoking the words *Castle Gate Domestic* received instant priority from his counterparts at the FBI and CIA.

This code word represented either the initiation of, or the response to, government destabilization on a broad scale with its scope to be determined.

CIA and the Defense Intelligence Agency were no strangers to initiating or responding to such initiatives abroad. Including the word *Domestic,* however, added a shocking and unprecedented dimension.

The stage was set.

The time would come when Director Mannheim would also involve his United States Cyber Command, but not yet. This would generate significant repercussions, and the president needed to know first.

Thirty minutes later, the director's secretary announced the arrival of Doctor Braxton in his outer office.

Greg Mannheim walked out to greet his guest with a warm handshake. "Thanks for coming, Sam. We owe you a debt of gratitude for bringing *Sword* to us."

As they retreated to the director's office, he asked Sam, "What kind of provenance can you provide us? We're seeing some very disturbing SIGINT, so we're setting the stage with the Bureau to deploy serious HUMINT assets. I need to know that we're not stepping into a muddy hoax."

Now seated in a small but sumptuous office on a button-tufted red leather sofa facing the director in an opposing chair, Sam delivered his assessment.

"Sir, it is my judgment that you must take this signal intelligence very seriously. I obviously can't vouch for its validity at a detailed level. I *can* tell you that its source, *Bandit One,* is likely every bit as skilled a SIGINT operator as any on our team. I would also assume even your cursory analysis justifies the deployment of human intelligence assets ASAP."

Sam continued with some urgency in his voice.

"*Bandit One* also earnestly believes the material he collected has broad and profound implications. This is a quote after we turned him: 'The Patriot Brotherhood's strategy is to subvert our entire American political process for profit. They're funding that long term strategy by skimming savings accounts of two hundred million Americans by way of Wall Street. It's a coordinated ruling class subjugating the rest of us poor grunts.'

"His words, Sir. Plus, we likely still command the element of surprise because per *Bandit One*, our copy of *Sword* is the only copy, and because he remained full black collecting this data.

"Further, I believe we should feel confident if we avoid names your guys have come across in *Sword*, we stand a reasonable chance of buying some time to weed the garden."

The word, *further* sounded like *fuh-thuh*. Sam could not conceal his southern roots, nor would he try.

"Okay, Sam. I'm headed to a National Security Council briefing at the White House in a few hours. Anything else we should know?"

"Yes, Sir. Another warning *Bandit One* issued that frightened me more than anything. He said, *'You won't be able to stop them, but maybe you can do some damage, slow them down.'* Now from this, we might deduce a few possibilities.

"First, the reach of this Brotherhood is so broad, and so intertwined with our political system, even central to our economy, that trying to arrest it abruptly could cause irreparable damage to our country.

"Second, he said, *'slow them down.'* That tells me there is some imminent time-based event yet to occur, and we need to exercise all possible urgency.

"Another notion, Director. By referring explicitly to a *long term strategy*, this organization has been around awhile, so you might aim a few antennae back in time, as a secondary source of potential insight.

"Spanning multiple administrations, and assuming it exerts as much influence as we suspect, we may not yet comprehend the magnitude of the conspiracy we've uncovered."

"How long were you with *Bandit One*?"

"About five minutes, Sir."

"So let me get this straight. You spent five minutes with a hostile, turned him, and gleaned all this from your conversation? Do I have this right?"

"Yes Sir… that's what I do. Well, that's what I did. I'm ostensibly retired."

"Okay, Doctor, I'm impressed. Director Fredericks was right about you."

"Sir, one more thing. I had a few unofficial assets deployed before we knew who could be trusted officially. One of them, a civilian, may still be subject to threat. His name is George Janis. He was *Bandit One's* boss at GGS, for *One's* cover job, that is.

"Mr. Janis is also the guy who fired *One* from that job and ultimately led to his capture—personally. He also happens to be one of *Bandit Three's* ex-employees, another high level Brotherhood operative, and was instrumental in pointing us toward *Bandit Two,* a Brotherhood assassin and a potential source of additional HUMINT.

"So George is the guy who initially broke all of this for us, and remains in the thick of it. I'd like permission to read him in on this, and solicit his continued unofficial assistance as we proceed."

"I trust you, Sam, and if you trust him…"

"Thank you, Sir. My recommendation to the president, if I were asked, would be to employ tactics which would pace the dismantling of this shadow organization over time, prioritizing specific actions based on urgency; I'd mask these actions under cover of prosecuting selective illegal business practices as opposed to broad-based charges of treason. The latter could effectively destabilize our economy and the country's confidence in his administration. With all due respect, Sir, that's what I might recommend if I were you."

Director Mannheim listened. Then his furrowed brow transformed into a devious grin. He spoke softly after fifteen seconds of silence.

"Doctor, do you still own a suit and at least one tie?"

〜

WASHINGTON, DC

Four hours later...

Lame duck President John W. Stevens reflected on his two terms in office. In a few months, his personal life could resume. He'd survived eight years of proudly serving the American people as leader of the greatest nation on Earth.

NSA Director Mannheim, General Flannery on his staff, with a retired Colonel Sam Braxton in tow as a consultant, conducted a private forty-five-minute briefing in the Oval Office for the President and his National Security Adviser, General Mason Renfro.

General Flannery addressed the entire group in a steady command-and-control tone of voice, although he aimed his remarks at the leader of the free world.

"Mr. President, allow me to state what is already obvious to some of us. Little doubt remains that *Sword* is an intelligence coup of monumental proportions, has been shown to be of iron-clad provenance, and mandates immediate and aggressive action. In no uncertain terms, we are a nation under widespread attack from within, supported by aggressive foreign sponsors and actors."

Sam watched the president's face. While he wore the practiced mask of a career politician, his micro-expressions only visible to an experienced interrogator revealed the president's unmitigated fury. Good.

Immediately thereafter, this same group met in the Situation Room in the basement of the West Wing for a ninety-five-minute meeting of nearly the entire National Security Council. Two members were conspicuous by their absence. *Sword* contained compelling evidence of their complicity with the Brotherhood.

Everyone in this newly established inner circle knew precious stealth would soon be lost. Time was of the essence.

The president addressed the room.

"Ladies and gentlemen, while I'd like to swing *Sword* to summarily line up each and every one of these SOBs in front of a firing squad, I know that would not be optimal for the nation.

"So I'm asking each of you to assist in the creation of an action team to address both domestic and foreign elements already known to be threats.

"As Doctor Braxton has recommended, select American citizens will be arrested and tried with due process on the basis of conducting criminal business practices, using SIGINT from *Sword* and HUMINT collected by the Bureau.

"Further, selected foreign targets will be... addressed... by trusted CIA and DIA assets. And to blazes with due process and my personal deniability."

Sam did not inquire as to the nature of intended actions against foreign targets, none of his business, but could imagine those actions would be architected to send the strongest possible message based on the strident tone the president conveyed to the group—zero ambiguity.

The president addressed General Renfro whose background included a doctorate in Political Science as well as an impeccable military career.

"General, I need you to personally establish and lead a cross-functional working group to define both tactical actions as well as a longer term strategy to guide us. I want the chairs of the House and Senate intelligence committees included in this working group. Just make sure their names aren't anywhere within *Sword* first. We need to stand united here.

"Let's do this in a way that mitigates the risk of eroding public confidence in our political system, and please, in a way that enables us to retain at least some government decorum in the process.

"I don't care if I'm spending every nickel of political capital in my personal piggy bank, but if the big picture got painted in full color on the front page of the Post or the Times, every voter in America would run for the hills. We cannot allow that to happen.

"You have two weeks, General, after which I'll expect your completed plan so we can start pulling triggers. Understood?"

General Renfro knew he'd just been presented with an immense task as well as a lofty honor.

"Yes, Sir. We'll line up the big guns for you—under the radar."

RED DOT

PUNTA GORDA, FLORIDA

George Janis stared at his old friend.

He and Doctor Sam Braxton enjoyed a peaceful lunch on the covered deck of Portobello's, a restaurant perched on pilings over the southern shore of Burnt Store Marina's south basin.

At high tide, diners could hear the waters of Charlotte Harbor ebbing and flowing, gently gurgling, underneath the deck's floorboards beneath their tables. The subtle but sometimes pungent smell of tidal saltwater might offend the sensibilities of someone unfamiliar with the ocean's perfume.

Sea gulls circled lazily, and an occasional black bird called a crackle landed on the nearby railing between tables on the deck and the water seven feet below them. Once in a while, one of them might strafe a table for an errant French Fry.

A pleasant setting, at first.

Sam had dragged George out of his condo where he'd been holed up for days nibbling on pain killers.

It is perhaps appropriate that the charred remains of the dock where our beloved Sojourn concluded her final voyage was visible, particularly within a marina that bore the word Burnt in its name.

Indirectly armed with intel from *Sword* as a starting point, Sam's network revealed that *Bandit Two* was somewhere in Southwest Florida. After the NSC briefing, Sam caught a direct flight from Baltimore-Washington International to RSW, rented an economy car from Avis, and drove out to the shore from Ft. Myers to brief George in person.

And if he survived the day, he'd be back in Washington late that same night. After all, life was all about managing risk and reward, wasn't it?

GEORGE SEEMED OVERWHELMED.

"I can't believe we're talking about meetings with the President, his National Security Council, working groups, action teams and pulling triggers. This is off-the-charts incredible information to a peon like me, Sam. Sounds like a Vince Flynn or a Brad Thor novel.

"But I'm glad these guys are deadly serious and aren't just sitting around on their bureaucratic butts. Tax dollars finally at work on something meaningful. And I get it, Sam. My lips remain crazy-glued shut."

Sam's other agenda: he knew that life-changing events of the last year threatened to consume his friend's psyche. George's strength of will was his last and most desperate line of emotional defense.

He lost four friends and his ship to a madman who made multiple attempts on his life, his wife's and his neighbors.

Everything he knew to be true about business, politics, and government dissolved to the core of credibility. Here was a man who ran his own gauntlet and survived.

What remained Sam was here to determine.

He had watched George harden from easily chipped porcelain to tempered steel fired in the forges of his new reality. He had weathered the remarkable transformation from victim to survivor.

So far.

He knew George—a good man who allowed himself to be guided into a tarnished cage of his own invention. Now he had become his own driving force—a force with which to be reckoned.

Sipping his club soda, George said, "Sam, I don't really know who I am these days. Everything I automatically assumed was true and good, and of value, has turned out to be a vicious mirage. Life was hard before, for my alcoholic and workaholic mind. Now I know too much. I know I can never go back. I'm hopeful for Kate and me, but all this other stuff…"

Sam's practiced interrogator's eye revealed the lad's last statement were epiphanies of the highest order. Major admissions of not one character defect in a single sentence, but *two?* Yes, George would be fine. He needed to be sure.

Otherwise, a loose end.

George told Sam he felt he could tell him anything.

"At any rate, new news! Kate and I are now active members of Alcoholics Anonymous, we're both working with sponsors, and engaged in *the program*, not only to sustain our sobriety but to improve our spiritual fitness, and to help others do the same. Can you believe it? Mr. Agnostic and Mrs. Atheist now possess a higher purpose!

"When I aimed your gun at Dent's chest that night out on the harbor, Sam, and I pulled that damn trigger, the raging storm around us was nothing but a trivial reflection of the naked rage in my heart and mind.

"Then when I realized he'd survived my attack, as corny as it sounds, I think I had what some might call a spiritual awakening. Look, I know it sounds weird, especially saying it out loud, but for the first time, maybe ever, I'm feeling pretty damn good. I'll always miss those who'll never be able to feel good again, but life goes on. Sorry. Sappy stuff, right?"

Sam just looked at George, head cocked to his left with the slightest hint of his enigmatic smile.

Too bad there isn't an organization called Executives Anonymous for kids growing up believing the American Dream is little more than a nexus to the Lexus and babies in the Mercedes. It is so much more, and less, as George is now finding out.

"Good for you, Old Son."

Yes, George would be okay.

The two homeland warriors seemed comfortable simply sitting in silence for a while when George noticed a curious red dot appear in the center of Sam's forehead. George heard a brief sound like wooden chairs scraping a concrete floor. Then that sound stopped and the red dot disappeared.

A dozen sea gulls flared up with raucous squawks overhead. Something agitated their annoying ritual of pestering incoming fishing boats that flushed their onboard bait wells overboard.

Sam's cell rang. George smiled at the ring tone—Peter Gunn's theme song. He touched the answer button on his Bluetooth ear piece, waited a moment, and simply said, "Copy. Thanks." He tapped the same button to terminate the five second call.

Lunch went on. George was confused. The odor of his now cold grouper sandwich, not to mention his curiosity, had obviously killed his appetite.

"Sam, what just happened?"

Sam smiled. It was a brittle grin. His ears and eyes, although geriatric, missed nothing, including the dark blue hull fifty yards away in the marina with a shattered windshield and vaporized pilothouse windows.

"An attempt was just made on our lives, George."

He took another measured bite of his Caesar's Salad. His digestive track required careful feeding these days.

"Too many anchovies in this dressing, I'm afraid. Too fishy."

George meant his response to sound cynical but came out rather casual, like such occurrences were everyday fare.

"Of course. Customary lunch at the marina with a friend who is a high-value target, assassin neutralized before extinguishing both our lives. End of job. Why am I not surprised? C'mon, Sam, seriously? Is hanging around you always going to be like this? Is this what retirement for spooks is like? Boredom is never the issue, is it?"

"Careful, George. You sound like the intelligence operative you've become. By the way, what makes you think you're not also a high-value target?

"Look, I will share a confidence with you. Ever since *Bandit One* blew up *Sojourn*, and your friend Maxine was killed, we've all been under a blanket of cross-agency protection, what we call *assertive surveillance*—your employees, Kate, you, me, my old friend Sergei... That means we've been carefully watched—each by multiple high-level operatives whose rules of engagement are to *protect, detect, and detain with prejudice if necessary.*

"In other words, they don't let anything happen to us, they watch for bad guys, and if there is a threat, they shoot to disable, not to kill. We're always looking for additional sources of HUMINT. Translated, we'd dearly like to have another opportunity to try out some bleeding-edge interrogation techniques on another soldier of the Brotherhood."

Sam's expression clearly broadcast the message, *don't ask.* This was just one operator chatting freely with another.

"We strongly suspected an outstanding contract on me personally, at least, after my name was carelessly linked with the initial NSA deep probe into *Bandit One's* background. This was when we were just dealing with a psychopath under a thin cover.

"After several of your team were, retired, we couldn't be absolutely sure who or what the driver might be. So, no chances."

Before George could react to the reference to his deceased employees who had become his friends before they were murdered, Sam quickly moved on.

"So we're flushing the pipeline, so to speak. You and I were once again the bait to flush out a potential outstanding contract. Apologies, but we needed to get this one behind us.

"While nothing prevents someone from initiating another contract, neutralizing this current threat sends a strong message. There are no more soft targets out here."

BOREDOM BECAME ENOCH SLATTERY'S FOE.

He assumed his team's role in the current gig would wind down soon. After all, that disgruntled foot soldier, Denton Canfield, no longer a factor. The report of his death at the hand of his old boss was welcome news—a freebie. One less tattered thread on which someone could tug.

Still troubling, however, was this annoying retired spook named Doctor F. Samuel Braxton. What kind of a name was that, anyway? Sounded more like the name of an assassin.

So after the good Doctor's location was pinpointed here in Southwest Florida, he decided to personally get in on the fun before it was too late.

Once on scene, he'd called off his other two operatives so he could deal with this part of the cleanup himself. No muss, just a little target practice to keep his craft current.

They'd had eyes on Canfield's old boss, George Janis, a known associate of Braxton's. Through his sniper scope, from his perch in a nearby high rise that overlooked Janis's building's entrance, he observed Braxton arrive at Janis's condo.

Enoch had disposed of his perch's geriatric owner who now rested in eternal peace in a bathtub of cool water to slow down the decomposition, as much as he enjoyed that smell.

Braxton exited the condo with Janis on crutches. He observed them slowly crossing a small parking lot before passing through a pedestrian gate, disappearing momentarily under the dense foliage of foxtail palms arched over the gate. Slattery once again caught sight of them entering the local restaurant down a short path on the far side of the gate.

Anticipating they'd be there for a while, he quickly packed up and relocated to an empty cabin cruiser in the marina's south basin, looking directly into the restaurant's dining room windows, *and* he commanded a clear view of the outside dining area under the covered deck. That was where he got good eyes on the prize.

He seemed to be totally undetected. Perfect. After setting up his beloved American-made carbon-fiber beauty, a CheyTac M300 Intervention sniper rifle, he gently inserted its precision clip containing seven .408 rounds, which should be more than enough. He cycled the bolt.

Then he waited.

Slattery stabilized his weapon on its bipod legs, its feet rested on the cockpit dash of the lovely thirty-four foot Albin, an enclosed raised pilothouse weekend cruiser with swing-up windshield panels. Less than three inches of the business end of his flat-black barrel protruded into the sunlight.

He spotted the two of them in the center reticle of his precision Swiss-made scope, as they lazily sat and chatted at a waterside table on the deck overlooking the marina, in full sun, no less, frontal view, and stationary.

The assassin gods were smiling on him today.

As he lit up the good doctor and began to relax his breathing, he was about to begin his slow squeeze of the M300's trigger between heart beats. Before he could increase the pressure of his trigger finger, however...

Slattery had no explanation.

At that precise moment, he just released the butt of his rifle; it fell heavily onto the boat's dash, seemingly of its own accord. Simultaneously, an unseen force threw him back and to his left side, instantly unconscious from massive trauma and shock. His brain just turned out the lights.

Had Slattery retained consciousness, he would have seen both his arms were penetrated by medium caliber rounds, but caused no major arterial damage.

The humerus of both upper arms, however, shattered with surgical precision, and left his trigger finger dangling at the end of a now-useless appendage.

HAT TRICK

OCTOBER 2008
POTOMAC, MARYLAND

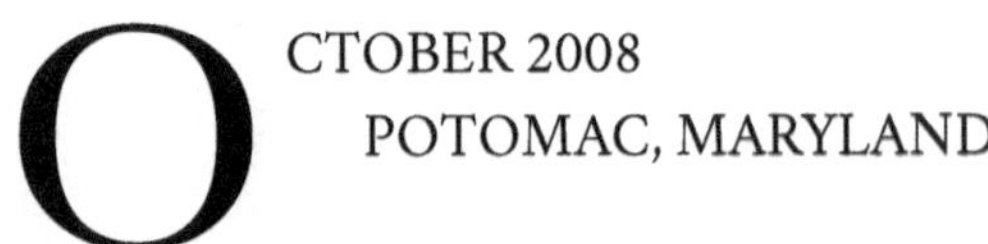

Malcolm Frieburg wasn't frightened.

But he was concerned.

Despite all his attempts to connect with his friend and counselor, he hadn't heard from Enoch Slattery in over forty-eight hours. That *never* happened.

Something was wrong.

He recalled a recent conversation with Enoch.

"Malc, I want you to once again recommit to me."

They'd had this conversation many times before.

"If you don't hear from me for more than seventy-two hours, ever, something is very wrong. We've discussed this. Execute *Hat Trick*. Promise me… Can you commit to that, one more time, unequivocally? This is vital."

"Absolutely, Bossman. You can count on me."

To Malc, it seemed an overly dramatic precaution, but Enoch was the man, a legend.

According to their agreement, a sacred oath between two high-level operatives, *Hat Trick* was a top-priority. Ever the operators, they code-worded this contingency plan.

Only Malc and a handful of senior operatives in their organization of mercs knew of its existence.

Early the following morning, clouded by dread for his friend and guide, he found himself giddy with guilty anticipation. The security guard opened the front door of the nondescript Wells Fargo Bank on Falls Road.

Hat Trick stipulated Malc would assume Enoch's mantle of leadership. Vital information awaited in a safe deposit box. The assumption? Something or someone compromised Enoch.

Malc would receive precise directives to destroy certain documents and files, to change keywords and passwords, to move funds and personnel. He would establish new double-blind communication channels with specific operators. And Enoch's written instructions would mandate that he move certain digital and hardcopy information to a location known only to Malc.

He'd then craft *Hat Trick 2.0* with a successor of *his* choice after the prescribed brief wait time. And so the covert chain of succession would prevail.

Malc wore that safe deposit key around his neck for almost a year. Should Enoch show up later, he'd resume control with Malc's close cooperation and they'd establish a new set of contingencies. No question. *Hat Trick* would then just be part of Malc's tradecraft.

The time arrived. After seventy-two hours of deafening silence, Malc opened the triple-briefcase-size box in the bank's opulent private viewing chamber. Stacked its contents on the small glossy table.

So began Malc's review with some bound paper journals. Then, less than a minute later...

"Holy shit!"

As many briefings as Enoch conducted with him, the cache of info carried Malc beyond his wildest imagination. He wasn't looking at dynamite. He was handling an armed weapon of mass destruction.

As Malc gazed at the materials scattered across the slick surface of the high-top table, what he saw paralyzed him. With difficulty, he arrested his reverie and continued to scan a phenomenal body of intel.

He scanned lists and descriptions of operations, financial transactions, small journals describing dirt on major public figures, pay-offs, including long-standing blackmail transactions with the title 'Annuities' going back years.

Now jittery, Malc backed off a step and surveyed the treasure trove. He guessed the DVDs and flash drives contained thousands of incendiary images. Enoch labeled each with provocative and descriptive titles in various colors.

A hard plastic case protecting each DVD featured copious handwritten tables of contents with legends for a simple but comprehensive color coding. They cross-referenced back to various hard-copy journals in the box.

There was more. Much more. This stuff had obviously been collected over *decades*.

He glanced over his shoulder to ensure nobody else was in the tiny room with the frosted green-glass door. The fancy gold-tone deadbolt remained in place.

Not seeing any cameras either, he shoved the array of explosive materials into the oversized briefcase he brought with him. The thing now weighed at least thirty pounds. More a medium-size suitcase than a briefcase.

Before departing the private viewing room, he once again donned a mask of neutrality. Difficult but not impossible. The volume of materials also forced him to pack every huge cargo pocket of his olive drab Army jacket—briefcase overflow.

Malc shivered. He exited the bank into the sunlight dappling Falls Road through the trees.

Even though the street appeared the same as when he had entered the bank thirty-three minutes earlier, he knew he'd just entered into another world that played by a very different set of rules visible to perhaps a handful of people... anywhere.

OFF THE BOOKS

W ASHINGTON, DC

General Renfro's working group met.

But they gathered in a conference room in the basement of the relatively obscure but secure Sydney Yates building, just off the National Mall, home of the US Forest Service. In other words, this was the last place anyone would suspect an Executive Branch working group to meet.

They could afford no prying eyes or ears.

There was to be no written evidence of these meetings on calendars or planners, electronic or otherwise, emails, text messages, desk blotters, legal pads, phone conversations, or Post-It-Notes. Neither was there to be any discussions outside the meetings between members, via voicemails or recordings.

Nothing.

Each member of the group personally heard from the president himself that any leaks of the group's membership or activities would be considered a violation of confidentiality, and would be prosecuted as an act of high treason.

The group comprised a well-vetted top- or high-level member from each of DoJ, DoD, NSA, FBI, CIA, State, and the Center for Anti-Terrorism, which was a cross-functional team of specialists in its own right.

The Republican Congressman from West Virginia, Charles Delaney, and the Democratic Senator from Texas, Matilda Hilley were also in attendance. Both members of Congress were Chairpersons of their respective intelligence oversight committees within the 110th United States Congress.

Select consultants included Colonel Sam Braxton and two others of whom Sam knew by reputation from within CIA and DIA Operations, respectively.

With this formidable panel assembled, they were briefed on President Stevens's directives and preliminary findings and draft recommendations to date. Each was astounded by the magnitude of the corruption and penetration into politics, business, military and law enforcement on a state, national, and international scale.

They knew the president demanded a comprehensive plan of action by the deadline, now just ten days out. Meeting twice each day, with each member essentially working around the clock offline to flesh out their respective assignments, this was already an exhausting beginning. But each member was invigorated by the profound opportunity to protect American democracy.

General Renfro summarized.

"Ladies and gentlemen, as we've discussed, the plan must satisfy a number of high priority objectives.

"First, at the highest level, confidence must remain strong in our system of government, and in the current administration. This is job one.

"Second, we need to craft a precise recommendation to pursue large scale criminal and civil actions with the appropriate optics. This means actions should not appear as a broad centrally coordinated attack on a single enemy. Rather, these actions must appear as decentralized as possible, and unrelated to job one.

"As we discussed with the president, even though a centralized campaign would be a major political coup for the administration, he demands that we place the health of the republic ahead of his own scoreboard. As POTUS put it, 'I'm just a lame duck anyway.' We will miss this president.

"Third, we'll flesh out a *visible* plan of action with specific accommodations for a *covert* layer beneath it. The latter is the weapon we aim at the most treasonous members of this Brotherhood.

"Some, like *Bandit Three*, a Palmer Xavier, whose treasonous connections appear to be at the highest levels, would be taken off the board, first by public means, that is, legal prosecution, for the purpose of public optics. Once indicted, we follow up with a covert interrogation by virtue of the Patriot Act of 2001, behind closed doors.

"In his case, and perhaps a few others, we see an opportunity to gain additional intel on the Brotherhood employing interrogation tactics with fewer constraints than, ah, more traditional law enforcement methods."

At this comment, FBI Director Martin Foreman winced. Admiral Mannheim from NSA simply retained his neutral mask, offered the hint of a nod.

The General continued.

"Other less public figures, like the Brotherhood's assasin *Bandit Two*, a certain Enoch Slattery, will be dealt with in a more straightforward manner. No need to manage public optics. Nobody who wears a white hat ever heard of this ghost except us. We'll keep it that way. Extraction of intel will be the top priority with this traitor and others like him.

"Fourth, the formulation of tactics and strategy with respect to international elements should be far simpler yet—search and destroy.

"The US Intelligence Community confirmed unmistakable evidence of a massive army of foreign trolls, that is, cyberspace operatives. Their primary focus is to influence the upcoming elections. These trolls are spreading disinformation online via social media, e-Journalism, activist blogs, as well as targeting secure government email servers. They also employ other channels, leaking false sensationalistic stories to web sites such as DCLeaks and WikiLeaks.

"Nearly all of these trolls' propaganda originates from erstwhile Soviet block countries, coordinated out of a central troll hole near Moscow, and reportedly enjoys sponsorship from the top.

"So diplomacy is not an issue here, ladies and gentlemen, only defining appropriate covert retaliation - non-lethal, but unambiguous. Details TBD. Quickly, I trust."

General Renfro was extremely confident of this international facet of the action plan since the US Intelligence Community, or USIC, a cross-agency group representing no less than sixteen government and private sector intelligence organizations, all came to the same incontrovertible conclusion. The Russians were coordinating an attack on America in cyberspace in an effort to sway American elections to candidates of their choosing.

Elizabeth Filbiss from State chimed in at the risk of interrupting the general's rhythm.

"General, we just need to be confident we are not viewed as violating any sovereign nations' rights. At the risk of stating the obvious, we need bulletproof deniability."

"Agreed, Elizabeth. Despite the risk of carrying out covert operations on foreign soil, we've all agreed to execute aggressive actions post-haste. Sending the strongest possible message to the Brotherhood's leadership, and more importantly, to meddlesome foreign regimes, one in particular, is vital to our National Security.

"But quite frankly, and this comes from our Commander-in-Chief, if the Russians are offended, let them go straight to Hell. We are *way* past sanctions and afternoon tea. All due respect."

The General looked slightly apologetic for his colorful use of language and strident tone, and his last phrase was issued in a more subdued tone; however, he left no doubt they were moving on.

"Bought and paid-for low-level domestic election officials and state law enforcement officials, on the other hand, will require specialized attention. All who have been identified as receiving payoffs for services rendered will be addressed in a staged fashion over a period of months; however, all will be placed on notice to cease and desist immediately, under threat of more direct means of prosecution, including corruption charges, or worse, that would destroy each of them personally as well as professionally.

"If they lawyer up, DoJ will cross that bridge on an individual basis as necessary."

Swift decisions chased brief discussions.

The nature and delivery of such a notice to hundreds of US citizens continued to be a sensitive and controversial discussion. Its necessity and urgency, however, was not. Most clear was the imminent threat the election officials' actions posed with respect to potential impact on the approaching 2008 national elections. In many cases, it was already too late, with the elections only weeks away.

Once again, Sam Braxton reflected.

He recalled the prescient words of Dent Canfield after his capture, *"You won't be able to stop them, but maybe you can do some damage, slow them down."*

The working group slaved prodigiously to meet the President's aggressive deadline. At the beginning of each meeting, General Renfro repeated, "Look, people, I'll continue to remind you of the critical importance of confidentiality and the element of surprise. Remember, screw up on this, and you *will* be prosecuted with extreme prejudice. That's firing squad material, folks."

He was not merely firing for effect. And everyone knew it.

AFTER EACH MEETING, THE SAME MESSAGE.

He'd repeat some variation on the theme, "We must deal decisively with a large group of players who wield tremendous influence, who would not only violate the Constitution of the United States of America but who would brutally murder Democracy and personal freedoms of our citizens in the process.

"We must convince POTUS we are proceeding assiduously, but once we deliver our recommendations to him, advise him to act aggressively.

"So let's get back to work on offline assignments to be completed before the next meeting. Thank you, ladies and gentlemen."

THEN A CALL SURPRISED SAM.

A few hours after the group's most recent meeting, he was invited to one of the more unusual dates he could recall. Usually he did the inviting.

The phone call arrived the previous day from someone on General Renfro's staff. A car would be sent for him. He was to wait in front of his hotel, a historical building now occupied by the Hampton Inn on H Street, just five minutes from the White House. At high noon, no less. He excused himself from the group.

When he stepped into the limo just fifteen seconds earlier, and his seventy-nine-year old eyes adjusted to its dim interior, the General himself greeted him.

"Sir, this is an unexpected honor. How can I serve?"

"An appropriate inquiry, Colonel Braxton. Consider yourself reactivated in the US Army."

"Um, of course, Sir. Toward what end, if I may inquire further?"

The last word came out a deep-south *fuh-thuh.*

"I have no right to ask, Sam, but I need your help. Recall our group's discussion with respect to foreign cyberspace operatives? We need to prosecute them, but the administration needs deniability, whether POTUS admits to that or not. That's where your, um, group of irregulars come into play.

"You've executed a series of master strokes drawing this massive conspiracy out of the shadows, outside any official sanction, or visibility. You have a sensitive hand on the wheel. Masterful.

"It occurs to me that you are just the man to pull together an off-the-books operation for the current situation, prosecuting these Russian trolls. What say you, Colonel?"

"I know better than to ask how you know about my irregulars." Sam displayed a knowing smile. "Rules of engagement, Sir?"

"Send them a message, Colonel, the origin of which they can only speculate, as we said in the meeting, in a conspicuously unambiguous manner. I'd prefer minimum casualties with maximum impact. Can do?"

This conversation made Sam very nervous, but he would never refuse an opportunity to perform his patriotic duty. That trait defined him. The General surely knew this.

Nevertheless, he'd need to do some homework.

"Of course. Sir, while we shouldn't need a safety net while in-country, the team may need some cover upon their return. If that's acceptable, I'll consult my guys, and will keep you posted. You personally, Sir?"

"My eyes only, Colonel. Thank you, Sam. I owe you."

When not in uniform, formal salutes were not required. That did not stop these two patriots from saluting one another out of mutual respect in the dim cabin of that limo that day.

The limo dropped Sam off in the precise location at which he'd been picked up six minutes earlier.

~

PUNTA GORDA, FLORIDA

GEORGE ATTEMPTED TO WEAN HIMSELF.

He was not a true obsessive-compulsive, but he did suffer, and sometimes benefit, from an addictive personality. When he did something, it was always in a big way: work, play, booze, pills…

So he was leery of overdoing the pain meds, the OxyContin in particular. He still suffered from Dent's attack—that nasty little bat. At least he could now walk without crutches, albeit with a limp.

Then his cell rang as he sat on the enclosed lanai of his Florida condo with the floor-to-ceiling glass sliders thrown open, enjoying an afternoon sea breeze off the Gulf. He glanced at the caller ID.

"Sam? Haven't heard from you since we were almost assassinated together down here. Are you in town?"

"Well, George, I'm delighted to find you sounding lucid. I'm still in DC. Sounds like you're recovering from your injuries, yes?"

"Ah, it seems my neurologist says nerve decompression surgery might be indicated in my not-too-distant future. This is due partially from the attack by our old friend, Dented Damage, which exacerbated a vintage service injury from 1972. That, and arthritis of the spine grown progressively worse over the last forty years. Oh well. To what do I owe the pleasure, *Dock-tore Sam?*"

This was in jest. Sam had told him that his old Russian friend, Sergei, called him some version of that.

"Funny you should call me that just now, George. Are you at home, are you alone, and am I on speaker?"

"Yup to the first two, nope to the third. Just enjoying my retirement. At last. Kate's playing a round of golf with the girls. What's up?"

"I've come to trust your counsel a great deal, George, and I need extremely unofficial help. Again. I remember you mentioning a friend of yours named Calvin. You shared with me several stories of his colorful history. Do you trust him personally? I mean, would you trust him with your life?"

"Calvin Pierce? Wow, ah, yes I do and yes, I guess I would, Sam… absolutely. I've never worked with him like I have with you, but I believe his stories are genuine and that his role in them were as he's represented. He's a good guy and has never let me down when I've asked for his help. He has always exceeded my personal expectations. So yeah, I do trust Calvin. He's just a little overwhelming to be around sometimes. Now I'm curious. Why, Sam?"

"Normally, I'd hop on a plane and come brief you, but I'm pressed for time. Do me the small favor of calling him. If you're willing, tell him you trust me like you trust him. Nothing else. I'll contact him in two hours. Can do, old friend?"

"Uh, sure Sam. Whatever you need. You know that. I'll give you his number. Will I find out what this is all about, sooner or later?"

"Of course, George, just not now. And I have his number, as well as his complete dossier. You forget who you're talking with, Old Son? Gotta run, and thanks again."

George's perplexing smile lasted long after he heard Sam abruptly disconnect.

This is gonna get good.

OD

C ALVIN *"OD"* Pierce was not ordinary.

He did, however, possess extraordinary appetites. Dubbed *OD* by his colleagues in days past, it was short for *OverDose*. If the average guy met him on the street, he'd think Calvin an exaggerated eccentric, certainly not a druggie.

His stories seemed like the most outrageous tales any cheap pulp novelist might hope to conjure. When George met Calvin twenty years earlier, he was short, loud, slightly overweight, wore coke bottle spectacles, and dressed like the blue collar mechanic he was.

He talked like a nerd, but a supremely confident nerd. He didn't swear much or use his arms to make a demonstrative point, and he was forever making a demonstrative point—mostly just with the force of his considerable lungs.

No, he didn't use drugs or alcohol. As he'd say, "That crap's for pussies." He just overdid everything, including political incorrectness. But the moniker *OverDo* just didn't do him justice.

This guy was a massive overdose of adrenaline-seeking reality captured in the heart of a soldier. Ironically, he'd never served in the military, but he did serve.

Thirty-odd years ago, Calvin married Matty. Both he and Matty were on their second marriages. She described her first husband as a *pussy*. He described his first wife the same.

Nobody could imagine how a guy like Calvin landed a gal like Matty. She was Calvin's bold beauty as he was her raging beast. But they were two of a kind.

Calvin, an exceptional jet aircraft mechanic of some repute, started with Boeing but quickly became bored. They didn't want to lose him, so they threw every weird and interesting job at him to retain him. A job in Saudi Arabia held his interest the longest.

He moved to Riyadh to supervise the application of a set of complex and necessary engineering changes to brand new state-of-the-art military jet fighters sold to the Saudis' Royal Air Force.

Sand country operations required certain modifications to these planes, designed in Washington state, where sand was as rare as a summer deluge in Riyadh. For a few years, Calvin's office was a hangar outside of Riyadh, at the heart of the Saudis' largest base.

Matty, despite her flamboyant Technicolor demeanor, went to live with Calvin, which shocked most of her hard-core feminist friends. They could not imagine Matty in a Muslim country, especially in *the* city of Muslim hardliners—Riyadh.

This was during the time when only a woman's eyes, particularly those of an infidel woman, were allowed public exposure. What was worse, Matty wasn't allowed anywhere without a male escort. Yet, Matty thrived. As usual.

Matty likened the experience to bringing herself to the delicious quivering edge of a frenzied climax but stopping just short so as to prolong the anticipation of the inevitable happy ending. She described their time in Riyadh as a three-year orgasm she carried around in a secret pocket underneath her black abaya.

Calvin's wife was larger-than-life-quirky, just like her outrageous husband. Both Matty and Calvin projected confidence and power. Matty reminded George a lot of Kate.

After Riyadh, once again restless, Calvin worked for a string of charter airlines, usually a few years at a time, before being courted elsewhere for more pay and more outrageous sorties.

Traveling with a small trusted crew of mechanics aboard large chartered aircraft for which he was responsible, he found his niche at Global International Airlines.

There wasn't a plane he couldn't diagnose and repair. Exclusively a charter business, GIA's wings-for-hire went anywhere, anytime, but most often, either their departure or their destination, frequently both, involved some third-world dung pit of which most civilized folks knew little or nothing.

Calvin could mix and carelessly butcher countless languages like nobody else, often blending them egregiously in the same sentence. We're not talking French, or Spanish or even Latin. Nor are we talking highborn dialects. Calvin's distinctive repertoire consisted of gutter slang and blasphemous profanity locals shouted to survive in the streets and jungles of Angola, Nepal, Laos, Viet Nam, Ethiopia, Tanzania…

His fluency in the language known as *American Express Black Card* with no credit limit, however, never failed to bridge any residual language or cultural gaps.

George remembered the first time he met Calvin. Back then, George hadn't heard his nickname—most normal folks hadn't. They met through Kate and Matty. Kate found homes for her pups under the auspices of the Irish Wolfhound Club of America. Matty purchased one. From there, the two couples became fast friends. It took a while.

The first time George met Calvin for an opportunity to just hang out, it was, ungainly, to say the least. At least for George.

From the living room of Calvin's very nice new but modest town home in the Minneapolis suburb of Burnsville, the two men sat in comfortable over-stuffed loungers angled toward each other in a rather small and minimalistic living room. They faced a bay window that overlooked a grassy micro-boulevard.

"So Calvin, you're a mechanic?"

Awkwardly filling a quiet moment after the girls abandoned them to go shopping at the Mall of America, George didn't mean to sound condescending, but it might have come off that way. Calvin didn't seem to notice. Apparently he flew at an altitude and cruising speed well above that. George would come to realize that the entire notion of *normal* was fiction. At least for Calvin.

"Yup. I fix planes. Took a nasty fifteen-foot fall off a slick wing onto a concrete hangar floor a while back. Now I'm on disability, so I rebuild vintage Porsche nine-elevens out in the garage. Pretty well known for that too, I guess. There's even one of those fancy coffee table books featuring celebrities' nine-elevens that I've restored. Most even credit my work. Not that I'm an egoist or anything, but to be blunt, I'm that good."

He delivered a crooked grin. Joking? No? Yeah, right. Oh boy. Who *is* this guy?

"Awesome... so you're a car guy." George wasn't a mechanic guy, an airplane guy *or* a car guy, obviously, thinking a grease monkey is a grease monkey, even if the grease is airborne or upscale German, but this grease monkey seemed articulate enough.

Okay, so George now *knew* he *was* acting like a condescending white-collar jerk, or at least thinking like one. He was, after all, only used to hanging out with other white-collar jerks.

Jeez, I gotta throttle back the careless attitude. This guy could be interesting, but it's gonna take some effort.

George reflected that he really enjoyed being around interesting people, as long as they weren't trying to deceive him. Sometimes even that was stimulating, but a little of that...

At that moment, however, his BS detector was begging for action.

Calvin continued.

"Yeah. I like to work on cars, planes, any kind of interesting mechanical device, really. But exotic cars really get me running through the gears. I spent some time in The Kingdom. Met quite a few young oil sheiks who had too many cars in their stable. Daddy says, 'Okay, you can buy another one, Sonny Prince, but first, you peddle one to make room. Our garage only has seventeen stalls, after all.'" Calvin tried to imitate a wealthy Arab, failing comically.

In his own voice, he said matter-of-factly, "So they'd dump a perfectly good, low mileage, Maserati Bi-Turbo, or an extremely limited edition Ferrari F4, maybe with a few 150 MPH sand pits in the paint on the nose, just to get rid of it, so they could buy their next hard-on with Daddy's bottomless well of oil bucks."

"So you were collecting exotic cars cast aside by oil sheiks." A statement, not a question. Incredulity crept unintentionally into George's voice. Again, Calvin seemed not to notice. It was almost as if he were used to folks not believing his fantastical stories.

"Nah. Don't be ridiculous. Wouldn't work... collecting. I didn't even have a garage. But, I'd buy 'em, ship 'em to the States in a container, spend ten grand to EPA-ize each of 'em, and then peddle 'em. I've acquired quite a few specialized contacts.

"My sweetest deal was a Ferrari Formula One, the 312 F1-69, chassis number seventeen. I loved that car, which was not at all street legal, by the way, but was strictly a one-off built by Scuderia Ferrari himself. What was particularly appealing was that 1969 was the worst year in Ferrari's long Grand Prix history. It was special because it was plagued by engine troubles, never finished, and failed to complete a single race in South Africa or in Spain, despite being driven by one of the world's best GP drivers. That car never even made it to Monaco."

*This guy has a perverted sense of what **special** means.*

"Ended up in a used car lot near Riyadh, abused and neglected, with a price tag scrawled on the windshield with white soap—just thirty thousand SR. That's Saudi Riyals. About a hundred grand US at the time. I knew they didn't know what they had.

"So I snapped it up and sold it as-is for a half-mil to a pretty famous GP driver. He still scored a helluva deal. Didn't actually have the hundred K at the time, so I had to move it fast.

"Matty and I went to Monaco for an extended vacation to the granddaddy Grand Prix that year. Pissed it away. Good times."

"Wow! Quite a story, Calvin"

"Yeah, cars are cool. I like unusual handheld stuff too because you really gotta design the heck outta something to make it functional and portable - especially weapons."

Oh boy. Here we go. George wasn't a *gun guy* either. He wondered, *Do we have anything at all in common? Doubtful. Definitely a rocky start.*

"Take the Russian RPG, for example. Those turkeys really screwed up a lot of their technology stuff, but they came through with *that* little trinket. Precision-effective, pretty lightweight, and unlike a lot of their crap, even reliable."

"You have a rocket propelled grenade launcher." A statement sopping wet with skepticism and disbelief. George only read about them in Tom Clancy novels.

Calvin picked up on George's blatant tone, seemingly shocked that his word might not be received as gospel.

Hook baited and set.

"Well, yeah, George. Wanna see it?"

True to his word, much to George's incredulity now laced with chagrin, Calvin limped down the hallway, disappeared into what George assumed was a spare bedroom, returned less than a minute later.

Awkwardly toting a Russian RPG with both arms, he held the vile tube vertically in front of him so as not to chip the narrow hallway's painted sheetrock. Complete with complex Cyrillic script on the side, red trigger lever, the works. It wreaked of violence and carnage. Chipped paint and a dented surface provided evidence that the weapon had seen action. Calvin offered it to George.

"Wanna heft it? Surprisingly light, for what this baby can do."

"Ah, jeez… son-of-a-bitch, Calvin! No, I'm good. Really."

Holy Hell in a surface-to-surface tank-killing grenade launcher!

Matter-of-factly, Calvin grinned, set it down carefully, leaned it against the sheetrock wall next to his easy chair. He explained that he'd picked it up from 'an acquaintance in the Kingdom' who specialized in such wares.

"Only cost me five hundred SR, including three rounds and a user's manual."

He was clearly very proud of that deal, especially that it came with the frickin' manual. In Russian.

George supposed he needed to look impressed at that point.

"I left the rounds in the bedroom. No need taking foolish risks, eh George?"

Calvin was now having genuine fun.

"When you fly your own planes, as we did, annoying customs crap is usually not a factor, unless you flirt with a major first-world airport, of course."

That nerdy lopsided grin again.

"Life is short. Matty and I decided we're just gonna enjoy the ride. Man, I could tell you stories."

He'd already burned through a half dozen stories in a half-hour. Barely believable, but apparently credible.

From then on, George was determined to listen to them all. He decided this guy was the real deal, unlike most of the people he knew. Close friends were different, of course.

This character and me? We could be friends, if he could put up with my snotty attitude, that is.

For the next twenty years or so, George devoured as many of the truly fascinating stories as Calvin was willing to shovel. Even though they rarely got together. Any time he felt a reading on the BS-detector register—and cried foul—Calvin invariably validated every outrageous tale of suspense and intrigue.

The guy even knew Ollie North. About him he said, "Oh yeah, intense guy, moved him around quite a bit. Pretty light on his feet. Said his boss, Nixon, was a gold-plated Dick though. Who knew, eh?"

George's favorite? One of Calvin's transport planes got caught on the ground in Angola. Calvin spun the yarn.

"While still airborne, our cargo of forty serious young men didn't talk much, were all heavily armed and in full blackout. My two-man crew and I were politely asked to repair to the cockpit with the flight crew and to close the door.

"Five minutes later, back in the hold with the ramp still open and the cabin depressurized, several dozen large crates labeled *farm equipment* were all that remained in the hold. I punched the red plunger on the bulkhead to retract the ramp.

"Ten minutes after that, we landed as directed. With the ramp down again on a darkened runway, we started rapidly sliding wheeled pallets down the ramp track and onto the tarmac, by the light of a huge half-moon. Op orders were, *AQAFP.*

"Then we heard, 'Ping… ping, ping, ping, thunk.'"

Now Calvin's arms waved around with fingers pointing here and there to illustrate rounds whizzing around in the hold.

"It took a few seconds for us to realize we were taking fire from the jungle. At that point, *As Quick As Freakin' Possible* made a lot of sense.

"The clincher was the moonlight visible through countless bullet holes in various places. We guessed most were about the size of vintage 5.56 NATO rounds. A few were from heavier stuff."

George had never heard stories like this but by now he knew better than to doubt their authenticity.

"With the cargo only partially jettisoned, and the ramp still deployed, we kicked loose the strap releases restraining the rest of the crates. The pilots didn't need prompting.

"Before we knew it, full takeoff power slid the rest of the stuff onto the ground. Some crates broke up. During that auto-dump, I was too preoccupied hanging onto my butt cheeks, spread out prone on the deck to notice what kind of *farm equipment* spilled out.

"Sparks trailed us where the ramp wheels dragged. I knew there was a bullseye painted on the outside of the fuselage precisely where that red plunger was bolted. I thought, *Screw the ramp!*"

Calvin went on, "Nobody got wounded. We called an agency base in Ethiopia to land for repairs, not knowing the extent of our damage. It was a big-ass plane, but there were a lot of holes.

"Anyway, we were cleared to land. During an exchange of status with final approach control, however, they abruptly waved us off at the last possible moment.

'Balked landing procedure. I repeat, balked landing procedure!'

"Apparently, once the controller consulted with his supervisor who learned we had been caught in the open on the ground in Angola, and our tail numbers were likely compromised, we were waved off. No plausible deniability, *no land-ee da plane-ee*.

"So we were rerouted to a black Israeli site somewhere else in Ethiopia for repairs. Those Israelis don't take shit from anybody.

"After landing safely, we learned we had taken 183 rounds, some of which damaged semi-critical systems for which I carried no spares. Of course, we took in the sights while waiting for parts."

Calvin was instantly prepared to launch into *yet another funny story*.

"Yeah, one time, we were hired to carry a bunch of village elders out of Nairobi to Mecca for Ramadan, and the jungle rubes started a cook fire between the seats in an exit row..."

Since those early days, Calvin, George, Matty, and Kate were fast friends.

More than friendship, they shared a deep trust in each other.

AIR PIRATES

B URNSVILLE, MINNESOTA

Doctor Sam was now Colonel Sam.

Again.

He caught a commercial flight to Minneapolis—cattle class—and drove out to Burnsville on a Monday afternoon in a rented Ford Focus to meet with Calvin Pierce. He was expected. Calvin's wife Matty went shopping. She knew the drill. She was gone before Sam arrived.

With one look and a handshake, Calvin sized up this guy as a high-level operator. "Nice to meet you, Colonel. George speaks very highly of you. So which agency?"

Sam smiled. He instructed George to tell this guy nothing more than his trust in him. Sam liked Calvin already. Perceptive.

"I'm retired Army, but have been reactivated for a specific operation: short term and off the books. Do you understand, Mr. Pierce?"

"Sure. And it's just Calvin. Somebody needs deniability, am I right? Old school. You're the spook who's been recruited to do the deed. Now you're assembling a team of ghosts. Yeah, I get it. Now, Colonel, no pretenses. Why are you here? In my home? I'm ancient history."

"Okay, Calvin, I'll lay it out. Highly confidential, et cetera. George and I stumbled onto something big. Here's what's directly relevant. Russia is polluting our election process. We need to send them the clear message: that's not acceptable. We've located a hard target that needs neutralizing. I need transportation for a covert team to and from."

"Okay. Location?"

"We've turned one of the opposition—one of George's ex-employees, actually. He assisted us in isolating the target. Is suburban Moscow an issue?"

"One of George's guys? Son-of-a-bitch. Didn't see that coming. Always knew there was a reason I like that boy. *Muscva* is lovely this time of year. Will require some planning, depending on an urban or rural landing strip. How about funding?"

"Probably not. The intelligence community is compromised. Maybe some on the back side. Will that be a problem?"

"Naw, don't think so. I know a crew who can scrounge, and they're used to operating *way* off the rez."

"Discreet?"

"Like a hole in the night, Colonel. I'll holler if any money issues, but these guys have their own resources, especially when it comes to sending a message to their old Muscovite buddies who are a bunch 'a hovering drones, for the most part. Worse than Washington, but more accessible." Calvin's playful smile made Sam slightly nervous.

Calvin continued, "Timeline?"

"ASAP."

"Got it. Do you have secure comms with you?"

Sam nodded, and within the time it took to pop the buckles on his beat-up old-fashioned top-loading briefcase, he decided which of his two satellite phones to offer Calvin. Since they were in a northern latitude, an urban area, and required sustained signal strength to complete encryption handshaking, he selected the Iridium.

After keying in the security sequence, Sam handed it to Calvin. The unspoken implication: Sam toted both a Plan A and a Plan B. He saw Calvin understood. Two experienced operators communing.

"Shall we repair to the patio?"

Calvin's head bobbled side-to-side as if top-heavy, mocking a pretentious aristocrat, pronouncing the words in an exaggerated Boston society accent. Not waiting for an answer, Calvin arose to relocate the party so the phone could find a strong signal to the geostationary birds necessary for a solid connection to most anywhere on the globe. Hadn't used one in a few years.

Sam followed, noticing Calvin's determined stride despite a pronounced limp as he punched in a number.

And so began Sam's one-sided monitoring of a most unusual dialogue.

"Hey, ya old bastard! How they hangin'?" Probably code for *Are you still a player?*

Sam was fairly sure this *was* some sort of street code. Code even while using an encrypted sat phone? Jeez, this guy's careful.

"Nah, just lookin' for something to do. Busy?": *Seeking transport for a mission. Are you available for an op?*

"Cool beans. Hey, we're havin' a party, and your sorry ass is invited, if you're interested, that is. The clubhouse seven p.m. tomorrow night. Hope you can make it. Bring the old lady, and BYOB, dude. I don't want you drinkin' all my booze, okay?": *Copy. Op planning rendezvous at our predetermined location, bring the rest of the crew and necessary equipment, needed or not, and come prepared to discuss contingencies. Need independent (untraceable) source of funding.*

"Okay. See you there, if you show up, that is. Anyway, you're invited. You gonna drive that jacked up Hummer convertible you built? You could show it off some. The gang would drool over her, I'm sure. Cool. Ciao, Dude": *Arrange for heavy transport ASAP. Very covert.*

In and out of a potentially hot zone. Will discuss cover, but full deniability essential. This looks to be fun.

At least that's what Sam speculated they *might* have meant underneath the testosterone-laden banter. He was not wrong.

Calvin handed the phone back to Sam who seemed very impressed.

"You're retired. So how long has it been since you've made contact with this operative?"

"'Made contact? Operative?' Jee-ZEUS, Colonel, you really are regulation red, hot 'n blue, aren't ya. This is just two old buddies gettin' an old fashioned thrill-fest together, starting *'mañana puta noche'*. Get your mind outta the guttah, Son!"

Calvin winked at Sam and smiled that intimidating smirk. Sam reflected just how far off the reservation he had trudged.

Sam smiled to himself. *This is how black ops get done, General Renfro. Starts when you know a guy who knows a guy...*

With just a few of Calvin's colorful but efficient phone phrases, *obscurum per obscurius*, or *the unclear explained by means of the more unclear*, Sam knew the foundation of the mission was already laid.

The two operators spent the next two hours discussing specifics. Sam would brief Calvin's crew on the preliminaries at the rendezvous the following evening.

Sam reflected he must thank George.

Very impressive, indeed.

<h1 style="text-align:center">RENDEZVOUS</h1>

MINNEAPOLIS, MINNESOTA

Calvin OD Pierce retrieved Sam.

Late the following afternoon, Sam stood waiting in front of his third-rate hotel, the LivInn off I-35W in South Minneapolis. Calvin screamed up and screeched to a stop in a fully restored 1965 Porsche 911.

*Now this is another reason why I've always avoided **official** government service all my life.*

It *was* near MSP, though, which was good.

"Hey, Colonel. Mind if I call you Sam? This Colonel crap was fun at first, but kind of a pain now, ya know?"

Sam found himself smiling a lot around this character, "I'd be honored, Calvin, as long as I don't have to call you OD. Fair enough?"

"Oh, you know about that old schtick, huh? I always thought that was a bit corny. Weird how these nicknames stick. My version of Colonel, I guess. An honorary title I spent big to earn, but who stands on formality in the pits, right Colo… Sam?"

"Precisely. So toward what covert rendezvous are we aimed in this subtle red rocket?"

"Ah, Sam, nothin' covert about a guy goin' to work in one of his trademark vehicles. Even though I'm retired, I still come out to trade hangar stories with the local boys I used to work with, before… Well, you know. I'm sure you've scoped out my personal odometer. No matter how you slice it, I'm not a down-low kinda guy. You may have noticed.

"My deal is hiding in plain sight when it doesn't matter, so that when it does, nobody much cares, or even notices. Simple head-on high octane. The highest compliment anybody can pay me is to think of me as a simple-minded purveyor of bullshit. I guess that's why I liked George from day one. Poor guy never knew what hit him."

That smirk again.

"Calvin, you're anything but…"

What a character.

Sam liked Calvin more as critical mission time marched into the past.

They were headed for a large old private hangar on the periphery of MSP, the official designator for the Minneapolis & St. Paul International Airport. As they passed through a security gate off the General Aviation service ramp, Calvin flashed his TWIC card at the TSA guard who passed them through.

TWIC, Sam knew, was an acronym for Transportation Worker's Identification Credentials. This coveted card is required for access to secure areas of airports and seaports within the United States and her possessions, basically ensuring the bearer is not a terrorist and is authorized to go pretty much anywhere within federal security's transportation domain. These same credentials are carried by airport security officers of the Transportation Security Administration.

THEIR DESTINATION LOOKED DESTITUTE.

The giant building appeared to be a little-used, but well-maintained hangar. At least on the inside.

Out front sat a medium-sized cargo plane with no markings on it whatsoever, illegal as Hell, but that didn't seem to matter right now.

Surrounding the sizable twin-engined jet aircraft Sam observed a group of five cars ranging from an older Nissan Sentra to a newer high-end Lexus SUV, along with a few rented pickups. A diverse bunch.

The younger Calvin limped heavily alongside the older Sam's lighter step. Calvin was greeted with hoots 'n hollers as they entered the small open metal service door set in the middle of a huge closed aircraft door.

"Hey! It's OD in the flesh. How they hangin' Bubba?" A repetitious staccato chant ensued, "Oh...Dee! Oh...Dee!"

"Hey, đi f**k mình, ya'll!" Calvin good-naturedly suggested demonstratively in Vietnamese slang that the group might want to attempt sexual selfies. The subsequent indignant cacophony reverberated within the huge hollow space.

After a round of gruff middle-aged man-hugs and fist bumps, they settled down into a tight semi-circle of molting easy chairs more threadbare than stylish. *Somebody* earned their title of dumpster-diver first class. Sam's surreptitious glance in that direction was not wasted on Calvin.

"Hey, they may look and stink like yesterday's onion casserole, but wait till you spend a few nights sleepin' in one of 'em, Colonel... I mean, Sam."

"Colonel?" an aging hippy-looking mechanic called Max Cramdon asked. "To whom, et cetera?"

"Max, guys, this is Colonel Sam Braxton, a man of few words... compared to us, anyway. Far as I can tell, he's a cat with serious juice. Says our country needs our help. Off the rez, by the way. Told him that's our specialty. Best damn crew this side of Ho Chi Minh City, Sam!"

What followed was a boisterous round of, "Freakin' A!" and "Who ya gonna call!" and *"Quá đúng!"* Of course, Sam understood the latter to be the rough Vietnamese slang equivalent of *Damn Skippy*—more by their boisterous tone than anything. Sam had spent some time outside of Da Nang back in the day.

"It's an honor to meet a crew with your reputation. Look, time is of the essence, so here's the pitch."

The group instantly transformed into all business. Sam entered sell and qualify mode.

"Russkis are hacking the American election process. They're succeeding. We need to hit 'em close to home and send a clear message, but it can't come directly from Uncle Sam, no pun intended.

"Gentlemen, I need non-stop no-hassle air transport for my team of a dozen covert operatives from Andrews to Sheremetyevo, less than an hour north of Moscow.

"Same for ground transport from the airport to a suburb called Novye Cheryomushki, half an hour southwest of Moscow. Quick in, quick out. As Calvin indicated, this is a rogue op, full black, but sanctioned by the JCS—with full deniability, of course. I did not tell you that. The Joint Chiefs would fire my ass before brunch."

Mention of the Joint Chiefs raised a few eyebrows. Juice, indeed. Mention of the word *brunch* brought snickers... who the Hell eats *brunch*? But no comment because this was now a serious mission briefing.

SAM CONTINUED WITH THE MEAT OF IT.

In his most efficient tone of voice he said, "There's a rundown building that used to be a research institute in the sixties, now occupied by a start-up software company with an unpronounceable name. That's a front. Our intel confirms this is a government-sponsored troll hole that we're going to convert to an ash hole. Questions?"

The team shook their heads side-to-side, but to a man, were grinning like it was Christmas. They could almost smell the pine needles of O Tannenbaum. Sam sat in one of the surprisingly comfortable eye sores that posed as an overstuffed lounger, still adjusting to the attack on his olfactories, but just listening now, personally observing the team's competence underlying all the swagger. The *sell* was done. Now came the *qualify*...

CALVIN: "OKAY, SHEREMETYEVO IS TRICKY.

"High profile compared to a rural strip, but we can generate the necessary tail numbers and bogus manifests of an international shipper or charter. Lots going in and out."

Max: "Yeah, pretty public. The passengers and their gear need cover. Us'ns too. Something that makes us painfully uninteresting to the authorities. Maybe GRU? Russki Mafiosi? Nah, too interesting."

They brainstormed and finally consulted Sam for cover ideas who said, "My guys can conceal their mission matériel. We have a few tricks consistent with almost any back story. So any legitimate mission that is not US Government-sponsored is acceptable.

"We also don't care if we pick up an escort. They're easily predisposed after arrival if we can complete our egress before they discover our true intentions. Rules of engagement: minimal human casualties. Ground transport should plan my team being on site no more than thirty minutes plus round-trip travel time on the ground, barring complications. But please plan for contingencies."

CALVIN SUMMARIZED SAM'S BRIEF.

"Okay, Sheremetyevo—a major airport with lots of surveillance, we pose as an NGO to provide the big boys in DC full deniability, a tail is likely, but not an issue, so we don't have to go native which is good. Quick in, quick op and quick out, barring more than a little excrement striking the reciprocating mass. *Plan for contingencies* means something's likely to go wrong. Don't worry, Sam, we live for this shit."

Sam remained skeptical that this much bravado could be one hundred percent backed up in the heat of action. He'd keep watching.

Calvin offered an idea.

"How about we get your troops to pose as U of M grad students on a field trip? I know a guy who can provide bona fides. I spent some time in *Muscva* back in the day.

"Novye Cheryomushki—how 'bout we just call it *Nosy Cherry* for Max here who hates those easy-to-remember Russian words. That area was one of Moscow's big experiments in mass-produced housing. Claimed to be the largest in history, if memory serves. They made a whole propaganda deal out of it during the Cold War.

"Let's appeal to these walking-talking egos, that your team of architecture majors wants to better understand how the Soviets achieved that *miracle* way back in the eighties. We'll be in and out before you can say, Nosy Muscovites. What say you, Sam?"

Sam's brow furrowed. "Not a bad scenario, Calvin, except that once our mission objective is discovered by the authorities, if sooner versus later, they'll be able to directly connect our flight to the incident. We need to buy several hours of deniability for a safe egress from their military air cover, which is some of the best in the world, once mobilized. But this is a good starting point. Let's refine from there."

Sam continued. "Let's say our architecture students have booked a cheap charter. They can only afford one day in Moscow to see the Kremlin, Red Square and the colorful onion domes of St. Basil's. Then they're off to the main event in a border town like St. Petersburg, known for its Baroque and neoclassical architecture.

"Assuming the team gets airborne post-op, it's only an hour's flight to St. Pete, but we don't land. We pass almost directly over St. Pete, which would be consistent with our flight plan. We bolt for Finland and land in Lappeenranta, the closest non-Russian international strip. If we have to, that is.

"We're blown when we don't descend into the pattern for St. Pete, but at that point, let 'em holler all they want. You guys decide whether we need to actually stop in Finland for fuel. Then we just retrace our flight plan back to the States. But this time, we actually land and disembark somewhere other than Andrews to go our separate ways."

Sam continued after he was rewarded with approving nods from this group of rowdy air pirates.

"So let's assume that can work. My guys tell me it's about two hours between the troll hole and Sheremetyevo, depending on traffic. Say another hour to clear out through their equivalent of Customs, and a maximum of two more hours to cross the border into Finland.

"We need to buy at least six hours after the op, better to plan for eight including contingencies before we're discovered, or we are toast. Caught on the ground means prison or worse. Caught in Russian airspace means a forced landing or getting shot down. Either way, finding us out too soon would spoil the rest of our day, for sure. What do y'all think, boys?"

Max chimed in, too loudly and too quickly. "Hell, yeah! That could definitely work!"

A forest of nods told Sam they had analyzed the plan from a flight perspective and found it adequate. They were anxious to start detailed planning and executing.

Their pilot and co-pilot were sacked out somewhere re-charging for a possible quick departure, and Calvin's crew would catch them up before detailed flight planning took place. A tight team.

Sam chimed back in before the inevitable bluster re-ignited in full bloom.

"Okay. You boys take care of the details to get our plane in and out of the CIS with that scenario as our base plan, and ground transport for our dozen, ah, students. I'll take care of credentials and materials for my team. A bunch of architecture nerds fascinated by overstated Soviet architecture? I like it.

"Calvin, any further comms are between you and me please, encrypted only. Keep the Iridium. I'll text the code key to your personal cell. You'll then work face-to-face with my ground team leader, Captain Derek Cheevers, whom you'll meet at Andrews. I'll also have comms with Derek. Can you and yours get to Maryland inside forty-eight hours?"

Max proudly said, "Twenty-four, if you need it, Boss. Our women get it, to heck with the day jobs. Laser-cut stencils for the fuselage are a piece 'a cake. And spray paint dries faster 'n printer ink. The hard part's done - gettin' this gang assembled in the Minny-Apple without a lot of questions.

"Believe it or not, Colonel, a few of us don't maintain very low profiles, at least not all the time."

Sam seemed to smile a lot around this crew.

"I have some work to do as well, gentlemen. Forty-eight hours then. Let me be so bold as to offer my thanks on behalf of a grateful nation. See you at the base Thursday night.

"Calvin, once the plane is papered and personalized, text me the specifics for approach control authorizations. I assume your flight crew's okay navigating military terminal control areas like Andrews?"

Calvin was juiced, barely able to contain his excitement at having something to do.

"Frickin' A, Bubba, I mean, Colonel, I mean... Aw Hell, Sam. You take the Porsche back to my place and pick up your rental. The address is in the GPS listed under the label, *Grounded*. I'll hang here, finish cookin' the stew with these assholes. A few of us also need some catchin' up. Have a good flight, Sir. Consider us your invisible wings 'n wheels. See you in Prince George County on Thursday."

Sam bid them adieu. The in-depth dossier he had earlier assembled and memorized on Calvin Pierce and every one of his known associates, including this entire bunch of irreverent sky pirates, was indeed impressive, despite all their comical sophomoric bluster.

He'd now affirmed the same with personal observation. Sold and qualified.

Colonel Sam Braxton, personally charged with responsibility for this op by the president's National Security Advisor, was imminently satisfied.

This op was shaping up.

A NDREWS AIR FORCE BASE,
MARYLAND

The team assembled.

Sam's team of cross-agency and civilian irregulars, including trusted agency and military insiders, ultimately created the cover for Calvin's transport as a matter of expediency. The plane itself, much like a gangbanger's Saturday night special with the serial numbers filed off, would remain untraceable.

On paper, the vintage aircraft was owned by a private company called BridgeCraft Charters, a US company Sam's team invented, including a fairly well-documented online history.

Also as a matter of expediency, Sam's guys posted a flight plan and passenger manifest with the info passed on by Calvin's crew. The flight would appear to originate from Portsmouth, New Hampshire to St. Petersburg, Russia by way of Moscow.

The twelve operators aboard were ostensibly graduate students at the University of Minnesota School of Architecture within the College of Design. Anyone digging deeper, as they certainly would after the op, would discover evidence of a not-so-subtle sponsorship by an American ultra-left organization called Democracy United.

DU was a fictitious activist group with a long and dubious history —all fabricated, of course. Officially, that narrative described DU as a small group of fanatical grass roots conspiracy nuts whose core membership resided within the US, but touted affiliates in several countries where democracy was revered and under attack.

They attributed the bulk of their resources to contributions from several well-heeled, anonymous international sponsors.

Sam's team received additional unofficial help to create a public web site for DU that appeared as if it had been around for years. In less than a week, the site received several hundred thousand legitimate hits, in addition to a few hundred thousand fictitious hits. The lightning response was both unnerving and affirming.

Calvin's plane touched down at Andrews with no issues using the clearances provided by Sam. The flight crew and Calvin's support team relaxed in a hangar lounge near the plane.

Upon its arrival, the aircraft seemed overly large to Sam for just a dozen passengers. Its markings looked to be old and indicated the plane was a Bridgecraft Charters aircraft.

Sam and Calvin sat in the spartan cabin of the aging Boeing 717.

Sam asked, "Why this plane, Calvin?"

"Well, we tried to accommodate as many of your parameters as we could, Sam. This is the same aircraft you saw at MSP.

"First, my crew and I know every bolt of the one-seven, so we'll require no external support other than fuel. We carry our own spares.

"Second, this plane is low profile, as ordinary and invisible as a rusty pickup in Minnesota. Easy to overlook.

"Third, making the trip non-stop would have required a stretched heavy like a forty-seven. It's not unusual for cheap charters to have lots of empty seats. But with a heavy, you'd have 260 empties instead of 90 on this baby.

"So the one-seven is big enough to minimize refueling stops, *and* at smaller, less inquisitive airports than heavies require.

"On the other hand, an aircraft smaller than this just doesn't have the range, even for short thousand-mile hops. We're cleared all the way through to Sheremetyevo with just three quick fuel stops en route, and then on to St. Pete."

"How about ground transport?"

"Well, that's trickier to arrange in advance in Commy Central. Involves even more volatility when you want to keep it full quiet. Unreliable sorts over there, but we're experienced in situational contingencies. I'm sure your team is as well."

Sam didn't ask or comment, just nodded. These guys were the best available, and he had no reason to question their competency. At least not yet. Besides, once they left the plane at their destination, his team would call the shots anyway.

Calvin asked, "Will you be along for the ride, Sam?"

"I'd love to, but I'm too old for fast-paced field ops. My, ah, physical shape could quickly become a liability. Bad ticker. I'll provide cover from here, best I can.

"Ah, here comes my team leader… Derek!" Sam waved a young man over to their seats near the front of the aircraft's cabin. As he approached down the center aisle, Calvin squinted. He was looking at a high school football player.

"Calvin, this is Captain Derek Cheevers. Derek, this is your aircraft crew chief, Calvin Pierce."

"Hey, Mr. Pierce. A pleasure. Colonel Braxton, the team is briefed and ready to board whenever you and Mr. Pierce give the word."

Lifting a single eyebrow, Calvin cocked his head as he stared. "Such a polite young man. Jeez, Derek, I feel old just lookin' at you, man! How old are you, if you don't mind…"

Sam patiently but firmly interrupted, "Calvin, Derek and the entire team are experienced operators, some of the best. They were chosen for their youthful appearance and non-military bearing. They're supposed to be college students. Remember?

"Derek, please coordinate with Calvin. Time continues to be of the essence. Questions? No? Good. I'll bid you, gentlemen goodbye and God's speed."

Sam shook hands with both men and departed the aircraft.

THEY FINALIZED THEIR PREPARATIONS.

Alone in the narrow cabin, sitting in two seats, one on either side of the single central aisle, Calvin asked Derek, "So what kind of cargo requirements do y'all have, Derek? This bus will handle anything, but we should expect to clear Customs on arrival. I'm sure Sam briefed you."

"No problem, Mr. Pierce. We know we're full black, and that the op needs the optics of a private sector organization with limited technology and expertise. We'll be using low-tech IEDs whose components are modularized and easily concealable. We'll even throw in a few at the party that fail to detonate. More authenticity."

"Okay, Derek, let's get a couple of things cleared up. First, my name's Calvin. Second, if you're toting improvised explosive devices on my plane, you're not gonna accidentally blow us up with bags of fertilizer 'n diesel 'n some-such shit, right? Just sayin'."

"Alright… Calvin. If you and your crew fly the plane and keep it operational, in and out, I'll run the mission and promise not to blow up you and your crew, at least until after we land at Commy Central. There will be minimal to zero ordnance remaining onboard once we exit CC Fair enough?"

"Fair enough, Son. Hah! CC? I love acronyms, man. You and I are gonna get along just fine. I'm gonna have another good story to tell old George after this!"

"Who?"

O CTOBER 2008
AIRBORNE

Calvin briefed Sam's crew.

He described the aircraft's capabilities for Derek and his team after they were airborne, heading north to New Hampshire.

"This bird's extended range of 2,000 nautical miles is a lot for an old ship. We carry extra tanks. Even so, a direct flight to Moscow is almost 5,000 nautical miles. For optics, it'll be farther.

"We'll make several hops for two reasons. First, we'll do a touch 'n go in Portsmouth to establish our flight's alleged point of origin, should anyone care. Then we'll take on fuel in Quebec City. Same in Nuuk, Greenland and Stavanger, Norway before we arrive at Sheremetyevo, North of Moscow.

"Specifically, we'll end up at their massive General Aviation terminal. We hope to get lost in the crowd, but you will still need to conceal your goodies from prying eyes.

"The flight plan will show less than one day there before hopping northwest to St. Pete so you guys can supposedly enjoy some real architecture, that is, *pre-Soviet non-bland*.

"At Sheremetyevo, a fifteen passenger van should be waiting to carry your crew to Novye Cheryomushki, code-named *Nosy Cherry*. That's about two hours south by surface roads, depending on traffic. It can be very congested, hopefully not so much within the mission window, coming and going.

"You'll loop around Moscow, so pee before you leave the airport. My crew and I stay with the plane, performing any necessary maintenance."

Derek picked it up.

"I don't like all the fuel stops. I guess we have no choice. Understood. For ground transport, I'd rather break the team into a couple of groups instead of clustering everyone into one van. Can we do that?"

"Whatever you want, Boss. Should be even easier to contract a couple of SUVs instead of one big-ass van or bus. We'll finalize that before we arrive."

Calvin also shared his concern about the potential need for *situational contingencies* he'd shared with Sam. Derek didn't even bat an eye. Yeah, an experienced operator.

He asked for more questions or discussion. Nothing.

These boys 'n girls were obviously used to unknowns.

NOSY CHERRY

M OSCOW, RUSSIA

An uneventful flight. A good omen?

From Maryland to Moscow nobody left the aircraft.

The ops crew talked quietly, professionally, drilling mission details and endless what-ifs.

The five female operatives all wore blousy brown and black goth-grunge threads designed to make them appear more collegiate and to hide their muscular physiques.

The seven men all looked fit and tried hard to look like studious geeks, succeeding somewhat. At least they all appeared age-appropriate. Calvin stayed out of their way because their type freaked him out a little, but mostly since this was now their gig. And they were focusing.

He and his crew just drove the bus and were just passengers now.

CLEARING CUSTOMS WENT EASY.

The Russian equivalent of Customs and Immigration at Shereme-tyevo seemed quite lax by Western standards, but Muscovites were no dummies. The ops team had shaped and shrink-wrapped small but deadly amounts of *det cord,* or detonation cord—a type of fuse mater-ial, essentially exploding rope—and the modern equivalent of old fashioned dynamite, all in small air-tight bags.

Once sealed, they rinsed these bags with bleach water, so no residue would be machine-sniffed, before being concealed in the construction of various pieces of shoulder bags and back packs. The volume of this stuff wasn't large and was stable.

They wouldn't need much. They planned to destroy critical components of the trolls' computer arrays, not to crater the entire building. The message would be unmistakable, and maybe even slow things down. They'd seize any additional targets of opportunity that might include collecting bits of portable intel, quickly snatched and concealed for the flight home.

Their first problem was immediate and not trivial. No ground transportation—in or outside the General Aviation Terminal. Stranded on the ground, carrying concealed explosives, in the heart of Russia? Another day at the office.

DEREK CHEEVERS NEEDED A CONTINGENCY.

Two-by-two, the team made their way to the long term parking area. Fortunately, they found an abundance of older vehicles, easily hot-wired. Ten minutes later they began their nine-minute route to *Nosy Cherry* in moderate traffic.

During the drive, Derek brainstormed with the team members with him in the vintage American SUV they'd hijacked. They needed a practical way to isolate an unknown number of Russian nerds.

They decided earlier to improvise this aspect of the op once in-country to leverage real-time circumstances.

"So how do we buy eight hours once we head for the ex-fil?"

"Obviously we cut comms going in to contain the facility's outgoing. What else?"

Darla Evans suggested, "Since broad application of deadly force isn't an option, detain 'n restrain like we discussed at Andrews?"

Derek still wasn't convinced that was practical. "Could be over a hundred of 'em. We *are* carrying a couple hundred zip ties. What else?"

Mick Sandstrom said, "Render the whole lot unconscious?"

"Ideal, but not practical. No means. Other?"

Darla said, "Get 'em offsite? A fire? Gas leak?" She knew this was improbable, but they were brainstorming. No stupid ideas.

"Possibly," said Derek, "but we wouldn't be controlling the situation. External services certain to be called in would quickly discover our handiwork before we exit CIS airspace. We'd be lucky just to get back to the plane. Might take them a while to connect our flight to the party, but... Other?"

Mick continued.

"Look, unless we come up with other options once we arrive, my vote is still with Darla for our original detain-and-restrain idea. Dispose of the guards so they're off the board, herd the nerds into a big-ass corner, hog tie hands-and-feet, maybe gag 'em with their own shirts, do the deed, get out. Still a risk some hero breaks free, but so far, best we have. Agree, Boss?"

Derek was convinced "Okay, Plan A: terminate the guards, cut the comms, detain, restrain, and intimidate. Let 'em see one of the guards' bodies to put the fear 'a God into them. Maybe have one of 'em hold a grenade with the pin pulled. We don't have grenades, but they don't know that."

They fell silent, visualizing the blueprints they'd studied of the old research institute supplied by Colonel Braxton, contemplating violent action.

Taking human lives never came easy, but they knew from experience that *ideals are peaceful, history is not.*

≈

NOVYE CHERYOMUSHKI, RUSSIA

Heavy security surprised them.

This was no private team of rent-a-cops outside *Nosy Cherry.* These guys were hard-core Russian regulars. Derek guessed *Spetsnaz,* elite troops of *special purpose* from Russia's Main Intelligence Department known as the GRU.

They made American special forces look like candy-asses by comparison, if you were to ask one of them in polite Russian. Same sort of training, but rumored to possess zero ethical boundaries to restrain them—only love of Mother Russia and unconstrained hatred of her enemies.

Their special purpose? They killed with lightning efficiency, and without mercy.

This seems overkill for nerd guard duty.

Somebody was serious about protecting this facility. There were six that Derek could see. Perhaps more inside. This was not good news.

≈

First, the team observed patiently.

For the next ten minutes they watched the institute's funky facade in the heart of this dilapidated district. Every member of the team knew time was of the essence, but impetuous action at this stage of any mission invariably foreshadowed failure.

A few nerds sauntered up the wide stairs between columns and entered. One of the stationary guards challenged each with the other looking on, weapon at the ready. Nobody exited. The few women they saw were young, plain, and unadorned.

"Darla, got any makeup with you? What am I saying? Of course, you do. Thank God you speak decent Russian."

Derek grinned.

She smirked, a non-verbal *kiss my darling ass* sort of expression. She could put down half the guys on the team between applying lipstick and delivering her kiss of death.

"Okay, go time. Darla and Mick, decoy."

All knew their assignments and moved into position.

It took Darla ninety seconds to look hot enough to tempt a eunuch. Mick Sandstrom looked goofier than a gold-plated ruble. She led the way, he trailed behind, bashfully.

As they neared the two grizzly monsters at the institute's front entrance, Darla smiled playfully and asked for help adjusting her backpack precisely where it compressed one ample bosom begging to bust out, barely constrained by several truant buttons on her split jersey top. The two guards closed in like starving wolves on a raw steak.

Mick, still half a dozen respectful paces behind but closing fast, appeared fearful of the weapon-toting wildlife.

With the palm and heel of her right hand Darla provocatively shifted her right boob upward and inward where it was compressed by her shoulder strap. They didn't notice Mick's surreptitious scan for other roaming guards.

In seconds, both guards were down hard with killing blows that drove their nose cartilage into their brain pans with the heel of their hands. Darla: one; Mick: one; guards: dead last.

THEY DRAGGED THE BODIES INSIDE.

But first they searched them behind the huge ornate columns just outside the eight-foot-tall double entrance doors at the top of the steps and scavenged everything useful.

Derek directed Flack Jackson to lead the six remaining team members to lay in ambush. Objective: decommission any other roving guards currently elsewhere on the grounds.

Four teammates, including Derek, waited for Flack's signal in the shadow of the building's columns. Forty seconds later, Derek heard *click, click.* That was Flack double-keying his comms to signal he and his team had secured all external hard lines—phone, computer, alarms.

Derek, Mick and Darla, plus three other teammates entered the facility dragging the two corpses and fanned out with their commandeered weapons scanning. Classic two-by-three offensive formation through the wide double-doors.

Not much cover once inside. A triple-burst echoed through the antechamber, and Mick spun off his feet. More shots—another triple. Derek neutralized the shooter with a single shot from one of the guard's captured rifles. All fell silent.

Mick arose and sheepishly shook off a flesh wound to his right bicep, but winced in pain after a grateful nod to his boss. Darla assessed the wound in less than five seconds before lightly punching it and Mick winced again. She grinned at him good-naturedly and said, "Pussy." He grinned back.

They cleared the antechamber. No more guards inside.

Flack rushed in less than a minute later while Derek was slapping a compression pad on Mick's arm. After smirking in relief at the sight of only one corpse, the opposition's, and just a bit of blood on Mick's sleeve, Flash reported.

"All guards outside down and concealed, confirming all external alarm, phone and computer hard lines cut, both SUVs now parked nearby, noses out. We have no gear to jam wi-fi or cell signals, though."

Derek peeked through a set of ornamental ballroom doors and

said, "Copy. Bring in the rest of the team. We're gonna need all hands on deck."

THEY ENTERED A HUGE HALL EN MASSE.

They saw the cavernous space divided only with chest-high movable partitions to create a gigantic array of small modular offices. And there sat a crowd of petrified computer users. Dozens of deer in the headlights.

Nobody dared leave their chairs after the shots rang out. The only operators here were keyboard operators. Some ducked and stayed down. These nerds appeared genuinely terror-stricken.

Flack and his wingman, Sanchez, dragged the exsanguinating guard by his armpits before unceremoniously dropping him at the top of the steps leading down into the ballroom. Blood drenched more than half his body from a pumping arterial wound. Only half his neck remained. The captured guard's rifle must have chambered hollow-point rounds. This poor schmuck's corpse became a billboard declaring, *Don't even consider messing with us!*

Within seconds of entering the room, Darla howled a guttural warning, almost masculine, definitely chilling. *"Ruki v vozdukhe! Teper'! I derzhite ikh, ili vy mertvy!"*

Derek wasn't sure but he thought Darla's command of Russian must be pretty good as he saw a forest of arms shoot straight up and stay there, all at the same instant.

He didn't know she'd been privately rehearsing that line... "Hands in the air! Now! And keep them up, or you're dead!" She couldn't wait to show it off.

Without another word, they rapidly searched pockets and drawers for cell phones or anything that looked capable of calling out or signaling. Before leaving each cubicle they zip-tied hands and legs.

Since Darla was the only one who spoke passable Russian, the others agreed to pantomime their directions by holding a pistol finger to the center of each captive's forehead (without pulling the "trigger") while shaking their own head side-to-side during the restraint process. Then that same gun finger transformed to a hush-hush finger in front of their own puckered lips that shushed. The message was clear: *you won't be killed if you just keep quiet.*

Most bobbed their heads up and down eagerly. They hadn't signed up to die. So they laid on the floor of their cubicles, quiet as a pulverized pager. This process took longer than expected. The second hand on the clock moved entirely too fast.

Several rack-mounted servers hummed in an unpartitioned corner at the far end of the long and narrow hall with high unadorned ceilings. While the crew secured the nerds, Derek pulled a handful of compact hard drives from their racks and stuffed them into his U of M backpack before deploying rudimentary fused charges they'd extracted from their luggage on the drive south.

He also found a newer Toshiba laptop on what appeared to be the desk of a supervisor near the server farm. There was a flash drive—a memory stick—protruding from one of its USB ports. The laptop and stick also disappeared into his backpack.

They agreed to leave a few subtle messages behind. With a little discomfort from his injured arm, Mick put to good use two small aerosol cans of spray paint that were not confiscated at the airport.

The team then assembled by the entry door waiting for Derek who claimed the honor of lighting several fuses with his Zippo-clone lighter. He took just a moment to admire Mick's crude but taunting graffiti: *PB Sucks!* and *DU Forever!* and *Mess with the Best!* All in English.

Those would only be understood by higher pay grades. That would take time. Perfect. There was even a drawing of a hand that formed a particular gesture, the universal meaning of which anyone would recognize.

~

THEY SPED AWAY, KICKING UP GRAVEL.

Moments later, they were rewarded with a rapid series of satisfying *whumps* behind them. The clock continued ticking, still way too fast. Over an hour had elapsed at the site, double their projection.

The team reached the airport in their stolen SUVs less than ninety minutes later; however, the security lines were long. Tension escalated, even for these experienced operators. Time continued to be their most deadly adversary.

Now to get through Airport Security.

Derek disposed of all but one compact hard drive, one laptop, and the memory stick en route. More than that would increase the risk of exposure even though they might contain useful intel.

The laptop was easy. Such a common item in Derek's student backpack passed unquestioned through the X-ray. The more unusual naked hard drive, however, wasn't easily concealed, so they'd agreed to also just hide it in plain sight in Darla's backpack. She'd claim it was in her pack when they entered the country, part of her studies in America.

This ploy worked, partially because of a long line of irritable passengers behind them, impatiently shuffling, and partially due to Darla's winning ways. She playfully scolded one of the TSA-type security guys.

"*Privet! Moi glaza zdes'!*"

Translated loosely, "Hey! My eyes are up here!"

And oh, that sparkling but lethal smile.

The memory stick went undetected.

Twenty minutes later, Departure Control granted their plane clearance. Moscow to St. Pete was an extremely popular sixty-minute flight for tourists. Number three for take-off, they spent less than ten minutes on the tarmac before lifting off.

So far so good. Until…

THE CAPTAIN'S GUT LURCHED.

They'd been airborne for less than twenty minutes under full throttle when the copilot received an urgent call on their guard frequency from Moscow Flight Control.

Suspecting they'd been discovered, after stalling for a precious minute or so, Calvin's veteran pilot, Captain Doug BS Orenson responded to repeated calls.

As the inflection in the controller's voice on the radio rose and fell, Captain Orenson sensed uncertainty. He decided to leverage that to buy a few more prized minutes.

"Moscow Control, please repeat… specifically, what is it you are requesting of us?"

"You will return to Sheremetyevo."

There was a hint of rising desperation in that youthful voice. The kid was under pressure. That was leverage.

"Moscow, I don't understand. We are now past the point of no return."

Orenson used the term to declare they were closer to St. Pete than to Moscow, even though, in fact, that point was still several minutes away.

"Captain, you are directed…"

"Son, I'll be landing in St. Petersburg in less than thirty minutes. If your people want to talk with us, we'd be happy to meet them there."

He wondered if he was already being pursued by one or more of the fastest jet fighters in the world, Russia's fleet-footed MiG-31 Foxhounds. Orenson knew they had perhaps only minutes to live if those piloted Mach 2.8 rockets were already airborne. He counted on the possibility they were not.

Orenson also took a calculated risk they might not yet feel certain enough to consider executing such dramatic action against an American civilian charter flight in a busy commercial airway.

The combination of these factors might just buy them enough time.

"Captain, I repeat…"

"Son, do you want to be responsible for an American flight running out of fuel over the Kremlin because you ignored the warning of the pilot-in-command of a foreign commercial aircraft?"

"Stand by…"

Orenson grinned. *No problem. All day long, m'boy.*

"Captain, you are directed to meet officials at Pulkovo's Terminal 2, per your flight plan. Over."

"Roger. Thank you. Out."

As a courtesy to Calvin's crew and the field team, Orenson had enabled the aircraft's PA system for his dialog with Sheremetyevo Flight Control. He knew the crew would be amused by his tactics, assuming they weren't about to go down in flames.

Besides, BS Orenson never missed an opportunity to show off.

Thirty-six minutes later, they were on final approach. As they touched down, Orenson announced to crew and passengers over the PA, "Welcome to Finland, ladies and gentlemen. You too, OD."

Calvin couldn't resist shouting from the first row just a few feet from the open cockpit door loudly enough so all their passengers in the first half dozen rows could hear him too, "Thanks, BS. What about scats and tray tables, Dude? You forget? Not very professional!"

The raucous laughter helped defuse the post-mission stress from which they were all glad to be distracted.

Captain Derek Cheevers had slept soundly throughout.

DEVIL'S DUE

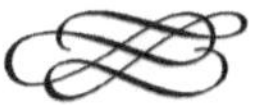

O CTOBER 2008
WASHINGTON, DC

PALMER XAVIER CONTEMPLATED THE FUTURE.

Sitting in the opulent study of his new home on Chain Bridge Road, Mr. X visualized the action list necessary to close the door on his job at GGS.

He repeatedly consulted with Mr. Z, whom he had come to think of as his *old* Number One Brother, concerning his early set of initiatives in his job as the *new* Number One Brother. He smiled inwardly, but as usual, the full impact of that smile never quite reached his eyes.

The pungent smell, the loud crackle and pop of the wood fire raging in his very own fireplace reminded him of Mr. Z's penchant for flames in his opulent club apartment. Very little smoke escaped the wide-open chimney draft and into the room. Just enough to enrich the ambience of this, his new favorite of thirty-six rooms.

He needed some comfort after receiving the shocking news that he was being indicted by the Securities and Exchange Commission for violating insider trading laws. Maybe his *friends*, the fund managers, weren't as loyal to him as he'd assumed.

Loose end. No problem. He'd ensure the Brotherhood's resources were applied to make this annoyance disappear as easily as the smoke of this fire up his new chimney.

His private security force on the grounds and in the house, courtesy of Enoch Slattery, provided him a measure of comfort. He'd learned these burly boys specialized in personal security, and swore an oath of loyalty to him. Promises of obscene bonuses for each sealed the deal. One of whom he now considered *his crew* remained at the perimeter gate, with orders to admit no one—no exceptions.

The remainder of the team did not patrol the grounds. It made no sense to attract unnecessary attention. Three more roved continuously within selected rooms inside the house. Panic buttons placed everywhere directly fed ear buds worn by each *personal safety representative*. The entire estate featured unsurpassed electronic security systems.

Except for the maelstrom raging in his mind, Palmer sensed nothing out of the ordinary beyond the demonstrative crackling of his soothing fire—hypnotic. Under the tutelage of one of Slattery's operatives who now patrolled *his house*, he'd acquired some rudimentary weapons training in the basement firing range somewhere beneath his feet, along with regular self-defense practice.

So it stood to reason that he was perplexed when the wood smoke from his snap-crackle-pop fire seemed to emanate the scent of cordite, the pungent odor he now knew was produced by gunfire. His senses flashed on full alert!

Despite no discernible sound for concern, he cautiously arose in the dark and moved to the library's archway that led to the grand entrance hall.

There, on his back not moving, laid one of his security team with a neat dark circular impression painted in the middle of his forehead. From ten feet away, it looked like a large mole he hadn't recalled seeing before. But that was no mole. That was a small-caliber bullet hole. But why a total lack of blood?

With his right hand, he reached for the panic button near the door jamb. Before he could punch it, however, something or someone jerked him backward. He felt the forceful jab of a needle into the left side of his neck from behind. Instantaneous dizziness and nausea overwhelmed him.

A black sack of coarse material slipped over his head. The foul smell of that sack pressed against his face was... what? Stale after-shave combined with the odor of week-old crotch sweat from unwashed gym shorts? Maybe. Then... Nothing, except...

There would be no funeral because there would be no body and no evidence of foul play. Slattery's guys were that good. It was just as well. Nobody would attend, as no one is willing to mourn for me. Win big or lose big, right?

The last sound Palmer Xavier heard was the hollow thud of total obscurity.

COMMANDER-IN-CHIEF

THE PRESIDENT WOULD NOT BE HAPPY.

NSA Director Admiral Gregory Mannheim and his deputy, Brigadier General Anthony Flannery, were accompanied to the basement of the West Wing via an underground entrance by Colonel Sam Braxton and Captain Derek Cheevers, leader of the Moscow mission code-worded *Nosy Cherry*.

The origin of that code word interested neither the director nor his deputy. The team's action report did. Besides, they had bigger fish to fry. Sam observed that both were more somber than the occasion warranted. He knew why.

Sam briefed Derek as they walked the tunnel. Hardened operator's demeanor notwithstanding, Derek's stomach churned at the prospect of being present in the same room as the leader of the free world.

This is far scarier than combat.

"Don't worry, Derek. These guys are all gonna be petrified by what they're about to hear as you are by the presence of POTUS. This is just a conversation between the president, his chief of staff, his JCS chairman, and the top NSA guy. We're just flies on the wall.

"POTUS asked to be privately and personally debriefed on this mission. I guess they've discarded the need for deniability. The gloves are coming off. They agreed his security council would be read in immediately after this debrief."

But Sam knew they had some ugly business to address first. Director Mannheim asked him and Derek to be present for that.

The four of them sat in the Situation Room and waited. When POTUS entered, they arose to greet their Commander-in-Chief. President John W. Stevens impatiently waved them to be seated.

"Let's start. Who's up?"

Director Mannheim made the introductions and continued.

"Sir, objectives of the mission designated *Nosy Cherry* included sending an unambiguous message to the Kremlin that tampering with our election process will not be tolerated. Great care was taken to ensure this op appeared to be sponsored by an international organization—fictional of course—called *Democracy United*.

"General Renfro, recall you personally re-activated Colonel Sam Braxton here to orchestrate a covert mission activating what he calls his team of irregulars, that is, a team completely off the books. Full deniability, no oversight. To date, Mr. President, there is nothing that connects this operation with your administration or any part of the United States government.

"Analysis of SIGINT acquired on site was confirmed by intel gleaned earlier from a flash drive recovered from a Mr. Denton Canfield, a Brotherhood operative who was subsequently flipped by Colonel Braxton. That yielded intel from which we've pieced together some disturbing revelations of which you and your staff need to be aware."

President Stevens had been given the nickel tour of the op beforehand by General Renfro. He now injected a question before the briefing resumed, addressing not Director Mannheim, but Colonel Braxton.

"So just to be clear, Sam, may I call you Sam? Good. Thank you... Sam, see if I have this right.

"You turned a hostile traitor into an ally and milked him dry, you then rounded up a bunch of private operators off the street, got them in and out of a secure facility in the Moscow suburbs, blew up some of their computers that were used to hack or influence our elections, had the team collect some hard intel and got them out of one of the most secure air spaces in the world without losing a single soul? Impressive indeed. Just out of curiosity, how much did this operation cost me?"

He asked, although he already knew.

Sam felt his face flush like a damn civilian, much to his chagrin. "Not a dime, Sir. We took up a collection."

The president's mask of neutrality cracked shamelessly.

"Well, I'll be a son-of-a-bitch… Sam, I would like to hear the rest from you and yours, that is if you don't mind, General."

"Not at all, Sir." This bit had been rehearsed.

Sam cleared his throat, not realizing he'd be asked to carry the debrief. "Well, Sir, I just got the right folks together. At some point, I'd appreciate a note of thanks from you to this group of patriots, especially my in-country team leader, Captain Derek Cheevers here who led the successful assault, zero casualties."

It was Derek's turn to flush and was rewarded by POTUS rising from his chair, chuckling under his breath, shaking his head, walking around the table and half its length to shake the Captain's hand with both of his own.

"Thank you, Son! You do your nation proud, even though we probably shouldn't admit that right now."

Wink.

"Please pass on my personal enthusiastic thanks to your entire team."

"Um, absolutely… Sir! Thank you, Sir!"

The kid actually snapped to attention and saluted.

Gotta love it. Adorable. Look at that stupid grin on POTUS's face. He deserves some fun too.

Sam waited for the president to return to his seat at the head of the table before continuing.

"Okay, now, we need to belt out some sobering facts for y'all. So here goes, Mr. President…

"First, there is now no doubt whatsoever that the Russian president personally commissioned these cyber attacks.

"Second, this ongoing attack is even more widespread than we initially feared.

"Third, the sophisticated cyber-weapons employed by these, ah, trolls, looked very familiar to our team of NSA analysts, with good reason. We discovered, by way of Moscow, that a small organized group of misguided misfits within the NSA who call themselves Shadow Brokers have been peddling our technology on the open market. Their most lucrative customer? Mother Russia.

"We believe their assumption was that these cyber-weapons would only be used against Ukraine, a weak ally of Washington's, a staunch enemy of the Kremlin. I don't believe these Brokers considered these weapons would be used against the United States, but they knew when they had, and said nothing."

Sam knew this was his cue to shut up.

To his credit, Director Mannheim hadn't hesitated once he'd learned of this from his own team and from Sam's irregulars. All he'd asked was twenty-four hours to round up as many of these traitorous mercs within his own house that could be identified and apprehended before briefing the president and his staff.

Greg Mannheim now stood and snapped to attention. He solemnly faced President Stevens and looked him square in the eye. He spoke in a loud and steady tone, with almost no inflection in his voice.

"Mr. President, General Flannery and I have rounded up seven traitorous dogs within our own ranks, have formally charged them with treason, and they await justice. We continue to interrogate them… aggressively… and have uncovered connections to other agencies and to the domestic private sector.

"We believe these traitors are a faction within the larger shadow organization we've labeled the Brotherhood that originally started us down this path, thanks to leadership from Colonel Braxton and his operatives. This Brotherhood seems to have tentacles everywhere.

"Sir, it is unforgivable that this happened on my watch, and I humbly offer you my resignation, effective immediately. I've let you down, Mr. President, and I stand ready to…"

Mannheim's cheeks burned white-hot, even as he fell silent with a blank look and lowered himself into his chair with a desperate slumped-over dignity.

This man served his country faithfully for almost fifty years. He could not finish his verbal walk of shame, but the act was complete.

President Stevens sat impassively, absorbing this bombshell, analyzing implications, consequences, alternatives… As he uncharacteristically ran his fingers through his thinning blonde hair, he paused for a few beats.

"Greg, I'm grateful for your forthrightness. This Brotherhood *is* everywhere, not just in your agency. If I accept your resignation, I'd have to sign several others, including my own. Please consider withdrawing yours so you can personally continue to hunt the rest of these treasonous bloodsuckers and prosecute them at my side. Can you do that for me, Greg?"

"Thank you, Mr. President. As you wish." Director Mannheim seemed to have aged ten years in the last thirty minutes but was still the battle-hardened veteran of four wars, and an appointee that the president had nominated near the beginning of his first term.

BROTHER RETIRED

ABRAHAM ZELOKOV LOOKED TO THE FUTURE.

Once again Mr. Z contemplated all possible futures, one of which was his precious Brotherhood without its new leader. This inconvenience had delayed his own retirement.

The uncaring perennial fire crackled apathetically.

He sighed heavily and squeezed shut his tired eyes. He regretted the need to retire Mr. X before he was able to contribute. Palmer possessed great potential. But they just couldn't risk him contributing to the opposition either.

Of late, Mr. Z took to conversing with a devil's advocate of his own invention. His was a lonely post, so it seemed logical to personify this imaginary colleague, at least in the privacy of his own library. In front of his own fire.

Abraham, was it really necessary to retire young Mr. X in such an abrupt fashion?

Mr. Z replied with an unexpected dullness in his chest.

"You know I had no choice. While the young man held great promise, he also held the keys to the Brotherhood's greatest vault of secrets. His most profound iniquity, however, was losing his veil of invisibility. You know the policy."

Still, he would not have betrayed us. Surely.

"No, perhaps not of his own free will, but remember Leningrad. Ultimately, everyone breaks, and lest we fool ourselves, Palmer would not have been availed of protection from due process of law, despite the mirage. Dark site interrogation under the American Patriot Act? With unlimited time to extract information? Yes, he'd have broken and told all. An absolute certainty, despite any sense of personal resolve which is a mere illusion."

Perhaps you're right, Abraham. So what now? Have we failed?

"Not at all, my friend. In fact, this will be yet another rallying cry for the Brotherhood. Oppressed profiteers simply sharpen their swords before commencing the next attack on the altar of Democracy, before the next sacrifice. Meanwhile, we re-group. We always do."

Sounds overly optimistic. Why should I continue to believe in you, Abraham?

"It does not matter. I'm already a dead man. But the wheels are already in motion for anointing my new successor. There is no question the Brotherhood appreciates the value of central leadership. So it will happen, without my further involvement. Besides, the very fact that you and I are conversing is visceral evidence that my time to retire has arrived."

With that ominous pronouncement, he casually raised his vintage 1971 Makarov pistol with a hollow-point nine millimeter round already in the chamber, pressed the end of the barrel firmly up into the wrinkled and jowled soft tissue just behind the bottom of his jawbone so hard it produced a single tear.

No matter. He cast his gaze on the lovely fire before squeezing shut his deep-set eyes under bushy white eyebrows and...

Retired.

HEADLINE BULLETS

DECEMBER 2008
PUNTA GORDA, FLORIDA

THE ELECTIONS CAME AND WENT.

A surprised nation experienced the highest voter turnout in decades. They responded positively to a negative campaign.

Fortunately, the American people educated themselves and voiced their displeasure by electing the most principled candidates, not yielding to poisoned pens and disinformation that seemed to run out of ink shortly before the election.

Congressional elections at the state and national levels, however, resulted in a mixed bag, although there was some good news regarding their new president. The candidate George favored would soon occupy the oval office.

Social media played a role as that technology's popularity exploded in America. George wondered what influence it would exert on future elections as more and more people interpreted broadly accessible but un-vetted opinions as journalistic fact, largely not challenging the reliability of their sources. He could not help but feel this foreshadowed trouble for what was now *his* democracy.

George was sure the war from within waged by the Brotherhood must continue. Or was it really from within? Would it get worse? Or would lazy voters re-emerge and simply listen to any candidate who'd feed them what they wanted to hear?

In any event, George feared for the integrity of future elections and for other valued cyber-infrastructure increasingly subject to hostile attacks—the twenty-first-century battleground.

Even more frightening, he feared how citizens chose to become informed, or simply voted based on information from a paranoid subculture that was often provided near universal and free publicity.

Or worse, would citizens simply become discouraged, not showing up at the polls at all? The paranoids *always* showed up because by definition, their fanatic commitment compelled them.

Worse still, generously funded lobbyists seemed to be exerting more influence on elections than America's voters. *But that is fodder for another cannon.* George now considered the threat the nation just averted.

From her stool near the condo's front door she watched George brew himself an espresso.

"Have you seen the headlines, George? Oh... I forgot. You don't read the paper."

She couldn't believe his unshakable disdain for news in print.

"Your old boss seems to have just disappeared, and his boss, Michael Martino, GGS's CEO, resigned, ostensibly due to health reasons. Trouble in Heaven, I wonder? Did that insider trading scandal claim his career as well?"

"I have no idea, Babe, but I'm sure it couldn't have happened to a couple of more deserving guys."

Perhaps the Brotherhood had cleaned up another loose end with Xavier. But Martino? A young and vital guy like that doesn't seem the type to just willingly leave center stage at the top of his game, unless...

Sam's words came back to strike him: *We must also look closely at his* [Xavier's] *closest associates within GGS.*

I wonder.

"Looks like the FBI is prosecuting election officials in several states. Some crazies are trying to claim election fraud, but nobody seems to be taking them too seriously. They say it might have been looked at more closely had Atherton's margin been narrower. From what you've told me, George, America dodged a bullet."

He smiled. Great minds of a single thought.

"America isn't the only one."

After a traumatic moment of silent reflection, they both shook from deep belly laughter. How therapeutic it felt to laugh about not getting murdered!

"Let's get ready for the party, Babe. We don't wanna keep our friends and neighbors waiting."

WASHINGTON, DC

WELL, IT IS TIME TO LEAD THE FREE WORLD.

President-Elect Stewart David Atherton found President John W. Stevens to be an honorable and competent man. Despite the responsibilities of the office he anticipated and the issues he would certainly face, he could not have anticipated a more shocking pre-inauguration briefing in his wildest imagination.

He and the president agreed to address each other on a first name basis. They also agreed to the need for absolute privacy.

Now he understood why.

"Stewart, you seem to have a reasonable grasp of the domestic and international issues after just a couple of hours. You'll do fine."

"Mr. Pres—, John, I appreciate your patience. I assumed my three terms as a State Senator would have prepared me for this job. I was mistaken."

Lame duck President Stevens offered some advice.

"It will be challenging, no doubt, but I'll share a little secret. I felt the same way eight years ago. To be blunt, to this very day, I still don't feel adequate to the task. Nobody could unless they're delusional. Surround yourself with competent people you trust, and then lead that team."

"But this thing about Jim… are you absolutely certain?"

"I'm afraid so, Stewart. Our intelligence is of ironclad provenance. Your running mate is in bed with a traitorous shadow organization whose tentacles are far-reaching. They pose a clear and present danger to the nation, and Jim Dilleford is in bed with them.

"I am sorry. I truly wish it were not so. But I don't expect you to take my word. I've asked our intelligence chiefs who will soon work for your administration to bring you up to speed in the coming days. You need to convince yourself, Stewart. We learned of this shortly before the election, and have been confirming and reconfirming our intel ever since. Dilleford is dirty.

"Now here's the deal, Stewart. We could have exploded your campaign, but the nation would have suffered a mortal blow from which it likely would not have recovered anytime soon. And your opponent, Mr. Redding, stole his nomination according to our intel. Aside from his radical views on leadership…"

Stewart was interpreting the strong nonverbals from POTUS. "Redding too? Certainly not… Omigod."

"Yup. Though you come from the other side of the aisle, you are now our nation's best and only hope, Stewart. You got my vote, by the way."

And there it was—the famous President John W. Stevens's confidence-inspiring smile.

~

Stewart barely clung to reality.

A conspiracy of this magnitude stretched beyond normal comprehension, but the president could see he was resilient.

POTUS continued.

"And Stewart, this next pill will be even harder to swallow. We're now collecting extremely reliable intel on this organization from multiple sources. You know there are different types of intel, ranging from solid actionable stuff to less definitive chatter.

"The back-channel chatter on this, of which we're becoming increasingly confident, is that sometime after the election, you were to develop a serious health issue from which you would not recover. They're planning to assassinate you, Stewart. Redding was their Plan A, Dilleford, Plan B."

"Oh!"

"Now it behooves us to formulate a strategy—*before* inauguration day. As far as we can determine, they don't know that we know. That's a critical advantage. But I must warn you it will be very difficult to maintain that advantage for long.

"Stewart, you're going to have your hands full as the nation's first black president, even without all this other nonsense, and I pledge to you personally, right now, even after January twentieth, I will do whatever is in my power to aid you in your office.

"Let there be no doubt. Our nation is under siege from within and without. It will get much worse before it gets better, Mr. President."

This pledge of allegiance from his soon-to-be predecessor unexpectedly brought a lump to Stewart's throat, especially by prematurely bestowing his new title of high honor.

These two political superstars spent more than a few contemplative moments in the shared reverie of a warm four-handed handshake, bonding as few men ever would.

Then they drew out their smiles as they opened the doors to the waiting press conference.

These reporters might never know that Stewart's smile was one of genuine gratitude to this incredible world leader who stood immediately to his left and had just vowed to continue his service to the nation even after leaving office.

He could only assume that President Stevens's smile was one of great anticipation in starting his next adventure from *behind* the scenes for a change.

KUDOS

P UNTA GORDA, FLORIDA

The bomb left dark reminders behind.

Scarred and blackened, the empty clubhouse pool and deck reminded South Shore residents of Dent Canfield's attempt to murder George Janis, along with most of his neighbors.

Repairs began, but a renovation of this scope took time. Especially in Paradise. Duct tape bordered expanses of somewhat clear plastic that temporarily sealed the blown-out clubhouse windows and patio doors poolside .

The community wished to show their gratitude to one of their own. Every last owner was outraged by this terrorist attack on their home. The realization that George had saved many of their lives created wave after grateful wave of enthusiastic ardor.

The party started that morning, and would continue well into the night. This group of seniors celebrated like tomorrow was but a mere possibility. The celebration had become a cathartic event for an aging community.

Many remained in shock. Several of their neighbors were injured by the blast. One passed away from heart failure—partly from blunt force trauma, and partly from a long life of excesses.

George mentioned to Sam before walking over to the clubhouse, "This party is both nice and a bit strange. There was a time when I'd have gobbled up this sort of attention, but now, I dunno…"

Doctor Sam Braxton had flown in. His wife, Mary, was too ill to attempt the journey but offered her heartfelt thanks and congratulations to George by phone earlier.

Sam said, "C'mon, George. This is what America is all about. Friends and neighbors hanging together, especially in the embrace of righteous outrage against murderous acts close to home. Tonight, they celebrate with one of their neighbors for engaging in mortal combat against the forces of evil and returning victorious on their behalf. You just might want to consider running for public office, Old Son!"

Kate's brown irises suddenly bloomed in a field of indignant white.

"I don't *think* so! We've had quite enough of corporate and political intrigue, thank you very much!"

Kate had heard a great deal about Sam over the years, but this was the first time she'd actually met him. Even during the preparation of *Sojourn* for shipment in Baltimore back in 1995, where George first met Sam, Kate remained in Minnesota. She immediately felt great affection for the little man who saved her own life and her husband's. That did not stop Kate from being Kate.

George said, "Nora, Frank, I'm so glad you could join us all the way from up north. You know a three-hour flight would have been faster than your two day drive."

The couple from Stillwater confided in them a more personal reason for driving. Frank was now inseparable from his deadly little twenty-two-caliber KelTech pistol not welcome in airports or on planes.

"We enjoyed the drive, George. Thanks for having us, and we're honored to be staying in your spare bedroom for a few days."

They had sauntered over to the clubhouse earlier.

George wanted them here. They were flattered. Sam indicated he wanted to share a few things with George and the survivors of Dent's attacks immediately following the party. But until then…

WHAT IS A CELEBRATION WITHOUT A SPEECH?

Never missing such an opportunity, the bald-headed but wiry South Shore Home Owner's Association President, Rand Parrish, offered a grateful nod of acknowledgment to Doctor Sam Braxton. George shared with him Sam's incredible role in recent events. At a high level only, of course.

Rand gingerly grabbed the microphone attached to the portable PA system in the main room of the clubhouse, the very room from which George had hustled Canfield's bomb.

"George, get your butt up here!"

Rand kept speaking as George gingerly limped to the front of the room, his back pain from the violent encounter with Dent still very much in evidence.

"Friends and neighbors, our home was attacked and we have survived."

Enthusiastic applause and cat calls interrupted him. Once the exuberant cacophony subsided, Rand continued.

"That's what Americans do. We survived, thanks to our own. George Janis acted decisively to save most of us from a grizzly end, risking his own life in the bargain. He didn't fall on the damn grenade, but came pretty damn close!"

More applause, this time more reverent.

"George, for your heroic efforts, you have been chosen to receive South Shore's highest level of recognition, the Swaying Palm."

Hoots and hollers from the standing crowd of more than a hundred residents filled the room. They all shared in the semi-serious joke. They all desperately clung to the opportunity to engage in a bit of weak humor. All having been shaken to their core, this event proved cathartic.

"Like a palm adapts to hurricane winds by bending, but not breaking, this symbol represents what we love about this little piece of the world, and about you, George. Wounded in the line of duty, you bent, but did not break. You stood for what's great in America: courage, selflessness and a steely resolve. Though there is little hope for your golf game—ever. Thank you, George."

Laughing too hard at Rand's joke, the crowd noise quickly subsided as Rand carefully slipped a shiny green ribbon lanyard over George's head. From it hung the silhouette of a palm tree of hammered brass at least a foot high and half as wide across. The atrocity looked ridiculous, but George's eyes teared up all the same.

Without saying a word, every person in the room saw this silly symbol represented to George the release of so much stress and so many regrets that no longer mattered.

His emotion was palpable and contagious. The room was suddenly heavy with passionate camaraderie among aging soldiers who had shared the field of battle, and survived. His weren't the only tears in the now quiet room.

To everyone's surprise, George sniffled once and then shouted, "Thanks. I love you all. Will somebody *please* put on some music so we can get this party started?"

Amidst cautious back-patting and throat-clearing and sniffles of appreciation, he limped back to a chair. Kate handed him a club soda before embracing him, anticipating their new life together.

Sophie Landers, the resident Jersey girl who never got along with Kate, approached. In her most flamboyant accent, said, "Kate, I still think you talk like a truck driver. I've come to realize this country needs truck drivers too."

She bent over to offer Kate a warm hug. Kate knew that's as good as it got with Sophie, and that was okay too.

~

THE AFTER PARTY WAS DIFFERENT.

An hour later, a small group sat comfortably in Kate and George's lanai. Frank and Nora sat together, as did George and Kate.

Sam stood as if he were about to offer the combination of an intelligence briefing and an epitaph honoring the deceased. The pervasive sound at that moment was the sheer absence of it. Sam struggled with how much to share with this little group.

Finally, as anticipation built, his eyes addressed Kate, Nora, and Frank with his mellifluous drawl.

"Dear friends. Even though we've just met, I feel I've known you all for years. This is a precious bond I've only shared with soldiers and field operatives in the past. Thank you for that."

With the briefest of glances in George's direction before addressing the trio of intent listeners once more, he continued.

"George and I comprised an improbable team over the last fourteen years or so, meeting again recently, now a not-so-short lifetime ago. You've lost friends and colleagues. I am no stranger to that as I've been in high-risk government service my entire career, *and* well into my retirement. For me, the harsher side of life is no friend, but no stranger either.

"For you, however, I know recent events changed your lives in a profound manner. You must be okay with that. And you will be. We honor our fallen by gratefully moving on. Taking any other course does them a disservice and admits defeat.

"Now, I owe you some context. George could not legally or ethically share this with you. I've been personally authorized by John W. Stevens, President of these United States to share a few specifics with you, but with the strict understanding that you will not share this information with anyone outside this room. If you do, you must know that would be a treasonous offense. Most serious. Is that clearly understood?"

He was rewarded by dumb-founded nods all around, and glances toward the boss they thought they knew.

"Good. Your ex-colleague, Dent Canfield, was a serial killer. You know that. He was a disturbed young man. His job as your teammate at GGS was only a cover. I can't share with you his real job, but when we discovered what he was doing, it led to uncovering treasonous acts he committed on behalf of others.

"Essentially, George and I went undercover—*rogue,* you might say —to expose Dent's involvement, and thwarted the efforts of this sizable group of traitors, with help from many other patriots. I am not allowed to be any more specific, so please do not ask. Suffice it to say we succeeded.

"When George took chase in a boat that stormy night to apprehend Dent after he tried to detonate his bomb where we attended the party tonight, George caught up with him and shot him after Dent attacked him. Dent survived.

"Thankfully, even though George is a quick draw, he is a lousy shot, because what we've learned from Dent since is most significant."

Even though jaws were dropping all around, this last remark snagged a few grins, especially from Frank, while Sam continued.

"Most of this you already know, but I wanted y'all to hear it from an official bonafide government official. Yes, I was retired, but they sweet-talked me back for one more mission.

"What you probably don't yet know is that after essentially being force-fed the medications that somewhat corralled Dent's insanity, at least temporarily, he cooperated.

"You should also know that your old boss, Palmer Xavier, was implicated, but when the traitorous dogs with whom he was affiliated discovered he'd been compromised by information obtained from Dent, thanks to George here, evidence points to his assassination."

Upon hearing this, Frank couldn't resist. He said in a low but dangerous voice, "Thanks for the memories, *Palmer*. May you rot in Hell. Karma's a vindictive bitch, isn't she?"

Then he said, "Sorry."

Sam continued, "You are not wrong, Mr. Lassiter. Yet another example was the shooting last week in front of the Federal Court-house in Washington. The convicted Dent Canfield exited the building under heavy guard—on his way to the super-max prison in Florence, Colorado—where he was shot at close range and killed by his erstwhile father-in-law."

It amused George that Sam was not using Dent's designator of *Bandit One* with his friends. *That sort of detail would just confuse them, not being operators like Sam and me.*

Yeah... like me.

Sam continued, "There's more that I'm not at liberty to share. Quite a bit more. Neither is George, so please do not ask either of us."

A profound state of sustained shock permeated the room as Nora, Frank, and even Kate considered what they just learned.

"Know this, though, my friends. George was instrumental in not only disposing of a bomb that could have killed dozens, he appre-hended our killer who subsequently provided pivotal national secu-rity information. Wish I could say more."

Sam turned from addressing the small group to his friend and fellow operative.

"George, I have been authorized personally by the President to *privately* thank you on behalf of a grateful nation."

George and Sam's warm handshake and subsequent soldier-to-soldier embrace lasted a long time, but not nearly as long as the awestruck little group's wide-eyed stares and glances at each other after learning of these astounding revelations.

Even Kate heard much of this for the first time as her eyes glistened.

Finally Frank broke the reverie by *shouting*, "Way to go, Boss! Jee-ZUS, man! Do you do *anything* half-assed?"

Nora finally found her voice, almost reverent in the wake of what she'd just learned.

"So what's next for you and Kate, George? Sipping martinis under a canopy on the foredeck of your next boat?"

"Naw. But Kate and I do have a little announcement of our own. We are now officially *recovering* alcoholics. We've resolved that we've taken our last drink, with a lot of help from Alcoholics Anonymous and understanding friends and family.

"As far as replacing the boat, we've talked about buying an RV instead. We're going to try *land yachting* for a while and travel around this awesome country of ours in a motorhome, get back in touch with the land, *our* America.

"Plus, I really enjoy writing, so maybe I'll start scratching out the great American novel. It's definitely time to turn the page, to write a new chapter.

"God bless us all."

SLEEP LIGHTLY

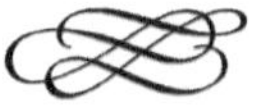

F EBRUARY 2009
WASHINGTON, DC

PRESIDENT ATHERTON SET TO HIS TASKS.

He began sorting out his house at the beginning of his first term. After the inauguration and a series of briefings with various intelligence chiefs now working for him, he continued watching his back as President Stevens strongly advised.

Protecting himself from assassination by his own VP seemed perverse and surreal. It brought to mind one of his favorite shows on television, *Game of Thrones*, but this was far more personal and far less entertaining. Jim Dilleford *was* a friend. Well, maybe not a friend, but certainly a trusted associate as well as his running mate. They *campaigned* together!

President Stevens had suggested taking no direct action too quickly, as that could prove disastrous to his infant administration. Rather, they agreed to this with counsel from a few trusted intelligence chiefs. President Atherton didn't even know if he could trust his newly appointed Chief of Staff, so a trusted few crafted a plan to deal with the VP downrange of their key one hundred-day checkpoint.

In the meantime, POTUS watched his back and trusted no one. He reflected the irony of trusting his predecessor from the opposition party more than his own staff, but pretended this wasn't the case at all. He did wish to stay alive.

Any action against the presidential nominee, Jefferson Davis Redding, seemed less urgent and somewhat trickier. That could wait.

Meanwhile, always the attorney, Stewart Atherton brushed up on the twenty-fifth constitutional amendment that defined the line of succession for the Presidency, but more relevant to him at the moment, it also stated that *"a president can nominate someone to become Vice President if that office is vacant, with the approval of Congress."*

The list of trustworthy candidates was short, with one name standing tall above the rest, the Democratic Senator from Massachusetts, the Honorable Norman Sealey.

After his unimpeachable twenty-three year balanced record in the Senate, he served with distinction as Governor of Maryland for the last three years. He was a passionate patriot and commanded broad political support. With him in mind, POTUS moved on to other items on his short-term agenda. The countless other necessary appointments could wait.

Next most urgent, given the domestic and foreign cyber attacks described by President Stevens, he laid groundwork in the strongest possible terms to establish policies and programs to mitigate the monumental risks now before them.

With the weight of his office supporting him, President Atherton lobbied for aggressive anti-cyber-terrorism funding and legislation. A sympathetic congress on both sides of the aisle did not stand in the way. How could they?

The fledgling president knew this was critical, but admitted to himself he wasn't sure if he was doing enough, or even taking the right steps. He kept coming back to John's advice—*surround yourself with good people you can trust and let them do what they do best.* But who could he trust? He felt smothered.

The alleged cyber attacks on the election were well-publicized. The fact that most of the population expected a landslide in the election, which turned out to be a close race despite the largest voter turnout in history, lent at least some credence to the allegations of voter tampering.

In fact, patriotic fervor and fear incited easy passage of important legislation that included unambiguous defensive and offensive measures, some more socially controversial than others.

At least they were taking a few steps in the right direction.

Next on the president's agenda, for many of the same reasons, came one of his own hot buttons, campaign contribution reform. He wanted to put power back into the hands of the voters more than into the greedy fists of high dollar lobbyists.

After all, there was a new sheriff in town.

EPILOGUE

J ULY 2009
WASHINGTON, DC

A SAD DAY DAWNED SIX MONTHS LATER.

A saddened President Stewart Atherton announced that Vice President James Dilleford had developed serious health issues and found it necessary to resign.

Vice President Dilleford passed away peacefully in his sleep less than three months after that. The nation mourned.

The good news, however, was that the popular Governor Norman Sealey of Maryland agreed to fill the post.

"Welcome to the team, Mr. Vice President."

"It is my honor to serve, Mr. President."

The newly minted VPOTUS thought, *To serve the Brotherhood, that is.*

It is not done...

- **Stewart David Atherton**: US President-Elect.
- **Doctor F. Samuel (Sam) Braxton:** US Army (retired) and retired Chief Medical Director NSA.
- **Denton (Dent) Canfield**: a psychopathic employee who works for George Janis at GGS, leads a double life; intelligence designator: *Bandit One*
- **Captain Derek Cheevers:** squad leader *Nosy Cherry* mission.
- **Charles Delaney (R-West Virginia)**: House Chairman Intelligence Oversight, US Congress.
- **James Dilleford**: Atherton's VP.
- **Darla Evans:** a member of Derek Cheevers' team.
- **Brigadier General Anthony Flannery:** Deputy Director NSA.
- **Malcolm (Malc) Frieburg**: Slattery's second-in-command.
- **Matilda Hilley (D-Texas):** Senate Chairperson Intelligence Oversight Committee, US Congress.
- **Flack Jackson**: a member of Derek Cheevers' team.

- **George Janis:** technology executive at Greater Global Solutions (GGS), Inc.
- **Kate Janis**: George Janis's long-suffering wife.
- **Frank Lassiter:** Nora Mathers's husband, works for Donny Segwell at GGS.
- **Admiral Gregory Mannheim:** Director NSA.
- **Michael (Mike) Martino**: CEO of GGS.
- **Nora Mathers**: Donny Segwell's software test team leader at GGS.
- **Captain Doug 'BS' Orenson**: Calvin Pierce's pilot.
- **Caitlyn (Cate) Potts:** Janis's boating friend
- **General Mason Renfro:** President John W. Stevens's National Security Advisor.
- **Calvin 'OD' Pierce:** air pirate (covert transport).
- **Sergei Rostov**: a cold-war-era Soviet defector to America; friend of Sam Braxton.
- **Mick Sandstrom**: member, Derek Cheevers' team.
- **Norman Sealey**: Atherton's replacement VP.
- **Donny Segwell**: manager at GGS and works for Maxine Sun who in turn works for George Janis.
- **Enoch Slattery**: sole proprietor, private dirty-tricks org; intelligence designator: *Bandit Two*.
- **John W. Stevens**: US President.
- **Maxine Sun**: a middle manager who works for George Janis at GGS Inc.
- **Zeke Wilson & Pete Moorhead**: Cleveland steel workers.
- **Palmer Xavier**: GGS Chief Operations Office & George's boss; later, Mr. X; intelligence designator: *Bandit Three*.
- **Abraham Zelokov:** aka Mr. Z. Disenfranchised Russian Jew, founder of the Patriot Brotherhood.

FRACTURED DREAMS

Look for the second novel in the Dream Runners series as the unintentional adventures continue for George and Kate Janis.
"Fractured Dreams" available March 2020.

George (Geo) and Kate Janis return. They hide in plain sight to avoid a bullet to the back of their heads.

Geo learns to ask the dead for advice, some of which is quite good. But his most daunting challenge? Culling out which conspiracies are real, and which are conjured by the traumatic brain injury he manages with some success.

As a veteran, a business executive who retired early, a best-selling author, and now a notorious podcaster, Geo fights the same battle every minute of every day. But nights are far worse. No more so than in the blast furnace of the Arizona desert.

Eight years ago, pulling a trigger to take a human life in the tropics altered Geo's mind. At the same time, a near-lethal blow to the base of his skull changed his body.

Now he and his wife fear discovery by the Patriot Brotherhood—a death sentence. But there is more at stake than their safety.

Janis awakens swinging at Kate with clenched fists and hates himself for it. And he pretends arthritis causes his back pain, his limp, and the headaches.

Regardless, friends in high places need his help—again—to defeat the Brotherhood and to defend democracy. He will serve once more, the risks be damned.

Turn the page for an excerpt...

FRACTURED DREAMS

HOMECOMING

~

2016

BLACK ROCK, ARIZONA

A straight line isn't always short.

The next ten seconds changed everything, and they changed nothing.

Too often in his life Geo Janis measured the distance between joy and terror in precious seconds. He was about to measure that distance at least once more.

Before he picked up Kate's surprise birthday pie at the tiny bakery in the eclectic desert town a half-hour away, he read the first of two text messages. His phone's screen lit the car's dark interior with a vague vision of his violent past overtaking him.

Eyes wide and bright, head thrust forward, the chords in his neck bulged and pulsed. He scanned the second text that appeared seconds later. Bile rose in his throat. He tossed his iPhone onto the empty passenger seat, his face a mask of horror. A violent U-turn aimed him back toward the campground, the pie now forgotten.

Geo blasted through the few stop signs and a single traffic light in the village of Quartzsite in Southwest Arizona. He merged onto Interstate-10 East with reckless abandon.

"Get out of the way!"

Left-lane dwellers gorged him with irrational anger. The campground, still fifteen miles ahead, wasn't getting *farther away,* was it? Worse than that dream of wading toward safety in waist-deep molasses while being chased by a monster...

Flashing lights appeared in his mirrors. A glance at the dash of his tiny four-cylinder Toyota surprised him. He wondered how much *this* ticket might cost—ninety in a seventy. Then he realized he didn't care. In fact, an Arizona State Trooper might back him for what could happen next.

Ten minutes later, Geo rocketed onto the desolate two-lane US 60 East toward Desert Wells with the trooper still in tow. He struggled to make sense of a jigsaw puzzle of events years in the making as he raced toward danger, maybe even death. Those two single-word texts brought the chaos back into his life he thought he escaped light-years earlier.

Always the adult in the room, Kate warned Geo not long after they assumed their new identities. She predicted their past would overtake them some day. Said she was okay with that. Geo drew from Kate's strength these days.

Their friend, Doctor F. Samuel Braxton and *his* friend, the retired senior statesman John W. Stevens, protected them—for services rendered to the United States of America.

Geo feared more for Kate's safety than for his own. He needed to reach her before they did.

Jeez God, what if...?

He'd made his choice eight years earlier when his country needed him. But he never envisioned life without Kate. Not after fifty years of marriage.

Geo braked hard at the last moment before colliding with the only other vehicle in sight, a dusty pickup that flashed across his headlight beams as it entered from a ranch road ahead of him. The truck belched out a black cloud of diesel smoke as the driver accelerated hard to escape collision from the rear.

Speeding up again, Geo's tires protested as he fish-tailed on loose gravel scattered on the asphalt. He passed the panicked kids in the truck, still pacing the Arizona Trooper behind him.

This ticket will cost more. Ninety-five in a fifty-five.

Why did the idea of traffic violations keep annoying him? Maybe because he wasn't used to breaking the law. He sneered in hapless defiance, then in perplexity *as the trooper passed him.* His blue and red rooftop light bar and taillights disappeared in the wind-blown dust and over a rise a half-mile ahead.

Eight miles later Geo drifted sideways into the gravel entrance to the obscure Black Rock campground on his left. He hoped no children played in his path. Not likely. Not at this time of night. Just retired desert dwellers out here anyway.

A piece of him perished as he saw the ocean of flashing red and blue lights surrounding the bus he and Kate called home.

"Oh, God, no!"

A fit-and-trim trooper stood in his way, maybe even the one who passed him, pumping his palms in front of him toward Geo. The little red Toyota's front bumper dived to a stop within inches of the trooper's legs. The guy's instincts backed him up an unsteady step or two.

His palms descended to his hips, elbows akimbo. Even though it was dark, with the lights all around, Geo could see his glare. He was livid. And something else.

But that was irrelevant. Their motorhome and attached trailer were still a hundred yards ahead. Didn't this guy understand? He needed to get to his high school sweetheart, to his soul mate, to the woman without whom he was adrift—lost.

Kate trusted her husband because she dared trust no one else. Not neighbors, not cops, only him. And her first text to him was their private 911 signal: *B-hood.* But it was the second that made him swallow his rising bile: *Run!*

Geo realized he was about to say something he'd regret but didn't care, *could not* care. His sweaty palms gripped either side of the padded steering wheel now sopping wet—pushing, then pulling to the wheel's breaking point.

His jaw hurt. He gritted his teeth so hard a few chipped. Realized he'd been doing so since he'd received Kate's two texts twenty-two minutes ago. Nothing since!

He even contemplated running down the trooper to get to her. But no.

Fit-and-Trim marched with purpose toward his window. A general malevolent demeanor hung on him like a shroud, and the heel of his right hand rested on the butt of his sidearm. He unsnapped its retainer loop.

With slitted eyes, he said, "Window."

Tinted red and blue in the ambience of reflected emergency lights, his gold badge glinted at Geo, taunted him.

Aside from an acute case of skin cancer, his eleven-year-old Yaris featured no options, not even electric windows. He found it impossible to keep eye contact with the menacing trooper while leaning down and forward to reach the crank.

"Freeze! *Do not move!*"

His weapon no longer remained holstered.

Geo complied, although now perplexity layered onto his fear and anger. It was all becoming too much to process. From his hunched-over position, he couldn't see two more troopers running to support their brother-in-arms.

One of them threw open Geo's driver-side door so hard it tried to bounce back. Stopped it with his hip. Pressed down on the back of Geo's head until his back hurt. The other dragged him from the car, head and shoulders and arms first, which made it impossible for Geo to keep his feet and legs under him.

On the ground, he felt rough hands jostling every part of him. He screamed, "I live here! I gotta get to my wife!"

He could taste musty desert dust in his mouth while gasping face down. It tasted gray and gritty. Had he not been near delirious with fear for Kate, his germaphobic nature would compel him to fret over the fungi likely present in that dust. Now in his throat, in his nostrils, in his lungs. In his mind.

"No weapons."

"Turn him over."

He looked up, straight into the blinding beam of a law-enforcement-strength flashlight and maybe the business end of a few gun barrels. He wasn't sure. Of anything. Not any more.

"Pick him up."

On his feet, strong hands gripped each of his arms, then released them. Geo raised his hands high without being told, but clenched his fists against white-knuckle fear, anger, and now rage.

"What the Hell?"

"Sir, state your name and your business here."

He noticed the original trooper held his open wallet.

Geo's voice projected but quavered. "My name is Lee Randle. That motorhome and trailer over there belong to me and my wife Charlotte. Now will someone *please* say something relevant?"

Trooper Fit-and-Trim's voice and demeanor softened as he handed over the wallet. His next words changed Geo's life forever.

"Sir, your wife is dead. Murdered."

He took a few moments of squinting to process the words. After torturing himself with this new reality, because he sensed the truth of it even as his mind ran away from it, his head jutted forward.

A feral sneer sculpted his face. Geo spit a guttering scream toward the trooper, his voice gathering volume and a fever pitch as the words tumbled out.

"No. You're lying! Why would you lie to me like that?"

He fought off the trooper's now gentle hands, determined to get to the only person who understood him, who awakened his deadened passion after… He needed to… He shook, trembled. Melted. Strong hands held him on his uncaring feet.

Then, something even more inconceivable happened. In a smooth motion, Trooper Fit-and-Trim raised his service weapon, aimed it at Geo's right eye less than an inch distant, and fired.

Geo dropped into a welcoming abyss.

Didn't even have time to wonder if Kate had suffered. So why were the trooper's gentle hands still jarring him as he once again lay there in that fungus-ridden dirt? Was this Limbo? Or Purgatory? Or another attempt to finish the job as he descended into Hell?

The shaking continued as he writhed in remembered pain.

Then…

"Sweetheart, it's just one of those dreams again. Wake up, Geo. A bad dream. That's all."

The fear remained. Not *only* in the dream. Kate was a saint. She put up with this.

But for how long?

WHAT'S NEXT?

If you like what you've seen of *"Fractured Dreams,"*
the second book in the "Dream Runners" series, please visit
GKJurrens.com
or purchase a copy from your favorite online retailer.

But before you go...

Please write and post a brief review
where you purchased this book.
Just scroll down to "Write a Review" and click to start.

*Remember, other readers and I need to know what you think. I am
grateful.*

Thank you.
GK

ABOUT THE AUTHOR

GK Jurrens writes with undiluted passion.

He also teaches writing on the road. With his wife Kay, he lives and travels in a motorhome. They find wandering North America a source of endless inspiration.

After four years of government service, GK earned several college degrees while mounting a successful three-decade career in high technology.

Now he writes, practices Yoga, paints, and plays Native American-style flutes, some of which he handcrafted while living in the Arizona desert.

His favorite quote? *"The difference between ordeal and adventure is attitude!"*

Subscribe at GKJurrens.com to be notified of new releases and giveaways.

Follow GK at:

amazon.com/author/gkjurrens

goodreads.com/gkjurrens

twitter.com/gjurrens1

facebook.com/genejurrens

instagram.com/gjurrens

www.ingramcontent.com/pod-product-compliance
Lightning Source LLC
Chambersburg PA
CBHW032205180726
48284CB00001B/203